CW01511913

To / Lisa
happy christmas
lots of love
Jennie & Joey
Hazel, Ethan, Layla
+ Macy
x x x

Once Bitten

Alexa O'Brien Huntress Book One

Trina M. Lee

Once Bitten

Trina M. Lee

Published 2009

ISBN 978-1-449-56145-1

Copyright © 2009, Trina M. Lee

All rights reserved. No part of this publication may be reproduced, stored in a retrieval system, or transmitted in any form or by any means, electronic, mechanical, recording or otherwise, without the prior written permission of the author.

Manufactured in the United States of America

Published by Dark Mountain Books

Editor
B. Leigh Hogan

Cover Artist
Stella Price

This is a work of fiction. The characters, incidents and dialogues in this book are of the author's imagination and are not to be construed as real. Any resemblance to actual events or persons, living or dead, is completely coincidental.

Chapter One

The taste of blood brought my wolf to the surface. I snarled up into the face of the vampire and braced for another blow. I welcomed it. The need for a good fight had my adrenaline pumping.

My bloody lip was quickly forgotten when the jackass grabbed me by the throat and banged my head against the ground. Light exploded behind my eyes. I brought an elbow up into his face before he could do it again. The crunch that followed was satisfying.

"You like to play, don't you, wolf?" With a backhand, he knocked the stake from my grasp and I watched with dismay as it rolled across the parking lot.

I followed up with a kick that effectively threw him off me. In a leap I was on my feet, braced and ready for him. In my mind, he was already dead. It was just a matter of when I tired of this dance. At the moment I was enjoying myself. His psychic attributes were weak, almost non-existent. So he was a full on physical guy. A good brawl was just what I needed on a hot July night.

I liked to keep things fair. I'd let it stay physical unless he got me in a bad position. Knowing he slaughtered Edmonton's homeless like they were cattle fed my eagerness for a nice, bloody beat down.

Patrick Morgan had been on my hit list for weeks. My partner, Jez St. Claire, had accompanied me on this hunt. I kept expecting her to jump in and help me out but she had yet to appear from her place in the shadows.

I rushed him, faking a punch but sweeping his legs out from beneath him with a kick instead. It didn't keep him down longer than a split second. He recovered fast and came at me with fangs bared. As if he really believed he'd get a chance to use them.

Just before he hit me, I threw my weight forward and leaned down low, effectively tossing him over my shoulder. I leaped on him fast, straddling him as I rained down blow after blow. I settled for dropping punches into his face. It wouldn't kill him but hurting him sure felt good.

"How many hits in the face do you think you can take before there is nothing left to look at?" I sneered with a bitter laugh. "My arms aren't even tired yet. I can go until sunrise."

Twisting his body suddenly, he threw me off, following through with a few well placed hits. I was going to be a mess of bruises after this. The struggle for dominance ensued. We each fought to gain leverage over the other. It was starting to feel like a hair pulling, bitch slapping kind of fight. I needed to take it to the next level.

He managed to put some space between us and sprang to his feet. I followed suit, circling back to give myself room to feel out my next attack.

The wolf's stamina and speed carried me when I came at him with claws ready. He moved swiftly and rather than take his head off, I merely scratched a few deep lines in his cheek.

Surprise glowed in his dark eyes. I must have caught him off guard on that one. Good. I lunged again but he was ready. He gave me a nice shove, one that lifted me off my feet. I hit the ground hard and rolled, getting back up. Glancing toward the stake, I made as if to move for it and the vampire stopped me with a well placed kick.

Taking a kick to the head stunned me. I fell to my knees, the stake just out of reach. I couldn't go for it and defend myself at the same time. Not when I was seeing stars. I still had all my teeth though so it could have been worse.

He grabbed me from behind, choking me before I'd recovered from the blinding kick. The son of a bitch was strong. I gasped for breath. Now might be the time to pull a psychic attack on him. I flung a clawed hand back behind me, groping blindly for his face. I felt the soft, vulnerable area around his eye. Success.

The scream that tore from him when I stabbed a sharp claw into his eye was almost feminine. It would have been funny if things hadn't just gone from feisty fun to death match. He released me immediately.

Blood poured down his face. His eye was a mangled mess. Rage rolled off him in giant waves. I never gave him the chance to recover. Lunging swiftly, I snatched the stake up and threw all of my weight at him. I hit him in the chest and we both went down. I called forth just enough power to help me hold him.

I still hadn't mastered my abilities despite having been born with them. What had started as basic telekinesis and energy manipulation had evolved over time. Becoming a werewolf had done nothing to hinder my power. In some ways, it seemed to enhance it. As far as I knew, I was the only living werewolf to possess power so close to that of a vampire.

Patrick Morgan gave a loud, angry cry and fought hard to throw me off. "Fucking bitch! I'm not going to beg."

"Good. It's probably better if you don't go out like a pussy."

With a perfectly timed head butt, he regained the advantage. I was skidding across the pavement before I could block the next hit. My back slammed against a parked car, knocking the breath from me. I braced, expecting him to try to finish me off. But when I looked up, he was just a blur in the distance.

He ran? *Coward.*

"Jez!" I shouted. In an attempt to stop him, I threw an energy ball, striking him dead center in the back.

He went down hard. Jez was a blur of black as she moved with supernatural speed. Bursting forth from the shadows, she was on top of Morgan before he could recover. I don't think he realized he'd been impaled until the hilt of her knife was pressed against the base of his throat.

Blood poured from the wound. Jez continued to wiggle and grind the blade. The vampire struggled to speak through crimson lips as blood flowed out of his mouth.

"Do you like that?" Jez growled into his face.

Her golden hair had fallen free of her hair clip, her brilliant green eyes were pure cat. Morgan just stared into those leopard eyes in horror. I guessed that he'd never encountered a werecat before. They weren't nearly as common as werewolves.

She was the only naturally born shifter that I'd ever known and one of only two werecats. Almost all Weres, like me, are infected through bite or attack. Of course, that was only if they managed to survive, which wasn't likely. I was a teenaged kid lucky enough to survive an attack. I was the only one in my family who did.

Growing in adulthood with a thirst for the hunt hadn't been easy. The man, to whom I'd looked for guidance, had been too wrapped up in his own self-absorbed world to notice that I needed him. Raoul Roberts had taken me in when I was sixteen. He had come at a time when I desperately needed him. My mistake was staying too long. Despite earning rank of Alpha female among my local town pack, I've done my best to cut ties with my former Alpha.

The title of Alpha had earned me little, least of all respect. My status did little more than provide minimal dominance over new werewolves. We were people first, and the animal hierarchy only crossed so far into our human world.

A much needed change had come several years ago when I was approached by Veryl Armstrong, paranormal investigator and vampire extraordinaire. Veryl had asked how I felt about taking out one of my own kind, a werewolf who liked little girls. I would have done it for free.

I worked regularly with Veryl and developed friendships with others who frequently supplied him with their services, like Jez. It just made sense to have someone as ruthless as me at my back. Hesitators wouldn't keep me alive while hunting rogues like Morgan.

The vampire stared into Jez like she was the angel of death who had come at last, and I realized that a part of him was enjoying this.

"You like this, don't you, you sick son of a bitch? Just like you enjoy cutting up pretty, little, rich girls while you drain them dry." Jez's right hand gripped the knife, and her left sprouted five perfect, razor-sharp claws. Morgan made a series of grunts and gurgles, but nothing coherent came out. He reached up with a strong hand for her throat, and she drove those claws into his guts.

This was getting too messy. I moved in to help her pin the vampire.

Morgan fought hard now, struggling against us furiously. I guess the game had lost its appeal. He didn't want to play anymore. Now it was a fight for his so-called life. With a sudden burst of desperation, he flung us both backwards.

He came at me then as he pulled the knife from his throat with a slick, wet sound. A sickening laugh bubbled out from around the gushing wound. I tapped the power nestled in my core, throwing everything I had at him. It was just enough to buy Jez a few much needed seconds.

Jez retrieved my forgotten stake and, with a mighty blow, slammed it into his heart. I let my power fall away and staggered with sudden weakness. I leaned against the nearest car and fought to catch my breath.

Patrick Morgan burst into dust and ash. His remains rained down around us. A grin danced along Jez's ruby red lips. It was infectious. I couldn't help but smile. I loved my job.

Chapter Two

The short highway trek between the city and my hometown of Stony Plain took all of seven minutes. My town was special. Though it boasted of big city luxuries, it had a level of safety the city could never claim.

The population reached about 20,000. The town was cozy enough that most families knew one another but not so cozy that a stranger seemed out of place. I was glad to call it home.

It was the perfect "grow old together" town. I no longer saw that kind of future for myself. My life didn't allow for normalcy of the picket fence kind. Of course, I still felt love, in more ways than I could understand. Love remained a confusing and wonderful thing, one power that no one truly harnessed.

I drove up to a brick building that beckoned to patrons with a simple fluorescent sign that stated the establishment's name, Lucy's Lounge. What the place lacked in the way of décor, it made up for in smooth whiskey and fine rock n' roll.

The walls were a drab grey. The carpet looked grubby, as if it had been filthy even as it came off the loom. In the center of the bar was a staircase that led to the second floor, which housed another bar and seating area. It was much smaller and less popular than the crowded downstairs.

Lucy's Lounge was packed when Jez and I arrived. Nobody

appeared to be in the mood for trouble making, but the night wasn't over yet.

We moved through the crowded club, an assault of scents battered our sensitive noses. I could smell everything from someone's jasmine perfume to somebody else's two-day-old socks. I was glad the club had gone smoke free. My keen senses informed me that Arys was there. I'd know his icy energy anywhere.

Arys Knight sat at his favorite table near the bar with his human card-playing buddies. Despite his casual posture and eyes on his cards, I knew he was aware of my presence.

While Jez made her way to the bar, I headed for Arys's table. He'd never let me avoid him.

"Alexa." He said my name as if it were a fine dessert. He brought my hand to his lips in a dramatic gesture of greeting, and the power rose between us as it so often did.

The part of me that was spent hungered for his cool, undead energy. The other guys around the table laughed as if his grand greeting had been for their benefit, but I knew it was for mine.

"Hello, Arys. Having a good night?" I gestured to the hand of cards that he held.

"Always." He flashed me the smile that he'd been perfecting for centuries, not even a hint of fang visible. He made it impossible not to smile back.

Arys came off as the cocky, egotistical type of man that I usually detest, but I knew there was more to him than that. He'd lived through things I could only read about and had known a world I would never know.

"Not making any trouble tonight, are you?" I asked as I glanced over my shoulder. Jez was still waiting in line to order.

"Trouble? Me? You've got to be kidding." He threw cards on the table and said, "Read them and weep boys." He looked up at me and grinned.

His forever-youthful grin indicated that he couldn't have been more than thirty or so when he was turned. The ladies loved him. With a smile like his, I couldn't blame them. However, when he smiled just for me, the sight of those fangs in that beautifully human face sent a chill racing down my spine.

I've known more than one vampire who dressed like a Victorian movie vamp but not Arys. Piercings in his ears, nose and lip revealed his edgy nature. He was casual in faded blue jeans and a black t-shirt that hugged his well-muscled chest in all of the right places. His eyes were a deep, drowning blue. His hair was slightly spiky and bedroom messy with just a hint of the early Elvis style. To say that I found him attractive would be putting it lightly. He was absolutely gorgeous.

I knew he was a ruthless killer behind that human mask, but thankfully, I wasn't on the menu. At least, as far as I knew.

"So what brings you in? Weren't you hunting tonight?" he asked, and I had to struggle to clear my head.

"Somewhat." I allowed my gaze to wander around the room and observed the other patrons. "I just had something to take care of."

When I looked back at Arys, he was watching me closely. Too closely.

"What?"

"Nothing. Just sensing you."

This wasn't anything new. Being a vampire, Arys had sensed the natural power in me the moment we first met.

"And, what is it that you're sensing?"

"You," he repeated but this time he caught my hand firmly in his own and forced me to meet his midnight blue gaze. "You're weakened." I was glad the loud music prevented anyone from overhearing. I couldn't help but be uncomfortably aware of his poker buddies watching us.

A small spark began in my hand, discernible only to those with the acute ability to feel energy. It flowed quickly up my arm and tickled as it went. Heat began in my palm as my power sought to draw him in. Against my control, it pulsed and began to grow as his power bonded with mine.

With a gentle push, I felt a surge shiver through me as Arys seemed to breathe energy into me through touch alone. He simply gave up that which I would never willingly take. I wanted to melt into the welcome sensation. Something about the vampire always made my power reach out for him. When the charge fell away, I was left tingling and craving more.

With a deep breath, I stepped back and pulled my hand away. Arys said nothing, but the look in his eyes said enough. I almost forgot we were in a public place. I shook my head to clear the haze that had developed.

"I should go keep Jez company in that line up," I mumbled, trying to find a reason to walk away. My heart pounded as a dose of adrenaline hit me. "I'll catch you later."

"Not if I catch you first," he replied.

I couldn't deny the meaning behind the look he shot me. His eyes held hidden promises of greater desires. Arys made no secret of his infatuation. He had made no attempt to deny his interest nor had he blatantly pursued me. He'd simply made it my choice. I could feel the hot blush that spread across my cheeks when I turned to walk away.

I thought back to a time when my best friend Kylarai Kramer had asked me if I was curious about Arys, curious about what it would be like with him and all of the power that went with him. Hell yes, I was curious. I was a living, breathing woman after all.

I was also realistic and cautious. I didn't want to jump in bed with the vampire just because it was the easiest way to see what we could do metaphysically. Energy just needed to be charged, it didn't have to be tantric. Arys gave our power exchange that flavor, and honestly, it freaked me out.

"That one has it bad," Jez said when I joined her at the bar. I carefully ignored the people behind her who thought I was cutting the line.

"What?"

"The smoking hot vampire," she nodded slightly in Arys's direction. "I can practically smell the lust from here."

"Shut up." I couldn't help but laugh. "Don't be ridiculous. I'm sure he has more than his fair share."

She just shrugged and overlooked my remark. "Do you want me to order you a drink? How are you feeling?"

"Thanks to Arys, I feel great. I'll take a whiskey. Just one though." I wasn't a big drinker, but I enjoyed the occasional cold one. Shifters process alcohol twice as fast as humans, so one drink would do virtually nothing to me.

"Energy games with the vampire, huh? Well, whatever works."

I didn't respond. She wouldn't understand, and I couldn't begin to explain it to her in the noisy bar. When it came to the rush and tingle of metaphysical power, some things cannot easily be described.

When we stepped up to the bar, Shaz Richardson flashed me a

smile almost as white as his naturally platinum blond hair. He had joined our small town pack as a newly turned and naïve eighteen-year-old after meeting Raoul by chance. He's since graduated to a twenty-three year old with a great loss of innocence and a new, in-depth awareness of what really goes bump in the night. My friendship with him was a special one. I trusted nobody else the way I trusted Shaz. He was my other half in so many ways.

"Hey ladies." He greeted us with a smile that appeared to have never known a frown. "What can I get for you? The usual?"

"Make mine a double," Jez quipped.

"I thought you guys were hunting tonight. That didn't take long." Shaz turned to grab a new whiskey bottle from the liquor shelf behind him and something bright red for Jez's fruity drink.

"No. Jez wanted to play cat and mouse with our target for awhile, but once he saw her kitty cat eyes, he changed his mind," I said and fished some cash from my bag. Jez waved it off as she produced enough to cover both drinks and a nice tip for Shaz.

"I would, too," he joked as he poured our drinks. His jade green eyes flashed bright in the bar light overhead as he met my gaze. "So, when are we doing breakfast?"

Once, Shaz and I had a routine of going for breakfast every morning. Since I'd started working independently for Veryl, I couldn't recall the last time I was actually awake during breakfast hours.

"Let's make it dinner. Why don't you come by the house one night this week?"

"Are you cooking?" He raised an eyebrow at me skeptically.

"No, I wouldn't do that to you. We can order in or go out. Maybe Kylarai will want to come." Kylarai and I share a house on the west side of town. It backs onto a farmer's field with a tree line of forest only a short run away. It's a perfect location for wolves.

"Sounds good to me." He pressed my drink into my hand, and the barest touch of his fingers against mine made the wolf inside me raise its head in recognition. For the briefest moment, our two wolves shared a wet nosed greeting. A longing deep down inside me sought the scent of the forest and the exertion of a good run on all fours.

We'd just left the bar and begun looking for a place to sit near the pool tables, when a few guys sitting nearby beckoned us over. When we ignored them, the ringleader of the three got up and approached us.

"What do you want?" Jez snapped. If he had known that she'd been knuckle deep inside somebody's spleen tonight, I doubt he would have tried.

"Take it easy, girl. I was just going to ask if you wanted to join us. We have some extra chairs at our table." He shifted his body in a lame attempt to flex his muscles. I could only imagine how many times he would try this in a night.

"No, thanks," I said. "We're fine."

Jez shot me this look that said she didn't understand why I bothered trying to be polite. There were a few reasons; one of them was that a bar fight would bring cops, which I didn't need.

"Come on, ladies. I'll buy you a drink." He looked at us expectantly, almost eagerly. Did he not realize that Jez was shooting daggers at him with her eyes?

"Save us the song and dance. You're wasting your breath here." I met his eyes when I said it so he'd see that I was serious. However, like most guys his age that are in a bar looking for women, he chose to disregard the fact that we were really not interested.

"Well, you don't have to be such a bitch about it." The minute the words left his lips, the energy level surrounding us tightened with the tension. I was suddenly very aware of Arys's eyes on us from across the room.

"What did you say?" Jez's tone was frighteningly similar to the one she'd used with Morgan.

"You heard what I said. I'd think you would have been flattered." His conceited words made me suck in my breath. If only he knew what he was dealing with.

Coolly eyeing the redheaded chick cuddled up with his buddy, she said, "I'll take her over all of you chumps in a heartbeat."

Before he could open his mouth again, there was a faintly cool breeze behind me as I felt Arys's approach. The young man's egotistical demeanor melted away.

"Is this guy making trouble for you, ladies?" The vampire's voice was low and velvety.

"No, Arys. It's fine." I said. "He was just walking away." I gave Arys an irritated look that he chose to ignore. I didn't need him coming to my aid. Not this again.

He said nothing, but I knew he'd heard me even if he wanted to pretend he didn't. He'd already gotten into a brawl here with a man who'd been dumb enough to drunkenly grab at me a few months back. That man hadn't been seen here since. Suspicious. I wasn't planning to make a habit of letting Arys save the damsel in distress.

"It isn't in my nature to allow a lady to be threatened." Arys looked directly at the guy who lifted his hands in surrender and quickly returned to his table.

"I'm not threatened, and nobody is threatening." My voice was flat. I meant it. I hate being treated as a weak female. I might be five foot one and counting, but that doesn't mean shit when it comes to what really makes you tough.

Arys stared down at me for a long moment before giving me a curt nod. Things were different with him than with most people. He was neither wolf nor human, the two things I knew best, and I found these situations uneasy. We were left to stare at one another like two dogs unsure of whether to wag tails or tear each other apart.

"Oh, come on you two, give it a rest. Alexa, you're so damn stubborn." Jez shook her head at me and took a long swallow from her glass while I wondered who the hell she was to talk. "What's wrong with allowing a man to defend your honor once in a while?"

I had no response to that. Hesitantly, I reached out a hand but didn't quite touch Arys's bare forearm. His aura was warm, and I could feel his power beneath my fingertips. He blinked dark ocean eyes at me, and I almost expected some kind of displeasure in his expression. Instead, his gaze remained calm and cool.

After a moment, he chuckled and said, "Damn Alexa, you should have been a vampire."

I wasn't sure if that was an insult or a compliment. "What the hell is that supposed to mean?"

As the words left my lips, my cell phone rang. A glance at the caller I.D. revealed it was Raoul. What could he possibly want?

He knew damn well that I had nothing to say to him. I debated whether or not to answer, but it gave me an excuse to momentarily avoid the awkward tension of the situation at hand.

"What do you want?" I growled into the slim silver phone.

"A ride, actually. If you don't mind coming down to the police station." The strain in Raoul's voice was evident. His wolf was clearly pressing the boundaries of his control.

Arys watched me silently while Jez's eyes were all questions, all curious cat. I suddenly needed some fresh air.

Chapter Three

Stony Plain only has one police precinct. Just my luck, it was on the same side of town as Lucy's Lounge. I took my sweet time getting over to the cop shop. My heart was pounding before I'd even left the Lucy's parking lot.

I wasn't fond of dealing with either Raoul or the cops. Even when I wasn't doing a damn thing wrong, I felt like they were picking me apart, searching for something to pin on me. That went equally for the police and my former Alpha.

The Stony Plain precinct was relatively small. It didn't have much in the way of imprisonment other than a few holding cells. This wasn't a high crime town. Vandalism and theft was the worst of what we see here, another reason the little town was home. Chances were good that, whatever pathetic little cell they had Raoul in, it had seen more drunk-tank guests than true criminals.

I parked a block away and used the extra walking distance to gain a few added minutes to gather myself. The air smelled faintly of rain, a shower before morning. A red flag waved in my brain, and I questioned if I'd been dumb enough to leave the sunroof open on the car. I considered turning back to double check, but I knew I was just avoiding the awkward moment. I just needed to get this errand over.

I couldn't imagine what Raoul had done to get arrested. Though, if I had to take a guess, I'd angle toward tax fraud or some kind of international embezzlement. With his love for money and toys, a financial crime seemed most likely.

Of course, he didn't need money. After fifteen years in real estate, he surpassed the million dollar net margin easily though I didn't know to what extent. So, I could only wonder what he'd been up to and why he'd called me to pick up his sorry ass.

We'd always had this one-sided relationship. He couldn't be counted on for a damn thing while I'd constantly been left to pick up the slack. Yet another of the many reasons that I'd packed up years ago and moved across town.

To be fair, it's not that Raoul is all bad. He took in both Shaz and I. He gave us a pack, a sense of belonging. The seventeen year age difference between Raoul and I cast him in the illusive glow of a leader that I could look to for guidance. By the time I moved out of his house, I had learned more about sex and bloodshed than living with my dual nature. Raoul was a manipulative player, and I couldn't take anymore of his bull.

I'd come to a point where I had to assume there was more to being a werewolf than I'd ever learn from Raoul. Of course, I was right. While he counted daily earnings and bedded multiple partners, I ran through the forest on four legs with the moon pulsing in my veins.

It was impossible to avoid someone completely in a town this size, but I'd done a pretty good job so far. The last time he'd bothered me was a few months earlier when he had asked me to run with him. I ran as wolf in the forest behind my house several times throughout the week. Knowing what he really meant, I had promptly told him to get acquainted with his hand.

I squinted in the harsh light as I stepped from the shadows to the cornea-bursting, fluorescent lighting. The first door led me into a very small hallway with a locked security door at the other end. Beyond that was the receptionist behind yet another layer of bulletproof glass.

A bright red, arrow-shaped sign clearly pointed out the button that I should push in order to ask for admittance. The woman eyed me from behind the safety glass. Despite having already noticed me, she waited to acknowledge me.

I rolled my eyes and tried to resist a glance down at my casual jeans and tank top attire. They weren't even dirty after the struggle with the vampire. I didn't think I looked like a hooligan, but the sharp once over she gave me led me to wonder. Well, my tank top did read, "This is so not my eyes," across my chest in big red letters.

What did she know? I thought smugly as I drew myself up to my full height plus the four-inch boot heels. I fixed her with a direct stare as I jabbed a finger at the button. There, I pressed it. Now let me in! I wasn't about to be intimidated by some old lady behind a desk.

After an unnecessarily long moment of consideration, she gave in and pressed the door release. Great, now I had to talk to her.

The station was even smaller inside than I expected. I entered a small room and the heavy door slammed shut behind me. The lock clicked, and I realized that one must be let out manually as well. Nice.

I didn't hesitate in approaching the woman, who glowered at me as if I'd eaten her Grandma. I pulled my driver's license from my wallet and slid it through the small hole in the window. I just assumed she'd request it.

"My name is Alexa O'Brien." I gestured to my I.D. card lying between us. I'd always thought that photo looked like a mug shot. "I'm here to pick up Raoul Roberts."

She cast a glance at my identification and shrugged as she picked it up. "Just a moment." With another suspicious glance, she'd moved down a hall to the right, beyond my view.

The quiet was deafening. I tapped my nails on the counter to break the silence, and then I chewed on a pinky nail in annoyance. *This had better be good*, I thought. If Raoul called me here over something stupid like a DUI, I was going to break his nose. If anything, he probably deserved to stay locked up.

The energy shifted, and I sensed their approach before the big man in uniform appeared from the hall. The incredibly depressing receptionist followed and twirled a strand of greying hair between her fingers. She still clutched my I.D. between her fingers, and I extended a hand to indicate that I wanted it.

Her gaze went first to the officer, who stood a full head taller than either of us was. At his nod, she dropped it within my reach.

"Ms. O'Brien, hello. I'm Constable Avery." He moved immediately to open the high security door and ushered me into the station.

Constable Avery was in his early fifties or so. He had a fit football player's build that had softened only slightly with time. His hair was cropped short, and his moustache was more grey than brown. Despite the gun at his hip, his crystal blue eyes were serious but friendly.

"Pleased to meet you." I accepted his offered hand. He judged my handshake as flimsy, but, if I'd been there to out strength him, I could have crushed his fingers with minimal effort.

"And you are Mr. Roberts's…?" The question hung between us, which left me to fill in the blank.

"Colleague." The word just popped out. The last thing I wanted was for anyone to assume more than that. "I'm a close friend and colleague."

"Alright." He gave me a quick once over and decided that I wasn't much of a threat. "Why don't you come on back while I finish up with some paperwork?"

His quick dismissal ticked me off, but I knew it wasn't personal. If he'd known that I could gut him with my fingers alone, I doubt he would have been so willing to turn his back on me.

I followed him past a series of rooms until they gave way to offices. The majority were empty at this time of night, save one. A uniformed officer spoke loudly into the phone, oblivious to our passing.

"I don't give a rat's ass, Jim!" Her voice dropped in pitch when she said, "If you blow this case for me, I'll bust your balls from here to Timbucktwo."

I smirked but resisted the urge to laugh. A lady needed special skills to work in an industry like law enforcement.

The last two doors were heavy iron with a safety glass window. Inside, Raoul sat at a small table, alone in the windowless room. He clutched a Styrofoam cup of coffee, but he didn't show much interest in it. He just stared straight ahead and drummed his fingers on the tabletop, while he whistled a jaunty tune. To me, this attempt at keeping his cool revealed exactly how close he was to turning wolf on these people and tearing a few faces off.

I did not hide my smirk when Constable Avery turned a key in the lock and swung the door open. I had a good mind to go in there clucking away like a distraught wife, just to embarrass him further.

His expression clearly stated that he was more than ready to leave. I noted how his first response was to glare at me, then Constable Avery.

I raised a questioning eyebrow and rested one hand on my hip. I stopped just inside the doorway. Coal black eyes fixed on me, Raoul raised the corner of his top lip in the hint of a snarl.

For someone who wanted my help, he sure wasn't doing a good job of making me feel especially giving. This was a complete joke.

Black hair hung long around Raoul's face. He'd gotten a trendy cut since I'd seen him last. It now rested just above his shoulders rather than well below. He looked damn good, as much as I hated to think so. His wide shoulders were squared, and he looked tightly wound, as if braced for trouble. He wore his usual dark suit, Armani or something equally pricey. My senses thrilled at his heady wolf scent mixed with aftershave.

A frown creased my brow. Why had I even agreed to come here? Was there really nobody else he could call for this? I'd bet my money that he had several women who would be more than willing to waste their time with this crap. Why me?

Avery lingered near the door as if awaiting my cue for him to leave us.

"Is he being charged with anything?" I asked outright. It earned me a grimace from Avery and a death glare from Raoul.

"No, not at the moment." Avery crossed his arms over his massive chest and looked down at me from his six-foot-plus frame.

"Then may we have a moment alone?" I followed up with a quick smile.

His eyes darted between Raoul and me as if weighing the odds of it being a bad idea. "I'll be right across the hall."

I knew he granted us the illusion of privacy, but it worked fine for me. I wasn't the one sitting in the hot seat.

"You want to tell me what I'm doing here at this hour of night?" I said when Avery left. "What did you do? Sell someone a shit shack and convince them it was a castle?"

"You're not funny, Alexa." He sat back in his chair and crossed one leg smoothly over the other. Raoul looked no less masculine for it. He made a show of fussing with the crease in his pants to avoid meeting my eyes.

"I'm waiting." I crossed my arms and tapped my foot in an exaggerated display of impatience.

"Julie Price was murdered last night. I was taken in as a suspect due to my previous relationship with her." He cleared his throat and dared me to make assumptions.

"And? If they're letting you out, then obviously, you got away with it." My lips quirked, but I maintained a straight face.

The look he shot me was absolutely murderous. Risking a glance at the open door, he growled. It was so low that it reached only my sensitive ears. My defenses kicked into overdrive, my instincts instantly went on full alert.

Ok, maybe I shouldn't have said that with a cop within earshot, but Raoul needed to know I wasn't at his beck and call. I hadn't been that girl for a long time.

Julie Price, I'd heard the name once or twice before. She had worked for the same real estate company as Raoul. The two became lovers, as was the usual for a guy like him, but it had ended some time last year. If I recalled correctly, they'd broken it off when her husband discovered the affair. That had been months ago.

"Alright," I sighed and shuffled my feet. I refused to take the empty seat across from him. "Give me the low down."

The look he shot at me oozed venom. "I didn't do it." He spoke through clenched teeth. "As of right now, I'm being released simply because they can't prove it was me. But, considering they can't verify my alibi, I'm still under scrutiny."

"Why can't they verify your alibi?" I had a few of my own sneaking suspicions why, but I wanted to hear it from him.

He glanced across the hall through the open door, cleared his throat and picked away at the edge of his coffee cup. "I was with Belle."

Well, that explained it, alright. Belle Listand was nothing but trouble. A mid-thirties werewolf with a fondness for sins of the flesh, she was on my list of least favorite people. Her elderly husband had been ailing for more than a year now. Since he had no living offspring and a whole lot of money in oil, she went to great lengths to keep him in the dark about her many affairs. The old guy had no clue, neither that she spent her nights with other men, rather than in her grand rooms on his sprawling estate, nor that she occasionally ran on four legs and howled at the moon.

If Raoul had no alibi because he'd been with Belle, then that meant she had refused to risk her husband finding out that she was a no good tramp. And, she most definitely was the type to allow someone else to sit in prison because she had a secret to hide.

"So, she left you in the lurch huh? That shouldn't come as a surprise."

"It doesn't." He got to his feet in one smooth motion, which brought Avery back with the sound of jingling keys.

"I've got some papers for you to sign. Then you'll be free to go." He handed a pen to Raoul.

He made eye contact with each of us in turn, and I had to admire his demeanor. Though he may not have consciously realized it, he was holding his body in a slightly defensive stance. Some humans sensed our unnatural vibe.

Though I didn't want to get into the close confines of a car with Raoul, the faster we left, the sooner I could drop him off and be rid of him. As I led the way to my car, Raoul made a point of keeping in step beside me rather than behind. I couldn't believe how pathetically fragile his ego was. I shook my head but said nothing.

"Thank you, Alexa." Taking a gamble, he laid a warm hand softly on my shoulder. I fought the urge to actively shrug it off. "I really appreciate your time. I mean it."

Now that he was touching me, I wished that I hadn't come. "So where am I taking you? Is your car at home?" I tried for nonchalance but failed miserably when the awkwardness never ceased. Uncomfortable and annoyed, I eased away from his touch.

"Yeah, home would be nice. I can take a cab to my car tomorrow. It's in the city, at the office."

So, they'd arrested him at work. Ouch. That one had to hurt. I didn't even have a scathing remark for that. Shame on me.

As we approached the Charger, I pressed the remote unlock. The lights flooded us in a sudden spotlight.

"When did you get the new car?" Raoul gave it an appraising once over but paused when he caught sight of my scowl. "It's not a new car?"

"You asked me that six months ago. I've had the damn thing for more than a year. Do you ever pay attention to anyone or anything outside of your personal bubble?" It came out fast, before I'd realized it. "Forget it."

Almost anxiously, Raoul reached for the passenger door handle. I knew he wanted to say something, most likely a bullshit apology, which I did not want to hear.

I started the engine and rushed to turn the volume down when the Hair Nation station on satellite radio blasted at us.

"Cinderella," Raoul commented as he did a quick survey of the roomy interior. "Good band in their time."

With the car in gear, I risked a glance in his direction. Our sudden close confines didn't sit well with me. A funny smile played along his perfectly shaped lips. I think it had something to do with the Cinderella song, a nostalgia of sorts.

"I didn't listen to them much myself." Driving was a good, valid excuse not to have to look directly at him. "I was always more of a Motley Crue kind of girl."

"Nice."

Silence fell, and with it, the tension grew thick enough to dance on. Just great. The ten minute drive to Raoul's house was going to feel like an eternity. I messed around with the air conditioner settings when we came to a red light. I'd take any excuse to focus my attention on something other than useless small talk.

The light turned green, and I pulled onto a nearly empty street. One lone car sped past going in the opposite direction.

"I didn't murder Julie." He spoke so fast that I almost didn't catch the words. His stiff posture looked uncomfortable, and I knew it couldn't possibly be because of my super comfy seats.

"Um, ok." Another glance at him revealed both fists clenched tightly on his lap. There was a desperation in his energy that picked at my senses.

"I think someone's trying to set me up. Probably that good for nothing husband of hers."

I didn't need to look to know that he was staring at me, gauging my reaction. Ever the careful driver, I focused on nothing but the road ahead.

"Well, no offense, Raoul, but perhaps you should make a habit of seeing single women." I shrugged a shoulder to emphasize the casual tone that I forced.

As we approached the train tracks, the red lights began to blink, and I hit the gas hard. I was not letting myself get trapped with him any longer than necessary. Railway tracks successfully bisect the town at three different points. If we got stuck on one side due to a slow moving train, there wasn't much I could do but wait. By the time I reached the crossing outside of town, I would have spent an extra ten minutes getting there.

The engine gave a mighty rev as we shot over the crossing well before the arms came down. Raoul's right hand gripped the door handle hard enough to turn his knuckles white. I was keenly aware of the sudden acceleration of his pulse.

He squirmed in his seat, clearly attempting to brush off the split second of fear. "Single women have too many hang ups. It's never just sex with them."

The tiny hairs on the back of my neck bristled, and a small fantasy played out in my head in which I throttled him with my bare hands. "God, do you have to be so callous? What's wrong with wanting more than only to be another nameless number on a list?"

He cast me a look that clearly said I just didn't get it. My temper began to rise, but I reined it in. In just a few more minutes, he would be gone.

"Don't be so dramatic." His ebony locks moved as he chuckled. "You always were the emotional type."

That had been a direct hit. "Which explains why you were getting acquainted with the booking process rather than me."

Maybe it hadn't been such a good idea to do this just one night before the three days of the moon began. The day before, the day of and the day after the full moon is a highly powerful time. Animal urges and instincts are at their strongest and many are unable to deny the call of the wolf. Of course, most of us learned to control it. The moon doesn't really have every shifter taking multiple partners or turning into a raging wolf in the grocery store checkout line.

Raoul watched me with eyes so dark they were nearly black. He was trying to unnerve me. A piece of shoulder length black hair fell across one eye, and he gave his head a toss. "Oh, here we go. I was wondering how long it would take for the gloves to come off."

A frustrated growl rumbled in my throat, and I had to look away before his smug smile made me to do something that I'd regret.

"You're a real piece of work, Raoul, you know that? In just a matter of seconds, you've got me wishing that I'd screened your call." With a quick shoulder check, I changed lanes and then signaled to take the next left after the golf course.

Instead of anger or irritation like I'd anticipated, the conceited jerk threw his head back and laughed heartily. "If only, huh?"

"You're an asshole." My fingers tightened on the wheel, and I forced myself to take a deep breath before I took out one of his eyes with a carefully directed claw.

"Well, I certainly didn't get rich by always being the nice guy."

Ain't that the truth? As I turned into The Fairways, the golf course neighborhood where Raoul lived, I turned the radio up a few notches. Maybe he would get the hint.

One of the old KISS songs from the 80s boomed out cheesy sexual innuendos. Not wanting to encourage that mode of thought, I hit buttons until I recognized Raine Maida's voice. Our Lady Peace was a nice non-sexual band.

The houses got nicer as we went. As we continued from street to street, the structure size grew substantially. We were nearing the east end of town, the rich district. My own house was directly opposite us on the town's west facing edge. *Just six more blocks to Raoul's.*

"So, is everyone still doing the lunar run?" He asked suddenly, and I frowned in response. Was this another lame attempt at casual conversation?

"If you showed up once in a while you'd know."

"It's flattering to know that I'm missed. Maybe I'll see you Saturday then. If anymore of my girlfriends end up dead, I'm going to need the alibi."

I laughed then. "Right. Just tell the cops you turned into a wolf with several others from the community and ran in the forest outside town. Then maybe they'll just lock you in a psychiatric hospital instead of in with the guys who just wait for pretty, well-kept men to arrive."

"That's not what I meant, Alexa. Somebody would back me, even if it isn't you." He practically snarled at me, and I glared my hardest.

"You know what, Raoul?" I swung the weighty car onto his street. The tires squealed, and I delighted in his sudden dirty look when a face peered out the neighbor's window. "You better watch it. Because if you go to jail, your secret is going to come out, eventually, and God forbid you wind up in a lab."

His eyes narrowed, but he obviously didn't consider the scenario a realistic outcome. "Spare me."

I let the car jerk to a rough halt in front of his giant three-level split. "That's fine. Disregard caution and common sense. But if you're such a big boy, then I trust you won't be wasting anymore of my time or my free evening phone minutes."

Raoul's door swung open silently. He fished a crumpled twenty from his pocket. "For gas."

I fumed so hard that, if steam didn't come out of my ears soon, the top of my head was going to blow. "You're offering me money? Why didn't you just call a cab then?"

His wide shoulders moved in a slight shrug, and he avoided meeting my eyes. He had only called me to see if I would come. My anger was nothing but a game to him.

I wanted to yell at him to get out of my car, but he did so before I could. When I wouldn't touch his money, he dropped it on the passenger seat.

"So, I'll see you Saturday, then." He glanced at his feet and then at the neighboring houses before finally looking at me.

I thought of every woman of all ages, colors and creeds who had trusted their heart to a man like Raoul only to have it handed back to them used.

"Kiss my ass, Raoul." My foot hit the gas and jerked the open door from his grasp.

I cut a U-turn in the middle of the street and closed the door with the momentum. A thrill shot through me when the tires squealed even louder upon my exit. In the rear view mirror, I could see Raoul hurrying up the walk, eager to get inside before the entire street was gawking out the window.

I switched to the local rock station and turned the volume way up. Finally, I pulled out of Raoul's swanky neighborhood.

The moment that I pulled into my driveway, I punched Shaz's number into my cell phone. I left a message for him to come by the house after work. Kylarai and I shared a two-level bungalow, a cute little white house with brown trim. It wasn't the fanciest of dwellings, but it's roomy enough without being too big or too small. The front walk was framed by one of those archway gates layered in flowers, courtesy of Kylarai. As always, I took a deep breath as I passed beneath it. That fresh flower scent was heavenly.

A glow beyond the living room curtains indicated that Kylarai was still up. Because of her career as a successful divorce attorney, she had little time for decorative ventures. However, when the urge struck her, the things that she came up with were simply amazing. Since she altered her schedule two months ago, she'd been doing her paperwork at home and just going to the office to meet with clients. I thought she did it so she'd have more time to dress up the house. I found something new almost every time I came home.

I frowned down at the new mat in front of the door that virtually screamed, "Welcome". I'd told her that there was no need to be welcoming anybody here. I'd prefer an unwelcome mat, myself. The time that I had found one at a novelty store, it had lasted a matter of hours before disappearing, never to be seen again.

Shaz and I joked that Kylarai was the mother hen of our little group because of her gentle, protective nature. She went out of her way to take care of us. I still found it hard to believe she was a thirty-three year old widow who'd torn out her husband's throat, but, she was, and she had. He'd beaten her into submission for the last time. After working for more than five years to hide her wolf from him, she unleashed it in a matter of seconds. I wonder if old Johnny boy had known his wife watched from within that furry face as his blood sprayed.

Endearing and soft spoken, but she'd eat your face off. That was Kylarai.

"How did it go?" She called to me when I came into the foyer. "Did you get rid of Patrick Morgan?"

"Yeah, he was no problem." I kicked off my boots and breathed a sigh of relief after each one.

Joining her in the living room, I settled into the leather easy chair near the large picture window that looked on to the street. "But, I have totally unrelated, stupid news."

"What now?" She asked with a worried glint in her grey eyes.

I told her about the bullshit call from Raoul. Her eyes widened as I spoke, but she didn't say anything until I'd finished.

"I wouldn't expect that from Raoul. He loves the ladies - there's no doubt about that - but slaughtering them? No way. There has to be another explanation."

I sucked in my breath and let it out slowly. Raoul and I were many things, but friends wasn't one of them. We rarely saw eye to eye, but due to status and power, we were the top two werewolves in town. Aside from that, we couldn't be more different.

"I don't know what to do, Ky. That son of a bitch had no reason to call me down there. What the hell is that about?" I took in her comfortable appearance where she sat diagonal to me on the full length matching leather couch. Clad in silky soft pajama pants and her favorite fuzzy robe, she looked the epitome of what I wanted to feel right then.

"I know there's no love lost between the two of you," she replied with a toss of her trendy brunette, Posh Spice-style bob. "But, did you ever think he does this stuff to reach out to you?"

I stared at her as if she'd grown two heads, and she shrugged. "If this isn't some kind of misunderstanding, if he's killing people, then he'd have to be stopped."

Her expression grew wary. "What are you saying, Alexa?"

"I don't know. He's driving me crazy. He is crazy. And, if he goes on a killing spree, then he'll have to be stopped before he endangers the rest of us."

Though I never breathed a word of it to Kylarai, I suspected Raoul would rat us all out if he was discovered to be a Were and put in a lab. He'd try to take us down with him simply so he wasn't suffering alone.

For a minute, there was only the sound of the wall clock ticking and quiet laughter from the television in the far corner. Kylarai's eyes took on a haunted look, and I could see that she'd thought the same when she nodded in agreement. I couldn't very well let Raoul bring murder and mayhem to our quiet little town. He would ruin us all.

"You know I agree with you," she said at last. As quiet as she was, she certainly wasn't known for being weak. She'd take out anyone in her way if push came to shove. "But, don't be so quick to jump to conclusions. You have to be sure he's doing this. There has to be more evidence than that to land him a death sentence."

"Well, the cops let him go, what does that tell you?" I forced my limbs to move and sauntered down the hall, around the corner, to my room.

After changing into fuzzy sweatpants and a clean t-shirt, I gave my long hair a halfhearted shove away from my face. Kylarai's muffled response sounded like, "He didn't do it." I made a face of disgust at my closet that nobody could see.

I re-entered the living room just as Shaz rang the doorbell. He was earlier than I'd expected. After savoring one of his perfect hugs, I retold to him what I had said to Kylarai.

"Why would someone want to kill Julie?" he asked. I found it odd, that was the first thought he had.

"Did you know her?"

"I met her once or twice when I dropped by Raoul's. But, that had to be almost a year ago, now." His eyes took on a haunted glow.

Being three years younger than me, Shaz is still finding out how much danger and death plays a part in our world. His remaining innocence along with his realistic acceptance is what I love about him.

"You don't think it was Raoul?" Was I the only one who thought that he probably did do it?

"Let's not go there," Kylarai interjected. "Not until we're at that point."

Shaz nodded, his lips pressed together tight. "If Raoul was to brutally kill someone, he'd have a damn good reason. And much as I hate to say it, he doesn't place that much value on past lovers."

"Which is exactly why he could do it so easily and feel no remorse." The bitterness was thick in my tone, and I ignored the look they exchanged.

"You look cold." Shaz ran a warm hand down my arm. My wolf responded by leaping against my inner core as if trying to break free. Closing my eyes, I could feel the pull of the wild in my veins and smell the pine and spice of fur.

"Actually, I think I need to go for a run." I didn't want to sit there trying to convince them what depths of scum Raoul really was.

We all knew him differently. This conversation had happened many times before. They assumed my opinion of him was strictly personal. Maybe it was, but my reasons were good.

I rose from my chair and stretched languorously. "Want to come with?"

"Always." Shaz was on his feet in a heartbeat.

"Count me out," Kylarai said and stifled a yawn as we moved to the sliding glass door off the attached kitchen. "I've been up for almost twenty-four hours. I'm going to bed."

The early morning air held a slight chill that caressed my naked flesh as I slipped out of my clothes. The sky was the color of absolute black, the darkest piece of night just before dawn breaks the barrier on the horizon. A thin cloud cover blocked out every star.

I stood at the end of the yard and looked out, onto the stretch of field behind the house. The tree line, which was about half a mile away, taunted my wolf. I longed to run and stretch my muscles to capacity. I needed to feel the burn as I pushed myself to the max.

Unlatching the gate, I turned back to see Shaz drop his t-shirt on the patio railing. His build was average but firm, and I allowed myself to sneak an extra glance at his well-formed body. As a werewolf, one certainly got used to being nude. Nudity came with the territory.

The grass crumpled softly beneath his feet as he approached, only to spring up again when he'd moved on. I knew he was going to touch me before he actually did. His energy was warm and seemed to reach for me. A hand gently traced the curve of my waist.

I raised my head to look at him. My eyes turned wolf in a blink; the deep brown of my irises filled the whites so they were no longer human. He smiled down at me and placed a quick kiss on the tip of my nose.

"Ready?" His low, smooth voice was a whisper. Those intense jade eyes held a teasing glint.

I gave him a playful shove. His closeness was undoing my last bit of resistance. I needed the change, and with the full moon only two days away, I was more than ready to run wild.

In response to his question, I threw my head back and looked into the sky, as if it were a dark velvet veil that hid the secrets of the universe. I held my hands out before me and just let the wolf inside break free.

The sudden blast of supernatural energy that shot through me forced me to my knees. A small cry escaped me. For just a split second, I was flooded with the most horrid pain. It flowed over me as bone and muscle shifted in reformation. In an instant, the pain had become soothing languor. In seconds, I stood in my backyard as a large wolf, with fur the same ash blonde as my hair.

Shaz makes the most beautiful snow-white wolf due to his insanely white-blond hair. He is much larger than I am, with green orbs that stand out in awe-inspiring intensity. He nuzzled me with a wet muzzle before bounding through the open gate.

We raced across the field at top speed. We always tried to beat each other to a particular tree at the far edge of the field. Shaz often took off fast and then burned out, so I planned to take advantage of that at just the right time to propel myself forward and win.

The wind in my fur was a cooling breeze that carried the scents of the forest to my sensitive nose. Blood on the air informed me that a few coyotes had managed to kill a small doe not long ago. The slightest hint of rain still indicated an early morning shower, and I savored the scent.

Just as I'd expected, Shaz began to lose his steady pace and dropped in speed. I took the opportunity to burst ahead of him, and he nipped at my heels. I stood in front of the victory tree with the best mocking, tongue-lolling, goofy grin that any lupine could muster.

When he arrived at the tree too late, his response was to wrestle me to the ground in a series of playful bites and nips. I could hear little critters running through the underbrush to take cover. I broke free of Shaz's grip and pounced on him to bite the tips of his ears. He feigned surrender and followed up with a nice bite on my flank, one that might actually bruise.

After we'd exhausted ourselves, we rested in the soft grass beneath a large evergreen tree. We easily fell asleep amid the sounds of the early morning birds waking and the last few hoots of an owl as he made his way home for the day. I rested my head on my paws and dozed. Shaz's head rested on my back, and before long, I heard the soft sound of even breathing.

To be a wolf wasn't hard. No, the hard part was to go back to being human afterward. In a world of noise, pollution and selfishness, I enjoyed the relief, the escape to something pure, natural and free. More than once, I had entertained the thought of living among nature as a wolf always and saying goodbye to the human world. However, it could never be so simple.

As a creature with a duel nature, to deny one risked the other. Several shifters had chosen one side, human or wolf. Most of them had driven themselves into madness. The balance in-between was often hard to find, but it was always worth it.

I sighed with contentment and allowed all human thought to blow away on the gentle breeze. Human worry had no place here, among the forest and its occupants. I was wolf and comfortably so.

Chapter Four

Friday night was the hottest night at Lucy's Lounge. I figured I would stop by for a bite to eat before making the short highway trek to Edmonton. The lounge kitchen made a to-die-for sirloin steak.

I touched up my smoky, dark eyeliner in the car. No lipstick, I rarely wore any. Tonight I'd decided to exchange my casual attire for basic black dress pants and a snug, corset-style, black top. My hair flowed long and loose down my back.

I preferred to park near the back of the lot. I didn't see the point in fighting for the closest space. By parking in the back, I had to walk past the alley that ran behind the building. No sooner had I approached it than I felt that cool, undead presence. Arys was down there.

I debated leaving the brightly lit lot and entering the darkened alley. Two guys whistled at me as they walked to their car, but I paid them little attention. My mind focused only on that cold energy drawing me in. That centuries-old power seemed to beckon to me on the still night air.

I have a natural distrust of alleys. They're not known for their safety. They are too dark with too many shadows to hide in. Anything, vampire or other, with any kind of psychic ability, can shield its energy. In effect, it can make as if it weren't even there and leave its victim unaware. What a big bad wolf I was, afraid of the dark. However, Arys was down there, which assured me that nothing else was.

I moved silently forward. I could feel Arys in the blackness. I had gone halfway down when another alley intersected, and the scent of fresh blood pulled me to the left. I wasn't surprised to find him draped in the shadows with a woman clutched tightly in his grasp.

Even in the dark, I could see the whites of her eyes as she struggled. He held her immobile, and my heart paused when her gaze landed on me. I was still yards away, but she saw me clearly as her vampire-induced disorientation loosened its hold. She gave a strangled cry, and Arys clamped a hand over her mouth. As she whimpered, I stood frozen, unable to come to her aid as she hoped. If anything, my presence only excited the vampire more.

Arys's pupils were a drowning black. His mouth was smeared with blood as he drank from her jugular. I should have been sickened, but I wasn't. Had becoming a supernatural creature made me immune to human suffering? Not entirely.

The fear in her wide-eyed stare bothered me more than her fading life. My own reaction to the scene bothered me more. Despite my own personal beliefs and born humanity, I am a predator, and in that moment, I enjoyed what I saw. The scent of spilt human blood tantalized my senses. The sight of the crimson splashes stirred things low inside me.

As the light began to fade from his victim's eyes, she ceased struggling and hung loose in his embrace like a forgotten rag doll. I watched in complete silence until she was nothing but an empty husk, and her vacant, dead gaze stared over his shoulder at me.

Arys stepped back and let her hit the ground with a thud that dropped my stomach to my knees. "Did you enjoy the show?" He wiped a hand across his full lips, and his tongue flicked over his crimson-smeared fang-teeth. "I always appreciate an audience." The predatory glow in his eyes began to fade as he came towards me.

"I see you've been a busy boy tonight," I commented casually, though I couldn't deny the rapid beat of my heart.

"Yeah, well, they're good for more than just one thing." He cast a glance back at the body, and I got an unwelcome visual of the vampire making love to the woman that now lie dead. He'd taken her to his bed, possessed her body, and enjoyed her heat, but intended all along to take it away.

The human side of me was shocked that I wasn't more appalled at Arys's nonchalance. He spoke like those guys in high school, the ones that most girls fall for before they realize their mistake. Though the wolf in me did not take life from its lovers, it did, however, appreciate his predator logic.

I swallowed heavily, suddenly apprehensive and too aware of the sweet scent of blood drying on the corpse. I'd never thought that I'd feel threatened by Arys, but I decided that maybe I should.

I knew that Arys killed with discretion. Vampires do not have to kill to survive. However, feeding without the kill was like sex without the orgasm, according to my colleague, Kale Sinclair. It explained why some vampires just quit giving a damn.

Arys watched me with cool blue eyes and a curious expression on his forever-young face. "What's your deal, Alexa? What brings you on a vampire hunt tonight?"

"I was just passing by. I felt you down here." I licked my dry lips, and my head filled with visions of tearing into warm flesh. I could almost sense blood, hot on my tongue, as its intoxicating scent filled my nostrils. I wanted to consume the life within the girl's blood. I shook my head, and my vision cleared. "You shouldn't be killing in town. It's dangerous."

"Let me worry about that, my lovely wolf." Arys studied me hard, and I wondered if he somehow knew what I'd just seen. With a hand on my back, he guided me out of the alley towards the glow of the light. "But, I am curious what had you hot footing it out of here so fast last night."

I told him about Raoul as we walked, giving him my best rant, one that would have been wasted on Kylarai and Shaz. The energy of his fresh kill buzzed around Arys, which gave me goose bumps and a constant tingle down my spine.

"You shouldn't have gone to him."

"I know. I thought maybe he was in real trouble. Lord knows why I'd even care."

"I certainly don't see why you do. Every time you give him a chance, he lets you down. There is so much more out there. Why limit yourself?" He laid a warm hand on my forearm and gave a gentle squeeze. I couldn't mistake the meaning of his words nor deny the warm heat that rose to meet his touch.

My breath caught as his energy danced along my skin and raised the little hairs on the back of my neck. His magnetic pull remained familiar, but the flow was different. The living, breathing power of my wolf rushed to the surface to meet the dark, icy power of the undead. If Arys's sharp gasp was any indication, he was as surprised as I was.

His hand moved down my arm until he had entwined his fingers in mine. With this more solid connection, our two very different powers joined into one that took my breath away. A warm glow hummed all around us. Pleasure raced through my blood, and I wanted more. Arys's pupils dilated in response. I could feel him peering into my soul.

I felt him in my head, a gentle touch on my mind. In the same moment, we shared a thought, a memory. He saw through my wolf's eyes as she raced through the forest, answering the call of the night. Bloody images flashed through my head and the rush of sinking fangs into a soft, slender neck entranced me.

I wanted more. I wanted to climb inside him and roll around in all of that power. He took a step and closed the remaining space between us. The heat grew into a fever, something I fought to escape before it consumed me.

"Arys, stop." With all my resolve, I pulled my hand from his and shoved him back. He blinked at me a few times but didn't step out of my personal space.

"That was amazing. I would never have guessed you could do that," he said. The look he gave me was undeniably full of desire.

"I didn't do anything," I stammered. He wasn't buying it.

"I knew you were more than a shifter, but I didn't realize how much more. This is more than a human's natural ability." His expression was serious, but he sounded drunk. The energy had buzzed me, too. It continued to throb through my veins. "You're a metaphysical dream, Alexa. I've known vampires like you, but never one whose mortal heart still beats."

"I'm not a vampire, though. I don't need to take from others to survive."

"Your energy calls like something that has never been human. It seeks something from me." He shook his head in wonder but never took his eyes off me.

"The energy, it's not always sensual," I offered lamely. I didn't know what to say, and I was feeling very ill at ease.

"No?" Arys raised an eyebrow, but a satisfied grin spread across his handsome features.

I did my best to fight the blush that crept across my cheeks. My face felt hot, and I wanted to offer any lame excuse just so I could escape the sudden awkwardness.

"Arys, I have to go. Duty calls." Not exactly a lie, but he looked at me like he knew damn well I was making a getaway.

I had to, though. He shared so many of my abilities, and my power seemed to really like him. The metaphysical attraction had been progressing over time, and I didn't fully trust myself around him anymore.

Needless to say, I skipped the sirloin steak dinner that I'd been anticipating. I made up for it by stopping by Swiss Chalet to grab a delicious chicken dinner on my way to see Lena.

She's one of just two humans that Veryl works with. She's a natural witch and a truly amazing spell caster. Lena was white witch to the core. All of her spell casting focused on things like healing, strength and protection.

Lena helped me learn how to focus, to concentrate. Without that, I couldn't control the outcome. She taught me plenty of tricks for both accessing and grounding excess energy. Without her, I would most likely still be a bumbling fool with little control or skill.

A few times a month, Lena and I got together to work with energy. As a spell caster, her manipulation usually required the use of an object as a conductor and storage point whereas I tend to be my own conductor. Though she uses the energy in a different way than I do, we call and manipulate it the same way.

I truly enjoyed the time we spent on focal exercises and female bonding. Lena reminded me a little of my mom, and I valued our relationship.

The office building we all used as a base was dark, except for the one light that blazed in the kitchen, where Lena was making tea. We'd have the place to ourselves, which was just as well considering we were going to be playing with energy.

"Good evening, Lena," I called from the entryway so I wouldn't startle the older lady.

"Hey Alexa, how's it going?" She smiled up at me when I entered the room. Her eyes sparkled, and she looked at least a decade younger than her fifty-three years.

"Pretty good. How about yourself?"

"Great, thank you. Just fixing a cup of herbal tea. Care for some?" Her long, dark blonde hair hung in a French braid to her waist.

"No. Thank you, though," I said as I dug into my Swiss Chalet bag. "You're not hungry, are you?"

"Oh, heavens no. I ate an entire pumpkin pie by myself for dinner." She patted her small belly as if it were enormous.

"How's the shop keeping going?" I asked. Lena owns a small magic shop on Whyte Avenue, in Edmonton, where she sells all kinds of neat new age gear, magic books, and trinkets.

"It's great. I had to hire a part-time girl to help out a few times a week."

"That's awesome. Good for you."

I sat at the table and chatted with her while I chowed down on chicken, potato and veggies. Dinner wasn't quite as succulent as a rare steak, but it was still damn good. After a long moment of quiet satisfaction, I gathered my garbage together and headed for the silver trashcan.

I asked, "So what have you got for me today?"

"Just some of the focal exercises from last time. I don't think there's much more that I can show you. You're a natural anyway."

"Aw, that's sweet of you to say." My cheeks warmed in response to her compliment.

She shrugged. "You've such an uncanny ability. Some of us have to work really hard to achieve what comes so naturally to you." She studied me thoughtfully, and I paused in mid-motion as I dug a piece of gum from my purse.

"What?" I asked when her brow furrowed in one of those worried looks that only a mother can wear.

She shook her head, and her braid moved like it was alive. "I don't know dear. I do hope you're careful though."

Lena often expressed concern for me. In our world, no shortage of things can get you killed. Power and ability are just two of many.

"I'm always careful, Lena." I tried to smile reassuringly, but she dismissed my phony attempt.

"Seriously, Alexa. Don't let too many people know what you can do. It's far better to be underestimated."

I knew that firsthand. However, the real danger was those with similar abilities. I can't hide my psi abilities from others with the same.

I leaned against the kitchen counter and crossed my arms over my chest. I watched as Lena pulled a small, blue velvet bag from her jeans pocket. She reached inside and withdrew a small green gem that I couldn't identify. Lena had more charms and amulets than I had hair on my head.

"I'm just going to draw a small circle on the floor so I can energize these charms." She shook two more gems out of the bag, one ocean blue and the other a deep purple.

She poured salt straight from the box on to the floor, which enclosed her in a protection circle large enough to sit in comfortably. I never joined her within it. Since I'd become a werewolf, I wanted nothing to do with that magical cage. Something in my wolf nature shied away from the magic of others. It gave me a strong sense of discomfort that grew with the unnaturalness of the intended result. Of course, I use metaphysical walls on others. I just don't want them used on me.

She told me once that she doesn't like being inside the salt circle either, due to claustrophobia, but it would keep her safe if something bad detected her magic and decided to drop by.

"What should I do?" I asked. I frowned at a splash of dipping sauce on the inside of my wrist. "You have nothing new for me?" I pursed my lips and watched as she laid the three charms on the floor so that they formed a large triangle.

"Why don't you work on that touchless psi ball again? You did far better than me." I had created a bigger ball than Lena, but at the size of a grape, I hardly found it to be brag worthy.

The no touch energy ball had taken a lot out of me. It involved creating the ball without the use of hands. The mind-only ball was much easier said than done. The fingertips are an especially sensitive tool in a psi exercise, a key factor in most energy conduction that united the body and the mind in creation. To do it with the mind alone was both uber advanced and damned hard.

"That was a hell of a task." I held my breath when she wiggled her fingers above the purple gem.

The energy she drew into her circle hummed on the air. She whispered a word of Latin as the stone began to glow.

"What are you doing to them?" I nodded toward the colorful

stones.

She held up a finger to indicate she needed a moment of concentration. I took the hint and left my next question unvoiced. I knew better than to chatter away when someone was trying to focus. Jez was famous for it.

Instead, I returned to the small round table. I pulled the wooden chair out with a scrape and angled it toward the front entry rather than Lena. I closed my eyes, cleared my thoughts, and took a deep breath. I actually put my hands behind my back, to resist the urge to use them. As I simply tuned in to my surroundings, I could feel the power that Lena had called prickle along my skin like pins and needles.

After two more deep breaths, I envisioned a tiny green spark. I watched inside my mind as the glowing orb grew to the size of a golf ball. I opened my eyes to find the psi ball hovering at eye level in front of me. I gasped, drawing Lena's attention. Lena was the only human that I knew who could see energy the way I or a vampire could.

"My heavens, girl," her voice was soft but incredulous. "How did you manage that?"

I shook my head silently. Hell if I knew. The psi ball should have glowed a faint green or gold. Instead, it shimmered in a deep, ocean blue. Energy often took on the same hue as the aura of the practitioner, but my aura is yellow-gold.

My heart surged as a thought hit me and, along with it, a small dose of adrenaline. Arys's aura was blue. I'd seen him work energy before. All we'd done was touch, right?

"I'm really not sure." I breathed, staring at the blue ball hovering a foot from my face.

I glanced at Lena. All three of her charms glowed brightly. I experienced the temporary sensation of wanting to touch them.

"Have you been up to something that I don't know about?" Lena's tone was disturbingly parental.

I turned back to my psi ball to avoid her accusatory stare. I noticed my yellow-gold lining the outside of the ball. As I watched, it swirled throughout the blue like the rainbow in an oil patch. Strange.

"Like what?" I replied. Too late, I added, "Of course not."

I could feel her eyes on me as I feigned supreme concentration. The little ball hovered as if awaiting instruction.

"It's much bigger than the last one you made."

My fingers twitched on the rung of the chair, and the little energy ball dissolved. The free energy buzzed around us like high-pitched radio frequency.

"Maybe that's something you should do outside." A hand flew to her temple where she rubbed lightly. "The intensity of that thing is giving me one hell of a headache. Now, tell me what you've been up to."

"I'm sorry, Lena. Are you alright?" I got up from the wooden chair and approached her circle.

She didn't answer me. She gathered up her glowing gemstones in one hand and broke the salt circle with the other. I took her silence to mean that she was insisting on an explanation.

With a shrug I said, "I touched a vampire. One with one hell of a pull. We've shared a metaphysical attraction since we met, about three years ago. But, it's grown since. It's like nothing else I've ever felt."

I felt silly saying it like that, but it was true. I had no idea why I would respond so strongly to Arys on a power level. It didn't happen with anyone else. Not like that.

"You touched a vampire. How? What do you mean?"

Lena reached for the broom in the corner, but I intercepted the action. I ignored the pointed look that she shot me as I turned to start sweeping. As I cleaned up Lena's salt mess, I told her about the exchange with Arys. I considered not telling her the color of his aura but decided the detail wasn't worth hiding.

The extended silence that followed worried me, and I realized a part of me was scared. I didn't do well when not in control. Whatever drew me to Arys was not within my ability to harness.

"Honey, promise me you'll be careful." Her tone took on a note heavy with worry, and my heart leapt into my throat when she added, "I can't believe what I'm hearing."

"Why? What? You're scaring me." I fought the urge to drop the broom, grab her by the shoulders, and shake out whatever she knew.

Her warm hand reached out to squeeze my arm. "Well now, I'm sorry. Look Alexa, there is plenty that I don't know and may never know. But, what I do know is this: Much the same as the attraction between the north and south ends of a magnet is the attraction between two souls cut from the same magical cloth."

I blinked at her. My mind was racing, but I wasn't following. I moved to empty the dustpan but continued to glance at her attentively.

"When drawn close enough together, their natural attraction makes it impossible for them not to join. Like a battery in a way." She shook her head and frowned. "It's hard to explain. But, two batteries on their own possess an impressive amount of power. If you put them together in the right circuit, they can become so much more than each was on its own."

A light bulb went on in my head as her words sunk in. "So this is just a power thing?" I tensed stiff as I returned the broom to its post in the corner.

Her thoughtful brown eyes were warm when she smiled. "It might be. But, I've never known of such a deep connection between two people without it meaning more." She gave me a wink, and my jaw dropped.

"Wait a minute." I held up both hands in a stop motion. "Please tell me you're not about to use a term like 'soul mates' in this conversation."

Her smile froze. "You're not interested in him? Don't tell me he has it out for you or something. Sheesh. That could only happen to you."

"No, it's not like that. He's a friend, sort of." My thoughts strayed to Shaz. "It's just really complicated."

The white wolf and I were close yet we had never been thoroughly intimate. The unspoken bond had developed quickly. We were fast friends from the beginning. Yet, we were not an item, despite the people who thought that we should be, like Kylarai. Like I said, it's complicated.

Lena nodded in understanding. "Matters of the heart often are."

"It doesn't happen with anybody else." I mused aloud.

"Nobody?"

"Well, I definitely am drawn to the energy of some. It's not the same, though. I vibe off them, but there is no feeling of need or resulting power high." As my thoughts wandered back an hour or two, my cheeks grew hot with embarrassment. Just remembering brought a tingle to the pit of my stomach.

A soft laugh shook Lena's shoulders. She opened her hand to reveal the three sparkling stones.

"Take the purple one. It's for meditation and inner peace. Good for the soul. As for the other thing, I'll look into it and see what I can dig up."

I stared into her hand in wonder. Ever so slowly, I plucked the purple stone from her palm with my thumb and forefinger, careful not to touch the remaining two.

"What are those two for?" I couldn't help but be curious. They were so beautiful. "And, thank you."

"Stress relief and healing properties. My sister tends to be a very high strung person." Lena chuckled and slipped the blue and green stones back into their velvet pouch.

The purple stone seemed to shine just a little bit brighter as I turned it over in my hand. Although the stone was shaped like a random rock, the surfaces shone where the jagged, cut edges split the light.

"Is there anything specific I need to do with it?" I hoped not. Spells and chants are not my forte.

"No, just drop it in your wallet. Keep it by your bed. Whatever. It should stay charmed until the new moon and then it can be re-energized."

"Awesome, Lena, thanks again." Though I wanted to continue examining the dime sized gem, I made myself drop it into my pocket.

"It's no problem. Really. A little positive energy at your side can make a world of difference."

She launched into a story about how one of her amulets saved Kale from a near fatal encounter with the sun. I recognized the story as one that I'd heard before from him. Her tale was interrupted when my cell phone rang.

"Speak of the devil," I murmured upon recognizing Kale's number on the call display.

"Tell me you're up for some fun and games tonight." He purred into the phone like a wanton lover. A shiver crept up my spine in response.

"What kind of games?" I hated the obvious note of curiosity that made its way into my voice. I was as bad as a cat sometimes, which was probably why Jez and I have such a great time together.

"Maybe a little good cop, bad cop. I'm digging for some information."

I contemplated his offer but not for very long. "Which one do I get to be?"

"Whichever one your little heart desires."

Damn vampires. Was there nothing they couldn't do? Each and every one of them whether male or female has this natural pull, to draw prey. Fortunately for them, it works pretty well.

"What's the deal?" I was getting the feeling that he didn't want to fill me in until I met up with him. He had an awful tendency to drag me into situations that I would have never entered otherwise.

"Like I said, I need a little information. No bloodshed, if I can help it." He chuckled, and I frowned in response, despite the fact that he couldn't see it.

I was trying to avoid Lena's fixed gaze without looking conspicuous. I knew she didn't have the keen hearing that some of us had, but the look she was giving me was driving me nuts.

"Where and when?"

* * * *

I practiced the touchless psi ball outside while waiting for Kale to pick me up. I refused to take my car and let someone tag my plate number. I didn't know who he was after or what they were capable of.

Lena sat on the doorstep sipping one of her herbal teas, as she watched the blue and yellow ball hover before me. I hadn't been able to increase its size, but it had been easier to form than the previous try.

"You should save your energy. Lord knows, you'll probably need it if you're out with Kale," Lena admonished.

I let the psi ball drop. The energy dissipated back into the trees and earth. She was most likely right. I'd faced certain death a few times with Kale and barely lived to tell the tale.

"He swears that there shouldn't be any bloodshed. Of course, that doesn't mean much." I chuckled. "I don't think a vampire enjoys a night that doesn't include fresh blood."

Lena gave me a hard, motherly look. "Maybe you shouldn't be running with that vampire so much. He endangers you because he has no mortal limitations. You're better off partnering with Jez."

I had certainly heard this before, but it was usually coming from Kylarai, our little den mother. "I'll be fine, Lena. But, don't think that I don't appreciate your concern. I really do. I trust Kale, as crazy as that may sound. Even though he's gotten me into some bad situations, he's also gotten me out of most of them."

She scoffed, but before she could reply, a sleek, black, 1973 Camaro pulled up to the curb. The windows were tinted so dark that there was no way of seeing who was inside. I was expecting the head of deep brown hair that appeared as Kale exited the car and approached us.

"Ladies!" He greeted us enthusiastically. "How are you this fine evening?"

Kale Sinclair was tall, dark and ridiculously handsome. A vampire more than five hundred years old, he was both a friend and that co-worker who drew me into more trouble than I get paid to deal with. A snappy dresser, he's always well put together. Dressed in a dark, trendy suit and his favorite black duster jacket, he wasn't hard to look at.

After spending a great many years suffering at the hands of the vampiress who turned him, Kale had sought solace by taking out supernaturals like her. Some of the stories of terror that I had heard from him had been enough to keep me awake, blinking in the dark.

"Kale, where in the hell are we going?" I was a cut to the chase kind of girl. Screw the small talk.

"For a business meeting, of course." He winked a puppy dog brown eye at me. The other was startlingly blue in contrast due to an intriguing gene condition, heterochromia iridium. His mismatched eyes were captivating. He had once told me that, as a child, he'd been treated like a monster. More than once, he'd been told that his different colored eyes were a sign of the devil. I thought they were beautiful.

He cast a critical glance at my attire. "Is that what you're wearing?"

I gaped at him open mouthed. "What? I'm wearing dress pants, you ass. And, how the hell was I to know we'd be going out tonight?"

"The pants are fine. Too much cleavage in that top though." He smiled when he said it, and I knew he was teasing, for the most part.

I flipped him my middle finger, and he grinned like the Cheshire cat. "Do you want my company or not?"

"I do, actually. I believe that my target this evening has a penchant for lovely ladies dressed in black." He cocked his head to the side and assessed my appearance. As an afterthought he added, "I'm sure he'll appreciate the cleavage, too. Enticing."

That summed it up enough for me. "A vampire then."

"Kale, you need to stop dragging this girl into your messes." Lena spoke up suddenly. The clink of her mug on the concrete was loud in the stillness. "You're going to get her seriously hurt one of these days. Or worse."

He took one of her hands in his own and turned it over so that he could examine the rings on her every finger. "Now, you know that I would never intentionally let any harm come to Alexa. If I truly thought there was that kind of danger, I would have asked Lilah to join me."

Lilah was a classic vampire loner. We don't interact often. In fact, she doesn't seem to interact with anyone more than necessary other than Veryl.

Lena eyed him with a look of disbelief. She gave her head a shake and shoved his chest playfully. "You don't know when to stop. Any of you. You may not be human, but you're not invincible."

Kale and I shared a look, which earned us Lena's frown. I smiled and gave her arm a pat. "No, we're not. I know that. Even if Kale forgets sometimes."

Which he did all too often. That vampire is a thrill seeker if I've ever seen one. If the chase wasn't intense and pushed to the limit, Kale wasn't having any fun.

We waited for Lena to get in her car and go safely on her way. We then locked up the office and left. Once I was settled on the soft leather seat of the Camaro, Kale pulled us into traffic with a chirp of the tires. I fixed him with my best deadly glare.

"You better not be using me as bait again, buster. Because, I, for one, am not about to play that role again. Especially without even being aware of it."

He chuckled in remembrance, and I punched his upper arm without holding back. His laugh quickly turned to a series of pain-filled noises.

"Alright, I deserved that."

"You deserve more than that." I couldn't help but laugh, even though a part of me held a grudge. My last experience as Kale's bait was certainly a memorable experience for all of the wrong reasons.

"Ok, I owe you one for that. I know. Call it in whenever you feel justified in doing so, and I'll be there to take the hit."

He could bet his lily-white ass that he would be. I was

anticipating the day.

"So, where are we going? And, what's the deal here? You better fill me in … before you blow it, like the last time you left me in the dark."

I gripped the door handle tightly as he zipped ahead of traffic to merge into their lane. I cursed myself for leaving my car behind. What was I thinking? As far as drivers go, I couldn't be sure who was more frightening, Kale or Jez.

"The vampire we're meeting is involved in a blood ring that profits from runaway youths and prostitutes. We will be posing as two potential partners interested in becoming regular buyers. Once we have the guy's trust, we torture information out of him. I want to know who's running the operation." Kale was all business now, speaking matter of fact as he wove in and out of traffic.

I hate it when people lane hop. I actively had to hold my tongue against the complaint that was building.

"Ok, well that's nothing new. We've dealt with crap like this before."

A car up ahead braked suddenly, which caused the rest of us to brake in succession to avoid a collision. I gasped and dug my fingers into the seats. The leather was tougher than human flesh and posed good resistance, but I worried that I would puncture them with my sharp nails.

"We're meeting the guy in the restaurant lounge of a hotel. Our goal is to have him invite us to his suite for a more private discussion, where we will beat some information out of him before leaving him in a pile of ash. It'll be fun." Kale reached to turn the volume up on the radio as the DJ ran through a list of traffic issues affecting the city.

I tried to relax as the scenery flew past. The job sounded straightforward, but I'd been doing this long enough to know that it rarely went as planned.

Chapter Five

The hotel was located on the west side of the city. It was busy due to a conference of some sort inside. That might pose a problem if we had to exit the hotel covered in vampire blood and guts, but I wasn't going to sweat the small stuff until we reached that point.

"He isn't here," Kale breathed near my ear as he scoured the lounge. Other patrons gave him odd looks as they noticed his eyes.

"Alright, I'm going to order a drink then." Without waiting for him to follow, I approached the bar.

After waiting five minutes for a handful of giggling forty-something women to place drink orders, I had a whiskey in my hand. When I turned to find Kale, I was surprised to see him sitting with a vampire that had been turned much later in life. I'd estimate his human years to have been near sixty due to the fine lines in his face and his shock of silver hair.

I hadn't sensed his arrival, which struck me as strange. My hackles rose instantly. I took my time strolling to their table as I delicately lifted the glass to my lips for a sip. Feeling for a vibe from his energy, I wasn't surprised to find that there was something more to it than vampire alone. What was Kale getting us into?

I put on my best artificial smile as I reached the table. Kale stood and held a hand out to me, which I accepted somewhat quizzically.

"Greg, please meet my girlfriend, Alexa. Alexa darling, this is

Greg. He's the one I told you about." Kale flashed me a quick wink as he spoke, and I could only assume he painted the picture of us as lovers to prevent the vampire from wondering why there were two of us. My being a werewolf probably had him wondering, but hey, many of us were known to enjoy the taste of human flesh.

"Hello, pleased to meet you." I reached out warmly to shake Greg's hand, careful to apply just enough pressure to be firm without squeezing.

Greg responded by pulling my hand to his greasy lips and making a few smacking sounds that turned my stomach. I resisted the urge to yank my hand away and slap him across the face, but it was harder than one might think.

Kale smiled right through the evil stare I shot him. He was so going to pay for this.

"Charmed." Greg's voice was thick and gruff. The suit that he wore didn't fit right. It was too snug over his middle and incredibly obvious. He was running blood victims but couldn't afford a well-tailored suit?

Kale posed as the perfect gentleman, which he sometimes was, and pulled out my chair. When we were all seated, Greg wasted no time. He cut straight to the chase.

"So, how much can I cut you in for?"

Kale could field that question. I was busy. I rubbed the slime off my offended hand and took a sip of my drink.

"That depends. What kind of deals do you have? Any regular client discounts?" Kale cast a glance around the place before looking pointedly at Greg. "Is there anywhere more private that we could discuss this? Alexa and I are well known professionals in our community. This has to stay quiet."

"Most certainly. Quiet is our specialty." Greg followed Kale's gaze around the room as if in agreement. "I can bring you up to the room, but I must warn you that, if you try anything funny, I won't hesitate to take you out."

I frowned in response but quickly shrugged it off. He wanted to play tough guy, which was only expected. In most situations, he likely was the most powerful creature present, but this time he was going to be sadly mistaken.

"Of course." Kale smiled through the threat, and I had to give him credit for not reacting with an outburst of temper like I tend to do.

The two vampires took a moment to stare into each other like two cowboys about to do a quick draw. I sat there feeling inferior because I wasn't being recognized as a threat. But, that would end all too soon, just a matter of waiting for the right moment.

Greg scraped his chair against the floor to create a squeal that hurt my sensitive ears. He gestured toward the exit. "If you would just follow me." We followed him, and I had the sinking feeling that this was going to get messy. The confined elevator proved extremely uncomfortable. An Asian family of four squeezed in after us so that I was virtually crushed between Kale and Greg. I tried my best to lean away from the ingratiating bastard.

We stepped off on the fourteenth floor and made our way to room 1423. I was more than surprised at what lay on the other side of the door. The hotel room was magnificent. Red carpet led from the doorway past a white marble hot tub to a round bed encircled by a white curtain. Mirrors lined every wall but one, creating the illusion that the room was much bigger than it was. It made the perfect honeymoon suite, although I would have enjoyed it more had there not been a pale, young woman tied to a chair near the window.

I hesitated at the doorway. A chill crept up my spine, and I unconsciously began to gather energy in the center of my being. Kale swept past me as if he had been dealing human slaves forever, which was disturbing in itself.

"Do you have a preference between men or women? Race? Anything?" Greg spoke casually, as if he were asking if we preferred red or white wine.

"Healthy and still beating," Kale chuckled wickedly, and I found myself looking at him with wide eyes. Greg joined in his laughter and swept an arm in the woman's direction.

"Do you want this one? You can take her with you tonight. She won't make any trouble. Will you honey?" He asked her. When she didn't acknowledge him, he gave her a resounding slap across the face.

I willed myself to rein in the anger that threatened to rip free of my control. Not yet. Soon.

"Yeah, we'll take her. What else can you get for us?" Kale casually strolled around the room and pulled back the bed curtain to admire the fine bedding. "Nice room choice."

His gaze focused on the white sheets and duvet, and I could almost see the wheels turning in his head. The room was incredibly white. How could we possibly keep this clean?

"Thanks. It's my favorite here." Greg pulled his wallet from his back pocket and produced a small sheet of paper that included a price and quantity list. "This is what we're running right now for this city. It should be more than adequate to feed your..." He risked a glance at me. "...appetites."

Kale accepted the paper. He read over it carefully and nodded every so often. In a motion faster than I could blink, he moved to pin the other vampire to the wall.

With an arm wedged against Greg's throat, Kale growled, "Tell me who you're working for, and I'll consider allowing you to walk out of here in one piece."

Greg's slightly chubby face seemed to swell with rage as he stared into Kale's wild eyes. He attempted a smirk despite the arm crushing his windpipe. "You've got to be kidding me, pal."

The girl tied to the chair made a small whimper low in her throat as she eyed us, unsure if we were her saviors or simply new masters. I approached the two vampires but kept a safe distance.

"Do I look like I'm kidding?" Kale's fist met the other vampire's face with a loud crack.

I didn't react, except to wince on the inside. The scent of blood quickly thickened the air. My stomach tightened, and the energy that I'd gathered seemed to grow hot.

Before Greg could respond, Kale followed up with another solid blow to the vampire's midsection. He grunted yet laughed again.

"Who do you think you're kidding? Do you really think I'd allow you two to back me into a corner like this without some kind of backup?" He attempted to wipe away the blood that streamed down his chin from his nose.

"If you don't start talking, I'm going to let my lady friend have some fun with your manly bits. And, I can safely say that she will be the only one enjoying it." Kale's tone dropped low, and the menace pulled another whimper from the victim in the chair.

Greg's expression faltered as he fixed his eyes on me. My lips spread slowly in a sadistic grin, and I gave him a wink. "Ready to play with me, Greg?"

"You wouldn't," he choked out, but his eyes clearly said that I just might. I was a werewolf after all, and a little bit of blood and gore was nothing new to me.

I held up a hand so he could watch as my long fingernails lengthened into five razor sharp claws. My smile grew even broader around the four fangs that filled my mouth, two on both the bottom and the top.

Vampires don't fear werewolves, in general, since we each have our own very respectable attributes. However, poor Greg was alive with fear. As he filled the room with terror, he fed the energy that I had gathered within me.

"Are you going to start talking, or is Alexa going to start tearing you to bits?" If Kale's eyes were any indication, he was feeling the effects of the fear as well. His pupils were so large that his eyes were solid black.

"I don't work for anyone," Greg ground out between a few grunts and groans. "I work for myself. Ask the bitch if she's seen anyone other than me."

I looked at the woman who sat in the chair and sobbed. She didn't seem to be paying much attention to what was being said as she pulled uselessly at her binds.

"You're lying," I said. "I can smell it."

And, I could. Though vampires may rival me when it comes to the sixth-sense stuff, my other five senses had one up on them. A lie carries a very distinct scent from the change in brain chemistry.

"And, who the hell is your so called backup?"

The impatience in Kale's tone caused me to wonder if he had fed yet tonight. He often prowled the underground vampire bar downtown for donors, something Arys frowned upon. Arys resented the imposition of being forbidden to kill. He stuck with traditional methods. Kale, on the other hand, made a point to kill humans only when necessary rather than simply from a snack attack. To each his own, I suppose.

Greg struggled in Kale's grip but the other vampire was both too strong and determined. A mocking smile played along Greg's greasy lips as he quickly rambled a series of unintelligible words, which I realized a moment later to be Latin.

Horror struck me. He was calling a demon. And, though my

experience with them is thankfully limited, it has never been a pleasant one.

"Shut him up!" I yelled.

Kale, not one to ask unnecessary questions, promptly snapped his neck. Unfortunately, vampires can live through that. The sounds that came out of Greg when Kale dropped him in a puddle were more wretched than those of the girl in the chair. I watched with satisfaction as he writhed on the floor and wished for death.

Though I was hoping we'd cut his words off in time, the growing scent of sulfur told me we had not.

"Alexa," Kale's voice was low as he glanced around the hotel room. "Get out of here. Before it shows up. Just go. Now."

"What? No way." My eyes went to the woman, then to Greg on the floor wailing. "I can't just leave you behind."

"Can and will." He actually moved as if to physically force me to the doorway.

Before he could attempt to lay a hand on me, a cloud of smoke seemed to billow up between us out of nowhere. My heart swelled as a lump stuck in my throat. Fear shook me. I watched the misty cloud evaporate until a man stood in its midst.

He was easily one of the most handsome men that I'd ever seen, a total Adonis. But, his eyes stopped me cold. They were the palest blue, almost white, so that the pupil looked particularly black. Even after Jez's and my own, those were easily the most eerily inhuman eyes that I'd ever seen.

I don't know if I was expecting him to speak, maybe introduce himself. But, when his first reaction was to backhand me off my feet, I knew that this fight was not off to a good start. My back slammed into the mirrored wall, which rained a shower of shards around me. Instinct placed my arms over my head. I crouched on my knees, motionless, until the glass stopped falling. I heard Kale move rather than saw him. With a growl, their bodies collided as I slowly got to my feet.

Shaking the glass out of my hair, I winced as I plucked one stray shard from the back of my hand, the only one that had impaled me. Lucky. The small cut would heal by morning. Of course, I had to live to see the morning, first.

Kale had launched a physical attack on the demon. Wrong move. The demon trapped him inside an energy circle that glowed with a red haze. My breath sucked in with an audible hiss. The demon didn't even look at me when he released a bolt of power.

If my reaction time were any slower, I would have died in that moment. I threw my hands up and pushed back right in time to meet the blast with my own energy. Hmm, and what appeared to be a little of Arys's energy, as well. My blue and yellow psi ball was tiny in comparison to what the demon had thrown, but it was enough to offset the impact and defer it from me.

Both the demon's power and my own crashed into one of the Roman statues near the hot tub. It burst into dust. Before he could throw another one, I surrounded myself in a protection circle. Since I used solely my own energy, that barrier wouldn't last long.

The demon grinned then, with his perfect teeth. He dismissed me and turned to Kale with a sneer. "Now look at what you've done." He pointed one long finger to Greg, who still writhed on the floor with his neck at a hideous angle. "He's no good to me like that. Damned pain in the ass vampires."

I watched in stunned silence. As the demon walked softly over to Greg, he carefully stepped around the glass on the carpet. Before I could even guess what he intended, he raised the heel of a fine Italian boot and brought it down on Greg's skull with a shattering blow.

A small scream escaped me, and the woman in the chair let loose with a loud, long wail. I turned my eyes from the gore on the floor and looked instead to Kale, who attempted a reassuring expression despite his prison of evil, demonic energy.

"Now." The demon whirled once again to face Kale. "Would you like a chance to explain why you're interfering with my little business venture, or shall I just gut you now and get it over with?" He made a show of straightening the cuffs of his Italian suit.

"Look, I can explain. We were acting on the assumption that he was running this little show. That is all." Kale was back peddling fast now, which had me scared. We were out of our league here.

"Is that so?" The demon walked around the energy cage so that Kale had to turn in order to keep an eye on him. "Now, who do you suppose is going to take his position, vampire? You?"

Things were very quickly going from bad to worse. Sweat began to trickle down my back, and I focused to maintain my circle as I tried to think. If only room service would show up right now, I thought.

Dammit.

Kale stammered but didn't speak. He knew as well as I did that a demon will literalize your words. Too easily, they could manipulate your words and effectively use them against you.

"You've carelessly allowed for a witness." At his words, all three of us looked at the sobbing woman in the chair. "She must be eliminated. Do it, vampire."

With a snap of his fingers the demon's circle dropped. Free, Kale stood there uncertainly. The demon waited, fully expecting him to do what he was told. When Kale didn't budge, the demon stomped his foot impatiently.

Oh God, I prayed. Please get us out of this one. The look on Kale's face said clearly that he didn't want to kill an innocent victim. He hadn't lived that way in hundreds of years.

"What are you waiting for? Bleed the bitch or consider kissing all three of your asses' goodbye." The demon spoke very matter of fact with a tone that held no room for argument.

"No." Kale spoke so quietly I almost didn't hear him.

The tension in the hotel room grew to the point of unbearable, as the demon stared into him, clearly unaccustomed to the word, "no." I took a deep, shaky breath. We were so dead.

Instead of replying to Kale like I expected, the demon strode silently to the crying woman. As he raised his hands, I realized what he was about to do.

"No!" I cried out. But, it was too late. He snapped her neck with the ease of breaking a dry twig in half.

"Save your enthusiasm, wolf. There is always room in hell for more hounds." He winked, and my guts shriveled in response.

He didn't wait for my reaction. He turned to Kale and lashed out with a sudden blow that rocked the vampire back on his heels. Blood blossomed from the fresh wound beneath Kale's eye, the blue one.

I could clearly see him fighting not to react. To retaliate would most certainly mean a death sentence for the both of us. I didn't realize I was holding my breath until my lungs began to ache.

With another abrupt blast of power, the demon sent Kale flying. He didn't get up. The demon turned on me with a gaze as black as night.

"How dare you involve yourself in my affairs? You are no more than a lap dog to my kind, werewolf. I'll show you what happens to wolves who don't know their place."

He raised a hand to me, and my blood began to boil as my circle dissolved. An intense heat, worse than anything I'd ever felt, coursed through me. I stumbled and fell to my knees. I believe his intention was truly to cook me from the inside out.

Thanks to Lilah, I never had to find out.

All of a sudden she was just there, framed in the doorway. Dressed in black from head to toe, she wore a long trench coat and army boots. Her unnaturally red hair shone with an ethereal glow. Eyes the color of a pale orange sunset stared into the fair-haired demon as if they could see out the other side of him.

"And, I'm going to show you what happens to demons who mess with my people." She said only one other word. The lady never even lifted a finger. "Die."

Those creepy white eyes widened in shock and the demon shouted, "You!" Before he could utter another word, he began to sink in upon himself. There was a puff of smoke and he was gone. Only a pile of soot remained where the demon had stood.

No fucking way. Demons don't die. They could be banished but with great difficulty. Incredibly unheard of, Lilah actually took this one out. I don't mess with demons for a reason. They are the biggest of the bad.

I stood unsteadily, dumbfounded, as Lilah went to Kale. I forced myself to move and joined her at his side. My heart beat so hard against my ribs that it hurt.

"Is he alright?" I asked. I looked down at Kale. His left eye was swollen, but otherwise, he didn't look too bad, just a little roughed up.

"Oh yeah," she glanced at me with a critical eye. "Are you?"

I shrugged. I'd be fine. Lilah grasped my injured hand gently and passed the blood stained skin beneath Kale's nose. I was too in awe of her to protest. I could feel the strange power in her touch.

Kale snapped upright suddenly and reached for my arm with a snarl. I jerked back, and Lilah put her hand on his chest. After a moment, he blinked a few times and relaxed. When she stepped back and dusted her hands off, I realized she was essentially wiping the metaphysical remnants from her skin.

She waited patiently, until he was steady on his feet, and then she gave us a nod and the briefest of smiles. It wasn't exactly friendly, but it worked for me. Before either of us could say a word, she'd retreated into the hall and disappeared.

Chapter Six

I didn't run as a wolf that night. Instead, I poured a glass of my favorite red wine and sunk appreciatively into a hot bubble bath. Blue bruises decorated my skin in a variety of places. The worst was my back, where I'd hit the mirrored wall. A good sleep would make a world of difference in the healing process, if I could get one. I wouldn't say that I'm an insomniac so much as sleeping took up time that I didn't have.

Kale and I had vacated the hotel immediately after Lilah, though we never caught up to her. We'd come closer to hell tonight than either of us had realized. I'd never been so glad to be safe inside my own home. Give me a vampire to deal with any day, but keep the demons in hell where they belong.

The water was cool by the time I pulled the plug. The approaching sunrise cast my bedroom in a faint, cozy glow. I turned the television on to a station that played sitcoms from the 80s and was asleep before the sun broke the horizon.

I hadn't dreamt about it for years, three at least. And yet, I recognized it as if I'd never left. I was right back inside my worst nightmare, the most horrifying moment of my life so far.

I was my sixteen-year-old self again. I stood at the top of the stairs in the house where I'd grown up. It hadn't always been the happiest of homes, due to ongoing conflict between my parents, but I'd learned to feign ignorance early on.

I looked down at the scene of destruction and death on the floor below, and for a minute, I couldn't breathe. The front door hung ominously on one hinge, and it was a mess of deep scratches. Bloody trails and crimson splatters adorned the white and taupe walls. My mother's screams thundered through my ears. My heart raced, and my breath caught in my throat, as I watched the next few moments play out in a wide-eyed stupor.

The large black wolf quickly silenced the incessant shrieks. It pounced on her back and sunk its powerful fangs deep into the back of her neck. Her blood covered its furry muzzle, and its eyes were wild, beyond monstrous.

My father and younger sister lay dead in the kitchen. I couldn't see them from where I stood, but I knew. I'd heard their dying cries as well.

My hand flew to my mouth in an attempt to muffle the sound of my loud, terrified gasping. Even as I told myself that, this time, it wasn't real, the blood-hungry beast below fixed me with cold eyes and darted up the stairs.

I turned to run as I had so many times before, but with a snap of great jaws, he caught my ankle in a crushing grip and threw me tumbling head over heels down the stairs. When I hit the bottom, I jerked awake with a start.

Sweat had my t-shirt clinging to me, and I accepted my aching muscles as a sign that I'd really woken up. I looked around hesitantly, half expecting the wolf to come snarling out of the shadows of my room.

Some nights the dream went on longer. In the years right after the attack, I never woke up until his fangs were buried in my throat, tearing skin and muscle away from my esophagus. That had never happened though.

By the time the wolf had gotten to me, it'd already had its fill. After landing at the base of the stairway, I had curled myself into the fetal position to protect my face and throat. Its fangs sunk into my back just twice before it disappeared through the broken front door.

I lay there for hours, alone with the cooling corpses of my loved ones. The call to the police had been one of the most horrifying moments of my life. I knew the authorities would think I was crazy if I told them the truth. I instead told them that I'd been out and had come home in the middle of the attack. I lied. I said I was unable to get a good look at the murderer.

I shook off the remnants of the nightmare. It seemed to cling to the fabric of my mind like age-old cobwebs. The kind that had been there long enough that they could never truly be dusted away.

The digital clock on the nightstand informed me that it was just past noon. I opened my bedroom curtain wide and allowed the sun to bathe me in its comforting warmth. My body ached and stiffness had set into my muscles as I slept. I stretched and groaned though my back already felt better.

"You look about as good as I feel," Kylarai said when I entered the kitchen.

"Thanks for that." I shrugged and went for the freshly made pot of coffee. "I think more people tell me when I look like shit than when I actually look good."

"Sorry, I'm not exactly at my best either. Didn't sleep worth a damn."

"I'd like to say I slept but I think I just went back in time."

"Attack dream?" Ky raised a questioning eyebrow. I nodded. "I don't think they ever really go away." She spoke as if she knew all too well. "Of course I can't imagine that it helps when you don't know whatever came of him. It might make a big difference if you knew he was dead."

Easy for her to say, I thought. She'd blown the head off of the werewolf who was stupid enough to attack her. It was the first and last time she had ever wielded one of the shotguns her husband kept around the house.

"Yeah. I suppose." I stared numbly out the window into the backyard as I stirred sugar into my cup.

A squirrel ran across a tree branch and leapt from one to the next. I wasn't fooled by their cuteness. My grandmother had once told me a story about finding squirrels in a bird's nest eating the legs off the baby birds. I've hated the little monsters since.

"Have you ever thought to talk to Veryl about it? Maybe he would know something." Ky suggested as I took a seat across from her at the table. "You'd think a werewolf like that wouldn't go unnoticed by him."

She had a point. Perhaps Veryl would have some information on the wolf that had attacked me. But, did it really matter now? And, what if he still lives? Would I be able to live my life carefree, or would I become obsessed with settling a score already a decade old? I debated giving Veryl a call, but as the sun would have it, I'd have to wait until dark. Pushing the thought from my mind, I sipped from the precious, steaming hot coffee.

"What's on your agenda for today?" Kylarai asked, successfully changing the topic.

I looked at her, prepared to deliver a mental to-do list, and realized I didn't have one. "Nothing actually. For once."

"I just have a few business calls to make, and then I'm free. Want to get out, do a little shopping or something?" Kylarai got up for a refill before rummaging around in her briefcase. "We can grab dinner after."

If I'd been challenged to remember the last time she and I did regular girl stuff, I'd lose. Kylarai had been working some long hours lately. It really had been some time since she'd gone out.

I couldn't think of a better way to spend the afternoon. Tomorrow night was the full moon and the most powerful twenty-fours of the lunar cycle. Most of us wouldn't be human, might as well enjoy it now.

"That sounds excellent. I wouldn't mind a little shopping. There was a really cute pair of heels at the mall a few weeks ago. I never had time to try them on."

When Ky disappeared into our small office and closed the door, I decided I'd better jump in the shower and get ready. I wasn't really keen on walking around in public wearing the worst pair of sweat pants I own. But, even as I massaged conditioner into my long, agonizingly straight hair, the scenes from my nightmare continued to replay inside my head.

* * * *

I stood staring at a lilac sundress. It would have looked great on me if I had legs a mile long, but, let's just say, I didn't add it to my collection of things to try on.

"Alexa." I heard my name whispered loudly from the changing room around the corner.

Kylarai stood behind one of the heavy, red velvet curtains. Only her face peered out at me. At my approach, she opened the curtain enough for me to slip behind it.

"What do you think?" She asked as she spread her arms, as wide as the small space would allow, and twirled. She wore a pale blue dress that ended just above the knee. The color gave the illusion that her grey eyes were also blue. A form fitting bodice and spaghetti straps made it simple but in an elegant way.

"It looks beautiful," I said, envying the other woman's height. She had a good four inches on me, which made all the difference when it came to buying pants. And, that lilac sundress. It's harder than one may think to find petites.

"Really? You don't think it's squeezing too much in here?" She indicated her generous cleavage.

"That's the point, Ky."

She cast me a playful glare and turned to examine her behind in the mirror. "Ok, you can go now."

I returned to browse through the sales racks and actually managed to think only about what I was seeing, particularly that silky red skirt. I examined the V-cut of it before shaking my head and putting it back. A long black evening dress near the doorway caught my eye. Though I did not intend to buy it, I was drawn to look.

My hackles rose, just for a moment, as if somebody was watching me. I cast a glance around the near empty store. Nobody. I glanced out the open door into the fast-paced mall beyond. A mother struggled by with three small children. A teenage couple holding hands and a pair of mall security guards passed by. No one stared at me. Even as the feeling began to fade, I couldn't shake the strange energy that taunted my senses.

I was relieved when Kylarai appeared, dress in hand. "I haven't bought myself something nice like this in ages. I know I'm going to feel so guilty about this later." I followed her to the cashier as she chattered on but stared back over my shoulder. "What's wrong?" She asked suddenly.

"Nothing. Just spaced out. Sorry." I shrugged. There was no point in ruining the day with some paranoia.

"My legs feel like jelly," I said when we finally flopped into the car with our bags stowed in the backseat.

I never did buy those shoes. Instead, I had come across a sexy, little black dress. A combination of silk with lace trim, it hugged my every curve, as if tailored for me alone. The fact that it was strapless had caused me some hesitation. After Kylarai's reassurance that my ample breasts would hold it up just fine, I succumbed and handed over my debit card. Aside from that, I dropped more money than I should have at the bookstore, one of my favorite places to shop. And now, I was ready to call it a day.

"Do you want to stay in the city for supper or head back to town?" I asked. When she reached to change the radio station, I smiled through the twinges of irritation.

"You want the steak from Lucy's, don't you?"

"It's been awhile. And, it is past supper time."

"That's fine with me. It's been a while since I've gone to Lucy's for steak and drinks." A few more turns of the dial, and she stopped on the local hip-hop station. I tried hard not to howl from the pain it caused me.

"Kylarai, I can't stand this station. My car, my radio. Why don't you ever drive anymore?"

"Your car is newer." She shrugged. "And, mine is a bitch on gas."

After some friendly bickering, we settled on a station that we could both live with, easy listening.

It was going to be the start of the full moon at midnight, which encouraged loose and reckless behavior. I could already feel the crackle of the moon's powerful pull on the air.

Upon pulling into the parking lot of Lucy's Lounge, Ky inquired jokingly as to why I wasn't wearing my pretty new dress. Not in a million years would I wear a dress like that to a place like Lucy's. I was more than happy with what I was wearing. The baby doll tee I wore stated simply "Bite me." My black velvet skirt was cut above my knees in the front, below in the back. It was comfortable and easy to move in.

The second we stepped through the doors, the sea of smells was an assault on the senses. My eyes adjusted quickly to the dull lighting, and though all I could see was a crowd of faces, I could feel every shifter in the place. Shaz was working the bar. Two other town Weres were shooting pool on the far side of the room.

Amateur exotic dancer night was always a hit with the guys, occasionally too much of a hit. It was only once a week, but it had a tendency to be the most interesting night to show up.

I knew that Arys was in the swarm, but I had yet to see him. I didn't doubt that he knew I was there.

We weaved our way through the tightly packed bodies. The side of the Lounge with the pool tables didn't have as many free seats, so we headed for a table on the other side, near the stage.

I followed Kylarai as she led the way through the thick mass of people. She looked great as always, dressed simply in pinstriped pants and a white, strapless top with her trendy locks framing her round face. Her eyes sparkled with the moon energy and her own lively nature.

Flashing lights battered my eyes from the stage, where a buxom blonde strutted her very topless self around to one of the latest Top 40 songs. Hoots and hollers followed her, and a handful of men crowded around the edge of the stage and waited for their turn to slip a bill into her tiny g-string. The testosterone was thick on the air. I wrinkled my nose at Kylarai in distaste.

I felt the vampire's eyes on me. He'd found me first. Once I felt him, I could pinpoint where he was. He sat closer to the stage, off to the side with a few of his poker buddies. He looked right at home in the bar, dressed all in black. His raven hair was just the right amount of messy. I could feel the fire in the smoldering look he gave me from across the room. I knew that, though his eyes were on me, he monitored the occupants of the room just as surely as I did.

He motioned me over, but I shook my head and crooked my finger, a signal to come to our table instead. After a few words to his buddies, he pushed his chair back and came our way. I wasn't sure why my heart chose this moment to beat so fast.

"Why are you so nervous?" Kylarai asked me. She leaned in close to be heard over the music.

Even if she couldn't hear my heart pounding, then she could surely sense my unease. Before I could reply, he was within earshot.

"Arys, hey. How are you?" Kylarai greeted him warmly. "Nice to see you again."

"Good, thank you. And yourself?"

I feigned interest in the show on the stage while they exchanged pleasantries. The blonde was now writhing on the floor sans g-string. I was willing to bet my money that most of these amateurs were not really so amateur after all.

"How about you, Alexa? I'm glad you stopped in tonight." He turned those deep blue eyes on me, and I tripped over my tongue a few times before I could reply.

"Oh really?" I gestured to the empty chair between Kylarai and me. I put on my best neutral expression and prayed that he couldn't hear my rapid heartbeat. "There isn't already enough here to keep you busy?"

He grinned and glanced briefly at the stage, but the spectacle didn't hold his attention long before he took the offered seat. After decades of dancing girls, I was sure he'd seen much better than this. I had a much bigger appreciation for classic burlesque myself.

"There are a great many snacks to be had on a night like this." He gave a low chuckle that seemed to stroke the nocturnal side of me. I was curious and drawn, as both human and wolf, to the sinister nature of his darkness.

"I don't find that hard to believe." I used my drink as a good distraction, a chance to look away momentarily. The waitress paused at our table so I ordered another.

When I looked back at the vampire, an obvious hunger burned behind his eyes. Was it my imagination, or did he study the pulse in my throat?

The blood of a shape shifter was intoxicating to vampires. Some had been known to form addictions to it, though that was rare. It gave them a hell of a high. I'd heard werewolves talk that way after their first taste of human flesh and blood, obsessed and addicted. It was unnerving.

"Tonight I'm feeling in the mood for something else, something…lupine." Arys let the words hang on the air between us as I tried desperately to swallow the lump in my throat. Kylarai excused herself to the ladies' room, and I felt my cheeks grow hot with embarrassment.

"Arys, what in the hell was that?" I hissed once she was lost amidst the crowd. "Don't talk like that in front of Kylarai. It implies something that we aren't."

"But should be."

"What?"

"Don't deny it, Alexa. You felt it. I know you feel it right now. The way the need pulls you. Your living wolf wants to touch my undead power and run through the world of the dark-,"

"It isn't real," I interrupted. I shook my head and downed the last of my drink. I used looking around for the waitress as a distraction. I was afraid to fall into those sapphire eyes.

"It is." He grabbed my hand, and I felt the urge that raced through my veins like fire. It didn't force the boundaries of my control, but it was unrelenting in its persistence. "It's as real as you and me."

It was. I could feel it under the surface of my being. The rush itself created a longing, and I was starting to learn that our own personal powers went much deeper than the surface.

Arys's fingers traced light circles in the palm of my hand. A heat wave flowed down my arm, followed by a tingle, the sensation of the energy building. Common sense told me to pull away while everything else screamed for more contact, more power.

"I can't do this." I whispered the words, but he heard me. Without replying, he leaned in and before I could react, turned my face to him as he boldly kissed me.

The roar in my ears left me deaf. As he deepened the kiss, a doorway opened for our two differing energies to meld.

He tasted faintly of blood, and I liked it. His fangs pierced my bottom lip, and an exhilarated thrill shot straight to my groin as he ran his tongue over the small wounds. The metal of his lip ring was cool against my tongue as I tasted him.

The power began a steady climb, but finally my rational mind took over. I broke off the kiss as the waitress returned with my drink.

When she'd gone, I turned to Arys. My heart pounded in my ears. "This is dangerous. We're playing with fire here."

"Then, let's extinguish the flame." Was Arys out of his mind? What was he expecting from me? "Let's get out of here."

"No. I'm not leaving right now. I'm going to find Ky, and then I'm going to shoot some pool." I needed to escape the situation.

The next girl to dance was one of the local Weres that ran with us on occasion. I certainly couldn't watch this. I used the moment to stand up and gather my things.

"I'm sure you should have enough to keep you entertained." I filled my hands with my purse and drink so that I couldn't possibly fulfill the longing to touch him again.

"Not a chance. You haven't seen the last of me tonight, Alexa." He leaned close. His breath felt warm against my ear. The heady scent of him tempted me to change my mind. "With a hunger like yours burning, I plan to be around when it burns out of your control, when you need someone to quench it." With that, he gave me a wink and sauntered back to his table.

I stared after him for a minute. I was hard-pressed not to just drop my things and abandon self-control. I did hunger. I'd attributed it to the moon, combined with natural human and animal instincts. But, this was different. This was a similar need with a different outcome. I wanted to know what that outcome might be, as frightening as it was.

I found Kylarai. She sat at the bar and visited with Shaz. I was suddenly stricken with worry, afraid that Shaz had seen Arys kiss me.

I had no commitments, but I was wary of hurting anyone's feelings. The smile, which he beamed at me when I walked up, told me that he'd seen nothing. Despite having no commitments, I couldn't shake the guilty feeling.

The customers never relented, so I didn't get a chance to speak with him long. Kylarai and I spent the next couple of hours shooting pool and enjoying some of that savory steak that I'd been eagerly anticipating.

In the back of my mind, I kept going back to Arys, to the wonderful way the power breathed over, around and through us. I couldn't stop thinking about it, which also led me to think about Shaz.

It was different with Shaz, different not only because we both shared the same supernatural power, but also because I feared an emotional attachment with him. I didn't feel that Arys would ever look at me that way. It was nothing more than a power trip for him, too, with nothing deep-rooted to destroy. I didn't want to take that chance with Shaz. He's family.

We'd decided to call it a night around one o'clock. I'd had more than my usual to drink. I got successfully tipsy. I didn't tell Arys that I was leaving. We'd just left the building and rounded the corner to watch for a taxi. I cursed about having to leave my car.

They came out of the dark. Three men moved to form a partial circle around us. One of them stepped forward to act as ring leader. The stranger stood before me and looked me up and down with a judgmental grimace under a greasy coif of hair. He looked almost forty, too old for stunts like this. He leered down at me and puffed on a cigarette.

"Tell me where to find Raoul Roberts." He ground his teeth together as he spoke. His eyes were extremely bloodshot, and he looked as if he hadn't slept in days.

"Who?" I blinked up at him with my best vacant-eyed expression.

"Don't fuck with me. Somebody told me that you would know where to find him. Raoul Roberts. Where is he?" His fists clenched and unclenched, and I fought the urge to head butt him right in his insipid face.

"I'm sorry, sir, but I don't know what you're talking about. Now if you'll excuse me-,"

"You're not going anywhere until you tell me where he lives. He killed my wife, and I'm not going to rest until I take him apart with my own hands. You don't want to be the only thing preventing that. I don't have a problem starting with you."

I said nothing and shouldered my way past him. What I should have done was drop him, right then and there. The slap came out of nowhere, and I tasted blood inside my mouth. I hadn't anticipated the hit.

Kylarai was in his face before he could blink. I don't think he even knew it was her that hit him before he was wiping blood from his broken nose.

He stumbled back, but his friends never budged. If things got ugly, I was more than sure we could handle it, but I always preferred to walk away when it came to foolish humans.

The other two guys looked at Kylarai uncertainly. They were second-guessing their choice in confronting us. As I braced myself for a fight, I cursed Raoul inside my head.

Julie Price's husband stared at Ky dumbfounded before he launched into action. He came at her fast, and I watched his eyes go from enraged to stunned as she easily caught his fist. With an audible crack, she twisted his wrist until he cried out.

"Is there a problem here?" A low, velvety voice came from behind me. The vampire had found me after all.

Price's two buddies wasted no time in fleeing. I guess they didn't want to have their faces rearranged by a girl, much less Arys. Price howled his pain but backed away at Arys's approach.

They fled under the watchful gaze of the vampire. I was amused and annoyed at the same time. I wanted them to be running from me, not Arys.

"Well, I guess we'll just be getting a cab then," I said, turning towards the street. Arys grabbed my arm and spun me back to face him. His eyes were serious and seemed to dare me to argue as he touched a hand gently to my stinging cheek.

"Correction. We will walk Kylarai to a cab. You and I have some unfinished business to attend to."

"You know this perfect timing stuff - riding in to save the helpless damsel in distress - is really getting old."

"You know I don't think you're helpless."

"Then why the sudden appearance every time some asshole with his dick in a knot makes trouble for me?"

Silence. He just stared at me with those deep blue orbs.

"Ok, Alexa, I'm out of here," Kylarai called from twenty feet away where a cab was pulling to a stop near the curb. "You coming with?"

I wanted to say yes and leave with Ky whether Arys liked it or not, but that was only to spite him, not because I didn't want to stay.

"No. I'm not." I didn't take my eyes off of the vampire. A devilish grin slowly spread along his handsome features. "Leave a message on my cell when you get home so I know you made it ok."

"I'll see you at home, Alexa. Be careful." The teasing look in her eyes said she meant the vampire.

When she closed the cab door, I was alone with my whiskey-encouraged, moon-inspired decision and a power-hungry vampire.

Chapter Seven

With Arys, I didn't have a sole intention in mind. I wasn't on the prowl for someone to relieve me of moon-related desires, and I wasn't lonely. What kept me walking beside him went deeper than either of those things: Power.

I declined his offer to get a cab. Instead, I insisted we walk the few blocks to his bachelor bungalow under the wide-open sky. I needed to feel the moon on my skin and the night in my veins.

We walked along a bike path and forced some aimless small talk. Energy shifted keenly between us as we ambled through the warm summer night. I could smell the common town jack rabbits in the empty playground across the street. The town was quiet.

I expected to feel awkward or uncertain as we drew closer to Arys's house. Instead, anticipation thrilled me, and my inner beast waited eagerly. As a heady glow enveloped me, my senses heightened to a painfully delicious extent. The faint evening breeze encouraged my wolf and called me to run.

I longed to touch Arys, to open that strange door between us. I ached to know what we were playing with. I yearned for a taste of his superhuman power, but the driving force wasn't really me. This was something bigger than the sum of our power, greater than the two of us combined.

We'd barely locked his front door when he pressed me against the wall. His body felt warm and ready next to mine. I'd resisted the urge to give in so many times already, but now I just let go. I needed to know the outcome of submitting to Arys's pull instead of fighting.

He allowed me no time to take in my surroundings. At his aggressive touch, my wolf leapt to meet him and a wave of adrenaline crashed through me. As his lips touched mine, our powers collided. Energy rushed around us, white noise that grew by the second. His soft tongue sought mine, and I knew that his need was as great as my own.

Arys tangled one hand in my hair, tugging urgently at my clothing with the other. His touch was possessive and rough. I gasped when he caressed my bare skin, stroking a bold path down my abdomen.

"Arys wait," I breathed. My lips fought to form the word. I wanted to move further into the house, away from the entryway. I had yet to take my shoes off.

"I know you want me, Alexa. I can feel your wolf calling to me." He buried his face in my hair, and I felt fangs graze the sensitive skin along the side of my neck.

I shoved him off me and kicked my chunky wedge heels off. "Let's go inside."

He stared at me like a hormone-fueled teenager who couldn't understand the word *no*.

Even as I sauntered into the heart of the house, the power tried to persuade me to reconnect the broken touch. I didn't get very far before Arys pulled me back into his arms. A gentle breeze of electricity stirred around us as I lost myself in him. The energy built with each touch and encouraged the next.

In the back of my mind, I wondered what exactly it was that we were conjuring up. Maybe we should stop. I made to pull away, but Arys kissed me. The passion sent a fire racing through my soul. I wanted to take him, right there in the living room. Instead, he led me to the bedroom.

The king size bed was in the middle of the room. With its lavish, fluffy pillows and deep comforter, Arys's bed looked like a marshmallow just waiting for me to dive in. I was disappointed when he steered me away, but desire and instinct drove me. I focused solely on the vampire that made my blood boil. I needed him to put out the fire that we'd ignited.

Engulfed in passion, I stripped off my own clothes. His hands caressed every piece of skin that I revealed. I couldn't recall if he'd rid himself of his clothing or if I had done it in my frenzy. I had no semblance of rational thought left at the forefront of my brain.

With dark, potent need, I clung to Arys. He picked me up and slammed me against the wall with a satisfying bang. Braced against the wall, I growled with hunger, ready for him.

As Arys slid deep inside me, a wave of power crashed over us. With our bodies joined, the power seemed to weld us together in our union. It was like that last puzzle piece finding its place.

I flashed back to Lena's battery metaphor, and a glimmer of fear crept in, but it was too late. I was in his mind, just as he was in mine. Images flashed through my brain like a strobe light. Arys's memories flooded me with too much information. I wished to close my eyes against the onslaught, but it ran deeper than vision.

I saw blood and pain in his memory, much that he'd taken and more that he'd given. And heartbreak. I was intrigued by the heartbreak. I'd never looked at him that way, like someone who had feelings beyond blood thirst. I had only seen the vampire, not the man.

I experienced the sensation of what he felt when he killed, the ecstasy that he felt each and every time. I saw Arys walk away from a kill with renewal and a grin, but I also saw the blood tears and the regret. The shame that he'd once again fallen into the trap of temptation.

Sweat dripped down the side of my face, and my hair was damp with it. I could feel him in my mind. I couldn't have shut him out if I had tried. Despite all of it, he didn't slow his pace as he thrust into me with a sense of desperation.

My fingertips were sticky with his blood. My claws had bit through his flesh as I held him to me. If it pained him, he gave no sign. I cried out as we spiraled toward climax. Our crescendo of buzzing power neared the breaking point.

I was painfully aware of the overflow of energy. It seeped into the objects in the room, as it sought a place to expend. A clock radio on the nightstand turned itself on at full volume and quickly fizzled out, fried. The ceiling light turned on before exploding, sending thousands of tiny shards onto the carpet. I gave a small yelp as one struck my foot. The lights down the hallway followed suit, and I could hear the TV in the living room turn on full blast and then a loud pop.

"Alexa, can I…?" Arys's breath was hot against my ear as he whispered my name urgently. His pace quickened, and I felt myself hurtling fast towards that ultimate finish.

When it hit, I climaxed with the greatest intensity that I'd ever experienced. It smashed into me with the heaviest metaphysical weight that I'd encountered during a physical act. The strangest sensation accompanied it, something that hurt deep inside my mind as it stripped away any barrier left between the vampire and I.

I heard the howl that tore out of my throat but didn't identify it as me. In the same breath, Arys sank his fangs deep into that soft hollow above my collarbone. I arched my back, and as the howl died out, it turned to cries of sheer joy. A sound low in his throat echoed me as he sucked and licked at the bloody wound. It hurt so badly but it felt so good.

I wrapped my legs tightly around him as he carried me to the fluffy bed, careful to check for glass before setting me down.

Everything in Arys's house that had run on power of any kind had been blown far past capacity. We had completely lost control. The disastrous potential of that much power alarmed me.

With our nagging metaphysical energy spent, we were left with the hum of residual power in the room and the continued sexual enticement of the moon, which I gladly gave into. Arys was more than happy to quench that thirst as well. We remained entangled in one another until just before dawn, when finally we lay exhausted.

I lay there amidst the down blankets and the satin sheets, breathless. My mind scrambled to make sense of everything that I'd seen and felt. I had been unprepared for the experience. A complete bearing of souls was not what I'd had in mind. Arys broke the silence first.

"That was a trip." He gave my hand a squeeze.

I lay, collapsed on the bed beside him, staring up at the ceiling. The blood still roared through my ears, and I shook slightly, whether from a chill or from aftershocks, I wasn't sure.

"Really Arys, what the hell was that? That was so far from normal."

"Why, thank you. You were damn incredible yourself." He laughed, and I gave his arm a halfhearted slap. With all that had just taken place, I was surprised that the atmosphere was so comfortable.

I knew the things that Arys had seen inside my mind. He knew my secrets, my hopes and fears. I said a silent prayer that I could trust him with that.

"Seriously though, did you know it would be like that? A complete sharing. I can't imagine how that could happen." I was insistent despite the fangs that now nipped playfully at my throat. When he bit at my breasts, I pushed him back to force him to reply to me, despite the tingle that grew low inside me again.

"No. I never would have guessed it would be something that I couldn't block. When our powers joined, it tore away any mental barriers between us. I'm not sure I can say I would have done it had I known we would share everything." He pushed my hands down and pinned them against the bed. "But now that it's too late, we might as well make the most of it."

Arys's lips made their way to one of my breasts. His tongue traced circles around my nipple as he chuckled wickedly. His eyes met mine, and he asked, "Can I taste you again?"

The fact that he wanted permission to bite me spoke volumes in terms of respect. I didn't need to answer, though, as I played with his feather soft black hair. Enough had passed between us that words didn't seem important.

After a moment, his fangs sunk deep into the fleshy underside of my breast. A sound escaped me that was both pain and pleasure.

"Do you treat all of your lovers this roughly?" I asked with a hint of teasing. My breath was stolen as his fingers sought out the warm, inviting place between my legs.

"Of course not. You're a werewolf," he replied as if that was explanation enough. His tongue lapped at the blood he'd spilled, and I strained against him, wanting more than he was giving.

"You're high. High on power and werewolf blood." My voice sounded terribly lazy. Arys looked up at me with a crimson smear on his lower lip. His eyes burned with a predator's glow.

"Funny comment coming from a lady with such stunning wolf eyes. Howl for me, Alexa. I want to hear how much you love this."

I did love it. His touch rocked me in ways I never thought possible. As much as I wanted him to scratch the itch inside me again, I wanted answers.

"Do you know what's happened to us Arys? I need to know. I don't know enough." My words stopped, and I dug claws into the sheet beneath me as his mouth replaced his fingers, hot against my core.

"What do you need to know? Power wants to be used." He spoke slowly, and his lips never left my flesh. "And enjoyed in the meantime."

"Ok, no more talking," I groaned. My questions temporarily forgotten, I urged him up so that he kneeled over me.

A sinful smile curved my lips as I gazed up at his hard body. He was more than ready for me again, and I growled my frustration when he didn't immediately take me.

"Arys," I murmured. "Don't play with me, boy."

"Still not satisfied, Alexa?" He rubbed his rock hard shaft against me playfully, and I made a noise that could have been a purr. I had been satisfied three or four times over now, but the hunger for him was far from fulfilled.

"Not yet. Why don't you hurry up and satisfy me? Again." The pleading note to my words made me grimace. The wolf would beg for it, under the right circumstance, but the woman in me never would.

If his snake-like grin was any indication, he loved hearing it. He wasn't as aggressive as the first few rounds. This time, the softness frightened me. I associated soft, gentle sex with feelings and emotion. After everything we'd willingly and unwillingly shared, insecurity was beginning to creep in.

Arys's room was heavily curtained to prevent even a sliver of sunlight through, so when the dawn broke, he paid it no mind. Around seven, I decided that I should be getting home.

"You know, Alexa," Arys said thoughtfully from where he lay on the bed watching me shimmy into my skirt. "This could be huge for us. Imagine what we could do with that kind of power." He grinned slyly.

"Like what? Wait. Don't answer that. I don't want to know what you're thinking." I slipped my shirt over my head and tried uselessly to finger comb the tangles from my hair. "Arys, about the memory thing…"

"I think that was a little traumatizing for both of us. Let's just agree to keep it confidential."

I nodded, uncertain. "Speaking of keeping things quiet-,"

"You don't want the wolf pup to find out." Arys nodded knowingly, and I cringed. "Don't worry, my lips are sealed."

"Thank you." I suddenly felt uncomfortable. I didn't know why it meant so much to me to keep this quiet. In part, the sex had a lot tied into it that maybe shouldn't be public knowledge. Also, there were certain people, like Raoul and Shaz, that, for very different reasons, I didn't want to know my personal business.

"I'll see you later, Arys," I called from where I'd stopped in the washroom. Pulling the glass sliver from my foot proved more painful than when the damn thing had gone in. I cursed and swore until the little shard had successfully found its way into the garbage. The debris and glass was appalling in the light of day.

"You can count on it. Do you need me to call you a cab or anything?"

I walked through the house calling back that I was fine with walking. I wanted to walk home rather than call for a ride because I needed the time to think. I dreaded the car retrieval of shame I'd have to do later. The night had revealed so much but had created more confusion as well. As I closed the door on the mess, I felt guilty about not cleaning up, but he'd insisted it was no big deal.

The second I closed the front door behind me and turned to face the day, my eyes burned and watered madly. I fished around in my purse until I produced sunglasses, which didn't do much to help other than hide my wolf eyes. I spent the first ten minutes of my walk furiously wiping my eyes. To passing motorists, it must have looked like I was crying.

I started feeling shaky and nauseous. I hungered, and it wasn't a fat, bloody steak that I longed for but the taste of human blood. My stomach hurt, and I had to pause near some brush where I heaved but threw up nothing. What was going on?

My shaking hands were again becoming claws, and I felt my fangs fill my mouth. The wolf was fighting to break free, and I wasn't sure why right now. I felt little control over myself suddenly, and I was scared. I began thinking that perhaps Arys and I truly had played with fire.

Chapter Eight

I'm still not sure how I made it home, but I did. I felt increasingly worse as I walked. More than once, I had to stop, wracked with pain in my abdomen.

Shortly after eight, I fumbled my way into the house with clawed hands. Claws are a real bitch for opening doors. The more subdued lighting inside was a relief to my burning eyes.

Removing my shoes proved such a difficult task that, in the end, I gave up and just kicked until they flew off. Each one smacked the wall with a thud that broke the morning stillness.

I was dizzy, and everything began to spin. Rocked with bloodlust, my stomach churned. It wasn't my hunger. I wasn't the one who thrived on the blood of the living.

I staggered to my bedroom. My clawed hands left scratches on the walls as I went. After hugging the toilet in my en suite bathroom did nothing to ease the pain in my guts, I crawled to my bed. I was overcome with weakness before being overwhelmed in a sea of black.

I was out for a solid nine hours during which I had the strangest dreams. Sometimes, I saw Arys's memories through his eyes, and others, I watched as a bystander. My brain seemed to be trying to make sense of the multitude of information that I'd absorbed earlier.

I saw Arys as a man, a human man. He'd been engaged to be married more than three hundred years ago. His fiancée had been a simple beauty, but he loved her dearly. She reminded him of his mother.

His mother… Everything changed, and now I saw his mother with her rouged cheeks and highly pinned hair. I was confused, and I wanted to wake up. Nothing was making any sense to me. It was so random.

I got a taste of Arys's horror and fear when he realized the woman who'd seduced him for the evening was a vampire with wicked intentions. She wasn't the one to turn him though. No, that was somebody else. Something was missing. What happened to the fiancée?

My sleep was fitful and disturbing, and when I finally awoke, I was slick with sweat. Kylarai was sitting at my desk using my computer. I sat up and threw my blanket off. My tongue was dry when I tried to speak.

"How are you feeling, Lex?" She asked. She approached me tentatively and perched on the edge of the bed. I could see the flood of questions in her eyes. "You better have a damn good story."

I still wore the clothes that I'd worn last night, but I was thankfully free of fangs or claws. I struggled out of my shirt and threw it on the floor near the laundry hamper. Then the skirt followed before I met Kylarai's eyes.

When I sat in my under things, I turned to her. Like a true best friend, she held a glass of ice water out to me.

"Thanks," I said, after wetting my parched throat. The word came easier than I'd expected. "I feel … awesome."

"Seriously Alexa, what happened to you last night? Did Arys hurt you?" Her gaze was fixed on the wound near my collarbone, and I could see the assumptions forming.

I reached up and touched the bite. It was crusty around the punctures, and it ached at my touch. I made an attempt to get off the bed, but my head spun, so I sat back down. "No, he didn't hurt me. I really need a shower."

"Ok, he didn't hurt you. So you've just recently become a donor?" There was no denying the vehemence in her voice.

"Ky, please. Don't be like that." I made a second attempt to get off the bed, and this time my head didn't swim.

"Well, forgive me for being suspicious, but wouldn't you be? You look like shit."

"Fantastic." I pulled some clean clothes out of my closet and turned to the bathroom. "I don't know what's wrong with me, but honestly, I don't think it was the physical nature of things. I think it was the metaphysical."

"How so?"

"If you'll be the best friend a girl could ever ask for and make me some coffee, I will tell you all about it after my shower. Promise."

The hot shower felt great even though it set fire to every sore spot I had. I shampooed my hair and lathered my body twice, careful to remove any trace of Arys's scent from my skin.

The vampire bite, however, had not entirely healed. If I arranged my hair just right, I could most likely hide it. The bite on my breast looked the same but both wounds were clean and should heal as if they'd never happened.

Kylarai stared daggers into me when I entered the kitchen. She looked at me as if I was hiding something. She listened attentively as I recounted the previous night's events from the time I left her.

I left out the most private and unnecessary details, but her raised eyebrows said she could guess. When I told her about the energy overload in Arys's house, her eyes really widened.

"I've never heard of any such thing. That's amazing."

"And bizarre. I don't know what to make of it. I felt terrible after. And so... hungry." I was hesitant to tell her that I had actually hungered for human blood, but I trusted her, so I shared.

She looked thoughtful for a minute, chewing her pouty lower lip. "Interesting. That could be something to play with."

"Could be dangerous, too. It really freaked me out. I'm going to ask Lena about it." I finished my first cup of coffee in a few large gulps and poured a second. "I'm sure I don't have to tell you this but-,"

"I know. Don't say anything. But, you still have to face Shaz with that bite mark. Better think of something good."

"I'll tell him its work related." Even as the words came out of my mouth, I felt bad about them.

"Do you think anything weird happened to Arys after you left?"

"No idea. Only one way to find out."

"He was an equal participant too. It should work both ways." Kylarai pointed out. My biggest concern was that he would dream of me as I had of him. It kind of creeped me out to picture it. "Therefore, he would probably experience some of your weaknesses like you did his."

"But what are our mortal weaknesses to someone who has passed beyond that?" It nagged at me because something didn't fit. She shrugged. She had no more to offer than I did.

I spent a lot of time hovering over the bathroom sink, splashing cool water on my face. My body was conflicted, and it shifted back and forth between a cold and hot sweat. I cursed a series of things all the while, needing a place to point the finger and lay blame.

I began by blaming Arys. This had to be all his fault. If he hadn't been after me, pursuing my living power as if it were a treat to snack on, this wouldn't have happened.

From there I moved to pinpointing the moon. The lunar cycle had influenced my poor decision. Inevitably, I came to rest my accusations solely on my own half-assed attempts to resist temptation. But, the power had called, and after resisting for so long, I gave in. Like a fool.

My face was still dripping over the sink when the doorbell rang. I sucked in my breath and willed my stomach to stop flip-flopping. I dried my face and prepared to leave the security of the bathroom. I sure hoped our visitor wouldn't mind my t-shirt and sweat pants attire.

"Shaz is here," Kylarai called. "It looks like he brought us dinner."

When I rounded the corner of the kitchen and was greeted by Shaz's characteristic grin, my hand actually flew to my neck to ensure the bite was hidden by the t-shirt. I was ashamed and afraid. Would he smell it?

Ky was already digging into the greasy bags of Chinese food and pulling out Styrofoam containers. The scent of ginger beef, rice and steamed vegetables teased my senses, and I was suddenly starving.

"You came to feed us? Awesome! I was just wondering what to order for supper," Kylarai said as she grabbed plates from the cupboard for the three of us.

"Well, I figured, since I never really got a chance to talk to you guys last night and we haven't done this in awhile, I should treat." Shaz replied as he helped himself to our cold beer stash in the refrigerator. Was it wrong to check out his cute rear end while he bent over?

"The bar was busy last night." I tried to sound casual and wondered if I sounded suspicious instead. Despite having showered, I worried that he would somehow scent Arys on me. "Julie Price's husband assaulted me in the parking lot. He was bound and determined to find Raoul."

"What?" Shaz looked up from the box of chicken balls he was attacking. "Are you kidding?"

"Hell no," Ky laughed. "The bastard slapped her across the face so I broke his damn nose."

"You just beat me to it." I interjected and stuck out my tongue at her.

"Holy shit. I always miss the good stuff being stuck behind that damn bar." Shaz shook his blond mane so that a stray lock fell into his eyes.

"It would have been better if Arys hadn't shown up so soon. That chicken shit Price took off too fast." My eyebrows must have risen in alarm at Kylarai's mention of Arys's name because she quickly went on. "But I guess its best that he took off. Things could have gotten really ugly."

"I wonder if he ever found Raoul." Shaz began to reach for a fortune cookie, but I playfully smacked his hand away. He knew it was bad luck to eat the cookie before the end of the meal.

"I doubt it. He didn't seem to be too coherent."

"Mmhmm," Ky nodded. "He was a mess. But, that makes sense considering he did just lose his wife."

"I would probably want a piece of Raoul, too, if I were him." I spoke between mouthfuls of beef. I felt like I hadn't eaten in weeks. "I already do."

"Well, you'll have your chance tonight. I'm sure the death of an ex-lover won't be enough to stop him from running during the full moon."

I looked at Shaz thoughtfully while I chewed. I could only assume Raoul would show up. Usually, we ran as a pack at midnight, which was still hours away.

The voice of the newscaster on TV carried to me from the living room. The news had been background noise until I heard the name Sheridan Boyd. I stopped chewing and, when they continued to chat, held my chopsticks up for silence. The news anchor rambled a little spiel about her body being found this morning in a dumpster behind a popular city nightclub.

"Isn't that another of Raoul's exes?" Kylarai's eyes were huge with incredulity. I merely nodded.

When we had finished eating, I dialed Raoul's number, effectively quieting Shaz and Kylarai. He didn't answer, but he screens his calls.

"I'm on my way over," I said when the voicemail picked up. "If you have company, get rid of them. You don't want witnesses for this conversation."

"Uh oh," Ky's tone was teasing. "Things are going to get ugly."

"Yeah," I couldn't prevent the sigh that escaped me. "Lucky me."

Before I left, my curiosity won out, and I broke into my fortune cookie. 'A new friend will prove too good to be true.' That was reassuring. I didn't have any new friends.

They offered to come along, but I needed to speak with Raoul alone. Too chicken to ask Shaz for a ride to my car, I called a taxi from my cell phone once I was outside. I was glad to see my shiny red ride waiting for me at Lucy's, untouched.

Raoul's house was dark except for one light that glowed faintly from deep within. The driveway was empty of cars so I took that to mean his Jaguar was in the garage. He couldn't put me off with an illusion that nobody was home.

I was careful to park a few doors down and scour the area. When I rang the doorbell, I called out that it was me. Inside, I heard nothing but silence. I sensed someone on the other side of the door just before it cracked open.

"Hurry up and get in here," he growled, stepping back just enough to allow me inside.

"Well, aren't you a grumpy old wolf?" I thought he'd appreciate that.

"I'm not old. What do you want?"

"That's no way to talk to someone who just fetched your ass from jail. And, may be stuck doing so again." I stepped inside and kicked my runners off. He locked the door behind me and frowned at my baggy sweatpants.

"Again?"

"Don't pretend you don't know. Why else would you be hiding here under lock and key?"

"All I know is that Richard Price has been asking around about me. He thinks I murdered his wife."

I couldn't help but frown. He didn't sound all that broken up about it, but his dark eyes were red rimmed. He looked tired when he added, "Yeah, I heard about Sheridan if that's why you're here. I'm surprised the cops haven't come for me already."

"Why would they?" I asked.

This is it, I thought. If he admits his involvement, I'm washing my hands of this.

Then, a memory hit me. During my first year as a werewolf, another wolf, older and stronger than I was, wanted me for his own. I had made it clear to him that I wasn't interested in being his pack run playmate, and he'd attempted to take me by force.

Raoul had stopped him, beat him until I thought he was surely dead. That wolf had never risked so much as a glance in my direction again. He left town soon after.

Perhaps, Raoul knew how to drive me absolutely insane. Perhaps, he knew how to piss me off royally. Still, he was pack, and as much as I hated it, I owed him one.

I was suddenly embarrassed. Arys had seen that memory.

"Don't they always blame the ex-husband or ex-lover?" He asked and startled me out of my thoughts.

"That's because it always is the ex." I met his eyes evenly. I had to.

"Do you think I killed her?"

The silence that settled between us was heavy and uncomfortable. But, in that moment, looking into his hard and unflinching gaze, I knew he was innocent. I couldn't scent even a hint of a lie on him.

I replied honestly, "No. I don't." He swallowed hard then, as if he'd expected to hear otherwise. "But because I don't, I need you to answer a question. Why would another one of your lovers turn up dead?"

Raoul paled considerably and took an involuntary step back. I could hear his quick intake of breath. "Is this an accusation? How the hell would I know?" His voice began to rise.

"Because if you didn't do it, then someone is setting you up."

I've never seen the poor guy look so distraught. I followed him into the kitchen, a chef's dream, where he poured himself a scotch on the rocks. When he offered, I declined. My stomach was starting to feel fluttery again.

"Julie was a great woman and fantastic in the sack," he said before draining his glass in one swallow. "But, I didn't love her. And, there's no piece of ass so good that it's worth a murder charge. I haven't even seen her in six months or more. Even longer with Sheridan."

"Do you have any idea why someone would want to frame you for either murder?"

He refilled his glass and seemed to stare off in thought. "No. I can't think of anyone."

I didn't like the way his negative energy stung my skin. It was similar to the irritation of a mosquito bite. My own personal power instinctively grew as if to shield the unwanted assault. "So, there is absolutely no way that you are involved."

"I told you that I was here the night Julie died. With Belle."

I chose not to address his words directly. "And last night?"

"In the city. At a business function."

"Alright then, Raoul. But, the question remains, who hates you enough to dedicate their existence to destroying yours?"

When he finished his third scotch and reached to pour another, I laid a gentle but firm hand on his. I pulled it away from the bottle. I saw something then in the ebony eyes of my former Alpha that I'd never seen before. Fear.

"Alexa, promise you'll help me if I tell you this." He gripped my upper arms in desperation. He surprised me, and I barely suppressed the urge to fight.

"I'm helping you by being here. Now, get off me." I shrugged out of his hands. "So, spit it out."

He nodded and stepped back. He rubbed his hands together as if my skin had burned him. "Someone broke into the house about a week ago, while I was at work. By the time the alarm company dispatched police, they were gone."

Now I could see where this was going. It wasn't looking good. "What did they take?"

"Personal belongings: A wristwatch, some photographs, and some jewelry, a ring with a wolf's head to be exact." He swallowed hard, and I was beginning to understand why.

"That's all? Your computer, TV, everything else of value was left untouched?"

"Completely."

"Ok, Raoul. I'm doing my best here to be loyal and supportive, but if there's something you're not telling me-,"

"You said you don't think I did it!"

"I'm just saying you can't hide shit from me. I will find out. And, then you'll be on your own." I meant business and felt incredibly annoyed. "You probably messed with the wrong woman, and this is the outcome. You know what they say, 'Hell hath no fury…'"

"Yeah, yeah."

Another silence ensued, but more comfortable than the last. I became aware of the itch starting beneath my skin. The pull of the moon created a warm glow in the pit of my stomach. Soon, the need to shift would be upon me. If I concentrated on Raoul, I could feel his wolf waiting. He needed the release, too.

"Why don't we grab a coffee and head back to my place?" I readied myself to leave and risked laying a gentle hand on his forearm.

His gaze fell to where our skin touched, and I resisted the urge to pull away. "I can't thank you enough, Alexa. I don't know how I managed to secure your trust, but I am truly grateful. Considering our history, I don't deserve this."

Alarm bells went off in my head. He wasn't sucking me back in, not now. "We're pack." I shrugged it off and swallowed hard. "Now, let's go run with our wolves."

Chapter Nine

Raoul wouldn't leave with me, but I refused to go until he promised to show up, with a tired, "I'll be in the clearing by midnight." We often met there in the years since I'd vacated his place. He offered no further explanation, and I didn't prompt for one.

I stood in the kitchen at home and gazed out the window. Across the field, the silver moonlight illuminated the outline of Shaz and Kylarai as they trotted toward the trees. I had said that I would be right behind them.

I wasn't feeling so hot. Since I had left Raoul's, the hunger had been carving out my insides like a dull blade. The craving for human blood tore through me like a sickness, and at one point, I doubled over in pain. Waves of nausea wracked my body, and I gasped for air, clutching uselessly at my stomach.

Arys's hunger ate at me like a disease. I began to understand why so many vampires chose to take the kill. I'd do anything to make the undying need stop.

The clock on the stove approached midnight. The part of me that was wolf felt confused and irritated. Tonight was supposed to belong to my wolf, who didn't have time for this.

Clad in only a velvet robe, I let myself out on to the back deck. Determined, I fought back the blood sickness that didn't belong to me and focused on the wolf that did. I closed my eyes and breathed the night air deep into my lungs. It was cool and crisp. It made me feel alive.

I allowed the robe to slip down my body and pool at my feet. The power of my wolf reached for the moon. The change broke over me, and I shifted quickly and smoothly. The pain in my guts ceased as I took off at a run.

Werewolves, my pack, filled the clearing. Most of the dozen or so local shifters waited there, many of them in human form. Some sat in the grass talking while others stretched or wrestled playfully.

And as he had promised, Raoul stood in the center of them all. I was glad to be in wolf form. I wasn't a fan being nude in close proximity to Raoul. He stood there beneath the moonlight, unashamed in his naked glory.

Belle began to make her way to him from where she sat with one of the younger males. Typical. I intercepted her just because I could. Her place will never be at the center of the circle with the Alpha. At least, not until she can best me in a fight, the good, old-fashioned way.

Raoul met my eyes and nodded. He didn't even so much as cast a glance in Belle's direction as he gracefully went to his knees. By the time, he touched the ground he was a striking black wolf. He fled the clearing with Belle hot on his heels in a pathetic attempt to keep up.

Kylarai and Shaz appeared out of the shadows behind me. Ky's deep brown fur contrasted greatly with Shaz's brilliant white and my ash blonde.

The three of us ran with a few others. We frolicked under the midnight sky until we picked up the fresh scent of a deer. I'd much rather hunt something a little less cute and a little more evil, so when they veered off to follow the trail I went my own way.

Shaz came back to me, and we soon found ourselves stalking small animals through the brush, just for fun. A good chase was exhilarating and didn't hurt anybody. We flushed out a few gophers and gave chase until they squeezed their fat little bodies down a hole.

Even as I enjoyed my time with nature, I regretted that my reprieve was only temporary. I welcomed the escape. I ran with abandon, but I could shake neither the phantom hunger for human blood nor the fear that raced through me.

Human blood. The thought called up a memory. I didn't like

seeing through Arys's eyes. His memories were beyond disturbing.

He was in bed with a young, dark skinned woman. I was looking down at her perfect, slender neck. Even in the pale light of an oil lamp, I could easily make out her pulse leaping against her creamy skin. Only the thinnest barrier separated my lips from the crimson river that flowed through her veins beneath. I bent to kiss that warm pulsating spot on her throat, and she pulled me closer, eagerly. I was going to kill her.

I bit deep, fatal. Enraptured by my power, my victim sought only to draw me closer as the life pumped out of her body. A struggle was preferable, but this quiet complacency was nice, too.

The grip of the vampire's memory was broken as my muzzle hit the dirt. Shaz had successfully caught me unawares with that pounce. His playful attack sent me sprawling, and when I got to my feet, I was angry.

Irrational rage filled me, and a deep growl erupted from my throat. Shaz's ears twitched, and he looked at me with confusion. Blood and death, they filled me, and I could already taste his blood. I could see only the invigorating rush of hot, violent death.

When I rushed him, I had very little sense of self and a need for blood that I had never known. He realized, as I reached him, that something wasn't right. He met me with his lips peeled back in a snarl, but fear shined in the depths of his jade eyes.

The impact of our colliding bodies broke the stillness surrounding us. The wind rushed out of my lungs as we went down and rolled. On my feet, I rushed him again, but a part of me asked what the hell I was doing.

The scent of blood hit the air, and my stomach cramped. Hunger swarmed me until I was drowning in it. I saw only through the vampire's eyes. Need drove me, and I fought hard for Shaz's throat.

His powerful jaws snapped inches before my face and drove me back. I circled wide and prepared to spring on him again. When I leapt, however, I quickly found myself going nowhere as pain shot up my spine. I thumped heavily to the ground and whirled around.

Raoul gripped my tail with strong hands. He was in human form, but he bared his fangs at me. With one great heave, he flung me away from Shaz. All four of my feet left the ground as I flew a good twenty feet through the air. So much for healing up those sore muscles.

Before I could get to my feet, Raoul was on top of me. He straddled my upper body and pressed my face against the ground. He had me trapped. I couldn't get up.

My every instinct screamed for me to remove him metaphysically, but in my wolf form, my skills were greatly restricted. Instead of struggling against Raoul, I stilled under his weight. I submitted.

My face stung, and my tail ached. I cursed both Arys and myself up and down. I needed to talk to Lena about this.

"Alexa?" Raoul's voice came low in my ear. "Have you lost your damn mind?"

I was hoping he didn't expect a verbal reply. There was no way that I was going to shift with his naked ass on top of me.

"What's gotten into you? You're beyond this kind of loss of control." When I made no move to fight, he slowly began to release his hold on me.

"Is she ok?" Shaz's voice. He'd shifted fast. Even after what I'd just done, his first concern was still for me.

My heart broke, and I knew, suddenly and exactly, how bad I'd really fucked up. Power like Arys's and mine was a curse before it was a gift.

"She seems fine. Other than the rabid bitch mentality."

"I'm not sure what happened. I was just playing around, and she snapped." I could see Shaz shrug as he came into my line of sight. "Don't poke the bear, I guess."

It pissed me off how they spoke as if I wasn't there.

"I think it's more like, don't tease the werebitch," Raoul said, and I felt my anger begin to bubble again.

He wasn't sounding like someone who needed my help. He looked down at me and said, "I'm going to let you up now. No sudden moves." As if to enforce his meaning, the jerk dragged a clawed finger across my throat before releasing me.

I have never felt as humiliated as I did right then. Without looking at either of them, I turned tail and fled into the night. I ran blindly for hours, until I could run no more. Nearing sunrise, I was thoroughly exhausted and finally headed for home.

Kylarai met me as I stepped through the patio door. She wore a look of concern and stood with her arms crossed over her chest. I could take a wild guess that she'd heard about my temporary loss of sanity.

Before she could open her mouth to speak, I burst into tears. I felt ashamed, and it made my gut ache to think about hurting Shaz.

"Alexa…" she was hesitant. It seemed as if she wasn't sure what to say. Her lips formed a small "o" of surprise, and when I wiped my eyes, my hands came away red.

Blood tears, only vampires cry blood tears.

"I don't know what's happened to me, Kylarai."

"You need to talk to Arys. Maybe he's not well either. Maybe he needs help, he could be dangerous like this."

I gave her a look that clearly indicated she wasn't helping. Arys was already dangerous. "I need to call Lena. She has to know something."

Ky nodded but said nothing. She seemed to be having a hard time meeting my eyes. I went to the bathroom to wash my face, but my reflection stopped me dead in the doorway.

My eyes were a sparkling vibrant blue. That sapphire blue belonged on someone else. Red streaks stained my cheeks, hideous and mocking. Unnerved, I forced my feet to work so I could stare closer into my face in the mirror.

"Holy shit," I breathed, horror struck. I didn't look like me. My deep brown eyes were now the color of Arys's eerie vampire orbs. A shiver crawled up my spine.

"How are you feeling?" Kylarai spoke from the open doorway behind me.

"Not like myself. If that wasn't already apparent. How's Shaz?"

"Worried. I had to force him to go home. He wanted to stay here until you showed up, but I wasn't sure that was a good idea." Ky shrugged and did her best to keep her expression neutral. "He was pretty torn up. He blames himself for setting you off."

"You didn't tell him about Arys?"

"Of course not."

I slammed my hands down on the counter in frustration. The sound of wood splitting did little to soothe me. I generally accept my mistakes, but this time, I'd really blown it.

"Son of a bitch! When was the last time I did something so stupid, Ky?"

"Are you looking for a real answer or a fake "there there"

answer?"

"Real."

"It's been a long time. Probably, the last time you slept with Raoul."

Ouch. I'd asked for honesty, though. Count on a good friend to never let you forget the dumbest things you've ever done.

"Ok. So there have been things worse than this. I just have to find a way to work through it."

Ky gave a scoffing laugh. "I'm glad you're being so positive about it, but would you mind sharing with me why you tried to bleed Shaz? What the hell happened to you out there?"

With a long, shuddery breath, I told her about Arys's memories and the insatiable bloodlust. Her expression never changed, but I felt the shift in the atmosphere. Was she putting herself on the defensive? A little part of me died when I realized Kylarai was afraid of me.

"Well, that sums it up," she said when I'd finished. "You need to speak with a few different people. But, it's up to you who is first on that list."

Despite sunrise being just an hour away, I couldn't sleep. I just couldn't stop thinking about Shaz. Long after Kylarai had gone to bed, this time locking her door, I lay awake staring at the ceiling.

Maybe, Shaz was awake. I rolled out of bed and pulled on some jeans. I grabbed my car keys and neared the front door, when I sensed him, on the other side. He lingered as if afraid to knock.

Afraid he would leave, I pulled the door open quickly. He just looked at me expectantly. Instead of stepping inside, he reached out with a gentle hand. His fingers deftly brushed the hair away from my neck. Before I realized what he was doing, he'd tugged the strap of my tank top down and exposed the vampire bite in the hollow of my collarbone.

He sounded resigned when he said, "We need to talk."

Chapter Ten

"How did you know?" I winced as the words came out of my mouth.

"Let's just say, when I found Arys gnawing the legs off a dog, he took a moment to mention it."

"What?" For just a split second, my heart seemed to stop. My mind had trouble making sense of what I just heard.

"Let's go grab a coffee. I'll explain in the car."

I couldn't believe what he told me, or at least, I didn't want to believe. On his way home, Shaz came across Arys on a side street. He'd killed his neighbor's dog, torn it limb from limb. According to Shaz, he'd exhibited all of the signs of a newly turned werewolf. He had been irrational and unsuccessfully fighting the urge to tear things apart.

"I'm not kidding you Lex. He had fangs on the bottom as well as the top. He blamed it on the two of you being together. I didn't believe him." Shaz risked a glance in my direction. "But, he told me the bite should be proof enough."

I didn't know what to say. I felt guilty. This was not how I wanted him to find out.

"Is he ok?" I hated asking but I had to know. "I mean, did he hurt anyone?"

"He's fine. I took him home. Other than the dog, I'm pretty sure no one was eaten."

We went through the twenty-four hour drive-thru at the coffee shop, and then Shaz drove us down to the duck pond on the edge of town.

We parked but didn't get out of his little Chevy Cobalt. The silence dragged as I struggled for words.

I stared at the large fountain near the center of the pond. I would have watched the sunrise from the bridge that crossed the pond, but unfortunately, I was lost amidst clouds of pain and uncertainty. The hurt Shaz tried to hide didn't escape me. His eyes betrayed him.

"Look Shaz-," I began. He cut me off before I could spit out another word.

"I don't want your apology, Alexa, or whatever excuse you are going to offer me. You don't owe me any explanations." He looked at me with ice in his gaze, which chilled me to the bone. "I know I have no claim on you."

"I'm sorry, but I have to explain what happened that night. I need you to know." I didn't say more than necessary. Shaz sat quietly and stared into me as I told him about energy bonding with the vampire. "Don't mistake the point here, Shaz, please. There is no emotional connection between Arys and me. It was just the power."

He blinked a few times before responding, and I wished I could snatch back those last words. "Just the power?" he asked. "You still have the mark from his bite, and you're telling me it was just an energy exercise. No Lex, that doesn't sound intimate at all."

I wasn't sure what he wanted from me, so I said as much in a bitter, sharp tone. I couldn't please everybody, and I was getting tired of trying.

"You know I have feelings for you," he yelled suddenly, and I sat in stunned silence. "I know you do. But, we are not together, and no matter how jealous I am, no matter how much I wish it was me in his place, I have no right to say so or act on those feelings." He wiped his eyes to destroy his unshed tears. "But, God, I need you to know."

A nervous sweat trickled down my spine, and I swallowed hard. Yeah, I was aware of the attraction between us. It was mutual on many levels. But, I was in no way ready for his confession. My heart pounded in my ears.

"I don't know what to say," I admitted.

"Don't say anything."

"I have to. I have to make this right. Or, is it too late for that?"

"What can you do, Alexa? Turn back time? I can't expect you to cater to my needs. You are your own woman."

The way he looked at me when he said that made me feel tainted, like damaged goods. My head ached in confusion, and I hugged myself tightly.

"I fucked up, Shaz. That's all I know. I don't know how to make it better. I don't even think it's possible. And now everything is all messed up, and I regret my stupid decision for so many reasons."

I blinked back tears, fearing they would be red. My eyes had been brown when I had crawled into bed, but the worry gripped me just the same.

"Is it because you made a mistake or because I found out about it?" He asked, knowing the answer already.

"Both." I was honest. "The last thing I want is to hurt you." I silently fumed at Arys. He had known damn well that I didn't want Shaz to find out, particularly not from him.

"It's not my place to be hurt. I feel like I'm over reacting by being as upset about it as I am."

"No, Shaz. You're entitled to your feelings. There is no sense in denying them."

The small car felt huge all of a sudden. The space between us felt like a canyon opening up, dividing us. The air felt fuzzy, and I needed to open the window to allow in a fresh breeze.

The sun broke on the horizon. We were awash in an orange glow, but the magnificence was lost on us as we both looked inward to personal wounds.

That moment cut deep. I had done something that could never be undone, and I may have effectively killed anything bigger between Shaz and me. I looked at him.

Sadly, I couldn't recall the last time that I had been in his arms. We had been so close. We had once touched one another with a familiarity and comfort reserved for lovers, though we never had been intimate.

When did it stop? I couldn't remember, and I felt all the sadder. I did this to us.

I felt sick with fear. Surely, he could smell it on my skin. Everything in me told me not to try, but I couldn't deny the sudden need to touch him, to feel his warmth and gain comfort from it. Selfishly, I needed to know we were ok.

He turned to look at me when my fingers brushed his, but he didn't pull away like I expected.

"Alexa, I can't…"

"Please, don't say it." I heard the tears in my voice. I couldn't hold them back. When they fell, they were just tears, crystal clear.

With a tender touch, he wiped each one away as it fell. He said nothing. He simply allowed me to release my guilt and sorrow with each wracking sob. Drawing me close, he stroked my hair.

"Tell me we're ok" I whispered as desperation seized me. "Can you promise we're ok?"

A deep sigh escaped him, and he slumped against me. Who was I to weep like the victim when I was the victimizer? He owed me nothing. But, what he gave me was worth everything.

"We're ok."

Chapter Eleven

I stared at Arys's house for a really long time before I got out of the Charger. I easily imagined striding up the walk and ringing the bell, but doing it was a whole lot tougher. The sun had just disappeared from the western sky. Only a pale glow remained at the start of another perfect summer night. I planned to catch him here before he left for the evening.

I was on my way to talk to Veryl and meet a new client about a potential job. I didn't have time to run around town right now. But, I needed to see Arys. A glance at the dash clock told me I should hurry, but I still had time. Or did I? Maybe I should just go to work and deal with this later. Duty called.

No. I was being cowardly, and thankfully, nobody was there to see it. My heart pounded from the anxiety, and a cold sweat broke over me. I stepped out of the car and steeled myself against the power inside me. It recognized his presence. I could feel him within the walls of the house. The little hairs on my arms stood on end, and I wished I'd brought a sweater to throw over my tank top. Dread settled in the pit of my stomach.

I rang the bell but got no response, and I wondered if he was trying to get rid of me. The door swung open suddenly, catching me off guard.

"Back for more, Alexa?" He greeted me with a big shit-eating grin plastered on his handsome face. His dark hair was wet and messy. He wore only jeans. I hoped that I wasn't gawking openly as I imagined running my hands over his hard, bare chest.

"Hardly," I managed to say despite the aching inside me. In that moment, I wanted to spill blood, his and mine, to bask in all of our power, to reach the heights that we hadn't yet dreamed possible. I went to take my first step towards him but snapped back to myself. I gave myself a shake to clear my head.

"Would you like to come in? I didn't really take the time to give you the grand tour during your last visit. I just had the place redecorated last month." His midnight ocean eyes spoke volumes. He made no attempt to hide his lust as he ogled me from head to toe and back up again.

Something didn't feel right. The air buzzed with our power, anticipating.

"Come on, Arys, you know why I'm here." He stared at me like a feline on catnip, and I resisted the urge to smack him upside the head.

"I assume it's to explain to me why I made a chew toy out of Mrs. Olson's dog last night."

"You say that as if I know."

"Don't you?"

"Of course not!" I was incredulous.

What the hell was he trying to insinuate? That I had done this on purpose? I shouldered my way inside and fixed him with eyes blazing with anger. "You're not the only one suffering, Arys."

"Oh?" He cocked his head to the side and studied me. I told him about the previous night: the blood tears, the eye color and the memories plagued with bloodlust.

He knew all too well. A glint of something new and unsettled haunted his eyes.

"I think the memories may have been the worst part," he said, and I frowned, insulted. My memories couldn't have been worse than his. His were much more gruesome. "But then again, perhaps it was the pain."

"The pain?" I asked. I wanted to hear his side now.

"After you left in the morning, I slept through the day. I woke, and everything hit me." He seemed to sober considerably as he spoke. "I was hungry but not just for blood, for the rush of running on four legs and the thrill of being one with nature. I couldn't shake the need to hunt, to tear into a fresh, meaty kill, so soft and warm." He paused for a minute.

He was sickened, but I found that funny considering his way of survival. I nodded and encouraged him to continue.

"That wasn't the worst part though. The worst part was the change."

"The change?" I was flabbergasted.

"Well, the need to shift would be more precise. It was like a wolf had been trapped inside me, scratching and biting to get out. Only I couldn't let it out, Alexa. It burned. God, it burned. I thought that was it for me."

I stared at him with a terror-stricken expression. We had been inside one another's minds, seen each other's souls, but I didn't realize the exchange had truly been to the core. This was so not funny.

"You had the need to change form?" I shook my head. This was dangerous. I anticipated a backlash of some kind, but a wolf trying to tear itself from a form unable to shift was downright scary.

"I'm surprised claws didn't spring from my fingertips. I could feel them, like torturous little needles pricking right beneath the surface." Arys shuddered then and stared at his hands as if they were foreign objects. "It ate at me for most of the night. I went to Lucy's Lounge but couldn't sit still. I had to get out of there."

I couldn't believe what I was hearing. I cast a glance around me as if searching for the unspoken answer.

I had called Lena earlier, but she'd been busy with her store and only had time to scold me for acting impulsively. Lena had used some pretty colorful language to describe our actions. "Loss of control is your undoing every time. It's all about security, Alexa, mental shields. I can't stress that enough."

Lena added that the real problem wasn't the power itself. We'd bonded. We'd joined on a metaphysical level, which could last forever or until one of us was dead.

"What do you mean bonded?" Arys's reply sounded similar to the one that I'd given Lena.

"We didn't just call power. We bonded our own personal powers which created something else entirely. Some of this is never going away." Why did I feel so insulted by the suspicious look he wore?

"How bad is it really?"

"I don't know." I shrugged and cast a glance around his country-style kitchen. It didn't look lived in enough. "I guess we find out."

"Well damn. I bet you could take down a lot of vampires with that tactic."

"What the hell are you saying, Arys? That I did this on purpose?" I took a step toward him, and he stood his ground.

Staring down his nose at me with those steely blue eyes, I remained unflinching under his predatory stare. It was my stare.

"The thought crossed my mind," he admitted. "I feel like I've been waiting for you forever and this is just too good to be true. I still want you though."

His admission was shocking. I went on as if he hadn't said that, but the pressure inside me was beginning to strip away my control. I couldn't be here. I had a meeting.

"There is a plus side to this," I stammered. "Lena said we should be able to call on each other's power now, like vampires can when they create a blood bond."

A vampire formed a blood bond at siring, by draining a human to the point of death then feeding the dark blood in return. However, two totally unrelated vampires could share blood. The bond would let them access one another's thoughts and power whether together or apart. Vampires never created a blood bond lightly.

"We didn't exchange blood. I took yours, you didn't take mine." His gaze dropped to my throat, and I felt my breath catch. My stomach knotted at the memory. He licked his lips, and I knew he was remembering the taste of me.

"I know, but I still took your power." My head began to cloud with the energy surrounding us. "I've got to get out of here. I have a meeting I'm going to be late for."

I turned to go, and his hand on my arm made me pause. I closed my eyes and said a silent prayer: *Please, no temptation.* The need to writhe naked in his arms was overpowering me.

"Will I see you tonight?" His hypnotic gaze stared into me, and my knees went weak. I knew what he was really asking. But, it was just power. There was no love behind it.

"Why did you tell Shaz?" The words spilled out of my mouth before I could catch them. I hadn't really meant to ask.

"How could I not? He found me eating a dog on the side of the road." Point for him, he had me there. I was just pissed about Shaz finding out from somebody else.

"Just forget it. It doesn't matter." I turned to go before he could lure me any farther into the house. "Did you get cleaned up, ok?"

Arys ignored my attempt at casual conversation. He reached around me and opened the front door. Before I could escape, he drew me into a warm embrace and just held me for a long moment.

I feared it would stoke the fire between us, but it didn't. The embrace was a need that my wolf could not deny.

Arys had a renewed sense of loss and longing that had not been there before. Gently, I disengaged myself from him and touched his cheek. With the barest touch of my lips on his, I turned to go.

After I left Arys's place, an unexpected flow of hot, guilt ridden tears seized me. I wiped my eyes and knew my mascara had run down my face. Son of a bitch. The last thing I wanted to do was walk into the office all cry–eyed. I'd either get questioned or comforted, or both. I dreaded the thought.

I had this nagging guilt that I couldn't shake. I had to put my personal life aside. This was time to be professional. Or, as professional as one can be when getting paid to hunt and kill things.

Jez got out of her Jeep as I pulled into the small parking lot. She paused and waited for me to park. Her gold curls were tied up in a high ponytail atop her head, and she wore little makeup. She didn't need much. She was stunning. I was momentarily envious of how great her long legs looked in blue jeans.

"How's it going?" She greeted me as she puffed quickly on a cigarette.

"That shit will kill you," I replied, sounding more like Kale than myself.

"So I hear." She ground the butt into the driveway with her heel and followed me inside.

On Sundays, the accounting business next door was closed, and the street was blessedly deserted. The only sound was Lilah's phone ringing down the hall.

Jez gave me a knowing wink and headed to her office, while I turned into the kitchen to make some coffee. I considered going after her to talk about Shaz but decided it could wait. I had an appointment in twenty minutes, so it had to wait.

The coffee began to brew, and I breathed in the wonderful aroma. There is no scent quite like that of fresh coffee.

Jez's voice carried to me faintly down the hall as she made a phone call. Minutes later, she turned up the steady beat of a heavy metal song. My head ached slightly from my brief crying stint, and I looked to the coffee pot for the solution to my problems. I poured a cup full of steaming coffee, and too lazy to add cream and sugar, padded down to Veryl's office.

The door was slightly ajar in open invitation. I poked my head in. He would have sensed my approach anyway. He sat behind his old, elaborately designed desk, my favorite piece of décor. Despite the phone pressed to his ear, he inclined his head toward the seat across from him.

Veryl was the type of man that nearly all women find attractive. His short chocolate brown hair was streaked with the barest trace of silver, which only added to his distinguished presence. His clear blue eyes beamed at me as he informed the person on the phone that he had to attend to business.

I knew that I had his undivided attention when his gaze swept over me slowly, agonizingly so. I was dying to spit my questions at him but felt obligated to make small talk first.

"You're in early tonight." He commented. His rich voice was deep and melodic. "Expecting somebody?"

I nodded, as I looked at the paintings behind his desk. "Yeah. I figured I'd take it easy tonight after the last few assignments I've had. Been a little on the rough side."

"I think you enjoy it, though." Veryl's slightly hawk-like nose was angular and intimidating when paired with the studious expression he now wore. "Standing so close to the flame can be hypnotizing in its draw. It can also kill you. Be careful with that outlook, Alexa. It has destroyed many that I have worked with in the past."

"I know. I blame my personal life for that," I offered lamely. When I didn't say more he knew better than to prompt. Veryl is absolutely the most professional person that I know.

"So what is it that brings you to my office?" He shuffled

through the papers on his desk and produced a copy of the day's paper. He handed it to me.

The headline screamed that police may be after a serial killer after the murders of two women in the past week. I skimmed the article. They referenced Raoul as a suspect, but the write up seemed to be based more on hearsay that factual truths.

"Not this," I said as I handed the paper back to him. "Raoul didn't do it. I've seen him a few times this past week. I know for a fact he could never have killed Julie Price."

Veryl shifted languidly in his chair, stretched his arms out, and cracked his fingers with a sound that chilled my bones. "I don't have to tell you what's going to happen if he is somehow behind this or if he ends up being convicted."

No, he didn't have to tell me. I knew that Raoul would be put on the extermination list, treated like the vampires raping young girls of both their blood and innocence or the Weres that just didn't know how to pass up fresh meat. A conviction would put Raoul behind bars where he couldn't hide his true nature.

"Someone's setting him up, Veryl. I can only ask that you let me keep an eye on this situation for now." I met his eyes, seeking the wisdom within. "At least until I can figure out who is behind it, and why."

"I can't make you any promises, my dear, but as of right now, it's in your hands."

Great. That was just what I needed to hear and more than a little irritating, since it had nothing to do with my questions.

"Ok, the real reason I'm here: I'm trying to find information on the werewolf who killed my family."

The blank look that passed over his sharp features was not quick enough to disguise the moment of recognition in his eyes. He knew something.

"Alexa, it's been years. Can't you just allow sleeping dogs to lie?"

"If you're trying to tell me that the bastard is still alive then no, I will not. I keep having the nightmare, Veryl, and if you know who it is, anything at all, I need to know."

Fingers poised into a steeple, he smiled softly as one might smile at a child who refuses to give up. "I cannot say whether I know of this wolf's existence or not, but, I can advise you to forget about it. I completely understand what it means to live out your life with doors that remain open and questions that are unanswered. But, trust me, this is better left that way."

I stared at him, stupefied. I couldn't believe he was giving me the whole "ignorance is bliss" crap. "You know who it is."

His brow furrowed as we stared at one another. I had the distinct feeling that he was weighing his words before speaking. What was he hiding from me? And most importantly, why?

"I know that you need to leave this alone. I'm sorry that I can't say anymore about this matter. If you choose to continue to seek this wolf out, that is entirely your business. But, I will not help you."

And, that was it. That was all he was willing to give me, and his answer only fueled my need to know rather than put a damper on it. What choice did I have? I had to accept his silence.

A thought came to me then, and I sat up straighter in my chair. "What about Lilah?"

He stared at me quizzically but gestured that I should continue. I told him about the demon encounter. A look of understanding passed over his strong features.

"And, what do you want to know about her?"

"For one, how the hell does she have that kind of control over a demon? Just how old is Lilah anyway?" I was being snoopy, but I was dying of curiosity. I'd seen what she did to that demon, and I wanted to know how it was possible.

Veryl smiled in amusement, and I felt like a childish student. "There is more history to that woman than you can imagine. Though it's not my place to reveal her business, I can tell you that not many things in this world have authority over demons. She is just one of the few that does."

Wait a minute, only angels have authority over demons. That and other, more powerful demons. Considering Lilah was a vampire, I doubted she was angelic.

"She's a demon?"

"Is, was, whatever you prefer. It's not something that should be common knowledge. I'm sure you understand." The phone on his desk rang, and he looked at it pointedly before meeting my eyes again. Yeah, yeah, I can take a hint.

I went back down the hall to my own office but left the door open so I could hear the doorbell. My mind was working in overdrive as I replayed the image of Lilah's quick dispatch of that demon. Who, or what, was she, exactly? How powerful could she possibly be?

I hit play on my voicemail. Two new clients requested a meeting, and the client that I was currently waiting for confirmed.

I was pretty sure she was a vampire, not only from the time-honed, silky voice but also the late hour of the meeting. I seldom had a vampire as a client. They tend to take care of issues with a personal touch, so I was intrigued.

I was clicking through my email inbox when the door chimed. I turned off the monitor, and I went to greet my latest potential business associate. Through the peephole, I saw a dark haired woman. She appeared to be alone. I didn't sense anything out there but her, and she was definitely a vampire. I slid the two dead bolts back and opened the door.

"Miss O'Brien?" That angelic tone poured forth from her as I grasped her offered hand.

It was tiny, smaller than my own but icy, cold, and strong. She had a grip that bragged of inhuman strength, yet she was gentle, careful not to squeeze too hard. She was a very delicate looking woman, petite with a ballerina's figure. Her dark brown hair, almost black, was layered so that it fell stylishly around her face and shoulders. She had a small but cute nose and strong cheekbones. A long black dress coat covered what looked to be a party dress. Her shiny, silver high heels gleamed in the bright overhead lights.

"Please, call me, Alexa. Come inside." As I stepped back to allow her entry, I felt strangely as if I knew her from somewhere.

"Thank you for agreeing to see me on such short notice. I truly appreciate it." She clasped my hands suddenly in her own as if to convey her gratitude. It startled me, and I took an involuntary step back.

"I'm sorry," she said, a pale hand covered her mouth. "I didn't mean to intrude in your personal space."

"That's alright." I resisted the urge to wipe my hands on my jeans. She could know neither the extent that I felt her undead power nor how it tickled me in places that couldn't be scratched.

I turned to lead her to my office and said, "Have a seat, and I'll see if I'm able to help you."

She froze at the entrance to my office door. Her eyes darted down the hallway to where Jez was working. The door to Veryl's office was now closed. Jez's music continued to scream down the hall at us.

"My partner is working down the hall, in her own office. Everything you say here, including your visit itself, is strictly confidential."

A wave of anxious energy trickled from my guest to me, and I was surprised that she'd let it escape her. She hadn't fed yet, which worried me. Vampires are much easier to talk to after they've taken care of their carnal urges.

Once she sat down, she began to relax, but a tightness in her shoulders told me that she was anything but calm. Her coal dark eyes peeked out at me from beneath a fringe of bangs. Her eyes were as black as Raoul's and striking against her alabaster skin.

"I must apologize, again. I haven't properly introduced myself. Please, call me, Cat." When I frowned, she supplied, "Catherine. It's short for Catherine."

I wondered why she preferred the shorter version, but I pressed my fingers together and asked, "So, what can I do for you, Cat?"

Despite possessing the grace and skill of her vampirism, I could easily feel her sudden anguish. I was concerned but not alarmed. She should shield better than that. I was perplexed. She was powerful enough to squelch such displays. Vampires don't exhibit a lot of emotion, particularly not around strangers.

"I'm not sure how to begin, Alexa. I'm a little overwhelmed here. I've been waiting so many years for this."

I leaned back in my chair, in an attempt at casual, and said nothing. I didn't dare read her aura like I wanted, knowing she would feel it. She took my silence as an invitation to continue.

"For several decades now, I have searched the western world for a particular vampire, the one who made me. I have finally found him and would request your services in extinguishing his undead flame permanently." Her words came in a rush as if she'd practiced them on her way over.

I noticed how her grip tightened on the armrests of her chair. "And, what did this vampire do that makes you want him dead?"

Cat's lips pressed together tightly. I could only imagine what she was seeing in her mind's eye. When she spoke, her words only formed with determination. I could sense her effort.

"He loved me and left me to die. I was a fool to believe his lies, but they sounded so beautiful. I wanted so badly to believe in him. He said we were to be together forever. Until the day that we were attacked, and he left me behind to save himself." Ouch. Cat looked as if she might cry. She bit at her lower lip, and I could see the tiny points of her fangs for the briefest of moments.

"Just say whatever you need to say. Don't force yourself." I slid a box of tissue across the desk to her. I didn't know what else to say.

Cat clutched a tissue tightly between polished red fingertips and attempted to give me a smile. "Thank you."

She blinked a few times, and the vampire control was back. "It's still emotional for me. I really thought he loved me, but then when our house was under siege, he escaped through a passage that he had never told me about. He arranged the entire attack as a way to get rid of me. I never imagined such betrayal was possible."

Her voice broke then, and I saw the weakness in her, oh so well. I'd never seen a vampire look so beaten. It wasn't in their nature.

"Why would he do that? Do you have any idea?" I shrugged and brushed a stray blonde strand away from my face. "I'm sorry, I don't know what to say."

When she met my eyes evenly again, I could see the pain etched in the depths of her ebony gaze. "He had no use for me anymore. I think he regretted turning me. I was no longer any more than a forgotten play thing."

The guy sounded like a total prick. I was shocked by what I was hearing. It just sounded so selfish and cold. But, I mean, we were talking vampires.

"And, what about the blood bond?" A shiver ran up my spine as I flashed back to my own recent bonding experience. "Could you not reach him that way?"

"Not at all. He shut me out completely. I've never been able to breach the block." That was interesting. This vampire must be incredibly powerful.

"Alright, so what is it that brings you to me, specifically?"

"I hear you're the only werewolf in the civilized world to possess some of the vampire's attributes. After looking for so many years, I've finally found him. Here."

She knew about me. Word was getting out, and that worried me. "And? You really want me to take him out?"

"Isn't that what you do?" She looked at me like I'd just told her the place was an ice cream shop.

"Yes, but I have a few general rules. First, you must fully understand that you're asking me to kill him. Another, you must really want irrevocable death, not simple retribution. Finally, my final decision is entirely based on my personal discretion."

Instead of replying, she slipped an envelope from inside her coat and pushed it towards me. "Is that enough?" She was all business. "I can get you more if you need it. I wasn't sure how much you would charge."

With a brief glance, I estimated twenty-five thousand dollars in cash. "No. It's plenty, but Cat, you must realize that I can't just randomly kill. I need more information on this guy."

She dropped a large manila file folder on my desk with a thwap. "Everything you need to know about him is in there. If that's not enough to earn him a death sentence, then I don't know what is."

Something triggered in me, and I looked more closely at her. "May I ask why you don't confront him yourself?"

She looked as if I'd slapped her. Her face paled as much as it possibly could, and her mouth dropped open. Recovering quickly, she cast her eyes downward.

"I could never. I have neither the courage nor the will to kill him myself. I loved him so deeply. To look into his unfeeling eyes after all this time may be too much for me to take. It's been so long." Her tone grew wistful as if her mind went to a happier time in her life.

I used her distraction as an opportunity to flip open the file folder, but the instant that I saw the photo on top of the sheaf of papers, I froze. I could barely keep my heart rate from soaring. I pulled the folder closer so that I could get a better look at the black and white picture.

It was old. From the style of dress, it appeared to be way before my time. The photo itself was from a wedding. Bridesmaids wore their hair in high curls and posed in extremely large skirted gowns. The bride, an unknown beaming blonde, smiled up at her handsome husband as he kissed her upturned hand. My eyes quickly skimmed over the groomsmen, each dressed in the same black suit with fringes of white lace peeking from beneath the cuffs. But, the groom held my attention.

Though his black hair was very short and he wore the same suit as the others, I stared at Arys while he happily fawned over his new wife.

I realized then I had recognized Cat from his memories. What in the hell?

"That was the most recent photo I could find of him." Cat said as she noticed my intent stare. "I think he started using a new alias shortly after killing her." She gestured at the photo in my hand, and I dropped it.

"And, what was his name when you knew him?" I murmured, as I fought to tear my gaze away from the picture. It mocked me from where it sat as surely as it mocked Cat. I was feeling both stupid and thankful. Thankful that I didn't take Arys's blood, didn't complete a blood bond with him. I'd fucked up enough without linking us mentally.

"His real name is Sindarys Ainsley Knightingale."

"Knightingale?" I heard myself say.

"An old family name. They were royalty once, or so he said."

She didn't continue, and I chewed my lip. "And, you're sure that you want me to kill him?" My voice squeaked, and I hoped that she didn't notice my unease.

"I don't suppose you'd rather bring me his naughty bits in a jar?" The faintest of smiles played around her lips, and I forced a small laugh.

"I'm sorry, Cat, but you sound like you still love him." I almost stopped when I saw her face fall. "Do you really want him dead?" Please say no, I chanted inside my head.

"I love who he pretended to be. But, I accepted long ago that was never really him. He's nothing more than a lying, womanizing murderer who thinks of nothing but himself."

I nodded slightly. I could agree with some of that. She looked like she was about to say more, but her mouth snapped shut, and she shook her head.

After a long moment, she sighed and said, "He needs to die so that I can finally escape him. He haunts me constantly, and I would give anything in the world to make that stop."

I could sense the weight on her, feel the burden she carried around with her, but I didn't know why. Was her hurt really never going to heal?

Was I really thinking that? If I were in her place, I would be on the hunt for blood, too. But I'd want to do it myself.

"Look Alexa, I appreciate your time, but I really should get going. I'll understand if, for any reason, you don't take the case." She stood, and I held the cash envelope out to her. She counted out five thousand dollars and forced it into my hand.

"Keep it. Read through the file and tell me what you think. I've included a few pages from my journal. It seemed better than reciting the past in detail."

I closed the folder and accompanied her out. "I will definitely read through everything and get back to you. But, I can't accept your money." I had difficulty swallowing around the growing knot in my throat.

"Please, I insist. Something for your time at least." She refused to take the bills when I tried to give them to her.

When she was gone, I sank against my desk in relief. What in the world would she think if she knew that I'd been in the arms of her traitorous ex only two nights ago? I felt sick.

"Holy shit," I said aloud to myself. I had to look at the photo again.

I had accepted jobs like this before. Vampires were monsters, and no matter what the situation, they usually gave me just cause to kill them. I kill rogues and eliminate problems. It's what I do. But Arys? I just couldn't do it.

I was still staring at the black and white, elegantly dressed Arys when Jez appeared in the doorway of my office.

"Hey, I heard your client leave. You want to grab a bite to eat? I haven't eaten in hours." She rambled casually, but when she saw my expression, she snapped her mouth shut and came closer. "Are you ok, Lex?"

"Hell no." I handed her the picture and waited for her reaction.

"This is Arys." She let out a low whistle. "He cleans up pretty good. Where did you get it?"

"He's my new target, if I decide to take the job."

"You're kidding." Her eyes never left the aged image in her

hands. "You didn't say no?"

"I didn't know how. Jez, he left her for dead. I couldn't very well tell her the truth." I sighed and held the file folder open for her to drop in the picture. "She left a bunch of dirt on him that I really don't want to know." Besides, everything was already hidden in my memory now. I didn't really want to access it.

"But you're going to read it anyway." There was no question in her tone.

I nodded. "She paid me to. She also said she'd understand if I don't take the hit. And of course, there's the whole curiosity aspect." I shrugged, and we fell silent.

After a moment of eyeing me, Jez cleared her throat. "Do you think there's anything in that folder that will change your mind about taking the hit? I mean, it may very well solve your little energy bonding problem."

I met her dark, golden eyes and found no trace of humor within them. She was dead serious.

"You're an evil woman, Jez."

"So I've been told." She produced a set of car keys with a loud jangle. "Let's go eat. I'll buy."

Chapter Twelve

The radio DJ spoke of sunshine ahead for the rest of the day with a chance of showers overnight, perfect sunroof weather. With it slid wide open, I cruised the streets with the summer breeze in my hair. The scent of rain was light on the air, hours away yet.

My bag, with Cat's unread file, sat on the passenger seat. I had yet to work up the gumption to read even the first page. I just wasn't ready yet.

Not only that, but I was on my way to see Raoul. First things first. He'd left half a dozen messages on my home machine after finding my cell phone voicemail full. Nothing linked him to either murder, but he was having kittens over the whole thing nonetheless.

I still wondered if he wasn't being melodramatic or putting on some kind of act. He wouldn't normally come undone, but I suppose if my exes were dropping like flies, I might be worried, too.

Somebody had it out for him, though, and I wanted to know why. That seemed like a better question than whom. A number of people could have a grudge with Raoul, and they would most likely be completely justified in it.

All too soon, I stood on Raoul's front step and crossed my fingers in the hope that he would have stepped out. The door swung open unexpectedly, and a large hand jerked me inside before I could blink.

My wrist stung where he grasped it, and I glared up at him until he let go. I rubbed the sore spot and frowned. I don't react well to being manhandled.

"I don't want anyone to see you here. They would probably just think I'm going to murder you and have the police here in a heartbeat." When I just gave him a suspicious look, he added, "I didn't kill anyone."

"Well that line is sounding more convincing every time I hear it, but if Belle is going to be your key alibi, consider it an open and shut case." I wrinkled my nose at Belle's heavy, lingering perfume. "Is she gone?" I couldn't sense her physical presence, but I had to be sure.

"Yeah. I asked her to leave before I called you." Raoul ran a hand through his disheveled hair. He looked tired. The dark circles beneath his eyes indicated he hadn't been sleeping well.

"I want to help you, Raoul, but we're running out of time here. No more games. Tell me who you think is doing this."

"Alexa!" The growl that spilled from between his lips made the fine hairs on my arms stand on end. "I don't know. Why are you so insistent that I know who is doing this?"

I studied him long and hard before replying. He met my gaze, unflinching and bold. I couldn't count how many times over the years we had stared at one another like that. Too many.

"I just get the feeling there's something you're not telling me. Why would anyone do this? Why not just kill you and get it over with, if they have it out for you so bad? Why go to the trouble of ruining your life first?"

"I've been asking myself that very same thing. I do not know," he said between tightly clenched teeth. "But, I'd sure like to get my hands on them."

I paced the length of the living room and then paused to examine some photos on the mantel. "If the killing continues, you're going to end up in prison. Or dead." Most of the pictures displayed a much younger, human Raoul with his family. He didn't see them much anymore. He was pretty touchy on the subject.

I knew he was being less than honest about something, but I couldn't place a finger on what. He may be telling the truth about his innocence in the murders, but I was sure I smelled a rat.

"How do you expect me to be of any help if you insist on

keeping me in the dark?"

"Who said I need your help?" The look he gave me was so full of scorn that I had to do a double take.

"You're kidding, right?" Staring at his childhood photos, I wondered briefly what had happened. Surely, he didn't start out in life as such a prick. "Well, forgive me for running over here when you called. Fool me twice, I guess. Shame on me."

He made a frustrated sound and rolled his eyes at me. "Don't get all female and defensive on me, Alexa. I should be able to take care of myself."

A laugh bubbled up and poured out of me before I could rein it in. So, this was about Raoul's fragile ego. Well, I sure as hell was not about to help him stroke it.

"Alright then. When this killer finally makes its way to you, then I'll assume you'll handle it yourself. After all, Lord knows how well you handle everything else."

My jibe didn't go unnoticed. Raoul grabbed my arm and spun me around to face him. I almost dropped the small wolf statue that I'd been examining. "And, just what the hell is that supposed to mean?"

We both knew exactly what I meant: he'd ruined our relationship. When Raoul had first taken me into the pack, I'd been grateful for the support and guidance. But, when I'd spent more time in his bed as a playmate than anything else, my innocence died. I distrusted him on every level. True, he had stopped me from being assaulted and abused, but that debt was paid, as far as I was concerned. I had no reason to forgive him for making me a toy. Over the years, Raoul proved himself a misogynistic chauvinist.

I glared pointedly at the large hand that squeezed my arm. "Get your filthy paws off me."

"I never let him hurt you." The energy behind his words shot through me like a scorching flame, and I jerked my arm away. I contemplated asking him who he was really mad at here.

"No, you just scored from me willingly what he was going to simply take." So much for asking questions. I'm a self-confessed sucker for an argument when I know, without a doubt, that I am right.

"What did you want me to do? Kill him?"

I blinked at him, dumbfounded. This was the man that dared to call himself an Alpha anything?

"Yes, Raoul. I was a teenager, for God's sake. Yes, I wanted to see the bastard dead! I wanted you to make him beg for death. But, you proved that you're full of empty threats and capable of nothing."

"And what did you prove, Alexa? That you're no more than a ruthless murderer, always ready to extinguish somebody's flame?" He smiled as if he believed he had me there.

"I proved that I get things done, and that I'm not afraid to get my hands dirty when it means taking care of business." I tsked and shook my head sadly at him. "Maybe you're not cut out for this werewolf gig after all."

"Oh, fuck off, Alexa."

I rolled my eyes at his blatant immaturity. I honestly wasn't sure why I bothered with him at all.

"And on that note, I'm going to keep this visit short and sweet before I overstay my welcome."

If I didn't leave now, I was going to explode. The fire inside me was nowhere near burning out, and his button pushing wasn't helping. If he touched me again, I was going to pop. Something about his energy set me off, in a way that nobody else's could. He left the bitter sting of betrayal in places that could never be wiped clean.

"You're leaving?" For the first time since I arrived, he showed an actual interest in my presence.

"Well, I sure don't want to get in the way when your soon-to-be murderer arrives to dispatch your egotistical ass to the dark side. But, if you cut me into your will, then I might come back to dispose of you properly when it's over." I resisted the smiled that tugged at my lips.

"So that's it then. Alright. I know you think I deserve as much." Raoul actually paced the length of the room once, then twice. I ignored him, turning to the doorway for my shoes.

The atmosphere grew smothered from his sudden anxiety, and I fought to resist it. Freely exuded, loose energy can become an intoxicant, and lately, it didn't take much to over stimulate my senses.

"It doesn't matter what I think, Raoul. It's a waste of our time to even have this conversation. Keep your secrets, but leave me out of it when they catch up to you."

I pulled my car keys from my pocket, and nearly lost a twenty dollar bill in the process, the one he'd given me. I had been planning on spending it on lottery tickets, hoping to win the big one so I could rub it in his face.

I continued, "Look, it's my pack duty to back you up, but if you don't want my help, then my hands are tied."

He seemed to weigh my words, scan them for sarcasm. Satisfied, he gave me a lecherous smile that I recognized with a sick feeling. This wasn't about to get any better.

"You really want to help me?" His low chuckle gave the room an eerie quality. The tiny hairs on the back of my neck stood on end.

With my defenses raised, I tensed for what was coming. "Don't waste your breath on my account. Please."

He must have moved when I bent to slip my shoes on because he suddenly felt much closer than before. Against my will, my heart began to race as the air shifted around us.

"What has it been, Lex, three or four years since you've been in my bed?"

"Is that all? I haven't kept track. It really doesn't mean anything to me anymore." I bit back all of the things that I wanted to say. I should have said nothing in the first place.

"Hey, you said you wanted to help. I'm simply refusing to beat around the bush. I'm not interested in rehashing the past either."

"You've got to be kidding me. Getting laid is your biggest concern right now? You, sir, are a lost cause."

"That's not fair. I could be a dead man walking, and you expect me to avoid the greatest things in life while I'm still able to enjoy them? Not a chance." He didn't really believe his days were numbered. His arrogance wouldn't allow it.

"Nice try. I hope you don't think I'm hard up enough to take you up on that."

His dark eyes narrowed, and the desire to leave was unbearable. I wished desperately for him to get out of my personal space.

"I don't suppose you would be with a young thing like Shaz. I'll bet he's a real aim-to-please kind of guy."

I made a sound somewhere between a snort and a laugh which earned me a dirty look. Of course, he would assume that Shaz and I were lovers. He wouldn't be the first to think so, but he would be wrong. Still, I didn't like being reminded of the awkward intimacy between me and Shaz. I hated the fear that I had now destroyed it for good.

Trina M. Lee

"I don't stick my nose in your many personal affairs. I'll thank you to stay the hell out of mine."

"Fair enough." With another step, he closed the remaining space between us. With a forward tilt of his head, his black hair fell like a silky curtain against my face. "How about we cut to the chase then?"

I fought to deny the resurgence of a memory, a time when I'd known the touch of that soft hair on my naked flesh. I was resisting the impulse to scream so intently that I expected my skull to burst into a million little pieces. I needed to calm down. Losing control wasn't an option.

His breath was hot on my neck as he nuzzled my hair and breathed in my scent deeply. The soft tip of his tongue was wet against my skin as he licked the sensitive spot beneath my ear. A sigh escaped me, and I flashed back to another time and place. Though it was the same wolf in the same house, it was all wrong.

Raoul thought he could seduce me with the lusty power of the werewolf. Perhaps he could charm the pants off a human or even a new Were, but I'd been seduced by the ultimate vampire, and Raoul just couldn't compare to that. At just the thought of Arys, Raoul's touch ceased to hold any sway over me.

"That's never going to happen." I gently pushed him with both hands. He resisted and pressed me into the wall. "I've got issues you can't even begin to understand. Trust me when I say, you don't want to play with me anymore. Stick with Belle, she's more your type."

The negative energy of his sudden anger pushed against me, and a menacing temptation to play with him taunted me from the cooled depths of Arys's magic. I wanted to manipulate him like the pathetic animal that he was, until I'd consumed all that he had to give: blood, anger, fear and sex. I just could suck him dry. The promise of pleasure encouraged the sadistic urge, and I licked my lips eagerly when he brought his face to mine.

I thought he was going to kiss me, so I was caught between relief and outrage when he bit my bottom lip instead. I tasted blood, which fuelled my sudden fury. The power flowed from me in a casual and effortless gesture that I'd seen Arys do many times. It had taken scarcely more than a thought to throw Raoul against the far wall.

I was pleased at the ease of wielding Arys's power. From the sound that Raoul made against the wall, I'd thrown him harder than I'd intended. I could feel an icy wave shoot through me, and I shuddered as Arys's power licked my insides.

I broke the energy that held Raoul, and he fell to his knees on the floor. He was speechless, a rarity for him. The weight of his wide, dark eyes bore into me. A series of emotions swam in his dark stare. His glare triggered my defenses, and I tensed. I wasn't sure what to expect, but I never expected what came next.

"Get out." Raoul got to his feet, unsteady.

"What?"

"You heard me. Take your secrets, your vampire powers, or whatever the hell that was, and get the fuck out. That certainly explains what you did to Shaz, you crazy bitch."

"You know it's not vampire powers. You've seen what I can do." I was so full of shit, and we both knew it.

"You couldn't do that before. And, certainly not without breaking a sweat. There's the door."

I stared uncertainly at him. I wasn't sure if I should leave or not. I wanted to refuse and force him to listen to me. However, the heavy scent of fear oozed from Raoul's large physique. He was afraid of me. The realization came as a shock. I had to turn away from his frozen black gaze. I'm not sure whose dignity I was trying to preserve, his or mine, but I wasted no time in getting out of there.

Though Raoul may not have known it, I was terrified too. I enjoyed it when Arys's power surfaced within me, but at the same time, I wasn't myself. Was living as a vampire always so Jekyll and Hyde?

Frustration rode me, and I drove half-blinded by anger. I didn't know where I was going. I just drove.

When I came to a stop, I was parked outside of Shaz's apartment building. I had instinctively run to seek solace from the only person that I felt I could. My finger froze, poised above the buzzer labeled 204. What was I doing here? Would he even want to see me? I thought about leaving, but I had nowhere to go with the burden inside me. I let my finger fall on the button.

I waited in stark silence. After a moment, I reached for the exit to the street, expecting no response. With a series of crackles, the intercom blared to life. Shaz's voice sounded fuzzy and far away.

"It's me," I said uncertainly. A deafening buzz indicated that the security door was unlocked.

I waited for the elevator as I nervously rubbed my sweaty palms on my jeans. I can't count how many times I arranged and then re-arranged my hair on the short ride to the second floor. My heart raced. I stepped into the hall, and the elevator doors slid shut behind me.

Deep breath.

He had cracked open the door in anticipation of my entrance. I worked hard to keep my footsteps even. My legs felt like jelly. As I grew near, I took in the overwhelming scents of coffee, fresh laundry, and Shaz. With a light knock, I went inside.

"Hey." He looked up from where he stood loading the dishwasher. His smile was friendly, but I could see the reserve within it. "How are you?"

I closed the door behind me, kicked off my shoes, and left the false comfort of the entryway. My smile was forced, and I knew that he would see right through it.

"I've been better. You?"

I willed myself to hold it together as my throat grew tight. He knew me too well. Despite the awkwardness, something in his stance changed. His eyes softened, and he put down the plate he was holding.

I would not cry. I repeated the words in my head as if to will them to be true. A guilty little piece of me didn't want his sympathy. I didn't deserve it. His compassion would be my undoing.

He crossed the small space between us in a few strides. A finger under my chin drew my gaze to his, and I looked into his calm, sea green eyes. I hated myself for the concern etched in their depths.

"Tell me," he spoke softly. He searched my eyes intently.

Between fighting the emotional outbursts that threatened, I told him everything: Raoul's advance and how I had scared us both, the strangeness of the power exchange, and the vampire who'd wanted Arys dead. I caught a glimpse of satisfaction on Shaz's face when I mentioned the hit job on Arys, but he hid it before I could be certain.

Before I saw it coming, Shaz pulled me into his arms. I expected his embrace to be stiff or distant, but instead, it was warm and inviting. The hand that gently stroked my hair was more possessive than I ever remembered it being.

"You are not Superwoman, Alexa," he said at last. "Stop feeling like you have to take care of everyone. It's not all within your control."

He took my hand in his and led me into the living room. I sat down on the noisy leather couch while he produced a mug of hot coffee from the kitchen.

"Thank you." I stared into the hot, creamy liquid. "I'm sorry, I shouldn't be here. I have no right to show up here crying on your shoulder."

"Of course you do. We're pack. We're friends." He smiled, and his voice had dropped lower when he added, "You know I always wanted to be your other half."

My heart twisted in my chest, and my next breath actually hurt. Unable to speak, I squeezed his hand and wished that he knew what he really meant to me, though it was still hard to come to terms with myself. Why must I make one hell of a mistake to realize what I should have already known?

"If I could take it back..." I choked on my words. "It would be you."

"Stop punishing yourself. Self-loathing doesn't look good on you, Lex. You're a free woman, and I don't have the right to make you feel like you did something wrong."

"But, I did. And, I'm afraid that it cost me more than I even know."

"Like what?" He edged closer, and I was lost in the clean, natural scent of him.

"You."

Silence. The beat of my heart echoed in my ears. I longed to touch him, but I feared that he would pull away. Instead, I kept my hands to myself.

Time stopped.

For one magical moment, he kissed me with such fervor that I spilled my coffee on the beige carpet. I pulled him closer but allowed him to control the kiss. My head was a mass of confusion, but right then, it just felt so naturally perfect. I felt like I was learning a lesson in head versus heart. He nuzzled my throat and breathed in my scent. I melted against him.

"You know what I think?" He whispered after what felt like a long time. "I think you should tell Raoul that he's on his own now. Don't risk yourself for something he brought on himself."

Shaz was ticked over Raoul's unwelcome advances, which pleased me regardless of our situation.

"I don't know what to do anymore."

"There's no sense trying to help him. For all we know, he really deserves what's coming to him."

"Maybe." I nodded. Raoul certainly wasn't the nicest guy. I could believe that someone would have a just grudge against him.

Since I continued to anguish, Shaz changed the subject. "Hey, why don't we order pizza for lunch? We can hang out here and watch talk shows all day like we used to. Maybe play some video games?"

I smiled at the memory. We'd once spent an entire week like that. In the heart of a Canadian winter, the blizzards had kept traffic off the highways. Commuters were stuck at home that week, a weeklong snow day for Stony Plain.

"Sounds great. Chicken and mushroom with honey garlic wings?" I was surprisingly hungry at the mention of food. "And some pizza bread."

The afternoon went by too fast for my liking. A couple episodes of Jerry Springer and a handful of court shows held our attention as we stuffed ourselves with pizza and wings. Shaz made another pot of coffee that we sipped, curled up together on the creaky couch. We laughed and giggled our way through a session of Guitar Hero. As I laughed with Shaz and pretended to be carefree, I felt rejuvenated.

After successfully beating him on battle mode for the third time in a row, I chortled, "In your face."

He responded by grabbing me in a move faster than my eyes could follow. Our plastic guitar controllers went flying. I squealed as his fingers deftly found that one ticklish spot between my ribs. To escape, I threw myself to the floor, but he followed me down and pinned me beneath his weight.

I looked up into his bright green eyes. They held an affection that I hadn't realized I'd been missing. He continued tickling and held my wrists above my head as I wrestled to break free.

"Shaz, please," I begged in a high, pleading note as desperation set in. Too much tickling could end very badly.

"Who's the dominant wolf now?" He growled playfully in my ear.

A series of soft knocks on the apartment door caused us to freeze. After a heartbeat, Shaz jumped up. The sudden absence of his body heat caused goose bumps to break out on my skin.

I didn't realize that I had been vibing off of him until the energy fell away. The metaphysical remnants remained like a coating of fairy dust on my skin.

Shaz flipped the lock, and I rolled over on to my stomach to push myself to my knees. I was in direct view of the door and didn't want to be seen splayed out on the floor.

A woman's voice called out brightly, and a brunette with a ponytail and a grey tracksuit burst into the entryway. She threw her arms around Shaz excitedly, and my breath caught. I tugged my top to cover my belly.

"How are you? I thought I'd come by and see if you want to catch a movie or grab dinner later." She stopped suddenly when she noticed me. "Oh, I'm sorry. I didn't realize you had company."

Shaz looked awkwardly at me and made a strange gesture in the air between the brunette and myself.

"Casey, it's nice to see you. This is Alexa O'Brien. She's a very good friend of mine. Lex, this is Casey Edmonds. She lives in the building here."

Casey's dark eyes flicked to me on the floor and noted the shirt that I tugged back in to place. I saw the assumption in her eyes, and I encouraged it. I fixed my hair as well, as if she'd interrupted something. Maybe it was catty, but Shaz hadn't mentioned any lady friend, and my cheeks were burning.

"Nice to meet you, Casey." I got to my feet and went to her, hand extended.

She tossed her wavy ponytail and sniffed. I knew she didn't want to take my hand and, when she did, it was with the barest of touches. I resisted the urge to crush her flimsy human fingers in my grip.

"You too," she murmured before turning back to Shaz. It was an obvious attempt at a dismissal, and I felt the energy around us begin to grow hot with my anger.

"Would you like to come in for coffee?" Shaz's fingers worked furiously through his platinum hair, a nervous habit that he'd had as long as I have known him.

His gaze jumped back and forth between us, and I knew he'd either dated her, slept with her, or both. Why did it make my insides churn? I squashed all feelings of jealousy before I had to admit to myself how bad it was.

"No, thanks. I'm just on my way to the gym. Why don't you give me a call sometime when you're free?" Casey slid a sidelong glance in my direction, and then she gave him the look.

I barely restrained the desire to tear her eyes out. Power began to hum softly around me, and both Shaz and Casey reacted to it.

He knew exactly what it was, and his jade eyes narrowed in warning. Casey began to fan herself saying, "It's hot in here, Shaz. You should turn the air conditioning on."

"It is on," he replied. He quickly added, "Maybe it's broken. I'll have the superintendent look at it."

"You should." She flashed me a brittle, cold smile and finally turned to leave. I sighed aloud. I hated her.

After she forced Shaz to promise to call later, he closed the door and turned to face me. Guilt defined his features, and I looked away, embarrassed by my jealousy.

"Sorry about that. I wasn't expecting her to come by." The moment was wretchedly awkward. The sound of the forgotten video game played loudly in the quiet apartment. "We only went out once. Nothing happened."

"Don't, Shaz. You don't owe me an explanation." And didn't I know it? It was hard to swallow even a taste of what I'd inflicted on him.

"I want you to know that I didn't mention it because there was nothing worth mentioning." He shrugged, and his voice grew soft. "I only went out with her because I thought you and I never stood a chance."

"It's ok, Shaz. I'm the last person in the position to be demanding answers. It's none of my business."

He accepted that reluctantly. He nodded slightly, but I knew that he wanted to say more. Less than ten feet separated us, yet I felt like we were a world apart. I'd gotten so used to keeping people at a distance that I still didn't know how to let anyone in.

"You want to finish the game?" He brushed past me into the living room, and the repeating music stopped.

"I'm done. I'll be seeing colors in my dreams as it is."

He chuckled and turned the PlayStation off. The apartment went silent. "I should probably start getting ready for work anyway."

"Well, thanks for entertaining me. It's been a while since we got to do this. It was nice." I was doing a rotten job of maintaining eye contact, but I felt weird and knew he would see it in my face. Of course, he could sense the rapid beat of my heart.

"It was." Shaz leaned casually against the wall as I gathered my things to leave. "So why don't we go out sometime? On a real date, I mean."

In turn, I sensed the blood rushing through him. His cheeks were flushed, and I couldn't hide my smile.

"You're asking me on an official date?"

Thinking back briefly, I couldn't recall ever having been asked out on an actual date. My teen years and early twenties had been chaotic enough without romance of the human variety. After the last week, I was astonished that he even wanted a date with me.

"Yes. I'm asking you on a date. Dinner, on me."

"And after?" I dared to ask playfully.

He shrugged. "Catch a movie, go for a run, park and make out. Whatever you prefer."

Energy shifted between us. At the core of me, where the power of my werewolf lay rooted, I felt him. Like a shadow that I could feel but not see, his wolf lingered, hesitant to reach for me.

The vampire in my energy made him pause, and I hated that. I knew the touch of his skin as well as I knew the silk of his fur or the musk of his scent. I longed to pull his wolf around me like a blanket to drown out the energy of the grave. Everything with Arys felt more wrong when I was this close to Shaz's pure, untainted aura.

But, I couldn't force out what I had allowed to become a part of me. It scared me to the tips of my toes to think that I might not ever be able to.

"I would love to go on a date with you, Shaz." I giggled slightly and felt like a total moron. I heard him release the breath he'd been holding.

"Great. How's Friday?"

I would have ditched anything to say yes to him in that moment. As I scanned through my mental calendar, I was already free that day.

When we'd confirmed that he would pick me up at nine on Friday, I crossed the threshold into the hall and turned back to say goodbye. I loved that he was just there, close enough for me to feel.

His breath was warm and inviting. His kiss was chaste but tender. Still, I felt his hunger leashed beneath his calm surface.

My heart skipped a beat when, just as fast as he was there, he was gone. Only his scent lingered to tease me as I waited for the elevator. I was one damn confused werewolf.

Chapter Thirteen

I simply didn't want to face anymore of Arys's evil. I'd avoided Lucy's Lounge and had carried the manila folder around for three days without cracking the cover. It did nothing to alleviate the growing confusion or the guilt over leaving Arys to fight the shift on his own. I wanted to pretend it would just go away. Instead, avoiding the vampire made the newfound power and the blood thirst more pronounced rather than subdued. It itched and clawed at my insides.

Rather than face Cat's thoughts on Arys, I screwed around for as long as I could justify it to myself. Menial tasks like tidying the kitchen counters and folding laundry grabbed my attention easier than ever before, and I dragged the chores out until I had nothing left to keep me from the folder. Well, the walls could use a fresh coat of paint but I had to draw the line somewhere.

I had no excuse to avoid Cat's evidence any longer. The cream-colored folder lay open on the desk in the small office I share with Ky. Sounds from late night television murmured quietly from the small TV set in the corner. A glass of my favorite red wine stood tall next to the sheaf of papers, awaiting my return.

Finally, I stared at the folder and thought, *Arys is a vampire who enjoys it. What more do I need to know?* Bothered by the prospect of a reason to take Arys out within those pages, I took a large, un-lady-like gulp of wine first.

Even my knowledge of the vampire's bizarre memories didn't prepare me for what I discovered on the series of crisp, white photocopied pages of Cat's journal. Before reaching the end of the first page, I was sitting up a little straighter in my chair with rapt attention. As I read, his memories began to take form inside my mind.

Catherine had written about her time as a new vampire with him. Her tales of seduction as a key component in inevitable murder resulted in a spattering of goose bumps along my arms. The wheels turned faster in my brain as I tapped into his memories of those same events.

Arys fed on much more than blood alone. Like a cat with a mouse, he drew out his excruciating game in order to savor it completely. Most of his victims were more than a quick snack. He used seduction and fear as an intoxicant, vital to his feeding process. Arys rarely took blood without the kill. In his earlier days as a vampire, he had little regard for the value of human life and used no discretion when choosing a victim.

As I read, I began to get the impression that Catherine had been nothing more to him than a victim gone wrong. He had never meant for her to survive him. Not only did he continue to bed his victims after forming a relationship with her, but he also encouraged her to do the same.

Arys loved to swim in the heady sexual energy of his lovers. I knew this personally. Their pleasurable responses generated higher energy production for him to consume. It made perfect sense, and yet I couldn't shake the heavy feeling that formed in the pit of my stomach.

Apparently Arys was no stranger to torture. Much of his enjoyment came from terrorizing his victims into hysterics. He took the most enjoyment from bleeding them tauntingly slowly. Though his methods were tasteless and cruel, they never crossed into the level of gruesome that I'd come to associate with human crime. How very reassuring.

My eyes flashed back to the previous page. I hadn't read anything that I hadn't already seen inside his memories. Even the girls who resisted ended up begging for fulfillment or death.

Bottom line, the vamp got off on the lust and terror of his victims before he killed them. In fact, he went to great lengths to draw it out for extended periods of time. Once he'd consumed all of his victims' sexual energy, a show of fangs and a little bloody torture generated a whole new kind of energy. Fear is the ultimate undoing of any predator. Feel it, and it's already too late.

Blood alone contains enough pranic energy for the sustenance of a vampire. Adding the often underestimated power of extreme lust and fear to the mix was like eating a five course dinner for every meal. It definitely explained his immense power but not his reasons why.

Chills ran down my spine at the thought of being his victim. Whether consensual or not, his victims loved every moment of the fire he ignited within them, just like I had. Even as I remembered, a tingle jabbed at my core, and a drizzle of adrenaline rushed through me. Had he ever intended to kill me? Or, was the obvious fact that I wasn't human enough to keep me off his food list?

Thinking back on every exchange between us, it had always somehow been about the metaphysics going on beneath the surface. I couldn't pinpoint one time when the energy hadn't simmered when he was near. I wondered how much of my attraction to Arys had been natural and how much was his metaphysical influence. With sudden realization, I noticed that I was gently caressing the faint scar of his bite.

"Son of a bitch!" I shoved my chair back with a squeaky roll of wheels and narrowly avoided knocking the wine glass over.

Now that I felt like just another conquest to the power monger vampire, I was both embarrassed and pissed off. Mostly at myself. I couldn't blame Arys for seeing me as something he wanted to sample. I blamed myself for letting him. I've played this game before, and dammit, I knew better.

I hemmed and hawed for a minute, uncertain about disturbing Kylarai in her room. I wanted to burst in there rambling a mile a minute about what a fool I am. Was it love I wanted from Arys? Hell no. But, I had expected respect.

"Power! That's all that the bastard wanted from me." I pounced on Ky the second I heard her door open.

"Excuse me?" She attempted to set a pot of coffee to brew while I waved papers in her face.

"Here." I shoved one particular sheet into her hand. "Read this one." Screw confidentiality. This case was personal, an exception to the rule.

I watched her eyebrows rise as she read about the night both Arys and Catherine had lured a young married couple home from the theatre. As she took in the tale, she didn't pause or look up.

Cat's description of the effects of so much energy had stirred a response low in my body. In the game Arys played, sex wasn't the main act at all, merely a method of foreplay.

"Well that explains why he's so damn powerful," Kylarai said, repeating close to what I'd thought myself. "But really, he can't be the only vampire acting as an incubus to increase the high."

"You're not surprised?" I stared at her incredulously.

"Not really, Lex. He's a vampire. Do you expect him to ask politely if he may drain your essence away with your life?"

I gaped at her open mouthed. Why did I suddenly feel like I was overreacting?

"Look." She touched my arm gently. "It makes sense that you feel betrayed, but you can't hold his nature against him. The past has nothing to do with you. If I were you, I'd tell this Catherine person that you can't help her. And, do it before she finds out you're doing her man."

"I am not doing him. All I was to that jackass was new power to consume." I crossed my arms over my chest. I shuffled my feet angrily and sniffed at the tantalizing aroma of brewing coffee.

"Would you rather have just been sex to him?" She eyed me skeptically, and I met her gaze evenly.

"Yes." I didn't even have to think about it. "That's what it was to me. I didn't go after him with ulterior motives."

Kylarai practically laughed right in my face at that, and I bit back the rant on the tip of my tongue. "You liar." She even went so far as to jab a finger at me in the air. "It was all of that spiced up power that had you so hot for him in the first place."

"What?"

"If he'd been human, there is no way you would have given him more than a passing glance." She turned to take two mugs out of the cupboard. "You're so hopped up on the juice yourself that you don't seem to realize that you're seeking it out, too. Though, perhaps, your reasons differ from a vampire's."

Dumbfounded, I stared as she poured coffee into each mug and handed one to me. "Do you really think that?" I spoke to fill the space, but part of me knew that she was right.

Arys could barely look at me without causing my senses to burn for more. Could it be that I wasn't a victim of his seduction, but an equal partner in my own right?

"You know it's true. It doesn't take a psychic to feel the energy increase when you're in the same room as a powerful man."

That was partially true. Both Raoul and even Shaz had stirred the metaphysical side of me. Not every vampire or shifter did though.

"So you're saying I got as much out of our encounter as he did." I nodded. The pieces were starting to fit. I didn't particularly like it.

"Exactly. Which means you could never have been his victim. He didn't kill you or even try because you aren't food. You're an equal. You gained as much as you gave. And, we both know you were a willing participant."

A sudden blush spread across my cheeks. I tucked the paper back into the pile and marched back to the den.

Dammit, Kylarai always got to be the insightful one. Something in me felt abused by Arys simply because I'd been unaware of his deep need of power. I was desperate to blame him for my wanton desire, for my betrayal of Shaz. Disappointed in the loss of my fury, I closed the folder. The rest of Cat's diary pages would stay unread.

After procrastinating for a few minutes, I called the number that she'd left for me and left her a voicemail declining the job. This case was about a broken heart that had nothing to do with me. In the meantime, I had a ton to think about, my own personal issues.

At half past one, the night was by no means over. After a ludicrous attempt to read a cheesy romance novel from Ky's bookshelf, I soon gave up. I couldn't get past the first page. I could do a million things to pass the time, but I couldn't invest myself in any one of them. Nagging thoughts refused to leave me alone. I couldn't help but wonder how Arys was doing.

By ignoring our mistake, were we simply making it worse?

The last time that I saw him, Arys was fighting a deep sense of confusion. Having something that he could not control was outside his realm of comfort. For my part, bouts of nausea and bloodlust alternatively wracked me, and though the moments were brief, they were frighteningly intense. But, I hadn't given in yet. I refused to crumple into longing the way that Arys had. I rode out every surge with willpower and sheer stubbornness. However, everyday, the need to give in to the bloodlust grew stronger. It grew harder to resist.

Determined and curious, I zipped a dark grey hoodie over my black t-shirt with a bright pink Playboy bunny logo. I changed into a pair of hip-hugging, black jeans so I could actually move comfortably. I double-checked that I had both my cell phone and wallet before calling out, "I'm going out." Kylarai's response sounded affirmative, so I locked the door on my way out.

I decided to leave the Charger for the night. I was in the mood for a walk beneath the moonlight. The late night walk through the quiet town felt magically soothing. During the twenty-minute stroll to Lucy's Lounge, I hoped to accomplish some productive thinking.

The nightlife in Stony Plain vastly differs from that of the city center. The streetlights here don't shine brighter than the stars. Traffic maintains a steady flow, but the vehicles are much fewer and farther in between. And, of course, the only businesses open at this hour consisted of the bars, the 7/11, and the McDonald's twenty-four hour drive-thru.

A fountain bubbled, and a creek flowed near the small, off-road path. I preferred to avoid the main walking routes. I sought the shadows. The path and the creek successfully wound the length of Stony from the north to the south end. Comforting and familiar, the sound of the creek held a soothing quality.

As I walked, several jackrabbits broke from frozen positions and ran for safety as I crossed through the playground of an elementary school. They didn't fear the trucks barreling through the street, yet they still feared me upon catching the scent of wolf. I paused to allow them to run without feeling as if I was giving chase. They were too small and helpless. I liked my quarry big enough to put up a fight. In fact, I preferred that they deserved it.

A group of teenagers looked up in alarm when I rounded a bend in the grey stone walkway. The joint they passed was frozen in midair. The kid holding it had the widest eyes. I almost laughed aloud. At their age, I'd been learning how to protect myself from true danger as well as my own predatory urges. What I wouldn't have given to be a kid with a joint instead.

I couldn't hide my smile when I passed them. One kid dared to give me a cocky sneer, a challenge. The youthful scent of his blood was tangy and metallic, inviting me to taste it. A brief thought flashed through my mind. How easy it would be to take him right here in a frenzy of blood and fear. The others would try to run, but I'd catch them, too. I forced myself to keep walking and the urge dissipated almost as fast as it had come.

No sooner had I vanished from sight than they resumed their laughter and juvenile jokes. Enjoy it boys. You'll have to grow up some time.

I ambled on toward Lucy's until the overpowering scent of fear made me stop in my tracks. Standing in the shadows, I was hidden from view by the tree-lined path as vehicles flew by on the four-lane strip to my right. I saw nothing out of place.

For a moment, I thought my nose was playing tricks on me, but then the scream came. High pitched and terrified, the helpless sound thrilled me with excitement, bringing Arys's smile to my lips.

I followed the sound down the gaping black hole of an intersecting path. I suppose I'm lucky that my night vision is damn good. It's better than that of the two humans that I had smelled in the darkness ahead, and that's what really mattered.

As I crept down the eeriest bike path in town, I stifled a giggle. My wolf didn't drive me forward. No, I had succumbed to the intoxicating temptation of the bloodlust. I suddenly wanted it so bad that I could already taste the sweet copper on my tongue.

I didn't need the whimpering to guide me to the couple. I could see them fighting near the thin tree line. The scent of fear hung thick on the air, as enticing as bread, fresh from the oven. But, there was also the heavenly scent of pain, which I despised myself for loving.

As I got closer, I realized how dire the situation was for the humans. They grappled in the dark for control, and one was fated to lose. The she-wolf in me reared her head at that, and a surge of rage hit me as the warm and cool energies of the wolf and vampire struggled for dominance.

"Please, David, don't!" I heard the shrill and terrified cry, and I saw his hand rise before the deafening smack followed.

"Nothing but a goddamned tease." Flesh struck flesh, and then I heard a muffled whimper.

The vampire may have gotten more enjoyment out of the fear heavily lacing the air. I on the other hand took greater pleasure in the cocky display of caveman mentality and knowing this guy would die for it.

The barest shred of realism appealed to my quickly fading sanity. I realized that what little was left of my humanity was falling away. Power rode me in an overwhelming rush. I knew such undeniable hunger when the vampire's appetite rose to the surface. The side of me that was wolf looked on the scene before me with apathy: he was a danger; he had to die. The scent of blood hit me, and the power building in my core broke free.

My head swam as instinct took over, and the beast within was unleashed. When I lifted my victim off his feet with one hand, I only wished he could see me better in the dark and fear me even more. With my fangs bared, a growl erupted from my throat. As I jerked the man away, the woman let out another ear-piercing wail.

Her fear fed my fire like gasoline, and I struggled to say, "Run," before I reached for her, too. She didn't have to be told twice. With David long forgotten, she ran screaming into the night. She would need a good twenty minutes to find someone even to look for the monster eating her loser boyfriend.

A cold sweat broke out on my skin, and I shivered despite the warm summer air. Conflicting urges toyed with my emotions, but all I felt was the hunger coursing through me.

David's attempt at a strangled scream was music to my ears. I smiled and licked my lips. Even in the dark, I could see the whites of his bulging eyes as he fought to breathe around my crushing grip.

"So you don't like to take no for an answer? Well, neither do I." I gave him a mind-numbing shake. His sudden resurgence of terror hit me like an overdose. I didn't need more fear to feed my inner fire. I saw through a red haze. The sky, stars and moon all shone down on us with a blood red glow. I don't have a clear recollection of sinking fangs and tearing flesh. I know only that David's noises stopped instantly as his blood sprayed in hot drops, like lava, and spattered my face.

My intention went out the window when I tasted his blood. Any remaining thread of my humanity broke. I blacked out.

It was absolute carnage, nothing like the two neat holes of a practiced vampire. When I came back to myself and took in the scene, a cry escaped me that sounded foreign, like somebody else. I'd killed the wretch of a man, and the remnants of David were strewn about everywhere, most of them unidentifiable. The fact that his head remained just barely attached to his torso was sickening enough. The pile of intestine near my feet had me scrambling backward. I clawed at the pavement in my haste to retreat.

Blood coated the back of my tongue bitterly, and I made it a few feet before vomiting a stream of blood and flesh. My hands and face felt sticky. My heart raced so fast that I expected it to give out. Silent tears zigzagged twin paths down my cheeks as I gasped for air.

My mind was reeling. What in the fuck just happened? Desperately, I tried to wrap my mind around what I had done. I was haunted by how good it had felt, better than any physical sensation that I'd ever known. Once I'd accepted the taunting lure of the vampire's need, there had been no going back.

I began to sob even as I spat blood and tissue. Crying wasn't going to help anything so I forcibly bit back my sobs, though the tears refused to stop. I recognized the copper flavor of blood, goddamn vampire tears. My stomach rolled again with nausea and bile rose in my throat. I had to get out of there.

I was scared shitless but not stupid. As soon as David's girlfriend reached the heart of town, she'd send someone. With any luck, he wouldn't be found before daylight, but I needed to get the hell away from the scene. I quickly checked for any personal evidence. No human dental records in the world would match any bite marks on the body parts.

My clothes, my face, and my hands were gory. I looked like I had been finger painting with vital fluids. I had to clean up, but the darkened path led away from the creek. If I turned back, I'd expose myself to the light from the main road. Out of the question. I'd have to get back home without anyone seeing me.

Deeper in the darkness, away from the main road, was another intersecting trail. That one however led only a short way to a residential sidewalk and ended. I glanced over my shoulder to the headlights on the busy street. I had no choice but to take the quiet residential streets.

My legs moved with Jez's speed as I hopped fences, ducked in between houses and slunk through the dark alleys. I stopped twice more to vomit. By the time that I arrived at home, I was dizzy and nauseous.

Trina M. Lee

I didn't even consider going inside. If Kylarai saw me like this, she might just kick my ass herself. I worried that I was losing my mind. I had to ask myself if what had just happened was real. It already felt like a faded dream.

Unfortunately, the moment I entered the garage and looked at myself in the Charger's side mirror, it became painfully real. My wolf eyes glowed with an eerie light in the dimly lit garage. Thankfully, they were my wolf eyes and not Arys's dizzying blue orbs.

The bright red smear across my mouth had turned brownish red around the edges. My blonde hair was chunky with red and pink tissues. I swore softly, but I wanted to pitch a damn fit.

I blamed Arys for all of this. He had to have known the risks far better than I did. Damn him for adding to my already screwed up existence.

Careful not to touch Kylarai's white Escalade, I went to the small sink near the workbench. For the first time, I was glad that the man who had built the place had thought of it. I stripped off my bloodstained sweater. My t-shirt beneath was unblemished. With a sigh of relief, I ran the water until it was warm and cleansed every spot from my hands and face. I wasn't happy about rinsing my hair with no shampoo or conditioner, and it really sucked that my precious toothbrush was in the house. But, if I went in, Ky would try to stop me from going back out, and I wasn't risking that.

Something was drawing me to Lucy's Lounge. Whether it was my inherent need to throttle Arys with my bare hands or something else entirely, I wasn't sure.

After stashing my bloody sweater in a gap behind the stairs, I studied my black jeans. The few splatters were barely noticeable on the dark denim. They would do for tonight and would join my hoodie in the burn barrel tomorrow.

I got in the Charger and backed out of the garage. I hoped that Ky wouldn't hear the mechanics of the garage door. I'd just have to explain later.

* * * *

Arys was nowhere to be seen, but I felt him as strongly as if I were standing right next to him. A strange sensation told me that he

136

sensed me, too. I cast my gaze around frantically for him. Something didn't feel right, like someone was out of place.

I felt Shaz's eyes on me, and I turned to give him a wink and a smile. I couldn't read anything in his expression, which gave me pause. I would have approached him if the pressing line of patrons hadn't stood in my way. He didn't look exceptionally distraught or beckon me over, so it couldn't be that bad.

When I didn't immediately spot Arys downstairs, I began to ascend the wide staircase. A rush of coolness stirred the hot bar air behind me. I turned to face him, suddenly on the offensive.

"You son of a bitch!" I cursed Arys from where I stood on the third step looking down at him.

His midnight eyes widened as he took in my blood-scented jeans and damp hair, now drying in dread-like chunks of blonde and gold.

"You killed a human." It was a comment, not a question. The Goth rock music boomed all around us. His words reached only me. "What have you been up to, Alexa?"

"Why don't you tell me? You're the one skilled in cold blooded murder." I glared at him. I tried so hard to blame him, even as I tasted the blood that lingered on the back of my tongue. He fixed me with a hard stare and, though my temper faltered, I refused to back down.

"What in the hell are you on?" Arys grabbed my forearm and jerked me down the stairs. He pulled me against him and forced me to crane my neck. He looked into my eyes. "I never forced you into anything, and you know it. Did I blame you when I slaughtered Mrs. Olson's dog?"

I raised an eyebrow at him and made a face that indicated how stupid I thought his statement was. After a moment, he relented.

Arys admitted, "Ok, I did blame you. But now, I blame us. But seriously, we have more important issues at hand."

"What the hell can be more important than the fact that I just tore a man apart? Literally! He's probably been found by now."

"When you say you tore him apart, you mean..."

"I said literally, didn't I? I mean just what I said. I left the fucker in pieces, ok?" His eyes sparkled with gruesome curiosity, which disgusted me enough that I had to fight back another wave of nausea.

"As much as I'd love to hear all of the sweet and, I'm certain, juicy details, I'm afraid we have bigger problems."

"Like what?" I didn't really want to hear what he had to say. In fact, I had made a mistake by coming to Lucy's at all.

"Like the hit job on me that you've been thinking about taking." He said it so matter of fact.

Dumbfounded doesn't even begin to describe my instant reaction. I stared up at him like he'd slapped me as I took a step back. Shit. Good news travels fast.

"What?" I mumbled, glancing around anxiously for whatever was out of place. My poor attempt at casual had bombed, but I forced myself to maintain eye contact. "I was never going to take the job."

"Don't even try it. If we weren't facing a shit load of trouble right now, I wouldn't hesitate to take a bite out of you. But, that will have to wait."

I was constantly finding myself thankful for the noisy din of the bar. Music, laughter and conversation created the perfect lull of background noise.

Before I could ask what he meant by trouble, my sense of unease grew as an angry energy swirled all around us. I felt vampiric energy approach me from behind and whirled to find Catherine descending the steps. She glowered at us with more hate than I'd had directed at me in a while.

"Alexa!" She was all too happy to see me. "I thought I sensed your presence. Good. Now I can kill the both of you, which only seems fitting considering the circumstances."

"Cat, please. We can discuss this rationally." I kicked myself for the remaining humanity that enabled me to feel compassion for a vampire that I seriously suspected of mental illness. "It's not what you think."

Her dark eyes narrowed on me, and I felt my chest tighten under the pressure of her fury. How I became "the other woman" was beyond me. I studied Catherine's absolutely evil stare and felt ashamed. I'd worn a similar expression no more than an hour previous. A shiver tore down my spine.

"Don't try reasoning with her," Arys said as he grabbed my hand. He yanked me behind him, away from the crazed vampiress.

His touch caused a visible spark of sudden power between us. It looked like an extreme static zap but much brighter and stronger.

"Whoa," I gasped, jerking my hand out of his grasp. Was he absolutely insane? This wasn't getting any better.

I couldn't tell if Catherine had even seen the spark. She was now staring so hard at Arys that I was glad to be the other woman rather than him.

"Cat, honey," Arys purred, and I couldn't help but look at him in surprise. "Let's not be irrational, my dear. We are in public."

Her glare grew in its intensity, and it took all I had to keep my eyes on her. Only a woman truly in love could exude so much pure venom. Either that or she was insanely obsessed.

I wanted to just let fly with a good smack up side Arys's head, but that wasn't going to discourage Catherine. Though, it might have changed me from foe to friend in her eyes.

"Don't waste your pathetic charm on me. I've come a long way since I was your play thing." A slow grin played about her ruby red lips.

"We're going outside, Catherine. Whatever you want to do, you can do there. I won't let you endanger innocent people in here." Arys's voice was low and firm, but she heard him as well as I did.

If looks could kill, he would have fallen into ash at my feet. She glared daggers that even made me want to squirm.

"How dare you speak to me as if you place such value on life? You're the devil who taught me to take it, ruthless and without mercy."

"That was a long time ago." Arys's voice was soft, persuasive. He was full of shit, and all three of us knew it, yet the pull to believe him was strong. The bastard was good. "Things have changed since those days. It's time to move on."

That was clearly the wrong line. Catherine's eyes seemed to sparkle suddenly, and she was alive with power, but not her natural vampire power. No, this was foreign magic, borrowed rather than owned. Where was she getting it?

"This has been a long time coming, my dear Sindarys." I saw him visibly flinch at her use of the name. "I cannot wait to watch you turn to dust."

Every part of me braced for the vampiress's blow, knowing it was coming. We had to get outside. I began inching away from the bottom of the staircase, toward the rear exit.

Instinctively, I wanted to lock eyes with Shaz across the bar but didn't dare. Like any supernatural, Catherine would be aware of every Were in the building. She had no beef with him, and I had no good reason to involve him.

"You don't think you're going to get away, do you?" Catherine turned on me. "You, who let me confess my heartbreak to you about the very man you, yourself, are bedding," she declared dramatically before holding a dainty hand to her mouth.

Passersby glanced briefly at the love triangle gone wrong. As a regular patron of the club, I was embarrassed to be involved in the dramatics. Of course, if I could escape the obsessive, manic vampiress unscathed, I could handle the judgmental humans.

"Hold on a minute, lady." I held my hands up defensively and took an involuntary step forward. Damn my indignant nature. "Don't be so quick to jump to conclusions. I never had any intention of taking the job, and I tried to refuse your money."

"But, you already had my man. Why ever would you also need my money?" She crossed her arms and tossed her layered locks. "Tell me, Alexa, what would a magically enhanced wolf like yourself want with a womanizing pig like him?"

Catherine didn't wait for me to answer. Instead, she sauntered down the remaining stairs until she stood directly in front of Arys. I was slightly envious of the five inches she had on me.

"I'll go outside with you, lover, but don't try anything funny. I'm not as unprepared as you might think." Her black eyes scanned the both of us. "Underestimating me would be a big mistake."

Arys looked pointedly at me, and I realized that he expected me to lead the way. That meant trusting him at my back with Catherine. In that moment, my worry kicked into overdrive, and I wondered if the two vampires weren't in cahoots against little, old, mortal me. Did I really think that little of Arys? Well, kind of, yeah. But, considering the scenario at play, I had no choice but to turn and head for the exit.

I took in as much of the freely exuded energy in the bar as I could. It felt warm and reassuring. I knew that she had an unnatural boost, but I couldn't be sure how psychically in tune she was. It wasn't the same for all vampires. Arys felt me absorb the energy in the room, but I had a feeling that she couldn't. Whatever was feeding her power, it wasn't good.

Relief washed through me when I saw the empty alley out the backdoor of Lucy's. Not even a group of smokers lingered nearby.

I was ready for her ... or them. I turned so that my back was to the building, and I faced them both head on. I wasn't afraid, not yet anyway. At this point, I was still more concerned with the mutilated body in the middle of town.

"Catherine, my love, why don't you and I leave Alexa to enjoy her evening, while the two of us catch up?" Arys wasn't fooling anybody, but he sure was trying hard.

His charm slid off Cat like water off a duck's back. I suppose when you've danced with the devil for decades, you learn a few of his tricks.

A blast of red light streamed between the two vampires for a split second as she hit him with a shot of power. When it was dancing in the air around us, I could feel the witch magic mixed with her own. So, Cat had stocked up her arsenal before coming here.

I hadn't sensed it in my office, so the magic had to be a charm or spell of some kind. I learned everything that I know about spells by watching Lena. I was really hoping that she wasn't hopped up on black magic, the crystal meth of magic, more or less. It didn't feel that dark, but one can never be too careful.

"Don't you ever learn when to shut the hell up? I'm not going to play your game, so save us both the embarrassment." Cat stalked to where Arys sat on his ass, dumbfounded.

She stood over him so that his gaze met her thighs, and he was forced to look up at her. An attack from behind, though good for me, wouldn't be good for Arys, and I could hear Jez in my head asking why I was hesitating. I was a jumble of nerves, wary of that moment when she would go too far, and I would have to react.

"Did you really believe that I would never live to find you? I thought you knew me better than that." She shifted slightly, so that he had to lean back to keep from touching her. Arys looked slightly pained, which I attributed to the proximity of her thighs, which were scarcely covered by her short, trendy dress. Despite the gravity of the situation, a nervous laugh broke free of me.

"What are you laughing at, wolf?" Suddenly, she half turned to face me and let loose with another metaphysical attack. I met it with the energy that I held hot and waiting.

The shot ricocheted back to her. A cloud of sparks erupted where the two energies met between us. The force threw her off her feet, to her knees in the dirt, which didn't do much for her temper. When she got to her feet, her eyes blazed red. I shouldn't have let her get back up.

A noise beyond the door of the club had me praying that Shaz would stay inside. I knew he wouldn't have missed the three of us leaving through the back way. If he thought there was trouble, nothing would keep him inside.

"And, to think, I considered sparing you. No, I guess Sindarys can now watch his lover die first," Catherine spat before another blast caught me off guard. The next thing I knew, I was flat on my back, staring up at the night sky.

"That's it, bitch," I said as I leapt to my feet. My body ached where the energy had struck, but I was otherwise unhurt. "I don't risk my neck every night just so I can deal with psychos like you." With a nasty look at Arys, I added, "Next time you leave someone for dead, make sure they actually are dead, first." With great self-restraint, I held back on shooting a slap of power at him.

Catherine gaped open-mouthed at me. "I knew you wouldn't understand, not until he does it to you. He'll take all you have to give until nothing remains that isn't bitter and cold."

"Only if I let him. Which from the looks of you, isn't going to happen." I saw her twitch, and with a snap of my fingers, an energy circle formed around me.

"This is between you and me, Catherine," Arys spoke up, his tone was furious as he wiped the dirt from his jeans. "If you want to finish this, then I'm ready. Leave Alexa out of this."

He shocked me by approaching the angry vampiress and grasping her tightly by both upper arms. He shook her hard enough to cause her to stumble into his lean frame.

"She should have goddammed told me!" Catherine's voice rose into a yell, and she fought to escape his grip.

She had a point. I should have told her that it would be a conflict of interest as soon as I saw his photo. But, I'd been curious, and my personal interests won out.

"Any woman I take to my bed is none of your damn business. It never has been." Arys's voice grew in its intensity, and pulsating anger swept through him. I could feel it from where I stood.

"Of course not. That's so very typical of you, Sindarys. Still very much the womanizing man-whore I see, even consorting with beasts now. I thought you enjoyed your women with a tasty, preferably dead, ending."

"What I enjoy is a woman who knows how to stay dead, at least in memory anyway." Arys spit the words into her face.

Even my guts hurt when I saw her face fall. I felt like I'd been kicked in the stomach. I took a clumsy step forward as if to break the painfully awkward moment. Unfortunately, it also broke the shield that I'd created.

Catherine's attack was instant. She didn't even look at me. Spitting dirt, I was on my feet again in a matter of seconds.

"Well shit, Cat!" I ground dirt between my teeth and lashed out at her simply from sheer spite, but she was ready for it. She escaped Arys with another assault against us both.

Now that Arys had successfully hurt and humiliated her, she had nothing left to lose. The onslaught of power that descended upon me in an offensive storm had me scrambling to create another circle. The atmosphere around us grew tight with all of us pushing the limits and laws of nature. Dammit, her power source had to have a limit.

Arys gave up the metaphysical fight and launched himself at her. The two of them went down, sprawled in a heap of fists and fangs like a wolf fight.

Any kind of energy attack risked Arys, so for the moment, I only watched because I sure as hell was not jumping in.

"Stop trying to force yourself on me," he growled into her face. "How many more centuries will you stalk me before I'm forced to extinguish you? This ends now."

Her sharp nails raked his face, and her pitifully small fists beat at his chest as he hovered over her, lying in the dirt. A struggle ensued, and they grappled until Arys held her tightly by the wrists.

"Have I ever been anything more to you than a nuisance?" Catherine never ceased struggling beneath Arys but from the way she wriggled her skinny ass, I guessed that she was trying to jog his memory. I rolled my eyes. I should have walked away and left them to it.

"Baby, a nuisance is all you'll ever be. You're backing me into a real corner here, you know." Arys's tone was low and smooth but as deadly as they come. "You're starting to take my options away. Pretty soon, I'm going to be forced to finally do away with you."

He said it so easily that I knew he would do it with no regrets. What did that say about how he looked at me?

"Do it then," she hissed. "It's about time you finish what you started. You killed me long ago. Finish the job, my love."

She leaned up just enough to brush his lips with hers, and I choked on the jealousy that was becoming too commonplace for my liking. I watched in extreme discomfort as Arys returned her kiss.

My attention was momentarily distracted by the vibrations of my cell phone in the front pocket of my jeans. A quick glance revealed a text message from Shaz that read simply, 'If you don't reply in two minutes, I'm coming to look for you.'

I managed to tap out a quick reply of, 'Wait, not yet.' My stomach flipped as the vampire kiss deepened, and I glanced around the alley.

I felt more than awkward and decided that I might as well leave. I'd just taken a step when Arys, in a blur of speed, sank his fangs deep into Catherine's throat. A strangled cry broke from her as the blood began to pour from the gaping wound.

Everything happened so fast then. Catherine propelled Arys a good thirty feet, where he landed against the back fence of a property across the alley. Judging by the sharp splinter of wood along with his steady stream of curses, that had to have hurt. I shook my head. The poor bastard was simply too much offense and too little defense.

When nothing stood between us, Catherine rounded on me, tattered and bleeding. Her red dress was caked with dirt, and I heard more than one pebble fall from her hair. A softly glowing red amulet had spilled from beneath the neckline of her dress. With blood streaming down her front, she gasped and choked.

Between her madness and her desperation, she was an unpredictable opponent, and I regretted mincing words with her. Still, the scent of her fear tantalized my inner predator.

"You," she pointed a bloody finger in my direction. "You got to him first. You warned him I'd come."

"Sorry to break it to you, but he's not afraid of you." I advanced on her with a psi ball, warm and pulsing with swirls of gold and blue, in my hand. "This is your last chance to leave here in one piece." I winced at my own choice of words as an image flashed in my mind of David's dismembered corpse.

What sounded like a war cry erupted from Catherine, and she rushed me like a mad woman, with her arms stretched straight out in front of her. The pungent aroma of her blood struck me, and my natural power began to grow in excitement but not from the heady elixir of prey. No, I vibed off my foe's impending doom. As her blood continued to spatter, I could feel her growing weakness.

I let the energy ball dissolve but took the energy back into me. I tensed for the impact of her approach. When she hit me full force, I threw my weight into her, which sent the two of us rolling in a tangled heap. With gritted teeth and years of experience, I ended the roll so that I was staring down into her face.

Blood was beginning to form at the corner of her mouth. I could clearly see the wound that Arys had made, a gaping hole in her jugular that would be hard to heal but not impossible for a vampire of her age. He should have gone for the carotid artery if he'd really wanted to bleed her. Could it be that the dark vampire was unable to dispatch the one that he had once loved?

Regardless, the wolf within me truly loved a physical fight to the death. I lost all control, letting fly a series of blows that would have killed a human. Catherine's head snapped back and forth, and I thought I had her until she suddenly threw me.

The amulet blazed, and I reached for it, but I was already airborne. I tucked and rolled painfully along the graveled road. Rocks and broken beer bottles cut and slashed at me as I tried desperately to protect my face and head. My bare arms stung as the gravel scraped and burned into my flesh.

I was running out of time. My white wolf was due to rescue me, and the chance of innocents stumbling across us was increasing by the second. There was only one way this was going to end quickly. I'd never had the guts to try it, but I knew it would work for me now. I'd witnessed Kale kill more than one vampire by forcing his energy inside them until the pressure built beyond capacity and the vampire's heart exploded.

As much as I wanted to lay on the ground in shock and let the rattling in my brain settle, my adrenaline had me up in an instant. I reached out for all of the consumable energy in the vicinity. I could gather some from the natural elements like the moon, stars, and air, but I needed a direct physical link for the attack that I planned to launch. In a dirty back alley with no fertile soil beneath my feet, my power reached out for the one steady energy source that was close enough to touch and achingly familiar.

Arys slowly approached. He looked rough. Deep red scratches formed a diagonal line from the outer edge of his eye to the top of his upper lip. She had just missed raking one of his damn eyes out. The dirt smeared on his face reminded me a little of war paint. His torn clothing added to the savage look in his eyes, so feral that even I grew nervous as he drew closer.

"Back for more already?" Catherine asked haughtily. The tone was forced and cost her a choking cough.

Unlike vampires, I'm not content to play cat and mouse all night, and I wasn't sure Arys could be relied on to finish her. Worried that she would recover if I waited, I reached out to Arys metaphysically before he was close enough to touch. Our link was going to help me take down Catherine. I drew on Arys's deep stores of undead power and fed it into Catherine. If I kept the connection, the sudden onslaught of energy would push her past capacity.

My phone vibrated in my pocket, and I cursed. Surprised that it even still worked, I had no choice but to ignore it.

At first, she just looked plain stunned. I think it took her a moment or two to comprehend what was happening. When the realization dawned on her, she panicked and tried to send the energy back to me.

If I deflected the shot, I'd have to break the attack, and I wasn't willing to do that. Refusing to lose the stronghold I'd gained on her, I decided to brace for the blow.

A millisecond before it slammed into me, I closed my eyes and tensed, but the impact never came. I opened my eyes to find that my vampire lover had intercepted Cat's attack with one of his own. A shower of hot sparks rained down all around us, illuminating the dark alley like a camera flash.

My energy was dwindling. I struggled to zone in on a focal point, to pump my power into her undead heart until it could take no more.

"Arys, I need you." My words were breathy, almost voiceless, yet Cat reacted to my plea as if I already held her heart in my hands.

She was on her knees now, beaten. Still, I pushed into her with all I had. Fire coursed through my veins, and I struggled to take a deep breath. The energy that I channeled pushed my limits, and I fought the urge to crumple beneath the burden.

I steadied one hand to direct the stream of raw power into Catherine. With the other, I reached blindly for Arys. Our link didn't feel complete. It wasn't strong enough.

As I sank to my knees, he reached me. He clasped my hand in his and pulled me to my feet.

Everything in me, all that is wolf or woman, reacted to the vampire's touch. His aura mingled with mine. He seemed to fall into me as if he had always been a part of what I am. A resurgence of strength filled me, and I focused on Catherine with a new fury.

Her mouth gaped, and her eyes grew wide with terror. Our mingled power danced with flecks of blue and gold as it flowed into her. Blood began to stream steadily from her nose and mouth. The whites of her eyes turned a grotesque shade of red, and I resisted the urge to look away. Sparks danced around our joined hands but I felt no pain.

The amulet around her neck went dark. Finally, the last of the fight went out of her. The amulet had supplied the majority of her power. As a vampire, she'd been mediocre at best. Now, she was at the point of demise, and nothing could save her.

No sooner had I wondered when it would be over, than a horrible sound came from her. She shrieked like a wounded animal and looked down on her body. She began to turn slowly to ash before our eyes. I closed my eyes and willed her to stop. I felt her heart pause and then burst.

Like a volcanic blast, her remains showered down around us. Her ashes settled on our hair and eyelashes. The sound of my heart beat loudly in my ears, and I allowed Arys to pull me close.

Catherine's amulet lay on the ground amid her ashes. Before Arys could take advantage of our intimate proximity, I pulled away and gathered it up in my palm. I turned the star shaped pendant over as I studied it. It didn't feel like black magic. I'd turn it over to Lena for proper disposal.

Shoving the charm into my pocket, I looked up to find Arys staring solemnly into the ashes. I wanted nothing more than to thump him a good one, but my back muscles ached enough to make me reconsider.

"Don't try telling me now that you wanted to spare her after all," I said. Hands on my hips, I dared him to try to placate me. "You could have gotten me killed by that psycho bitch!" I scattered the ashes with a kick.

Arys held up a hand as if to silence me. "I had no idea she would be this foolish, Alexa. I'm truly sorry that you got mixed up in this, but it was purely by chance. Perhaps if you hadn't been so eager to get some dirt on me, she wouldn't have made you a target."

So that's where this was heading. Of course, that was to be expected.

"You are so absolutely full of shit, my friend. She wanted to take me out because she thought that we're lovers, which you made no attempt to clarify." With a raised eyebrow, I added, "If I didn't know better, I'd think that you didn't have the balls to off her, so you had me do it for you."

A dizzy spell hit me, and I swooned, suddenly light headed. As one whose biological clock was still programmed as living, I couldn't withstand the same level of exertion that he could.

I blinked, and he had already crossed the small space between us. Strong hands steadied me, and I looked up, into his clear blue eyes. The emotion in their depths spoke louder than the words that he'd never let himself say. One hand gently stroked the side of my battered face before he wrapped his arms around me.

Shaz! I had to pull away before Shaz made this strange moment completely awkward. He should burst through the door any moment now.

"Stop resisting me." Arys's lips were warm as they moved against my ear. "We belong to one another. Why deny that?"

Before I could voice my protests to that declaration, he kissed me with an intensity that burned through my body. Our two energies were strangely one, and a comforting calm filled me. Already my strength returned in a relaxing ebb and flow.

I could taste Catherine's blood on his tongue as it traced a moist line along my lower lip before dipping back inside my mouth. Things tightened low in my body, and I wanted to beg him to take me right there. Knowing how irrational that was, I still had to remind myself that I'd just killed his ex-lover as well as a human being.

A part of me was so pissed at him, and I struggled to allow it to come to the surface. I had to chase him away from me.

I succeeded in breaking the kiss. My hand on his chest kept a small space between our bodies. "Don't do this right now. I need to be angry with you."

"No, you need to tell me why you killed a man before you came here tonight."

The cuts marking his face looked red and angry, and I reached tentatively to brush my fingertips over them. He closed his eyes and leaned into my touch.

"I couldn't deny the bloodlust," I whispered. When he looked at me again, his expression was pained. "A young couple were arguing. He was trying to force her-."

My voice broke and tears pricked the back of my eyes. David's strangled screams echoed inside my head, and I reached to cover my ears in a vain attempt to shut out the noise.

"Hey, it's ok." Arys's voice was softer than I had ever heard it, and I hated him for his tenderness even as tears rolled down my cheeks in two crimson lines.

He reached out with a gentle finger to catch them before bringing the bloody drops to his lips. "The fucker deserved everything he got then. Don't feel bad about dispatching a sorry piece of crap like that."

I shook my head and took a small step back. "That kind of kill, it isn't my life. You've done something to me that I don't know how to live with."

The rear exit door to Lucy's creaked open then, and Shaz appeared, silent and white against the night. He made no move to come closer when he saw the strange tension and Arys's crestfallen features.

I half expected Arys to blame me, again, for the slaughter of Mrs. Olson's dog, but he said nothing. Instead, he nodded and let his hands drop as if just noticing that he still reached for me.

"Then tomorrow night, we visit your witch friend together and learn how to live with it." He made no question of it.

He turned to Shaz and beckoned him to where we stood. "She needs you now. I believe you will be of more use to her than I am."

Arys turned to go but paused to kick at what remained of Catherine's quickly dispersing ashes. I made no attempt to stop him. I had nothing left to say. I had blamed him for all of it, and he hadn't argued.

Shaz came to stand behind me and pulled me into his warm, living embrace.

"Are you ok, Lex?"

I was at a loss for words. I was physically injured, but the worst of my agony was mental and emotional. I turned in Shaz's arms, to face him as I attempted to tell him what had happened to me that evening. A rush of emotion overcame me.

"Don't try to explain right now." He tucked my head under his chin and attempted to stroke my tangled, filthy hair. "Just let me hold you."

With the hem of his t-shirt balled in my fists, I buried my face in the warm, familiar curve of his neck and fought back bloody tears.

Chapter Fourteen

Kylarai was ticked at me. No, she was pissed. She cussed me out good. I heard how very stupid I was in more ways than one. I should have talked to her after slaughtering the human. I should have let Shaz keep me out of Arys and Catherine's fight. I should have done anything except what I did. It really was a shame that she hadn't had children of her own.

She would forgive me. Shaz on the other hand...I wasn't so sure.

Shaz and I had sat in the parking lot. Through my tears, I had told him everything. He had listened quietly, nodding and patting my hand as needed. Not once did I find the judgment that I deserved in his eyes. He had already forgiven me for everything.

Apparently, one mother hen wasn't enough to keep me straight. When Kylarai got tired of chiding, I called Lena. Without telling her that I'd eaten a human, I told her enough to have her insisting that I stop by her apartment. She even agreed to help Arys.

By evening, I was a nervous wreck.

"I can't believe you're taking him to Lena's. Do you think that's safe?" Kylarai tapped her long, manicured nails on the kitchen table, where I sat looking into my portable makeup mirror. "And, why do you need to look so good anyway? I thought it was just a onetime thing with you guys."

I glanced up at her. She wore a long, sandy brown suede skirt with a blue V-neck sweater. "What are you all dressed up for? Or should I say, who?"

"Don't even try that change the subject crap on me. Answer my questions." She tossed her trendy bob and smiled. "I have a date. With Tom from my office."

I wasn't one for Weres playing human with real humans romantically, but I'd be damned before I'd burst her bubble. "That's great Ky. Why is this the first I'm hearing about Tom?"

"Because, I turned him down the first three times he asked me out. And, you still haven't set me up with that sexy vampire you work with." She leaned across the table and picked through my open makeup case. "So, how did Shaz take all of this killing a would-be rapist and dusting your vampire lover's ex thing?"

"Like a trooper." I paused to apply mascara to my eyelashes after lining my dark brown eyes with smoky black eyeliner. "Actually, every time I screw up, every time I think I've driven the final wedge between us, he proves me wrong."

Kylarai studied me as I picked a glop of mascara from one lash. "That's because he's in love with you." When I looked up she added, "Note that I said love, not lust."

"Yeah, yeah, I know. I don't deserve him. Believe me, I know."

"You really don't." She chuckled and played anxiously with one of her dangly hoop earrings. "More coffee?"

"No thanks." I'd had enough coffee in the past day to last me a lifetime.

Ky got up to refill her mug, and I noticed her energy felt as nervous as I was. I smiled to myself. It was kind of cute seeing her all aflutter like a schoolgirl. Maybe I should have set her up with Kale when she'd first hinted at it ages ago.

"Is Arys picking you up tonight?" She asked casually.

"No. I don't trust him to drive. I'm picking him up in half an hour. When is Tom coming?"

"Any time now." She glanced at the wall clock that read ten minutes to eight. "This is the first time I've been out with a man in ages. I can't remember how to play the dating game."

"I don't think I ever did. But, since I have a date with Shaz coming up, I'd better crack open an issue of *Cosmo* and get informed."

I shook my head at my reflection and rubbed some red lip-gloss on. "I don't know how I got so lucky."

"Did you take that lip gloss from my bathroom?" Ky leaned closer in order to read the label. I pulled away in a gesture of mock defense.

"No. Back off, lady. If you want the lip gloss, all you've got to do is ask."

We laughed together, then froze when the doorbell rang. Her grey eyes grew wide, and she sputtered a sip of coffee as she launched into action. She grabbed her purse, stuck a breath mint in her mouth, and threw her coffee cup into the sink.

"Damn, I'm nervous. Wish me luck." She hurried toward the front door but called over her shoulder. "Be careful tonight. Don't let that vampire ruin you for somebody more deserving."

"I love you, too, Ky. Have a good time." I smiled as I carefully ignored her pointed statement. I didn't feel the need to add any words of caution. I knew she could take care of herself.

When the soft clicking of her heels in the driveway had faded, I ambled to my bedroom. I just stared into the closet for a solid five minutes. I was leery of sending Arys mixed signals so I steered clear of any cleavage baring halters or tank tops. Instead, I chose a pale blue Aerosmith baby tee and paired it up with my favorite blue jeans and black leather ankle boots. After running a brush through my long hair, I decided to leave it down and natural. With a spritz of my favorite vanilla perfume, I was ready.

Well, physically, I was ready. Mentally, a piece of me never wanted to face Arys again. I wasn't sure I could resist him every time he made an advance toward me. Kylarai had been right. I was power hungry, and Arys was a prime source. Together we were dangerous, but we posed the greatest risk to Shaz, and I couldn't accept that.

With one last glance in the mirror, I checked that my make-up hid my bruising. My cover up was doing a good job with the lingering bruise on my chin. The majority of my abrasions and bruises had healed as I slept, and the remainder looked acceptable.

On my way to Arys's, I got a good case of the jitters, complete with shaky hands on the wheel. Worries that I couldn't banish plagued me as I drove. I expected the twenty-minute drive from Arys's to Lena's to be uncomfortable closeness and unwelcome discussion.

I'd worried about forcing myself to ring the bell, but Arys stood on his front deck chatting with Mrs. Olson while feigning to sip lemonade. A big wave in my direction told me to stay put. Just as well, I couldn't look that little, old lady in the eye knowing what really happened to her dog.

Arys quickly wrapped up his visit. He beamed a fangless smile at the tiny lady as she turned to go. I noticed the small bundle tucked under her arm, and a tiny puppy poked its head out of the blanket.

My heart melted. I couldn't believe that the vampire had done such an unselfish act for another. I was touched, and I resisted the urge to break open my head and forcibly remove the part of me that reacted so strongly to him.

"You disgust me." The words spilled from between my lips before he'd even closed the car door.

"What? Why?" His eyebrows raised high in surprise. "Because I bought Mrs. Olson a puppy? We both know that Benny can never be replaced, but she's alone. She needs a companion."

What in the hell was wrong with me? I'd done so much worse than kill a neighborhood pet, and here I was persecuting the vampire.

"I'm sorry. I'm just a little on edge today. I didn't sleep very well." Or very much. I'd been haunted by the attack dream again.

"I hope the wolf pup was able to comfort you last night. I felt he may be more calming." Arys reached over to grasp my hand briefly in his. His fingertips were cool. He hadn't fed recently.

"Bullshit. You didn't want me to leave with him, and you know it." A few sparks leapt about our joined hands, but they were minimal and did not grow further.

"True. But, I know that he loves you in ways unheard of to both you and I. And, that means more than my personal jealousy."

An admittance of genuine caring from the vampire? It astounded me to realize how little I really thought of him. And really, who the hell was I to judge? I threw the car in gear and pulled away from the curb.

I wasn't completely naive. I wasn't falling for the amazing, sweet guy gimmick. The next twenty minutes were going to involve a lot of swatting.

He took advantage of a minor traffic distraction and slid his hand across the furry seat covers to brush the sliver of skin showing on my lower back. I struggled to pull the back of my t-shirt down but couldn't because of the angle of my seat.

"You just can't sit still, can you?" he asked.

He flashed me a cocky grin and reached up to hit the button that opens the sunroof. It irritated me that he helped himself to my controls. I wasn't surprised when he reached for the radio next.

"It looks more like you can't sit still," I said pointedly. We were at a red light, so I gave him a nice, hard glare.

He made a slow melodramatic show of switching the radio station. "You should calm down, Alexa. Your anger is giving me a hard on."

"What?" My eyes dropped to his lap. I looked away quickly, but it was too late. He'd already seen me do it.

"You heard me. You're mad at yourself, and you want to be pissed at me. But you can't, can you?" He poked me in the side, and I flinched.

"Ow, careful. I took a pretty good fall last night. And stop distracting the driver."

"Tell me what I want to hear." His velvet smooth voice dropped lower, and I felt it caress me.

"And what might that be?" I stared straight ahead, anything to avoid eye contact, and silently pleaded for the light to turn green.

"That you don't blame me any more than I blame you. That it takes two to tango and all that jazz." I saw his casual shrug in my peripheral vision.

Green, finally! I hit the gas pedal, and the Hemi roared. I left a tail-gaiter behind me in the dust. Shoulder checking, I moved over two lanes of traffic as we merged on to the highway.

"Does it mean so much to you? That I believe you didn't manipulate me into bed because you're a power hungry player who doesn't know when to stop."

"Yes," he said, "It does. I think you greatly underestimate the respect that I have for you."

I didn't know what to say to that. I took a deep breath and focused on the warm summer air as it whipped my hair around my face. The air smelled faintly of rain, and I expected a shower before the night was through.

After five minutes of strained silence, Arys leaned forward and popped open the glove box. My mind raced a mile a minute. I didn't think I'd stashed anything personal in there.

"Arys," I said sharply and swatted his arm. "Get out of there. I don't come to your house and rummage through the drawers."

"Be my guest," he replied and held up a portion of a joint. "I didn't know you were into the mellow stuff. I didn't taste it in your blood."

My eyes widened in surprise at his find. "I'm not. I haven't smoked the stuff since I was sixteen. That's got to be Shaz's. Make sure there isn't any more, will you?"

I noticed a small, European sports car racing up behind me, and I maneuvered over to allow him free rein of the fast lane. Regardless of my night vision, I'd prefer not to bite it in a car crash.

When the little European model had sped by, I glanced over at Arys. In his hand, illuminated by the glove box light, was a speeding ticket I'd received a few weeks prior.

"You're quite the little bad ass, huh Alexa? I knew it."

"Would you put that back?" I sputtered, grateful the dim interior hid my embarrassed blush.

He gave me a wink and a grin that I felt to the soles of my feet. By the time we reached Lena's condo, I was in a hurry to escape the close proximity of the car.

Even as he followed me dutifully into the lobby, I could feel the weight of his hunger like a target on my back. She buzzed us in. The elevator felt too confined, and I practically leapt out when we reached the fourth floor. He merely smiled and gestured for me to lead the way.

Lena greeted me, as I knew she would, with open arms and a warm, friendly environment. "Alexa!" She pulled me into a tight squeeze. "It's nice to have you over."

"Thank you so much for seeing us on such short notice. I can't tell you how bad I feel for intruding on your evening."

"It's no intrusion at all, my dear." She waved us inside. The gold bracelets on her wrist jangled loudly. "I'm more than happy to help you as much as I possibly can."

Lena wore her characteristic braid down her back and more jewelry than I could ever wear at once. A long denim skirt and a tie dye t-shirt reminiscent of the 60s completed her vintage flower child look.

The small condo apartment was cozy and meticulously clean. The air had a false but refreshing pine scent. She led us into the living room where we sat on an old sofa with a patchwork quilt laid over the back.

After rushing back and forth to the kitchen and refusing my help, Lena had laid out an elaborate tray of tea, coffee and baked goods.

With an apologetic smile, she turned to Arys. "I'm afraid I must apologize, dear. I have nothing to offer that would feed your appetite."

"Think nothing of it. I appreciate your desire to make me feel welcome." With an aged grace that I both envied and despised, Arys captured Lena's small hand within his own and raised it to his lips in a grand gesture. I fought hard not to sigh in exasperation and roll my eyes.

"Oh my," Lena giggled and turned to me with a smile. "Now what exactly can I do for you?"

I recounted everything for her, editing the details of David's murder but including the rest. She nodded as I spoke but said nothing. When I finished, she drew in a long breath and looked carefully at each of us in turn. When her eyes landed on Arys, my heart rate began to climb.

"It's not so different from the blood bond forged between vampires when one creates another. You've allowed your passion to draw you into a true sharing of power." Lena's features were pinched in thought. "Like I told you before Alexa, sometimes this is the natural order of things, as hard as it might be to believe, it's meant to happen. A bond like this lasts to the death."

Negative energy swirled around us, and I noticed Arys suddenly stiffen. I tried to shake off the unease that filled me.

"So a onetime fling is a lifelong hassle?" I almost choked on the words as they spilled out.

Lena rounded on me with a look that had me backing up in my seat. "Hearing those words from you is like a slap in my face. I taught you better than that. You know not to take your powers lightly. I know you do."

My face burned, and I couldn't look at either of them. I noted the four different shades of brown in the carpet as I stared at the floor. I did know better than that.

"In Alexa's defense, madam, the power that results from an encounter between the two of us is extremely potent. It's unlike anything I've known in my three hundred and twenty-eight years." Arys spoke up, taking my hand in his and banishing my insecurities.

Lena blinked at him, unconvinced. "I'm sorry, dear, but after centuries of sampling the wares, I wouldn't expect you to resist Alexa. However, I did expect her to resist you."

Her comment both inflated and deflated my ego. "You're totally right, Lena." I stared into my tea. "I was drawn in by the lure of power, and I didn't look back."

"It's in your nature, dear." She leaned forward and patted my hand affectionately. "Those with innate powers often long for more. It's as much a part of you as the very air that you breathe. However, like any bonding, there can be repercussions. Selecting the wrong partner can change your life."

I'd been an idiot to throw caution out the window. Immune to physical risks, I had arrogantly ignored the other potential dangers.

Arys said, "Alright, so we live with it. But, how do we deal with the weakness and urges we've picked up from one another?" I gave him a warning look. Ignoring me, he looked directly at the friendly witch.

Taking a long sip of her tea, she gave a little shake of her head. "That is something I'm not quite familiar with, my dear. Many similar stories end with somebody losing their mind, often committing suicide." Worry creased her brow when she fixed me with eyes full of concern. "Promise me that you'll be careful."

"I promise." I flashed back to the bloody scene on the bike path. Arys looked at me sharply, and I wondered if he had shared my vision.

"My only suggestion is to learn all that you can about each other's personal strengths and weaknesses. Power must be controlled. Otherwise, it controls you. I'm afraid I can't help more in that regard. I'll do what I can to dig up more information for you," Lena promised with an encouraging smile.

Bound to Arys until death. How was Shaz going to understand this? How in the hell was I going to live with a bloodlust that chose to strike me at random? And, Arys suffered with the agony of the wolf's need to break free. We were so screwed.

"On the bright side," Lena added thoughtfully. "I would imagine that if you were able to control the power, you kids would be a mighty force to reckon with."

I couldn't help but chuckle when she referred to us as kids. Despite Arys being centuries older than her, he looked young, and so she treated him that way just like Kale.

"Oh," I said, jumping up to reach into my pocket. "Maybe you can tell us a little about this." I produced Cat's red star amulet. It lay cold and inactive in my palm.

I passed it to her, expecting some kind of scrutiny but she merely glanced at it. "It's just a run of the mill charm. I'd say it was spelled to boost the wearer's power supply."

"It certainly did that. The wearer was a vampire. She's dust now," I said.

"Then it can be charmed again for another purpose. It's quite simple really."

"By all means, it's yours," I said. I still had the charm she'd given me last week and had little use for more.

She smiled broadly. "I can always use another charm." The phone rang from the kitchen, and she excused herself to take the call.

I forced myself to down the rest of the tea. The cogs and pulleys in my brain worked overtime, as I tried to piece together how I'd live with a constant tie to Arys.

"Did you catch the bottom line? She said this could make us a power house." Arys winked at me, his voice low. Go figure that would mean more to him than anything else.

"Is that all you think about?" I hissed. I could hear Lena in the other room talking in low tones.

"Baby, you know that's not all I think about." His smoldering gaze swept over me. My breath caught. "In fact, you've already got me thinking along other lines."

I blew a stray hair out of my face and flashed him a dirty look. "You are so inappropriate."

He considered me with a self-satisfied smile. "And, yet you love it. I'd be willing to bet that you're ready for me right now." He raised an eyebrow and shot me a look that oozed sexuality. A heat swept through my body that nearly knocked me breathless.

If I hadn't been done with my tea, I would have gagged on it. The energy rose between us, and I knew, if we touched, I would lose control.

I hungered in more ways than I'd ever known before that night with Arys. I could smell his blood rushing hot beneath the surface of his skin, and I longed to taste it.

When Lena hung up the phone with a small clatter, I realized I'd been leaning toward Arys as if I would have crawled out of my skin to get to him.

"Sorry about that." Lena returned to the living room, noting my empty cup immediately. "Would you care for more tea, dear?"

"No, thank you. I probably have more caffeine in my veins than anything else."

I helped her clean up the dessert trays, but the time grew late. "We'll get out of your hair now. I'm sure you'd much rather be in bed." Arys took my lead and ambled to the doorway.

I drew Lena into a quick hug, but I could smell the blood in her veins. Hunger soared ravenously, and I sent a panicked look over her shoulder to Arys.

"Thank you, again, for all of your help," he called from the entryway. The heady swoon of bloodlust shattered, and I stepped away from her before it hit me again.

"I don't know how much help I was, but I'll do some digging and see what I can come up with."

I slipped into my shoes and thanked her again. We turned to go. I'd been holding my breath. The hallway was empty and unnaturally quiet. I stumbled and fell against the wall, but Arys steadied me.

"Are you alright?" His gaze searched me.

I had to think about my words. The bloodlust picked away at me, but I shoved away from him to hit the elevator down button. When I heard the mechanics engage, I turned to face him. A light sheen of perspiration broke out on my brow, and I wiped it away with the back of my hand.

"I am not alright. Why didn't you feed tonight?" I gulped the stale hallway air and longed for the fresh outdoor breeze.

"I didn't think I needed to." He eyed me carefully as I slumped against the wall.

I held tightly to my stomach as it cramped and growled. The hunger was intense; much like it had been the previous night when I'd lost control. A mix of emotions stormed my system.

I smiled wickedly and crooked my finger in invitation. The elevator arrived with a ding, and the doors slid open. Arys grabbed my hand and pulled me in after him. He eyed me carefully, as if I were the unpredictable one.

"I wonder if feeding would have kept this from happening to you," he said thoughtfully.

"And me shifting will alleviate your need." I felt giddy, as if I'd had too much wine.

"Possibly." He appeared thoughtful but was easily distracted when I licked my lips in obvious invitation. "You're a dangerous woman, Alexa. I don't think you know how powerful your allure is."

"Well, it's not my allure that has me itching to feel you."

I reached for him, the contact of our skin producing an electric tingle throughout my body. A gasp escaped me when a jolt filled me with pleasure. He sighed. All resistance left him as he grabbed me tightly in a bruising kiss.

The elevator slammed to a stop, and I startled until I realized he had stopped it. I wasn't keen on the locale, but with the silky softness of Arys's skin beneath my fingers, I could make do.

Where our skin made contact, the sparks burned. My fingers pushed under his t-shirt, and ten steady streams of energy hummed against his bare skin.

The warmth of his mouth found what remained of the previous bite wound above my collarbone. My pulse beat hard beneath the surface. He lingered there, and I froze. I remembered what his fangs felt like buried in my flesh. The matching scar on my left breast throbbed in time with the other. Pressed tight against him, I still didn't feel close enough.

His hands were low on my hips. They brushed the sensitive patch of skin just below my bellybutton. If I were a werecat, I would've purred right then.

I knew he wasn't going to bleed me right there, but damn, I wanted him to. The hunger swept through us like a hurricane, and I tugged at his shirt to feel more of him.

His lips hovered over the healed bite, his tongue played lightly around it. As I neared the point of no return, he pulled back.

"If you do this now, you're going to regret it later."

For a moment, I was confused. My thoughts followed the wolf's instincts rather than logic. Why would he stop now?

I blinked at him. "What?" I asked in a sultry tone.

"Think about it, Alexa. You don't love me. You love the wolf pup. If we keep going down this path, you will lose everything with him."

He was pulling away because of Shaz? I fought to wrap my mind around my white wolf. He was in my heart, but my feelings for Shaz were drowning in a sea of power and hunger.

"Since when do you care about Shaz?" I challenged him to have a damn good reason before he rejected me.

"I don't." His tone was short and clipped. He moved away from me and pushed a button. The elevator resumed its descent. He added begrudgingly, "I care about you."

The genuine affection came as a big surprise, like a sudden slap in the face. He was in this for the high. The woman in me wanted to believe that he spoke the truth, but I knew better. My wolf, on the other hand, was outraged. I was an unclaimed female with needs and desires.

The elevator reached the main floor, and the door slid open. Arys glanced at me and headed for the lobby.

"You can't just leave me like this," I called after him. "You did this to me."

Outside, the rain fell in a steady rhythm. I caught up to him halfway to the car. I was pissed that he could just walk away from me. His hunger was bringing me to my knees, and I wanted to slap him or bite a nice chunk out of his thigh.

"Come on, Alexa. This isn't the time or the place. Get the keys out." He walked a few steps ahead of me.

The night air was warm, which made the rain bearable and even calming. Though, the coldest shower on the planet wasn't about to cool me down.

I pulled my keys from my purse, grinned mischievously, and said, "Is this what you want?" I dropped them lewdly into my bra, and I heard myself say, "Come and get it."

Arys crushed me against the front of the car, and I loved it. Laughter pealed out of me, tinged with the growl of a wolf. On tiptoes, I leaned up to taste him.

He pulled back so that I only made contact with the soft indent beneath his lower lip. As I gently traced his bottom lip with my tongue, I felt him shudder. The power grew between us. He leaned into me again until I lay nearly flat against the hood.

"Stop pushing me, wolf." His eyes were intense as they bore into me, and he bared his sharp fangs, white in the darkness. "You know damn well how bad I want to give it to you right here. We make the most beautiful combination in every single way."

I held my breath as he inhaled my scent ever so slowly. Raindrops hit my face and soaked my clothes, but I didn't care. The car keys spilled out of my top onto the hood. I grimaced inwardly and hoped they didn't scratch the paint.

I forgot the paint when his sharp fangs grazed the soft spot inside my elbow. He licked the sensitive skin, and tingles raced up my arm. When he broke the skin, a rush roared through me that echoed in my ears.

"Oh, come on," I pleaded, frustrated with the fire burning out of control inside me.

"There's one thing, Alexa, this mortal love you have. You need it." His tongue slid across my skin, hot and wet, and I wondered why his words so greatly contrasted his actions. "In so many ways, you're mine, but I feel your need for that pup. I won't selfishly take that from you."

"Who are you trying to convince?" I asked. My throat was dry, and I licked my lips. The cold rain was doing nothing to cool the heat that continued to rise within me.

"Ok, fine," he said, meeting my eyes. Drizzle plastered his hair to his forehead. I brushed it away from his eyes. "I know I'll be the one you blame. The one you resent because you messed up too many times. I don't want to see that happen."

"So even pushing me away now is selfish and based on what suits you best. So typically the vampire."

"That I am," he growled even as he spread my legs and pressed his hard length against me. "Never forget it, or you'll be mine forever."

I considered debating that but thought better of it. He was firm against me, and I drew a shuddery breath, conflicted. The energy buzzed hot around us and contrasted strangely with the rain.

The comforting rhythm encouraged a partial shift. Fangs filled my mouth, and I clawed red lines in his arms with my nails. I was ready to beg or demand, when laughter rang out from eight floors above.

"Hey buddy," a drunken voice called. "Do your girl already. It's getting cold out here."

Four guys stood on a balcony, gawking down at us. A streetlight gave them a perfect bird's eye view. Arys grasped my hand and pulled me upright. He swiped the keys off the hood, pressed the unlock button, and shoved them into my hand.

"Let's go downtown. I need an easy victim, and you need-," he stopped suddenly. He pressed his lips to mine, and his tongue tasted of my blood. "Well, this isn't the time or place to give you what you need."

I gave the balcony gawkers a Hemi burnout as I cursed myself for messing around outside Lena's. Thank God, she hadn't caught us.

My first stop was the nearest Tim Horton's for an extra large coffee. All nerves, I couldn't stop running my hand through my hair. Though the coffee did nothing to calm me, it was soothing nonetheless.

After that, we hit a particularly seedy district of the downtown core, a prime locale for drugs and prostitutes. He promised to be quick. He'd dispatch one of the local vermin, and hopefully, ease my hunger. I didn't think it would work, but I had my fingers crossed.

"So you want me to wait here?" I asked for the second time since we had parked behind the dingy bar.

"Yes, just wait here. I won't be long. And, lock the doors."

I thought he was full of shit but nodded anyway. "Will do, chief."

Arys blended into the shadows so well that even I could barely spot him. The stereo played softly, which eased the heavy feeling that I was about to watch a murder.

I waited. The scent of coffee filled the inside of the car. My wet clothes left me chilled despite the heat at full blast. The headlights were off, but I wasn't killing the engine in this part of town for anything. Soon enough, a shape emerged from between the bar and the vacant building next door.

As the shape approached the obscured vampire, it revealed two people. A woman that looked far too young to sell her body, and a man old enough to be her father. Arys grabbed the man by the shoulders and jerked him hard enough to lose his footing. The woman screamed and turned to run. I held my breath, afraid that Arys would stop her, but he let her go. Screams in this part of town rarely garnered response.

The noise from the radio seemed to fade away. I felt like I was watching the scene before me on an old movie reel. The rain and the vampire brought to mind a classic horror film.

I didn't flinch. I didn't even blink when Arys pulled the man into his embrace and sank his fangs deep into the human's throat. Time seemed to stop, and I remembered Arys killing the nameless woman behind Lucy's. I had liked it then, and God help me, I liked it now.

My predator grew hungry, and I should have been alarmed at my pleasure, but it just felt so right, so natural. My wolf thought nothing of my arousal at the kill. I, however, felt ashamed to be turned on as I watched the vampire take the man's life. My self-control barely kept me from jumping Arys the moment that the passenger door opened.

"You reek of lust," Arys commented. The fresh energy rolled off him and tantalized my senses. "What have you been doing in here without me?"

"Shut up." My cheeks burned hot. I felt stupid and awkward as two very different natures warred inside me with their differing views.

Arys chuckled, and I used driving as a welcome distraction. I cracked open my window to allow the breeze and raindrops to hit my face as I gave myself a mental shake.

Lena was right. This was about control. Right now, I worried about that snarling wolf who didn't enjoy being told no.

"Do you need another coffee? Or just a cold shower?" Arys smirked and even in the dim car interior, I could see that he wore not even a drop of blood. That must come with experience.

"I don't think even the coldest shower would help me now." I navigated a construction detour before glancing at him again. "Thanks to you."

"Oh please," he replied with a dramatic lilt to his voice. "You flatter me too much. Really. It isn't good for my ego."

"Isn't that the God's honest truth?" I made a sound of absolute disgust, and he laughed merrily.

I got on to the freeway exit that would lead us back to Stony. Before I could cuss out the guy who cut me off, my cell phone rang, startling me. I grabbed the noisy thing expecting Shaz or Ky. Instead, the number on the display made me cringe.

"It's Raoul," I muttered. "I wonder what he wants. If my vampire magic is so corrupt then maybe he can just leave a voicemail."

Arys cocked his head to one side. "Maybe you should answer it."

I raised an eyebrow to question his sanity, but he just shrugged.

My curiosity piqued. Against my better judgment, I answered.

"Hello?" I sounded properly sharp and impatient, but Raoul completely ignored me. His frantic ramble came loud enough for Arys to hear. At first, the only words I could decipher were "Belle", "shower" and "dead". Whatever he'd said, it didn't sound good.

"Ok, you've got to repeat that. I can barely catch what you're saying."

"Oh fuck, Alexa, I'm so screwed. I should have told you." His terror put my heart in overdrive. Adrenaline hit me full force. Raoul was a professional, a businessman, and a self righteous jackass. I had never heard him speak like that.

"What in the hell is going on?" I put the phone on speaker as I sped down the highway.

"I'm at home with Belle. We'd been in bed together. I just went to the bathroom ... to shower." His voice broke and he paused. The silence in that moment was deafening. "When I came out ...fuck, Alexa, she's dead. In my bed, as I speak."

My driving went to shit, and I was thankful for the deserted highway. I was stricken. I felt my face pale. I was at a loss for words.

"Um, ok," I said, stalling to think. "How long ago was this? Is anyone in the house?"

"I just found her. Nobody's here. Not anymore anyway. I know I'm a jackass for saying this but, will you come?"

I met Arys's calm gaze and found no answer within it. "Alright." I white-knuckled the wheel. "We'll be there in twenty minutes. Hang tight."

"We?" Despite his fear, that one didn't slip past him.

"Yeah, Arys is with me. And I'm not walking in there without him." I was hoping he didn't mind that I'd volunteered him.

"Fine, whatever. Just come. I'm calling some of the guys for added security. See you soon?"

"Yeah, see you soon." I turned my phone off with a beep and focused on the dark road.

"And you're perfectly certain that this werewolf isn't offing all of these women himself?" I could hear the grin in the vampire's tone.

"Well, I was. I mean, I really don't think that he is. You don't mind coming with?"

He dragged out the silence to make me sweat. I thought he was declining until I sensed him reach for me in the dark. I didn't wave him away. I was worried, and I let myself take comfort in his touch. His fingers lingered softly on the small bite inside my elbow.

"Anything you need, Alexa, I'm there."

Chapter Fifteen

When we pulled onto Raoul's street, two of our pack, Zak and Julian, approached the door. They were best buds who clashed over every little thing. Raoul glanced outside suspiciously before he rushed them inside. He paused when he noticed the Charger crawling along the block.

Without burnouts or tire squealing, I parked three doors down. I shivered when the breeze hit my damp clothing. Arys ambled casually as he followed me up the walk.

"Hey," I said before we reached the door. "I'm sure I don't have to tell you this, but nobody in this house needs to know all of the ways we're connected."

Raoul wasn't quite sure what to think of me as it was. If he knew that I had full access to Arys's power, he'd probably tell me that he could handle impending doom all on his own. Or, would he? Raoul knew he needed help, or he wouldn't have called, not this time. Raoul's face was visible from the window, and he looked like a nervous hen rather than the bold wolf.

"So, you don't want them to know we're sleeping together and can share power like a vampire and wolf hybrid that even Hollywood couldn't dream up. Got it." He flashed me a sly wink and pinched my ass.

"No, no, no." I held up a hand. "We are not sleeping together.

We slept together. Past tense. And, funny comment coming from a guy who turned me down less than an hour ago."

"Right." Head cocked to the side, he studied me pensively. I didn't like it. "That was different. You needed your hunger quenched. Your desire was under influence. When you come to me under your own free will because of your own feminine wants, that will be different."

"Oh," I scoffed. "Like it was my own free will the last and only time?" It had seemed pretty power influenced to me.

"Wasn't it?" He asked with a grin that spoke volumes of wickedness. Before I could reply, he rang the doorbell, which left me to choke on my retort.

The scent of death struck me, and my heart rate increased. Arys glanced at me with a puzzled expression. I wondered what he was sensing that I might not be. There was a negative energy lingering around the place that screamed of hate and vengeance.

I swallowed hard. Inside, I would look at Belle's dead body. There was certainly no love lost between us, but this was not what I wanted.

"Thank you for coming." Raoul attempted to play nice but eyed the vampire skeptically. "I wouldn't have if I were you. Not after the way I treated you last time."

I waved off his apology before the moment got more awkward. Blood and violence coated the atmosphere inside the house with a thick, uncomfortable energy, and I wrinkled my nose in distaste. One of my own lay dead.

When Arys followed me inside, both Julian and Zak did a double take. Few Weres liked dealing with the notorious vampire. He was known for his ability to make life unpleasant for others when the urge struck him. Not one of them offered him a hand in greeting.

"So what the hell happened exactly?" I looked around, but the elaborate sitting room hadn't changed since I'd been there last.

"You guys want to man the front and back doors?" Raoul's dark eyes flicked back and forth between the Zak and Julian. "I'm going to show Alexa upstairs."

I swallowed hard and stared at Raoul. The most powerful werewolf in our pack was pale and shaky. Even a human could have smelled his fear. He knew what was really going on here, and I vowed to get it out of him before I left.

He led the way upstairs. The air was thick with Belle's blood. My stomach tightened, and I fought the urge to cover my mouth to avoid tasting the air.

"I swear, Alexa, I just left her for a few minutes." Raoul hesitated outside the door to the master bedroom. "The only evidence that someone else had been in the room was the open window. We'd had it closed."

It had been a long time since I'd been in Raoul's bedroom. Thankfully, this was no time for embarrassing memories.

To my absolute astonishment, Arys stepped forward and laid a hand gently on Raoul's shoulder. "Don't feel like you have to go in there again. We can take it from here."

"Yeah, Raoul," I added. "Don't torture yourself. Maybe you should call Fox to get a place prepared for Belle."

Fox Matthews, a city werewolf, specializes in medicine. He helps with injury, illness and, unfortunately, death. We can't go to human doctors with vampire bites and claw marks. With Fox's help, we had laid more than one wolf to rest within the trees and forests beyond town. Belle would be in good company.

Raoul looked at us with obvious relief but slowly backed away from the door. "Sure." He nodded and grasped the railing at the top of the stairs. "I'll make some calls. Maybe make some coffee. Do you guys want any?" He paused, looked at Arys then shook his head. "Sorry."

"Make coffee. Use the phone. We'll be down in a few minutes." I rushed him downstairs. His nerves created a raw energy that bit at my skin in all the wrong places.

He descended the stairs and turned the corner before I reached for the door handle. The knob was cold and smooth in my hand. I must have held it a split second too long because Arys tried to step in.

"Do you want me to go first?" he asked. When I shot him a dirty look, he added, "It's not personal. I never knew her. Well, except for that one time."

My cheeks grew hot, and I shoved the door open with more force than was necessary. I couldn't believe he was joking at a time like this, or at least, he damn well better be joking.

I took in the sight of the bedroom and forgot my irritation. I almost slipped on something slick as I stepped through the doorway. If Arys hadn't been within grabbing distance, I would have landed on my butt in the mess.

"Oh, this is a nice one," Arys remarked, completely unaffected.

He gave the murder scene before us an all-appraising glance, like an artist surveying the latest creation of another. I knew the things that he'd done in his time. I saw them through my own eyes. Arys had done so much worse than this.

I started at the foot of the bed, unable to look at her face yet. I could only recognize Belle's bleached blonde hair, well, what remained blonde anyway. Most of it was stained a tragic red.

Blood covered the duvet on the bed as well as the wall behind it. I wondered how Belle had that much blood. A trail of splatters fell in a line across the expensive grey Berber carpet. Even her pretty, pink toenail polish was dotted with scarlet smears. I was dying to take a deep breath but the air was rank with the sickly sweet scent of werewolf blood.

Two gaping wounds caused the entire mess. One ran straight down, from her surgically enhanced breasts to her pubic region. Although exceptionally straight, a few jagged tears indicated that a clawed human hand had created the slice.

The other wound was in her neck. Her throat was torn wide open, exposing gruesome tissue and bone. Her vacant blue eyes had rolled up to stare at the ceiling.

"Oh God, Belle." The words slipped out, and I reached to touch her but didn't.

I stared at Belle for a long, silent moment. Finally, I pulled the blood stained sheet to hide her nakedness. My hand lingered, and I trailed it through her silky locks simply because she was one of my own. As I gazed down into her dead stare, I was livid. Someone dared to take what Raoul and I protected. His human lovers weren't mine, but Belle, she was pack. Somebody was going to pay for this.

"Tell me what you feel," I breathed.

"You don't feel anything?" Arys asked and stepped nearer.

"I feel a lot of things. But, there's so much here, and the smells are overwhelming." The energy in the room created a swarm of sensations, a fuzz inside my head. I waved a hand to indicate the carnage around us. "I'm not quite sure what I'm feeling. Something is off."

He studied me as he slowly walked the room's perimeter. "The blood scent overpowers your Alpha's fear, but the rage... It lingers everywhere."

He stopped near the bed and looked down at Belle. He saw something that I couldn't see, which created a metaphysical itch that ate at me. His thought taunted me like an idea on the tip of my tongue.

"Who would do this?" I asked, not expecting an answer, but I felt the weight of Arys's questioning stare.

"Somebody with a serious vendetta. Your Alpha has been a really bad boy. You really can't pick up that energy?"

"He's not my Alpha." I crossed my arms over my chest, which only drew the vampire's eyes to my breasts. "Yes, I can feel something, Arys, but I can't identify it. I have been around for two and a half decades. You've seen centuries. Don't make me feel inferior just because I don't know what I'm sensing. It smells human, but it doesn't feel that way. It's hard to pick out anything beneath the blood and death."

His hands came to rest on my forearms, and he gazed deep into my eyes. The now familiar heat within my core began to grow at his touch. He pulled my arms apart despite my childish resistance and gave me a slight shake.

I frowned. "Arys, what are you-,"

"Shh." He placed one finger lightly on my lips to silence me. "Loosen up. Concentrate. Seriously, Alexa, listen to me."

I wanted to listen, to allow his voice to draw me in. I leaned into his touch and savored his cool power.

"Shake off the need to be wolf," Arys continued. "Smell, sound, sight...these things won't serve you here. You have to go beyond those senses. Tap into what makes you more than wolf or woman."

Even amid the death and destruction, my eyes closed of their own accord. The overpowering smells that crowded my sensitive nose seemed to dissipate as I saw the world through an aural haze. I opened my eyes, and Arys's midnight blue aura shone faintly around him. My own yellow gold surrounded me. I gave a small gasp. The two energies reached for one another. They formed a small arc between us like a rainbow of swirling golden blue.

I shook off the fascination of our entwined auras and

concentrated. I was able to clearly isolate the remnants of energy left behind by both Belle and her killer. I felt Arys. He shielded me from the trauma that danced among the energy shadows. I could see nothing, but I didn't need to see her because I could feel her. The killer I sought was female and neither human nor wolf but both. The energy was new to me, but with Arys's touch, I found the idea: Hybrid.

I must have said the word aloud because Arys nodded and repeated it. I blinked a few times, and my link began to fade. I lost sight of our auras.

"Did you see that?" I asked with a giddy excitement in my tone. "Our auras joined together like some twisted, poison vine? I mean I've seen it in the color of my psi balls but that was crazy."

I felt a little silly. The metaphysical high hit me on a physical level. Arys's serious expression only enhanced my self-consciousness.

"See it? No. I can see it when we work energy, but just now? No." Ever so slowly, he ran his hands over my aura, scant inches from my body. He didn't touch me, but I felt his touch inside me, like a tickle. "I can always feel your aura drawing mine, like magnets."

Arys's eyebrows drew together. I could see the wheels in his brain turning. He was intrigued. Why could I visibly see it, and he could not?

"You never saw the colors just now? Blue and gold? Nothing?" I'd so easily slipped into third eye view, and my nerves buzzed, as if needles poked every inch of my body. I squirmed.

"What? No, nothing." He paused, glanced down at Belle and then back at me. "I think it's because I am undead, on the other side of the plane from the living."

Nodding, I turned to the bed to draw the dirty sheet up over her head. I would have closed her eyes, but the shock in her frozen expression made me reluctant to touch her.

"Ok, let's go talk to Raoul. See what he knows about a wolf hybrid." I'd seen enough.

"What does it look like?" The vampire's cool touch on my arm caused a small spark. "Our auras, I mean."

In his jaded gaze, I clearly saw his envy. I had an ability that he did not. I hid the smile that caused my lips to twitch as we descended the stairs side by side.

"They arc like electricity between us, connecting us in the

center." I vaguely indicated the lower chakra region on my body and didn't miss his sly grin and nod.

"Of course," he purred low in my ear. "That's only fitting."

"Get off," I growled playfully with an elbow in his side.

We followed the short hall to the kitchen where Raoul and Julian spoke in hushed tones. Zak stood on the front deck with his cell phone pressed to his ear.

They all turned to look at us expectantly, and I hated that I got sucked into this crap. Raoul offered me a cup of coffee, which I took out of obligation, not because I wanted any. Surprisingly, he remembered my three creams, two sugars.

I glanced at Arys who met my gaze with an intensity that I didn't like. Not here, not now. Sure, that wasn't what I'd been saying before.

"Would you mind running some security while I talk with Raoul?" I asked with a look said this wasn't the time or place for energy games.

With a wink and a slight nod of his head, he replied, "Of course. Anything for you, my love."

My face turned ten different shades of red. What was it with men? Why was it necessary to make it so obvious?

"Raoul, if you and I could have a moment of privacy?" I carefully ignored the other Weres' appraising glances. So, Arys was willing to share with Shaz but no one else? How thoughtful.

"Sure, let's go in the den."

I followed him into his cozy office. Small and windowless, it held only a sofa, desk and bookshelf, but we could sit and shut everything else out. When he closed the door, I took a deep breath and spoke with my voice low.

"A hybrid killed Belle, and Julie and Sheridan, too." I shuffled from foot to foot, nervous of his reaction.

Raoul's face drained of all color, and he sat heavily on the edge of the desk. His wide shoulders slumped, and I read in his coal black eyes what I'd suspected all along.

"You know who it is," I declared. "If you expect me to put myself on the line, then you'd better start talking. Now."

I crossed my arms and fixed him with my best "take no shit" expression. He stared at my feet for what felt like an eternity.

I was ready to hurl a tirade of irritated curses, when he forced his eyes to mine. I could feel his anguish and shame like a worn cloak of bitterness settling about my shoulders.

"God, Alexa, don't hate me. I've made some really big mistakes in my past. Bigger than you'd ever imagine." He ran a hand through his damp hair, which trailed water droplets along the shoulders of his grey t-shirt. I said nothing, waiting for him to go on.

"I was so afraid that she was behind this. After all this time. I should have known better." His eyes took on a haze that indicated he was reliving a memory, and I was keenly aware of the way his bottom lip trembled ever so slightly. The wolf in me was curious what he would do if I bit it.

"I swear to you, Alexa, I never thought she would hurt innocent people to get to me. You have to believe that."

"Listen Raoul, if you dragged me into some scorned-lover on the warpath bullshit, I'm going to be super-pissed. I've had enough of that shit for one week."

He looked puzzled. "No, no, it isn't like that."

"Then why don't you give me a little more information before I decide you're wasting my time?" His nervous jitters made me anxious. His energy prickled along my skin like hot sparks from a fireplace. "We both know how hard hybrids are to come by. Let's just cut to the chase."

He swallowed hard and cleared his throat. "Her name is Zoey Roberts. She's my daughter."

Chapter Sixteen

"Oh, this just keeps getting better." I did nothing to hide my exasperation. "When were you planning on mentioning this, and why the hell would your daughter be on a murderous rampage? What did you do to her?"

My words ended on a squeak. Instinctively, my hands balled into white-knuckled fists. Adrenaline blazed through my veins, and I forced myself to breathe deep and calm.

"Oh, that is so typical." He fixed me with his black stare, but instead of vehement, he was only weary. "You immediately assume it's my fault that somebody else chose to take lives? I'm not pulling the strings here, Alexa. I didn't think your feminist side went so far as to condone murder."

He was right. I was out of line. "Hey, I am not a feminist. I'm an equal." I took an awkward step back but didn't apologize. "You're right though. I shouldn't automatically accuse you, so keep talking."

With a half-hearted shrug, he said, "I met her mother more than twenty years ago. She was the first of only two women that I truly loved. I'd just turned twenty-one. She was a few years younger, and though I knew I should stay away from her, I just couldn't resist." He smiled then, but it lacked his usual arrogance and sarcasm.

"Her name was Naomi," he continued. The love in his eyes shocked me. "She sparkled with such life. I'd only been a werewolf for two years and was still struggling to come to terms with my wolf, but it was worth learning to have her in my life."

A long heavy sigh escaped him. He sounded so defeated, and I reminded myself that I had no reason to feel sorry for him. Not yet.

"So what happened?" I asked with feigned casualness.

His eyes roamed around the small room, and I could feel his blood pressure increase. "She actually fell in love with me. We dreamed of having a picket fence life and living happily ever after." He laughed bitterly and wiped the corner of one eye. "I was an idiot to think I could have that."

"She didn't know, did she?" I could see where this was going.

"No. She told me she was pregnant, so I had to tell her. I was so goddamned scared."

I would have been too. Weres are generally sterile. However, rare fecundity led to offspring like Jez, a natural full-blooded Were, and hybrids, a wolf and human combination. Neither is common by any means.

I sat as Raoul paced the office. I perched on the arm of the couch and followed his movements with my gaze. "So, you told her."

"And, she hated me. She screamed and cried. She thought I was crazy until I showed her." His voice grew thick with unshed tears. "Then, she simply feared me. Her pregnancy was full of complications. Zoey was a parasite that tried to consume her. Still, Naomi refused to see me. She finally called me during labor, when she realized that it was killing her."

Raoul stopped pacing with his back to me. I said nothing, as his heart-rending pain reached me. My heart ached for him, but I didn't let his emotions influence my reactions.

He took one long shuddery breath. "By the time I reached her, she was barely hanging on. She begged me to take care of Zoey, no matter what, and I swore that I would."

When he turned to me again, unshed tears glittered in his ebony eyes like diamonds. I couldn't imagine how hard it was for him to face me like that.

"I failed her, Alexa. God help me, I thought I was doing the right thing for her at the time."

"Tell me what you did with her, Raoul." He trembled. How many had he told this secret to?

The need to comfort him won out. I went to him, bridged the distance between us, and reached out to grasp his large hand. It was warm and slightly damp. I leaned in, just enough to rub my face gently alongside his. I nuzzled him with a teenage affection that wouldn't die after all these years.

He surprised me by grabbing me in a big hug that pulled me off balance. The scent of shampoo, cologne and musky wolf filled my nostrils, and the sudden desire to run on four feet struck me.

"I went to an older wolf that I trusted for help," he continued in a sudden rush. "I didn't know how I'd manage to work and raise a baby while being a damn shifter. I was overwhelmed. I didn't know what to do."

When I pulled back gently, he allowed me to disengage myself from his grasp. I was afraid to speak, afraid he would stop sharing.

"She helped me locate a tight-knit pack down south that was willing to care for her while teaching her about her mixed blood. They had women to nurture her in ways that I never could. But now, it seems like a mistake."

It didn't sound like a bad choice to me considering his options at the time. But, I wasn't Zoey, and she obviously felt betrayed. The girl was on a damn rampage.

"You made the choice you thought was best for her. How can that be a mistake?"

"She apparently thinks so. She's single handedly destroying the women that I've been involved with. I knew she was upset, but I never would have guessed she'd take it this far."

That made me snap to attention. "What? So you've been in contact with her over the years?"

The look he gave me was full of scorn, and he scoffed. "I'm not a dead-beat dad, Alexa. I didn't just dump her and run. I stayed there for two weeks with her before I felt right about leaving her. I wrote and called and went to see her up until a few years ago when she asked me not to."

With a shrug of his massive shoulders, his short-lived defense evaporated. "She can't forgive me for not keeping her. But, she was blossoming there, and I didn't think to bring her here. I'm a bachelor. My lifestyle isn't right for a young woman. Sometimes, I think she hates me for being wolf while she cannot without risking everything."

Part of me was astounded at how completely clueless he was. I turned it over in my head. Hybrids have a much harder existence than the average Were. A hybrid is born missing a piece of the puzzle. Their half-human blood inhibits the ability to change forms. The urge to shift could never truly be fulfilled. If a hybrid did manage to change forms, they rarely shifted back. Many were trapped in wolf form forever. It made sense that a hybrid could be driven completely mad from resisting their natural urges.

"How was she doing with everything? The full moon and the wolf urges." I moved across the room to feign interest in the bookshelf. The puzzle had come together, or I thought it had.

"Good, for the most part. Or, at least I thought she was. It wasn't until the past five years or so that things began to change with her. I'm not going to give you the long version but you can see where it's led to." He gestured wildly at nothing, but I nodded just the same.

"She sees you from a distance, pouring your affections on other women. When you said you live the bachelor life, you weren't kidding."

"Do you have a point?"

"Yes," I bared my teeth at him. "In her eyes, you have all of this love and attention to shower on other women, but you've abandoned her. Is this making some sense to you? Throw in the whole being a hybrid thing, and it's no wonder she's lost her marbles."

Raoul gave me a blank look that told me my words weren't registering completely. I chalked it up to purposeful ignorance on his part. He can be the kind of guy that will blame you for his guilt after he screws you over.

A thought suddenly occurred to me. "You said that Naomi was one of two women you loved… Who was the other?"

Raoul's eyes narrowed in a glare and a chill stole over me. The atmosphere shifted so dramatically that I was momentarily confused.

"Why?" He asked, suspiciously.

I stared at him. His demeanor told me to be wary. "Because you said she was the first of two. I just thought that maybe the other woman may have something to do with Zoey's mental decline."

The heavy silence that followed made me wish I hadn't asked. However, I wondered why it was such a touchy subject. He stared daggers into me. He blinked, took a deep breath, and ran a hand through his hair. Ultimately, he turned away with his head down.

"I really don't want to talk about it, Lex, but believe me, those are two entirely separate times of my life. I don't believe Zoey could have known anything about the other woman anyway." The way that he said that spurred even more interest in this mysterious second great love of Raoul's life.

When I refocused, another thought struck me. I'd been involved with Raoul at one point, on and off for a very long time.

"I'm sorry, Raoul, but I've got to warn you, if she comes after me-"

"Don't say it!" He interrupted. "I know. I would expect you to defend yourself. But promise me, if you come across her before I do, you won't kill her. Please."

After years of imagining Raoul begging me for something, the reality wasn't at all satisfying. It didn't really feel good in any way.

"I can't make any promises to you. If it's me or her, I'm walking out of it alive. Hell, maybe what she really wants is someone to put her out of her misery after two decades of torture."

Wow. When had I become so cold? The words froze on my tongue, and I briefly wondered if Arys's attitude had rubbed off on me, another lovely parting gift from him. That was ridiculous, and I knew it. I was bitter enough to kick Raoul when he was down, but I don't play that dirty.

"I'm sorry, Raoul. That was a nasty thing for me to say."

I felt guilty and crude as I waited for him to say something. His disgusted look spoke volumes, and I wished I could drop into a hole and hide. Couldn't this moment just end already?

"Clearly, you have your own issues with me, Lex." He spoke softer than I'd been anticipating. "I suppose I should be thankful you haven't already taken me out. Or tried to."

Something about that last sentence. Was that a challenge? I couldn't believe his audacity. I moved to go, and he blocked the door in one smooth motion.

"Don't walk out on me." His voice, now a low growl, sent a delicious shiver down my spine, and the wolf within me responded in full.

I suspected that Raoul didn't want the sharp ears beyond the thin door to catch our exchange. Though, if Arys had caught the challenge in Raoul's voice, he was already on alert.

"Don't try to stop me." I wasn't growling yet, but instinct had blanketed me in warm Were energy. In one blink, my eyes shone with the blazing brilliance of my wolf.

I watched Raoul's black eyes bleed to wolf, and my heart began to pound.

"I'm not going to. Alexa, you've had years to get the closure you need. Instead, you hold it inside and allow it to feed your bitterness and anger." He advanced on me so that we stood just inches apart. "If you need to hash out the past, if you want to tell me exactly why you loathe me so much, then do it, but stop dragging it into every encounter we have."

I stared into his eyes with amazement. I admired him for calling me on what, I have to admit, was the truth, but I was pissed that he allowed his voice to rise so those beyond the door might hear. I opened my mouth to speak, but he kept talking.

"I asked for your help because I know you're a true survivor. I thought I could count on you. Despite everything, we are pack. Or at least, we were."

His words rang in my ears, and I recalled my very similar thoughts about Belle upstairs. Shit.

I hate when Raoul's right. I had agreed to help him, and he'd thrown me out of his house. Yet, here we were, together, pack.

"I was a young, scared girl who counted on you, and you let me down." I was surprised as the whispered words left my lips. I was more surprised when my voice cracked. "You taught me about blood and sex, but I needed more than that."

Unnerved by my words, I understood. Zoey had been better off wherever she'd grown up. Raoul's life had always consisted of fulfilling his many urges and desires. She would have hated him more had she been here, if only she knew that.

His gaze softened, as if he never had a clue how bad it had been for me.

"Alexa," he breathed my name and reached for me, but I stepped away. If he touched me, I might cry, and I refused to give him the satisfaction of my tears.

"Don't," I said, a growl rumbled low in my throat, barely audible. "Don't you dare try to placate me. You didn't care then, and

I'll be damned if you care now."

The tears on my cheeks were warm and silent, and I didn't recall the first one falling. I wiped them away with an angry motion, infuriated that I would cry over this. Maybe I still harbored more of that frightened teenager inside me than I realized.

I didn't expect Raoul to challenge my withdrawal. He caught me off guard when he backed me up against the desk. I craned my neck to look up at him as the hard wooden edge dug into the back of my legs. My body reacted defensively. My fangs extended, ready for a fight. My nails dug into the wood, as they became claws.

I expected an attack, but he leaned down and buried his face in my long blonde locks. One well-muscled arm went around my lower back and pressed me to him. He nipped my neck lightly, just below my ear. It didn't hurt. He hadn't meant it to. I realized that he was trying to comfort me.

Both of his large, warm arms went around me. He held me with an odd intensity. He nuzzled deeper into my hair, and when the first hot drop ran down the side of my neck, I realized he, too, shed tears. Unsure of what to do, I let him hold me, even though I was vibing off his pain. I just wanted to hide my feelings. I felt too exposed.

That close to Raoul, I was damn glad to be free of Arys's hunger. Amid the excitement of the evening, I hadn't noted that I had been completely free of his hunger since he'd fed.

"I know that I wasn't what you needed me to be. But, there's just so much you don't know. I'm sorry. It doesn't mean anything now, but I am."

Time seemed to stop with his small confession. My wolf was content to rest in his arms, but something deep down began to ache for Shaz. We both needed this moment, but people were waiting for us, and a dangerous hybrid was on the loose with a taste for blood and vengeance.

"Raoul?" I said tentatively. He didn't release his hold, so I prodded him gently. "It's ok. We don't have to do this right now. It's not the right time. We have to deal with Zoey."

In slow hesitation, he let go and stepped back. His ebony wolf eyes were hauntingly beautiful with tears, and I allowed myself an extra moment to fall into their depths. I wanted him to tell me the things that I didn't know, but I didn't dare ask. Call it cowardice, but an inner voice warned that I really didn't want to know.

I pushed away from the desk, past him. "So, do you have a picture of her? You know, so I actually know what she looks like if I happen to see her." Or get jumped by her, I added silently.

He relented with a shrug. "We have to find her before she does anything else."

"Do you think you can track her down?" I forced a casual tone while he produced a large envelope from the desk. I felt ill at ease.

He pulled a wallet-sized photo out and handed it to me. "I'm not sure, but I damn well intend to. There isn't a distinct scent to a hybrid, though. It's all human."

I nodded in agreement and focused my attention on the picture. Zoey was absolutely striking. She had her father's dark hair and defined features. Her eyes were a pleasant blue that I couldn't even picture on Raoul. She was smiling in the photo, standing beside a wishing well with the countryside behind her. A pale blue sundress adorned what appeared to be a tall but slender frame. I could take her.

"I think Arys and I can locate her by her energy. He immediately knew she was a hybrid when we were upstairs." I wiped a hand across my eyes to eliminate any last traces of tears. A glance around the room revealed a much-needed tissue box on the corner of the desk.

Raoul's eyes narrowed, and just like that, the tension was back. "I don't want him involved in this. He isn't pack. Hell, he isn't even a werewolf."

Was this more male-hierarchy bullshit or what? "If you want me involved then you accept who I choose to bring in."

I met his defiant gaze with my own. The decade old rift between us was back. I didn't think we'd ever truly banish it. The past was the past, but our resentments remained fresh and bitter.

"Just because you're bedding the vampire does not mean you can make him a part of this. This is my daughter we're talking about."

"Don't start the macho man shit with me. I'm in or I'm out. If you prefer to deal with your daughter yourself, that's fine with me." We stared into one another until the angry heat became too much. "I could be making money, right now, for a job like this, rather than screwing around here for free."

This time, I didn't hang around to get sucked into another

argument. I threw the office door open and strode back into the kitchen.

Raoul appeared behind me. He clutched my coffee mug in his hand as if he'd shatter it by sheer will alone.

"Sorry," I offered lamely.

Arys stood in the front sitting room while Julian paced in the large kitchen uncomfortably. Zak still stood on the back deck and shouted into his phone. He had great timing for a lover's quarrel. Before I reached the doorway that connected the kitchen and front room, Raoul grabbed my wrist hard enough to bruise and spun me to face him.

"Fine. Have it your way. But keep him on a leash. No funny stuff. This is my flesh and blood we're after."

I couldn't help but risk a glance at Arys in the neighboring room. He might not appreciate the leash comment. I certainly did not miss how Arys's eyes were riveted to where Raoul's hand gripped my wrist. Not good.

"You need to remember," I jerked my arm from his grasp. "That your daughter is losing her mind. And, one thing about crazy people, Raoul, sometimes they don't want to come back. The brink of insanity suits them just fine. Don't go into this expecting to save her. You'll just be fooling yourself."

A series of emotions crossed his face, and he successfully squashed them all. "I'm aware of the circumstances, but nobody is going to kill her. Clear?"

I wasn't getting into this again. I mustered an exasperated sigh and shrug. I rubbed the rawness out of my wrist. He manhandled me because I was wolf and not human, which aggravated me all to hell.

"I'll call you." I turned to go but paused as a smile quirked my lips. "You're not afraid, are you? To stay here alone?"

If looks could kill, I would have been dead three times over. "Ok, ok. Forget I asked."

Arys launched into motion as I walked into the room. I gestured for him to join me as I approached the front door and let us out. I stopped at the bottom of the front steps. Nothing was amiss.

"There's nobody here. I've been keeping tabs." Arys pulled the door closed behind us with a soft click. "He made you cry. I can't tell you what it took to keep from going in there, but I knew how pissed you'd be if I came riding to your rescue again."

I took a few steps down the front walkway and turned back to look at him. My eyes must be red and puffy.

"How did you know?"

The vampire fixed me with a dark blue stare. The intensity that burned there sparked a fire low in my core, and my breath caught when he said, "I could feel it."

His hand went to his still heart, but his eyes never left me. "Right here. I can't even begin to tell you the last time that I felt anything that didn't include blood, sex, or death."

When he descended the last stair and stood before me, I didn't shrink away. His soft kiss spoke to a side of me that Raoul had long ignored and Shaz just didn't yet understand. Arys had lived brutality, as both a giver and a receiver, and so had I. I responded to him in full, and our power swirled around us in a dizzying embrace. I drank in his sweet taste and smell hungrily.

With great reluctance, I pulled away, all too aware of the spectacular view of us from Raoul's big picture window. I really wanted to cast the world aside and enjoy the forbidden pleasures that joined me to this lovely, dark creature. The need to shift was a poignant ache in the pit of my stomach as I turned to lead the way to the Charger.

"So am I correct in assuming this hybrid is your Alpha's offspring gone wrong?" Arys asked when we were in the quiet confines of the car.

I looked at him sharply. "You could hear us."

"I've merely been putting the pieces together myself. That seemed to be the most logical assumption."

"He's completely adamant that nobody kill her unless it's more than necessary. He's carrying around a lot of guilt regarding her childhood."

I started the car and headed for Lucy's Lounge. I didn't want to part ways with Arys at his house. I didn't trust myself to say no to him tonight.

I really wanted to see Shaz. Tomorrow night was our official date, but at this rate, I could see it being postponed. I was a jumble of nerves, and I needed the quiet solace that I only found with my muzzle buried in Shaz's thick, white fur.

"So, no hybrid fun for the vampire?"

I shot him a scowl, and Arys laughed. A pleasurable thrill

tingled in places that simply should not respond so strongly to something so miniscule. Damn him.

"Keep your hands off of her. And, anything else that may come to mind, too. Seriously." I narrowed my brow in my best no nonsense face. "Grab her if you see her, but don't do anything but detain her. Capiche?"

"Relax, Alexa. I won't bleed the half breed, promise."

When people tell me to relax, it only serves to tick me off more, but I stifled a yawn and blinked through watery vision. I hadn't been getting enough sleep. The digital clock on the dash read 2:17am, and I knew today would be another long one.

"It's not you bleeding her that concerns me."

I smiled upon noticing that the rain had stopped. I already knew how fresh and inviting the forest would smell after a warm summer shower. I wanted so badly to be there with Shaz.

Arys squirmed uncomfortably in his seat. "The heavy presence of your wolf is like a weight inside my head. You need to shift." The way he said it was so casual, as if our fates were not inextricably entwined, as if his perception of my wolf were perfectly normal.

"I know. That's my next move. I can't focus on anything else until I clear my head with a run."

"Why don't you let me out at the 7/11?" He said suddenly. "You can go to your wolf pup, and I'll do a little scouting around before I head home."

I felt a little strange that he could sense my intentions so clearly.

Before I could form a response, he continued with a grimace. "My fingers are itching. Get your ass out of that skin and turn furry before I lose my mind. I swear I'll keep a better rein on the bloodlust from now on."

Sharing our power was hard, but sharing our weaknesses was a new kind of hell.

"If you kill that puppy you just got for Mrs. Olson, I will personally kick your ass." I teased. The 7/11 was right on the corner up ahead, near the main thoroughfare.

"Oh God, Alexa, don't even joke about that. Did you see how damn cute he was?"

I chuckled and shook my head at the big, bad vampire who melted over puppies. "What I did see was that poor old Mrs. Olson didn't have a clue that you tore the head off of her little Benny." I made a tsking sound, and Arys gave my thigh a playful pinch that had some sting to it.

"Up here is fine." He pointed to a crosswalk a good block or so before the twenty-four hour convenience store. The crosswalk was flanked by nothing but the darkness and only led to the Brown Street walking path, a ten minute walk from where I'd killed David. I was suddenly stricken with anxiety.

I pulled over. My heart began to pound as I stared out the window into the dark. My chest tightened, and my breath seemed to come short. Somebody had to have found the grisly remains of David by now.

Arys leaned over and drew me close. With a soft kiss at my temple, he whispered, "I took care of it. Nobody's going to find a thing."

I had to pull back to look at him. The lights of an approaching vehicle flashed in the rear view mirror, and I flipped my hazard lights on so they would go around.

"You did what?"

"I took care of it," he repeated as I stared at him stupidly. "There is nothing left to be found. It's your dirty little secret."

I swallowed hard as my pulse raced. Did I want to ask what he'd done with the remains? The images of what I'd done to that man flashed again in my mind, images that could never be erased. It hadn't been pretty.

"I can't believe you did that." A long, shuddery breath left me, and I felt both relief and shame. "I can't believe his girlfriend didn't send somebody to find him." My laugh bordered on neurotic.

"You know I've got your back." Arys looked at me gravely, all serious. "It was partly my fault that you lost control. We can only maintain control of this by keeping our hungers sated."

"I hope you're right."

"You've been fine since I took blood. Me? I'm starting to itch on the inside. The burning comes next. You need to let the beast out." He gave my hand a squeeze before adding, with a fang flashing smile, "By the way, you owe me two hundred bucks for half of Mrs. Olson's puppy."

I gaped, open-mouthed, at him, and he took advantage of the

moment. He pressed his lips hungrily to mine. The distinct taste of pine and wolf almost made my heart stop.

When he pulled back, I said breathlessly, "You taste like wolf."

With a bitter smile and a pained expression, he nodded. "Hurry. I'll see you soon."

He disappeared like vapor into the night, a timely and dramatic exit, and I was flabbergasted by his strange and intoxicating devotion. I wasn't quite sure what Arys was up to, but I trusted him. And, I sincerely hoped that he would never make a fool of me for doing so.

I turned off the hazard lights and eased down the street. I whipped a U-turn at the 7/11 and went back the way that I'd come. I drove straight to the lounge.

Lucy's brimmed with people despite the line of patrons that ambled out, talking and laughing amongst themselves. Though the bar was now closed for drinks, many people continued to down their last, content to stay until closing. They finished that last game of pool or sought a potential bed partner before closing time.

Shaz's platinum hair caught my eye amid a cluster of women who sought his attention. This was a regular occurrence on cheap drink night. These women looked forward to hitting on the bartender all week. As I drew near him, my wolf fought to break free of my restraint. Over the toxic combination of cologne, perfume and alcohol, I honed in on Shaz's scent and energy. If my wolf had been a separate entity, she would have run ahead to knock Shaz to the ground and shower him with wet wolf kisses.

He felt me, too, and broke away from his adoring fans to come to me, grateful for the escape. No fear or disgust showed in his beautiful jade eyes, even though I expected it. Guilt washed over me in a crashing wave. He knew what I'd done in the shadows of the walking path, and his feelings for me remained. I did not deserve this.

"Lex! My lovely wolf queen." His grin tickled me right to the bottom of my feet, and I reached for him but stopped short. "How are you doing tonight? Better, I hope."

Every woman turned to see the intruder that so easily captured the attention of their bartender. I flashed them a fake smile before dismissing them completely.

"I'm fine, Shaz, but boy, do I have a story for you." I tucked a stray chunk of dyed gold hair behind my ear and cast a glance around the bar. I stayed on full alert. Zoey could be anywhere. "Are you up for a run? I really need to unwind. And then, I can fill you in on everything. I just came from Raoul's. It's not good."

He searched my eyes briefly and then nodded. "I'd love to go for a run. Just give me a minute to finish up here and grab my things."

He gave my arm a gentle squeeze before disappearing behind the bar. On his way back, he was intercepted by a large, older lady. Though I couldn't hear their exchange, the look on Shaz's face spoke volumes. The lady produced a card from between her heaving breasts and pressed it into his hand, and I couldn't hide my laughter. She blew him a kiss and sauntered away, while he looked on, dumbfounded.

"That was strange." Shaz said as he rejoined me. He fished in his jacket pocket for car keys. He really had no idea how good he looked in that leather jacket and blue jeans. He could pass for art. "She told me to call her if and when I'm looking for a sugar mama."

"Oh yeah?" I raised an eyebrow in question and smiled. "Sounds like somebody's moving up in the world. When's your first date?"

"Ha ha, funny." He rolled his eyes, but I caught his sudden blush. "So, I'll just meet you at your place?"

"Yeah. I'm going straight to the backyard. I'll meet you there."

I turned toward the exit, and I could have sworn I heard Shaz say, "Right behind you, sweet thing," but when I turned back to him, he just winked.

Chapter Seventeen

I needed the release of that run. When I ditched my clothing in the backyard and dropped to all fours, the shift had never felt so right. I wondered if Arys shared my relief as my body reformed itself into an ashen wolf. I felt the gentlest touch on my mind, and for just a moment, I heard the vampire's soothing laughter.

As Shaz and I raced through the trees, the magical scent of fresh rain swept me away. We rolled amid the wet leaves and moss. I felt a greater joy than any human experience. In this form, I felt my connection to nature so much stronger. Rich soil streaked my fur and filled my nostrils with fertility, while my sixth sense reveled in powerful earth energy. Nothing competes with what I feel as wolf.

We ran. We chased each other and wrestled amidst the underbrush. We lifted our voices to the sky, howled together in a crescendo of harmony that haunted my rapidly shrinking human side. Miles away, a farm dog took up the howl in acknowledgement of our mighty declaration.

Dawn streaked Shaz's white fur with a colorful glow as he ran ahead. I loped along behind him and watched as he gave chase to two ravens that dared to settle too close to his path. We had run so far out of town that we needed the better part of an hour to trot back to the field behind my house. A brilliant golden glow crept over the town with the promise of another hot summer day.

I wondered if Arys could sense the magnificence of the sunrise, which he would never again experience himself. His presence returned, heavy in my mind. He'd been there before my change to wolf. Our connection crossed physical limitations. I felt I could call out to him, and he would hear me.

As we crossed the field to my house, I felt eyes on me, not from my house or even my street but from the street that ran perpendicular to mine. Shaz's startled expression indicated that he felt it, too. A scan of every backyard on that street showed nothing. We were a good distance off though.

I stopped where I was. I just stared in the direction of our watcher. I could feel Zoey. No way in hell was I going to lead her to my house if she didn't already know where it was. Unfortunately, five in the morning was not a good time to give chase through the streets of Stony Plain. I maintained my stare across the field, until I felt her go.

Why she was following me? I didn't know, but if for one minute she thought that she was going to take me out for stealing Raoul's warped affections from her, she had another thing coming. Of course, my nagging human side pitied her. The sight of Shaz and I together as wolf must hurt her more than I would ever know.

Shaz's furry eyebrows raised in question, and I nuzzled him briefly before breaking into a run. I wasn't too keen on having the neighbors witness our approach in the early morning light.

Within half an hour, we both lay sprawled across my bed, sipping coffee and watching the morning news. I'd slipped into a plain black tank top and wrapped my favorite silky leopard print robe around me. I thought of Jez every time I put it on. Shaz reclined beside me clad in just his blue jeans. His slender body was well muscled and firm, inviting me to touch.

"Now, let me get this straight," he said in between mouthfuls of refreshing java. "Raoul's estranged half-breed daughter is running amok, murdering his lovers out of jealousy. He expects your help but refuses to believe she's too far gone to ever come back."

I picked a fluff off my fuzzy bedspread and watched it float down to the grey carpet. "Yeah, that more or less sums it up."

"I wonder why she was watching us," he mused, staring thoughtfully into his cup. "She's a complete idiot if she's jealous of you."

"Thanks for that." I sneered sarcastically as I punched him in the arm.

"No, I mean that you and Raoul can barely stand each other. It's not like he's pouring a whole lot of love on you."

"True. Who knows what's left of her mind now? I'd just as soon not be involved in this mess. But, she killed Belle, so now it's personal." My grip began to tighten on my coffee mug. I took a sip and frowned when it burnt my tongue.

"I can't believe she's gone. It doesn't seem real." Shaz's voice grew soft.

I tried to hide my disgust. Belle had been a lady that every male werewolf in this town had gotten to know very well at some point. Shaz was no exception.

"Yeah, well, it looked pretty real to me." I pictured the bright red splatters in her bleached blonde hair and grimaced. I don't care how rotten your existence is, serial killing isn't the answer.

Who are you to talk? A little voice taunted me. *You murdered David in cold blood. And it wasn't even personal. So what's your excuse? Getting your kicks from sating your vampire lover's borrowed lust?*

I shuddered, and Shaz asked if I was cold. I shook my head and said, "I don't think we can make our date tonight. We have to find this crazy chick. Can we reschedule?"

He beamed a grin that set a butterfly to flutter in my stomach and reached for my hand. "No problem. Let me know what you want me to do. I'm at your service."

"You're too good to me." I felt silly, but the words were out. Before he could reply, the news lady began to talk about the missing man from Stony Plain.

We both sat up straighter, instantly alert. The police currently had no leads or clues. The man's girlfriend had told police that she'd parted ways with him earlier in the evening, that they had each taken the path that led to their respective homes. Anyone with information was asked to call local authorities.

"Holy shit." My heart raced a mile a minute, and I had to take a deep breath. "She didn't tell the cops anything. That is so fucked up. She knows damn well something got him, and she's not talking."

"Maybe she's afraid you'll come and eat her, too," Shaz

laughed, and I gave him a look. "Sorry. Still too fresh, huh?"

Fatigue began to set in as the night's events caught up with me. I emptied my mug and set it on the night table, and then I got comfy on the bed beside Shaz. His scent was easily among my favorites, and it lulled me quickly.

I remembered the days when we would fall asleep together after a run, entangled in one another's naked limbs. Thinking back on it, I couldn't quite recall when or how it had come to an end.

"If you're ready to get into bed, I can head home. I probably should anyway." He made as if to rise, and I stopped him with a firm hand flat on his bare chest.

"No, you don't have to. I want you to stay." That came out a little more forward than I'd intended. "I mean, you're tired, too. Why don't you crash here? Like you used to."

He looked at me so long and hard that I began to regret my choice of words. I was getting ready to back track, but my tongue turned heavy and hard to manipulate.

"I'm not trying to suggest anything … I just need you here."

I was feeling successfully foolish and more than a little vulnerable. I hadn't really meant to blurt out that last part.

Instead of responding and adding to my moment of awkwardness, he simply got comfortable beside me. He pulled my silky black sheet over us and drew me against him so that my back pressed against his chest. The comfort was so surreal that I made a point of taking note of every sensation.

With all that I had to think about, I expected my mind to be in overdrive. However, once we got settled, words were no longer necessary. I was out like a light.

* * * *

Just six hours later, I was awake and drinking more coffee as I spoke with Kylarai in hushed tones in the kitchen. Shaz continued to snore softly in my bed.

When I filled her in on everything from the previous night, I was momentarily afraid she was going to lose it. Anything to do with men mistreating women in any way had Ky on the offensive. She turned four different shades of red before counting backwards from ten.

Her unhappiness with Raoul couldn't have pleased me more.

"How dare he think for a minute that it's ok to bring you into this while withholding that kind of information! Why are you helping him? He's never gone out of his way for you in a way that's even remotely comparable to this." Her grey eyes blazed, and I couldn't recall the last time I'd seen her so angry.

"This isn't about Raoul anymore." I shook my head and caught the faint scent of Shaz in my hair. "He fucked up. He knowingly endangered Belle, and now she's dead. If Zoey comes back for him, he's on his own."

Kylarai looked hesitant as she twirled a piece of chin length hair absently around one finger. "You think she's that powerful? A hybrid?"

"No. I think she's crazy and dangerous. Sometimes that counts for more than power and strength."

Kylarai only nodded. We both knew what it was like when sanity snaps, when chaos is fully embraced. How much harder might it be to never come back from that?

I mentioned my plan to scout the town for Zoey later, as well as how I'd felt her watching Shaz and me. Kylarai's eyes widened, and she choked on her coffee.

"Well, I'm coming with you," she declared. Her tone was defiant, daring me to argue. "She's messing with pack now. And, don't forget about your history with Raoul. You might be on her hit list, too."

"If she's got her facts straight then she'll know I'm president of the I hate Raoul Roberts fan club. Anyway, I'm going to give Kale and Jez a call. We can cover more ground that way."

I was calling up a lot of manpower for one crazy ass hybrid, but I wasn't willing to wait for another murder, particularly since Zoey had me in her sights. I'd kill her if I had to, but I expected that I'd have to kill Raoul, too. He wasn't going to stand by and let me take her out.

"Kale, huh?" Ky grinned mischievously.

I met her gaze with a quizzical look. "Didn't you just have a date with Tom last night? How did that go by the way?"

"We had a nice dinner, alright." She rose to put her cup in the sink before fetching her keys from their hook above the microwave. "But, I don't see much more than that. He is human, so how serious can that really get?"

I watched her gather her purse and straighten the jacket of her dressy skirt suit. "You're working today?" I asked.

"I have to meet a client for lunch in the city. She caught her husband, red handed, in bed with his lover, so the divorce should be a pretty open and shut case." She smiled then. "I love those. And, what might you be planning to do in my absence? Catch up on some much needed sleep?" She inclined her head toward the hall and winked.

I knew what she was getting at and so would Shaz if he was awake and listening. I forced the best scowl I could muster and pursed my lips. "You'd better hurry, Ky. Wouldn't want you to be late for your meeting."

"You're in denial, Alexa. But, I'm sure you'll come around." She laughed and turned away in time to miss the finger that I held up for her.

"So, I'll see you later then," I continued as if she hadn't spoken. "Around sundown. Drive safe."

Before returning to my bedroom, I poured a fresh cup of coffee for Shaz. If I was lucky, maybe I could grab a bit more sleep before hunting down Raoul's nut-job offspring. When they say the apple doesn't fall far from the tree, they weren't kidding.

Shaz was sprawled in the middle of my double bed, with his eyes closed and the blankets pushed down to his waist. I stole a moment to admire the view. He was gorgeous, lean and finely sculpted. He was such an amazing contrast to Arys's dark beauty, and I blushed as an image formed in my mind of the two of them awaiting me in that bed together.

Under the weight of my gaze, Shaz slowly cracked open his eyes. His lazy smile enticed me into the bed. I leaned across him to place his coffee on the nightstand. His arms encircled my waist and he pulled me down on top of him. I startled and spilled the hot liquid on the back of my hand.

"Sorry about that." His voice came out low, barely above a whisper. I could sense his wolf lurking there behind his eyes, and I licked my lips invitingly.

Our faces were inches apart, my breasts crushed against his bare chest. I gasped as the energy of our wolves entwined and danced together. Shaz's wolf stroked a part of me that was all about the beast within.

"Shaz, I-,"

He cut me off with a warm finger pressed lightly against my lips. The temptation to run my tongue along that finger was strong.

"Don't talk. We don't need to." The intention in his green eyes had my pulse racing, and I found myself at a loss for words.

I wanted to ask him if he knew what he was saying, but he kissed me with an intensity that washed away my concerns. He tasted faintly of pine and wolf with a hint of cinnamon. I reveled in it.

I gave a small shriek when he rolled me over and pinned me beneath him. My heartbeat echoed inside my head as his tongue sought the soft hollow beneath my ear. He sought to dominate me, and by God, I was going to let him.

My nostrils filled with the scent of him, and an undeniable tingle started between my legs. Despite the ache, the urge to have him inside me after years of teasing torture, I wondered if we were making a mistake. Every part of me that was both human and wolf responded to him in full, and I knew that I'd be an idiot to open my mouth now. Words would break the spell that held us in its thrall. The last four years had been leading to this moment, and I'd be damned if I was going to be the one to stop it.

When he kissed me again, his warm, wet tongue slid between my lips. I threw myself into it whole-heartedly, no going back. He deftly slid a hand inside my robe to my breasts, and a thrill shot through me simply from his uncharacteristic boldness. I returned his kiss with a hunger that I hadn't known was possible. I moved to accommodate him as he pulled at my robe. He tossed it to the floor with careless abandon. My tank top followed, which left me clad in only my pink thong underwear.

This was happening so fast. Or was it? The anticipation had been building for years. After my night with Arys, I'd assumed Shaz would never want to touch me like that. The possessive nature with which he caressed me indicated that he felt quite the opposite. He wanted to claim me even more now.

We were rushing toward that most crucial moment, and though every human part of me insisted we should slow down, our wolves set and kept the pace. Neither lust nor undeniable animal urges rushed us. We rushed forward because we feared that it just wouldn't happen if we paused to enjoy the building momentum.

Shaz maintained his role as the dominant. His lips on my breasts brought a small growl out of me, and I gripped him tightly in response as his fingers sought the warmth between my thighs. I tore my thong off. I needed to feel his persistent touch without the barrier between us. When he lingered hesitantly and brushed the most sensitive part of me, I arched my back and reached to free him of his remaining clothing.

I reached to stroke his velvety smooth shaft as he hovered above me. When our naked bodies pressed together, nothing remained between us but our own personal worries. He paused, and we shared a thought: Was this going to ruin us? Either way made no difference to us in the heat of the moment.

I rubbed myself against him. Delicious jolts of pleasure coursed throughout me. He made to kiss me again, and I nipped his bottom lip, drawing a small bead of blood. I licked it away with the tip of my tongue and wondered when my fangs had shown up. The blood hungry vampire energy low in my core seemed to raise its head the moment his tangy blood hit my taste buds.

Shaz's green eyes were all wolf. He drew away slightly, and I worried that he changed his mind. When his mouth made contact with the sensitive skin of my most private of places, I couldn't stop the moan that broke loose, edged with a hint of a growl.

His wet tongue had just barely stroked my moist flesh when something inside me demanded that this union be made now, *before the vampire comes back*. That last thought didn't feel like me at all. Whatever it was that made me wolf, it wasn't keen on losing this moment.

"Shaz," I gasped his name around my four fangs.

I looked down my body, into his wild eyes, and a shiver of excitement engulfed me at the untamed hunger I saw there. Could he feel the growing metaphysical swirl that stole my breath and reached out for that, oh so sweet, werewolf power? The blood hunger rose up inside, and the scent of him overwhelmed me like too much perfume.

I never had to say anything more than his name. He wasted no time. If I'd expected him to stall further, I was happily disappointed.

The moment that Shaz slipped inside me, the urge to howl rocked me. The sex wasn't anything similar to being with the vampire. Shaz and I didn't join on a metaphysical level. We were all about the carnal wolf and the personal emotion between us.

Shaz's fangs grazed my shoulder as we developed the perfect

rhythm. I gripped his lower back where I could encourage the depths he reached for. My clawed nails easily broke his skin.

Our lovemaking was frenzied but not rushed. We each had a need for the other that quickly took over, and the world outside faded. A series of growls, snarls, and moans filled the silence around us. His breath was hot against my ear as he panted my name. I met each of his thrusts in perfect rhythm as if we'd done this so many times before. Instinct led, and we followed.

I cried out in both pain and pleasure as he bit at my neck and shoulders. When the sensations grew to be too much, when I knew we were hurtling towards a thunderous finish, I braced myself and surrendered as the point of no return claimed me.

My back arched involuntarily, and I grabbed at him as if to pull him closer than he already was. The energy was like a tornado that had us successfully trapped in the center.

We resisted the return to a normal state of being. We lay there panting, wrapped in one another. We were both equally afraid to move and risk breaking the spell. I stroked his sweaty, disheveled hair. Laughing contentedly, I hugged him to me tightly. The tension, which he'd been holding in his shoulders, eased, and he kissed me lovingly. I inhaled the musky scent of sex that filled the room.

Shaz buried his face in my hair and took a deep breath before sighing, "I'm so in love with you."

My breath caught, and the pinprick of tears assaulted my eyes. I knew how hard the admission was, now, in light of last week.

"Shaz?" My voice was rough, edged with wolf. "I love you …. you know that, don't you?"

Silently, he nodded. We lay there wrapped in the comfort of each other until the sun began to sink in the western sky.

Chapter Eighteen

After two more vigorous rounds of intense lovemaking and a shower thrown in the mix, I was ready to go hybrid hunting.

I had invited Shaz into the shower, since getting clean was more fun with two. When we'd finally emerged from the shower, we were dripping wet and had goose bumps appearing in all the right places. After some aggressive bathroom sex, we had moved back to the bed and slowly, deliciously loved each other again.

I pried myself, reluctantly from the sanctity of his love. I wanted nothing more than to shut the world out and stay in bed enjoying him all night. I was stricken with fear that I may never get another moment like this one. Suddenly, Raoul and his mentally-ill daughter didn't feel like my problem.

However, nobody else was going to clean up this mess.

So, when ten o'clock rolled around, Shaz and I were waiting at the Tim Horton's coffee shop, a few blocks from Lucy's Lounge. Kylarai arrived minutes after us, and we waited on Jez and Kale who had both graciously donated some of their evening to my pathetic little cause. Ky and Shaz each sat across from me at the small table. I watched traffic as I sipped the heavenly strong coffee.

I left a message for Arys but didn't really expect him to show up. Part of me was downright terrified that he would. I'd be stuck in the awkward hell of having him, Shaz and me in close proximity.

I'd gotten lucky that evening, no pun intended. Jez hadn't been free until last minute, when her latest flavor of the week girlfriend had cancelled on her. Since Kale now owed me for that little brush with the demon, he had no excuses.

While Shaz and Ky made small talk, I feigned ignorance to my and Shaz's mingled scent. There was no fooling a werewolf's sense of smell. Detecting our intimacy took barely a sniff, but knowing Kylarai, she was thinking that it was about damn time already.

"Don't you think so, Alexa?" Kylarai asked with one eyebrow raised. I had a feeling the question had been repeated.

"Sorry." I shook my head and took a swig of the perfectly brewed coffee. "Don't I think so, what?"

"I knew you weren't listening." To Shaz, she added, "Maybe you guys should have stayed in bed. I think it's all she can think about."

My cheeks warmed instantly in a blush, but Shaz turned cherry red, which made me feel better. I kicked Ky lightly beneath the table, and she responded with a smirk.

"Anyway," I said. "What were you asking me?"

"I was just commenting on how fast Raoul's mental state will decline if you take out his kid. He's going to freaking lose it."

"If he ever had it." I commented.

Actually, Raoul's sanity was a nagging sore spot. He believed Zoey was savable despite her killing spree. I didn't tell him about this little excursion.

"He'd kill me before he'd let me lay a fang on her." I dug around in my purse and produced the photo of Zoey, with her haunting, sparkling eyes, and I passed it to Ky before I could feel guilty.

"She's a pretty thing." She forgot her coffee as she stared at the picture.

Shaz leaned over to get a good look. "She looks a lot like Raoul."

His expression darkened as he glanced behind me. He pointed, as I felt the approach of the cool, undead presence that I knew so well.

Adrenaline surged through me, and my heart skipped a beat. I couldn't hide anything from the vampire. He would know instantly about the romp with Shaz, and despite the fact that he had encouraged me, I was afraid that he would be less than enthused. Considering the timing of the flings, I was bordering on tramp territory, as far as my own personal standards went.

Those blue vampire eyes landed on me, and the look sent such a rush through me. I felt short of breath.

Across from me, Shaz reacted to my increased heart rate by brushing his leg against mine under the table. As wrong as it was, the urge to pull away from him was strong, and I fought to resist it.

Arys sat next to me, across from Kylarai and Shaz. I'd expected him to do something to embarrass me, but I was disappointed and thankfully so.

"Nice to see you, Kylarai." He greeted her with a grin and the briefest flash of fang. She just nodded and smiled.

That small glimpse was enough to thrill me in places beyond physical touch. I quickly felt guilty and tried my best to hide behind my coffee cup.

He then nodded to Shaz, and I froze. "How's it going?"

My jaw clenched, and my breath sucked in as I waited for Shaz's response.

"Great," he said with a smile that was more forced than Ky's had been. "You?"

Their attempt at casual should have been normal, but it smacked of phony. I got a sick feeling that they'd discussed me at some point without my knowledge. Had they both just been waiting for this awkward moment, fully aware that it would arrive?

Arys turned to me and smiled like a hungry cat. His voice dropped low enough to soothe when he said, "I've got to warn you, I haven't fed tonight. Let me know if it becomes too much for you."

I had felt the slightest hint of bloodlust when I'd first opened my eyes at noon, but Shaz's earthy Were energy had shifted the focus of my energy. Only now, within touching distance of that cool blue aura, did I feel that sickly twinge in the pit of my stomach.

I rushed to think of something to say. Awkward silences are the worst.

"Could you feel it when I shifted last night?" I glanced furtively around to make sure no one was obviously eavesdropping. I was incredibly aware of the heat in Shaz's energy. He hated this thing with Arys, and I couldn't blame him.

"You know, I can't say that I know the exact moment, but when I went to bed this morning, I swear I saw you in my dreams, two enchanting wolves with the scent of pine and rain in their fur." His tone dropped as he spoke, and my heart dropped along with it. Shaz looked perplexed, and Kylarai made no effort to hide her raised eyebrow.

"That was real." I didn't know what else to say. He'd seen us in his subconscious. I'd had strange dreams, too, though they had been random flashes of Arys's memories. I was annoyed that he'd earned extra insight through our link.

He nodded his acceptance of the reality. "You were beautiful." Those deep ocean eyes looked into me, and I fought down the energy that threatened to keep rising. Just as the moment became awkward, he looked at Shaz and said, "Both of you. Together. I've never been so envious of any creature."

That was carefully worded, suspiciously so. I couldn't help but wonder if there had been a double meaning to it. I'd felt him in my mind. Just how much had he seen?

"Thank you," Shaz said softly. I was painfully aware that something unspoken was passing between them. Arys was conceding that Shaz had something on him. I didn't like it one bit.

As I floundered for words, Kylarai cleared her throat, and all three of us looked at her. I hoped that neither of the guys noticed the grateful smile I shot her.

"So, what's our plan? We find her, and then what?" Kylarai downed the last of her iced cappuccino and fixed me with her grey eyes.

I slapped at a mosquito that had strayed inside. "Honestly? I'm not entirely sure. I'd kind of hoped we could hand her over to Veryl. He might have a safe place to keep her."

"Like imprison her?" Kylarai's tone said that she found the idea ridiculous.

"I don't know what else to do right now." A strand of hair kept escaping from behind my ear, and I huffed in irritation.

"Kill her." Arys spoke matter of fact, and though I agreed, death wasn't my first choice at this point.

"No. Nobody is killing her unless there is absolutely no other way. I want to talk to her."

"Where's Raoul tonight?" Kylarai grew thoughtful, judging my reaction.

"I don't know," I admitted. "I ignored his call earlier." He hadn't left a message, so I felt justified in my choice to screen his call.

"So, he has no idea that we're hunting his daughter tonight?" Shaz sat up straighter in his chair, his features pinched in disapproval. "Oh Lex, that's not cool."

I couldn't resist looking to Arys. I wanted him to validate my choice. His gaze bore into me, and I felt my power reach for him.

Like the humans in the coffee shop around us, neither Kylarai nor Shaz would see the power, but they'd be able to feel it. The growing power struggled to break free of our control. Maybe Arys should have fed after all.

"If Raoul knew, he would never let us find her." Kylarai pointed out. "He's really just afraid for himself. Typical selfish bastard." Her tune had certainly changed lately. She turned around and stared at the line. She didn't get up for more coffee. "Let's just grab her and take it from there. If worse comes to worst, we can just give her to Dracula, here." She gestured at Arys who smiled. "He can make short work of her in no time, and she'll die with a smile on her face."

Shaz gave Kylarai a disapproving look, but she just shrugged. The two of them often disagreed at random. Shaz couldn't understand how Kylarai could go from being the nicest person around to a ruthless, no nonsense killer. She on the other hand understood that he had yet to come to that point. That remaining innocence was part of Shaz's charm.

He wasn't completely naive. He simply couldn't relate to what Kylarai and I had lived through. Every one of us walked a very different road, but at the end of the day, we were still pack.

"Nobody is going to bleed her, except for maybe me. I might be on her hit list, and it may come to that." I gave everyone at the table a look that said I meant business, though I doubted anyone took me seriously.

Jez's white Liberty passed by on the highway just beyond the parking lot. I watched distractedly while she pulled into the Travelodge parking lot next door. Kale's dark haired silhouette was clearly visible in the passenger seat. My tension eased simply knowing that we could get moving and stop sitting in an awkward little circle.

"Let's just meet them out there." I waved to the Liberty through the large window, grabbed the coffee that I'd bought for Jez, and turned to lead the way out.

"Excuse me," I murmured as I squeezed between two ladies in line for coffee.

Outside, my shoulders eased and I realized how tense I'd been. I had to force myself not to run out of the building in a desperate attempt to put space between Arys and I. The pull was so strong that I wondered if he was encouraging it purposely. I blamed it on his hunger. If that was part of some pissing contest between him and Shaz, I planned to be seriously ticked.

In the parking lot, Jez reached for her coffee before she shut the Jeep's door. "Thank you. Damn girl, you can read my mind. I swear." She winked and licked her scarlet lips before sipping from the steaming cup.

She looked smoking hot in tight black leggings and a black tank. The golden hair piled on top of her head shone like she'd stepped out of a shampoo commercial. A glance down at my blue jeans, black ankle boots and basic black halter-top made me feel drab in comparison. It must be her golden hair. My ash blonde was not nearly so brilliant in contrast. Next to Kylarai and Jez, I felt like the girl next door. I'm attractive, but they are striking.

"I really appreciate you giving up your night off. I hope it's not a waste of everybody's time, but I need to deal with Zoey before she decides to deal with me."

I resisted the urge to take a step back when Jez leaned in close to breathe my scent. "Oh, you naughty girl," she purred as she glanced at Kale, who was greeting my small crew with the best fake polite act that I'd ever seen him pull off. "You finally did it." She grinned and winked slyly. I shot her a warning look that went ignored.

I waited patiently while everyone exchanged pleasantries, and the two vampires sized one another up. They'd met before but only briefly. The fact that Kale and I were strictly platonic seemed to be enough for Arys. His good behavior was surprising. So, he could be civilized and abandon the tough guy routine on occasion.

"What's your plan for nailing this target, Alexa?" Kale stepped up beside me. His mismatched eyes stood out in startling contrast against the black of his long jacket. "I'm hearing that this is a no kill hunt. Could you possibly be more boring?"

"Please, stop," I waved a hand dismissively. "You're going to make my ego positively huge with these sugary sweet compliments. And yes, for now, it's a hunt and detain. I'll sort out the killing stuff as we go."

I perused the five people who waited for my clearly thought out plan. Other than tracking Zoey down, I didn't really have concrete details.

"I guess we'll split up." I shrugged in response to their expectant expressions. "Three groups of two should make it easy to cover the whole town. Zoey's energy feels hybrid but she smells human."

"So pairing a shifter with a vampire would make sense," Kylarai spoke up. She gave Kale a roving once over. The first time that she'd met him at my office, she'd told me that she found him hauntingly beautiful with those eyes.

I nodded and surveyed the possibilities. I shouldn't be paired with Arys. I wasn't willing to gamble with being alone with him right now. His allure was too strong. Our energy worked on its own science. It didn't give a damn who I loved or why. It just wanted more of our power.

Kale's differently colored eyes darted between me and Arys. He sensed the bond between us. I wanted to ask if he could see the aural colors, or if all vampires were unable, but this was hardly the time.

I didn't have to look at Shaz to know he hoped to come with me. However, the testosterone-laden air spoke of envy.

To keep my focus on business, I didn't want to go with either Shaz or Arys. I considered pairing the two of them together, but that didn't sit well with me, either. Frankly, I didn't trust the vampire alone with my wolf. In the end, I smiled apologetically at Kylarai.

"I'll go with Jez. Shaz can go with Kale, which leaves Ky and Arys. Is that cool?" After they all nodded, Ky somewhat begrudgingly, I continued. "Since Ky brought her Escalade, we have enough vehicles to easily cover the whole town." I turned to Jez, indicating Shaz and Kale. "Do you want to give them my car or yours?"

"Yours is newer," she shrugged, her eyes on a leggy blonde exiting the Travelodge. "They can take mine."

Kale made a scoffing sound, as she tossed the keys to him, before flipping her off.

I delegated everybody to a different section of town and stressed again to take Zoey alive. "Kill her, if it's you or her, but I think we should all be capable of overpowering her."

In my hurry to get moving, I almost forgot about the photograph. When everyone had taken a good look and exchanged cell phone numbers, we were ready to move.

"What if we run into Raoul?" Shaz asked softly. He was so quiet that I couldn't be sure if he was upset or his usual, soft-spoken self.

"Try to avoid him I guess. Call me if you do see him. If we don't find Zoey within a few hours, we'll call it quits."

As everyone turned to go, Arys told me, "Be careful."

He surprised me when he kissed my hand in a way that made my blood run hot. A slip of his tongue on that soft stretch of skin between my pinky and ring finger made me shiver.

I was painfully aware of the wide-eyed horror etched on Shaz's face before he successfully forced neutral expression. I forcefully pulled my hand from Arys's and gave him an absolute death glare for his trouble.

"You, too." I did my best not to scream when he smiled in satisfaction and turned on his heel towards Kylarai's Cadillac.

Shaz quickly turned to the Jeep where Kale sat fiddling with the radio knobs. I grabbed Shaz's elbow and forced him to face me.

"Please, don't let him get to you. It's just in his nature. He's used to getting what he wants."

Shaz ducked his head so that his white blond hair hid his eyes. "I know. It just makes me crazy knowing he's bound to you."

"I know. But it's metaphysical, not emotional." I raised his chin up so that he met my eyes. "As good as all of that power feels, it isn't like what you and I have. You need to believe that."

"Don't worry about me, Alexa." He glanced at Kale, waiting in Jez's Jeep. "I'm not as fragile as you seem to think I am."

"This isn't about being fragile. This is about me needing you to know that, no matter what happens with Arys, he's not the one." My voice caught.

Did he know what I was trying to say? I couldn't possibly guess how deep this thing went with Arys, but I searched Shaz's eyes for some kind of confirmation that he loved me regardless.

As he pulled me to him in a soft yet strong embrace, I basked in the wolf scent of him, reluctant to let go.

"I'm not walking away from this, Alexa." He breathed into my hair. "Not now."

The emotion in his voice tugged at my heart, and I pulled back to look into his youthful face. His smile warmed me in places the vampire's cool touch just couldn't reach. It was all Shaz.

"Alright," he leaned in for a fast press of his lips to mine before turning to the Jeep where Kale feigned interest in a family parking their motor home across the lot. "We better go find Raoul's offspring and tidy up another one of his messes."

I had to laugh. He knew Raoul almost as well as I did. The back of my neck was stiff, and I just wanted this all to be over. Both Zoey and Raoul needed a supernatural psych ward. Did such a thing even exist? From what I knew of Veryl, he liked to take out the trash, not put it in a care facility.

The sun had set a while ago, yet the faintest pink glow remained in the western sky. Heavy metal music pumped out of the Charger, and I frowned. She was so bad for that. Jez had slid the sunroof all the way open, and I glanced nervously at the circling seagulls overhead. My footsteps quickened, my boot heels clicking loudly as I hurried to the car. I was not at all surprised to find her chatting up some ginger haired girl in the truck next to us.

Shaking my head, I used my hair to hide my smile as I climbed into the driver's seat and turned down the speaker volume. As Jez fished in her purse for her card, the girl's boyfriend, or so I assumed, returned with two coffees and a bag of muffins.

"Just in case." I heard her say as she handed the card through the open window.

"You're unbelievable." I tucked a gold chunk of hair behind one ear and started the engine.

"Why, thank you, Alexa. To what do I owe such a fine compliment?" A few stray strands of wavy hair had come loose to frame her heart shaped face.

"You put guys like Arys to shame." I tsked and looked over both shoulders before backing out of the narrow parking space.

"Good," she quipped.

I directed her hand away from the volume knob and signaled into traffic. She gave my hand a light slap, exactly the way a cat would, not quite enough to hurt but enough to exhibit her displeasure. Since she gave up on the volume, I didn't slap her back like I wanted.

"How can I not put them to shame? Most of them really don't know the first thing about women: How to understand them, or what to do with them." She pulled out a box of nicotine patches from her purse.

"So you always say." I glanced at the box in her hands while waiting for a red light to change. "Finally trying to quit?"

She strained against the confines of her seatbelt in an attempt to turn partially around. Fumbling with the waistband of her leggings, she peeled them down enough for me to see the milky white of her left butt cheek. I didn't notice the clear patch until she hooked a long nail under the edge and removed it. I did notice that Jez enjoyed going commando.

"Try me, Alexa, just once. You'll give up both of your men in a heartbeat. And yes, quitting again. Every time I turn around, Veryl's wagging a finger in my face." She slapped the new patch on to her ass and settled back in her seat.

My heart sped with an anxious beat. I'd heard her come on many times before, but she'd referred to both Shaz and Arys as my men.

"They are not both my men," I said tersely.

The guy in the next lane revved his engine, and I recognized the truck with the girl from the parking lot. Not wanting to encourage him, I eased off and allowed him to race ahead. "And why do you put it on your ass? Does it absorb into your bloodstream any better?"

"Which one of them isn't your man? Hmmm?" She winked a cat eye at me when I glanced her way. "No, it's just a good place to keep it out of sight."

I sighed. Technically, neither of them was mine but figuratively? I had to acknowledge the territorial claim I felt over each of them. I suck. I knew Shaz felt that Arys didn't deserve any piece of me, but I felt that I didn't deserve Shaz. He deserved so much more than what I could give him, but as long as he wanted me, I had no intention of cutting him loose.

I followed Golf Course Road through town towards Raoul's neighborhood. I wanted to check out some of the alleys and side streets. Hopefully, we wouldn't pass his Jaguar anywhere.

"If I were you," Jez began, as she reclined her seat, "I'd enjoy it. Two fine looking creatures that want to ravage you, how can you go wrong?"

"One of those creatures is a self-absorbed vampire and the other is someone sensitive and sweet that I don't want to hurt. This can blow up in my face, Jez. Stop thinking with your..." I realized what I'd been about to say and censored myself with a chuckle. She laughed, a musical sound like the tinkling of wind chimes. "What I meant is that the physical and especially metaphysical fun can lead to some real emotional distress. It already has."

"Well, you have a very strong energy. Honestly, I'm surprised that you don't have more power hungry wannabe lovers as it is."

As Jez spoke, her eyes lit on me with a weight that I could feel. She studied me intensely for a long, drawn out moment, and I saw her lick her full red lips. I didn't truly think Jez was into me. We're friends first and foremost. The flirty "try me once and never go back" was a running joke she had with many of her straight lady friends. However, did I think she might be attracted to me as a power source? I did now.

"Well, one is more than enough. At least with Shaz, there's a real foundation." I huffed impatiently at the guy in front of me. Could he possibly turn any slower?

"I like him. He seems like a good guy. And Lord knows, you could use one." She picked at one of her perfectly manicured nails, oblivious to the frown I wore.

Unsure if I should feel insulted or not, I said nothing. I scanned the streets and sidewalks, scrutinizing everyone we passed.

"So, where are we headed?" Her cell phone vibrated loudly, and she flipped it open to read a text message before punching buttons in response.

"Cruising the streets near Raoul's then heading to Lucy's. I know she's been in there even if I haven't seen her myself." A thought struck me, and I added, "There's another area, too, adjacent to my neighborhood. That's where she watched Shaz and I run this morning."

We cruised every street but Raoul's. For that one, I parked down an alley, and Jez took a quick stroll around the block. When I asked if

Raoul's Jag was in the driveway, she said no. The kitchen light had been on, but she'd seen no one.

Just after eleven, we pulled up at Lucy's Lounge. The place was already pretty packed.

"Is this place ever dead?"

Jez eyed the small group of ladies in the parking lot. An eyeful of short skirts and cleavage enhancing tops had her ogling like a kid in a candy store. We weren't even inside yet.

"Aren't you seeing someone?" I raised a quizzical eyebrow.

"I see a lot of people. There's no ring on this finger." She wiggled the fingers of her left hand too close to my face, and I slapped it away. "I'm not dead, Alexa. I'm always open to meeting that one lady that just knocks my socks off."

"Just one huh?" My wry smile wasn't lost on her, and I chuckled at her exasperation.

"Who are you to talk about having just one?"

"Ouch. Nice, Jez."

Inside, the aggravating sounds of a recent Top 40 hit made me long for Jez's heavy metal. The joint was packed with humans. It was strange to see the bar without Shaz. Most of the staff recognized me and nodded. A few of the local Weres were usually there, but I didn't feel their energy anywhere.

"Go ahead and grab a drink if you want," I said close to Jez's ear. "I'm going to use the restroom." I didn't have to tell her twice. I knew I'd come back to find her with a brightly colored cocktail in each hand. She just couldn't resist a fruity beverage.

After using the facilities and washing up, I was walking down the small hall back towards the bar when I felt someone's eyes on me. Before I could turn to look, the lightest touch on my elbow had me startled into a defensive stance. It was just a human girl, and I relaxed until her scent hit me. It was David's girlfriend, the one who had lied to the police.

"I'm sorry," she shouted to be heard over the bar noise. "I didn't mean to startle you."

Mustering the best, forced smile that I could, I replied with a lame, "That's ok."

"I wanted to thank you." Her eyes were downcast, and the scent of fear and anxiety trickled from her. I was keenly aware of her heart accelerating, the blood rushing inside her, just waiting for that perfect puncture to release it. Goddamn it Arys, I thought briefly. You've made me a monster.

I considered playing dumb. How in the hell could she recognize me? It had been dark, and I hadn't looked this human.

Oh, God help me. I'm such a fool. I should have killed her, too. The thought came unbidden, and I knew that it wasn't mine. However, I had to acknowledge that the vampires' logic kept them touted as fictional. They have to be ruthless to stay alive.

"Oh, that's alright." I felt more awkward staring into her beaming smile than I had sitting with Arys and Shaz earlier. I was at a loss for words. My eyes went over her head, searching for Jez's shock of gold hair in the crowd.

"No really. I probably shouldn't have approached you, but I didn't want to risk losing my only chance to thank you. He made my life a living nightmare. I was ready to kill myself."

I had to give her credit for being wise enough to avoid saying David's name. There was obviously no use trying to convince her that she hadn't seen something she knew damn well she had.

"Anyway," she continued, suddenly in a rush to finish. "I can't tell you what you've done for me. I don't regret a thing about any of it. And, whoever or whatever you are is no business of mine. My lips are sealed." Her eyes took on that wide solemn look of a child making a sincere promise.

My smile felt small and tight, but it reached my eyes. I had to appreciate her guts. I can't say that I would have approached the person that had grown claws and fangs before eating my boyfriend. Courage was an admirable trait, though it could be stupid.

I offered her a hand. "I'm glad you're alright."

"I'm Amanda." Could her smile possibly get any wider? "It's nice to meet you."

I didn't like the spark in her eyes. I'd seen humans like this. My supernatural power and allure enticed her. This was often temporary but could be potentially dangerous. Fanaticism is a form of insanity.

"Likewise." I spotted Jez who was making her way to a group of college girls shooting pool. From where I stood, I could see the electric blue cocktail in her hand. "Look Amanda, I'm sorry but I need to get going. Have a really good night, ok?"

I excused myself before the strange moment could drag on any longer. I hoped she didn't take it the wrong way when I hightailed it across the club to Jez.

Yeah, I felt like an asshole, but really, what could I possibly say to the girl? Thanks for not telling the cops that I ate your boyfriend? The bastard turned my stomach anyway. Besides, the scent of her blood was giving me a cramp.

"I saw that you found a pretty thing to chat up so I wanted to have some fun, too." Jez raised her glass in greeting, downing half in one sip. "No sign of our target. Think we should move on?"

I pulled my cell phone from my pocket and found one missed call from Raoul, which likely meant that he was looking for Zoey, too.

"Yeah, we'll go as soon as you're...." My words broke off. Her glass was empty. "Ok then. We'll go now." That was fine by me. I wanted to get out of there before Amanda thought to approach me again.

"Raoul called about ten minutes ago," I told her when we were back in the car heading down the near empty main strip. "I think he's looking for her."

"No voicemail?" Jez looked longingly out the window as we passed the 7/11. She was thinking about cigarettes.

"Nope."

"Then, it couldn't have been that important."

Typical of the small town, those who were not out for the evening were at home in relaxed comfort or already sleeping soundly. Most of the homes we passed were dark or dimly lit. I got back on to the main drag and followed it to my end of town. Once, that section of town had been the rich part, but over the years, it melded into the other old parts of town. Main Street, no longer the main drag, is a tiny business street and older than dirt. Buildings with painted murals give it the impression of being part of an old movie backdrop.

"What a cute house," Jez commented as she perused the houses with real estate signs on the front lawn. "This looks like a great place to live. So cozy."

"Yeah, well, it used to be. It's growing a little too fast for my tastes, but it's still home."

The last thing I wanted to see my little town turn into was a city with a condo on every block. They were already beginning to make an appearance on the outer edges of town where the land had been sold for development. We were just minutes away from two cities, was it necessary that we be one?

A town like Stony is perfect for new Weres. Put one in the busy city center on their first full moon and see what happens. Not pretty. As long as I have the field out my back door linking me to the forest, everything is all good. If they developed it into a Starbucks and a shopping center, I was moving to a rural location on the double.

I turned into The Glens, the neighborhood with the street that ran adjacent to mine off the field. We still saw no sign of Zoey anywhere. When I got out, to get up close and personal with the area, I could sense the remnants of the hybrid energy that Arys had tuned me into, but it was long faded.

She hadn't been here recently, and I couldn't tell where she'd gone since. I growled in frustration and scanned the field from this angle. I tried to picture Shaz and I as both Zoey and Arys might have seen us, but I couldn't do it.

"That's a pretty negative energy, even for a hybrid," Jez said, following my gaze to the empty field.

As a full-blooded Were, she could feel supernatural energy stronger than the average shifter though she wasn't adept at manipulating it.

"You known a lot of hybrids in your time, Jez?" I slid a sidelong glance at her, curious now.

"A couple." She shrugged as if it was no big deal. "I didn't know either of them very well, but I can safely say they weren't the happiest of people." Her gaze drew distant. "A suicide and an accidental overdose. I guess it's not the easiest existence."

An image of Belle's brutalized corpse flashed behind my eyes, and any sympathy that I might have felt for Zoey vanished. Her personal vendetta with Raoul was strikingly similar to my own, but I wasn't willing to murder over it. She had no excuse.

"That's terrible." I breathed. "I almost wonder if Zoey is doing all of this so that someone will take her out and end her misery."

Jez studied me. I met her cat eyes evenly. "Do you think it's a good idea for you to be so wrapped up in this? I mean, a hunt shouldn't be personal. You know?" Her tone was carefully neutral, but I bristled at her judgment anyway.

"No, I guess I could just go home in time to catch some good late night TV and paint my toenails. That would take care of everything." The sarcasm in my tone came out far heavier than I'd intended. I had to bite back a further snappy remark that came unbidden, dancing on the tip of my tongue. "I'm sorry, Jez. I'm stressing out. This growing damn vampire bloodlust doesn't make it any easier." I tried for an apologetic smile and lifted my hands in surrender. "That's no reason to be a bitch, I know. Pun intended."

"You are so lucky that I don't just kick your ass right here." Her crossed arms and narrowed eyes betrayed the joking tone she forced into her words. If she'd been leopard right then, that gold and black tail would have been twitching like mad.

"I know." Even though I said it, we both knew that a real fight between us would be a pretty tight match that would never happen. Sure, we had faced off for fun, but we never went beyond sparring, thankfully. I couldn't imagine anything really causing us to stand against each other in a true fight to the finish.

When my phone rang, we both jumped. A bad feeling settled into the pit of my stomach, and I went cold. My palms were damp when I flipped open my phone.

Arys was on the line rather than Kylarai. Adrenaline coursed through me when he said calmly, "Alexa, you better come to Squires Sports Bar. Kylarai's been stabbed, and Raoul's half breed is on the run."

"What happened? Is Ky ok?"

Jez and I dropped our minor bitch session. I turned back toward the car, and Jez was already a step ahead of me.

"Just get over here."

The phone went dead in my ear as Arys hung up. I had the car on the road in seconds with a screech of tires.

"Kylarai's hurt. They found Zoey." I mumbled to Jez who nodded as if she already knew. "I don't know how bad it is."

Squires Sports Bar is a billiards bar near the highway. It's a place to catch the latest hockey game and consume pizza and wings. It definitely wasn't a regular part of my evening experiences.

"I didn't think she would turn up in public so obviously. She must be asking for it."

"Me neither. Arys said she's on the run. We have to hurry."

The five-minute drive felt like forever, and I gave a little cry of frustration when we approached the train tracks on Golf Course Road. A slow moving train effectively blocked the two closest crossing points. To access the one near Raoul's neighborhood, I'd have to make a U-turn and cut around town in a partial circle. The trip would be faster if we waited it out, but waiting is not one of my strong points.

"Just relax, wolf girl," Jez murmured with her voice low and soothing, a cat's soft purr. "It'll be less than a minute."

She reached over and gently stroked the back of my hand with one finger. It wasn't a human urge, but our animal instinct to comfort another. Despite our difference in animal form, Jez and I had forged a pack bond.

The thought that Kylarai was hurt because of Raoul's dirty little secret had my gut clenching. I was scared and pissed. Then, suddenly, the sweet copper scent of leopard blood was at the forefront of my senses. I fought the rising bloodlust as it fed on my fury.

"Fuck!" I slammed my hand angrily against the wheel. "I've got to get out of here."

I made a motion as if to take off my seatbelt, and Jez grabbed my wrist. "Where in the hell do you think you're going? The end of the train is right there."

When I threw the car into park and opened the door, she held firm. I panicked, and anxiety choked me. I couldn't fight Arys's demons and help Kylarai. The close confines of the car smothered me in the alluring scent of blood pumping from a healthy leopard heart. I was sick with worry that Jez may have to kick my ass yet.

"Close the door and drive, Alexa." Her voice was icy cold, as if she was aware that she was dealing with something more than me.

The end of the train passed. Two vehicles came from the other side of the tracks, and I shut the door rather than risk losing it. Resigned, I shifted into gear.

"I'm losing my mind, Jez. Don't hold it against me. It's that damn vampire. I can't get him out of me." One hand gripped the steering wheel until my fingers tingled, while the other hit the button for the automatic window.

"I slaughtered a man two nights ago," I rambled on, staring intently at the road. "A human. He was abusing his girlfriend, and the hunger hit me. I lost it."

When Jez spoke, her tone was carefully neutral. However, not a drop of fear rolled off her. "We do that all the time, Lex. We take out the trash."

"The supernatural trash though, the ones with a chance to fight back. This guy, he didn't even see it coming." I laughed bitterly. My anguish did nothing to ease the cramp in my guts. "His girlfriend did though. That pretty little thing chatting me up in the bar was his girlfriend, thanking me for setting her free. She lied to the cops, you know."

Jez's sudden chuckle startled me, and I looked at her. "Shit, it doesn't matter what monster you are, humans will always be the worst of the bunch." When I lifted an eyebrow and shook my head, she added, "Take a look around. Everything humans do is destructive and for their own selfish gain."

"Hey now," I admonished. "Just because you weren't born human doesn't mean none of us were. But yes, for the most part, I agree."

As we talked, I focused on the scent of Were rather than the scent of Were blood, an important difference. The hunger that chewed at my guts simmered down to a nagging but dull roar. Interesting.

As we got closer to the sports bar, my temper returned. I was outrageously angry with Arys for allowing this to happen. We were supposed to maintain our weaknesses, not inflict them on one another.

A dark figure moved in the shadowed parking lot across the street from the sports hangout. I recognized Arys when he stepped into the beam of a streetlight. He motioned for us to pull behind the building to the back alley where we'd be out of sight from those passing by.

Jez called Kale, read the street address off a sign and snapped her phone shut. Kylarai's white Escalade sat with the rear facing us with both doors open on the driver's side.

Arys jogged up as I cut the engine. Time seemed to stop and crossing the short distance between our vehicles felt like slow motion.

Kylarai slumped against the back seat with one hand pressed tightly to her side. Blood seeped between her fingers. She was fully conscious, but her small smile did nothing to ease her pained expression.

"Oh, she's Raoul's kid, alright." Her voice came out strained. I reached to touch her but stopped short as the scent of her blood hit me. "Who else would throw such a low blow?"

"Don't talk, sweetie," Jez crooned as she crouched in the dirt beside the big Cadillac. "Let's have a look."

The interior light was dim, but I saw the oozing gash when Jez gingerly lifted the hem of Kylarai's shirt. The scent beat down my control, and I whirled on Arys so fast that I almost lost my balance.

"Tell me what happened. And when you're done, you can explain why you let this happen to me tonight."

His dark brows drew together, and he looked down his narrow nose at me with a cool stare. Perhaps he felt the bloodlust less intensely than I did. Due to his power and age, he should, but Arys was the insatiable type. I couldn't determine what he was feeling.

"We found Zoey Roberts inside the sports bar. She took off the moment she realized we were there. Kylarai chased her down in the parking lot, and the crazy bitch pulled a blade." He sniffed lightly at Ky's powerful werewolf blood.

Every one of my cells raged at me to lash out at him, but the vicious shadow dancing behind his eyes held me in check.

"I couldn't go after her without leaving Ky behind," he continued, his gaze unwavering. "So I let her go. But, Ky sure put the attack on her first. Once the knife was pulled, all bets were off."

"So Zoey's injured too?" I felt hopeful.

Going easy on her was no longer on my agenda. She blew it. Raoul's plea to keep her alive meant nothing to me now. With the way I was feeling, Zoey would be jealous of poor dismembered David when I was through with her.

"Oh yeah," Arys laughed low and smooth, tickling my insides. "Ky got in a few good digs. She didn't try to play nice. Wherever Zoey is headed, she is bleeding and roughed up. We can track her."

I understood now and felt absolutely moronic. "That's why you haven't fed? So that you can track her easier?"

"Of course." He looked at me like I was asinine for asking, and I shot him a dirty look. "I'm a vampire. It's all about the hunt and the kill for me. Appeasing the hunger eliminates the driving force of the hunt. You're a predator; you should know."

217

I did know but not the way he meant. My predatory urges were more inclined to slaughter anything nasty that walked with a human form rather than the deer and bunnies of the world. Kill Bambi and Thumper? No thanks. However, supply me with a psychotic vampire or child abuser, and I'll gut them with a smile on my face. My predator had a logic that Arys's bloodlust did not.

I turned back to Kylarai. She patiently allowed Jez to bind the wound with shreds of Ky's shirt. The blood was slowing. She should be fine.

"I offered to try healing her injury but she wasn't comfortable with that." Arys shrugged as if it made little sense to him. It made sense to me. Kylarai wasn't comfortable with vampire power in general.

"So, what are you waiting for?" I directed my words at Arys as Kale and Shaz rounded the back of the building in Jez's Liberty. "Get tracking Zoey."

"Not without you." Arys squinted against the headlights and raised a hand to shield his eyes. "We can track her on foot while they attend to Kylarai. They can meet up with us once we've found her."

My gaze went to Ky. Her grey eyes sparkled with determination, but her jaw clenched in pain. "Go get that bitch, Alexa. I'll be fine. Go now before she gets much farther."

Shaz and Kale climbed out of the Jeep. Shaz ran to join us around Ky.

"Did you call Fox?" I asked at the same moment Shaz said, "Fox is on his way." I had to smile, just a little.

"Great. Have him head to my house. Kale, please go with Kylarai and Shaz-,"

"Don't tell me to go with them. I'm not sitting this one out." Shaz gave me a look that I knew well, the one that dared me to tell him otherwise.

"Fine, but I'm going on foot with Arys. Zoey is bleeding, and we can track her. Drive my car and keep your phone handy. Head to Raoul's. I think she might go there." I didn't give anyone further chance to contest my instructions. I wanted to get moving while the blood hunger was still within my grasp rather than the other way around.

Jez stood up from tying the strips of cloth around Kylarai's middle, tight across the healing wound. "I'll follow Shaz with my car so

Kale can jump in here with Kylarai. See you on the other side." I nodded and gave her arm a friendly squeeze.

Shaz accepted the keys that I placed in his hand. The buzz of his wolf prickled my skin unexpectedly. He was wound tighter than a guitar string.

"Alright, I'm taking off. Give Raoul a call on your way." I resisted the urge to rub my hand where we'd touched. "He's been calling my phone."

"He called mine, too, but I didn't answer."

Ky raised a blood-covered hand silently to indicate that she too had gotten and ignored a call. Raoul had to know I was hunting his daughter. Well, he could save his temper tantrum for when I got there to kick his ass personally. Hopefully, Zoey didn't beat me to it.

I leaned down to face Ky and squashed Arys's hunger deep inside me. I nuzzled the side of her face, similar to what Raoul had done to me. I wished we were in fur on four legs.

"Take it easy. I swear she's dead for this," I assured her.

Her eyes pleaded with me to hurry.

"Alexa?" Shaz caught my elbow, and I met his eyes. "Please be careful."

I reached up to tousle his hair gently. "I will. I promise." There was nothing else that I could say. "I'll see you soon."

Because I couldn't sink into his arms the way I wanted to, I grabbed my phone from the Charger and gestured to Arys to lead the way.

Chapter Nineteen

We started in the parking lot of the sports bar. Zoey's blood hung on the still, muggy night air. With Arys's bloodlust, I easily picked out the scent of human amid Kylarai's pure Were aroma. With no rain or wind to interfere, tracking Zoey was almost too easy, barely a challenge.

She most certainly headed towards Raoul's end of town. I dialed his number as we went and hailed his voicemail with a litany of my favorite curses. A sick sensation of dread settled in my stomach.

"There's no answer." I was hot and itchy in my skin. The instincts that drove me commanded me to ditch the restrictions of a human form and go as wolf, but I had to wait until the time was right. As great as the advantages were, pulling fur in the middle of town wasn't something I wanted to add to my list of stupid moves.

"Maybe she's already there," Arys mused with his head cocked to one side as he studied the stars.

I hesitated for just a moment when her trail led across the golf course. It was the fastest way to Raoul's. The well-maintained green was soft and springy beneath my boots. It felt good enough to roll in.

Though Zoey ran only ten to fifteen minutes ahead, she was long gone. She was faster than the average human, but she was injured. That didn't seem to be slowing her down though.

I suspected that she'd already made it to Raoul. I considered letting them battle it out. Raoul was impossible to talk to, and I wouldn't be surprised if she killed him before we arrived out of sheer frustration.

On any other night a trek through the dark, deserted golf course would have been nice, maybe even a little sexy. The silver moon shone brightly against the dark backdrop of the sky. No one was in sight.

As if reading my mind, Arys nudged me playfully. "Do you think Raoul can take care of himself if we take a five minute time out?" When I raised my eyebrows and shook my head he added, "Alright, alright, a ten minute time out."

"Very funny."

"Would you do it with the wolf pup?"

His question nearly brought me to a halt as I stumbled in the grass. "What's it to you? Don't tell me you're going to get all jealous male on me, too."

"He was jealous?" I heard only amusement in his tone. I didn't have to look to know he wore that amazing grin of his.

"That's not the point. You told me to go to him. Don't start playing the territorial card or so help me, I'll knock out a few of those perfect teeth."

He laughed loudly, and I jumped. I was a real ball of nerves tonight.

"Don't get me wrong, my love, a part of me is a little envious, but we have something that extends well beyond sex, deep into the power of our metaphysical make up. Something that so many will never know." In a motion so swift I barely saw him move, he caught me up in a kiss. It was brief but sweet, leaving me breathless. "But, I also know that I must be realistic."

He turned away, walking ahead, but I'd already caught the somber note in his dramatic words and action. Drawn to him, I took a hurried step to catch up.

"Wait. What do you mean by that? Realistic."

When he stopped, I got the feeling that he didn't want to look at me, but he did anyway. I think he was afraid that I'd see the emotions lurking behind his eyes, waiting to betray him.

"You're an incredibly complex creature, Alexa. A strange combination of the compassionate human heart and the ruthless leadership of one of the finest animals on earth. Our journey together is far from over, but I know that you will never long for me at the end of the day."

I found no trace of regret or anger in his voice, merely acceptance of the fact. I was tongue-tied and unsure of what to say. I looked eagerly to the street ahead as we neared the end of the golf course.

"Shit, Arys," I poked him lightly in the side. "Why are you getting all sentimental on me? Is it because you think she's going to kick my ass?" I forced a laugh in a lame attempt to sound like I was kidding.

We came out in a gated community just a few blocks from Raoul's street. We hopped a wall. Dogs started a chain of barking, which had me hauling ass over the stone wall onto the street beyond before the ruckus brought people out on their doorsteps.

When we stood at the end of Raoul's street, I called him one more time. A shiver raced up my spine when somebody picked up.

"Alexa O'Brien," purred the most sensual female voice that I'd ever heard. "The woman my father both loves to hate and hates to love." There was a pause, and I heard her take a ragged breath. Ky must have got her good.

"Have you killed him yet?" I cut to the chase, sounding both bored and irritated.

"What?" She snapped, and I stiffened.

I fixed my eyes on the darkened house down the empty street. Arys, tense and ready beside me, brought me more relief than I wanted to admit.

"You heard me. If you've already killed him then I won't waste my time by coming in there."

"You're sick, bitch." Her reply was snide.

The need to kill grew overwhelming. I snapped my phone shut and strode angrily down the street. My boots clacked loudly, announcing my arrival.

"It's not that I don't think we can easily take care of this pathetic little problem, but where is everybody?" Arys gestured to the empty street. No Charger or Liberty was in sight. The mournful sound of a train whistle blew. They were stuck on the other side.

"Don't tell me you're nervous about facing a human half breed without back up," I teased.

I couldn't help it. I was anxious as hell and having a hard time thinking about anything that didn't include blood and violence. Even the presence of the powerful vampire at my side was trying my patience, encouraging me to quench the undying hunger that cut up my insides.

"Hell no." He didn't miss a beat. "Just afraid of being in a house with two wild women." I felt his gaze suddenly narrow on me. "Are you going to be alright?"

"I don't know," I admitted as I shoved my shaky hands in my pockets. "Just don't let me kill the wrong person."

He nodded. "Let's go inside."

The curtains were drawn in the front window, but a light shone beyond. I thought I saw a flash of movement.

I reached out instinctively for Arys's cool, inviting hand. Our auras wasted no time mingling, and I welcomed the cold vampire energy.

When I reached for the doorknob, it wouldn't budge. I hadn't really expected an open invitation. I glanced at the doorbell but didn't bother.

I braced myself with the stair rail. I focused on the soft spot below the knob and let loose with a high kick. The door frame splintered in an ear piercing shriek of tearing wood. The door hit the wall so hard that it bounced back at me, vibrating on its hinges. The front sitting room was empty. I wasn't looking forward to venturing inside.

"Beautiful," the vampire breathed.

A jolt of his power rushed through me, and I embraced it. I wanted to go in there tapping every power source I had. If the crazy bitch thought she was going to knife me, I'd blow her through the damn roof.

"Do you smell that?" Arys stalked past me into the house while I lingered uncertainly near the doorway.

He had a lilt to his voice that indicated the effect our combined power was having on him. I can't say that I wasn't happy that it was a battle of control for him, too.

Zoey's blood was thick on the air inside. Drawn by the scent of injured prey, I followed the tall, dark vampire.

Muffled voices reached me. They were in the windowless study off the kitchen. They had to know we were here. The front door had been anything but quiet.

Our footsteps were silent as we made our way into the large kitchen. I paused in the threshold between both rooms. Raoul's beloved wolf tapestry hung in tatters. Only claws would do that.

As I took in the damage of Zoey's rage, the energy in the house shifted. At Raoul's office, Arys stopped mid-motion as he reached for the doorknob. He risked a glance back at me and his pupils were huge.

I panicked when I saw him vamping out. I needed him to maintain the power that we'd called. I opened my mouth to tell him not to blow this when the office door suddenly burst open.

Raoul crashed through the opening, narrowly missing Arys as he tumbled and rolled. The vampire appeared at my side with his body positioned to defend an attack.

Raoul was gracefully on his feet in an instant. With one hand outstretched, he pointed an accusing finger at me.

"You," he snarled. "It's because of you that Zoey's hurt. If she dies, I'll fucking kill you, Alexa. You promised!" A harsh cough wracked him, and he spat blood on to the pristine white tile.

In an instant, I held a psi ball in my palm. "She stabbed Kylarai!" My voice was shrill enough to hurt my own ears. "I'm not playing by anyone's rules here, Raoul."

He was pale, the bruises lining his eye and nose appeared darker in contrast. He licked a drop of blood from the corner of his lip. He'd been letting her smack him around. Pathetic.

"I can't be held responsible for Kylarai's choice to get involved in something that doesn't concern her."

Though he was speaking, my eyes were on the study door. I could feel her approach, and I licked my lips eagerly. I felt that same crazy smile, Arys's smile, that I'd worn when I'd slaughtered David. It adorned my features so naturally. The blood hunger seemed to hone in on the creature in the house that I wanted the most.

I had a good mind to tear out Zoey's throat while Raoul watched, before letting Arys go at him. Wouldn't that just be the most delicious fight?

Zoey appeared in the doorway to the small office. Her black hair hung to hide most of her round face. She didn't look much like the smiling young girl in her picture. This version of Zoey Roberts was anything but striking. She looked like a Japanese cinema ghost.

Her skin was whiter than Arys on a bad day. Dark circles lined her eyes, and her dark blue wolf eyes were glazed. Her clawed fingers were bloody but the absence of fangs was a good sign. If she went completely wolf on us, she'd never come back.

Her clothing was all black. The rips and dirt on her jeans marked her scuffle with Kylarai. I didn't see a weapon, but I assumed it was there. A jagged, blood-caked slice marred the white skin of her throat. The inside of her forearm showed bone where Kylarai had got her.

Zoey held her injured arm carefully at her side as if trying to hide how much it hurt. Her strange, blue wolf eyes blinked at me appraisingly before going to Arys. She believed him to be the bigger threat. I loved how wrong she was.

"How dare you barge in here like you own the place?" Zoey spoke to me but seemed reluctant to take her gaze off Arys for longer than a split second. "This has nothing to do with you, Alpha bitch."

"Oh no?" With a flick of my wrist the swirling blue and gold orb exploded against her and showered colorful sparks overhead. I grinned when she went down on her rear end with a pained cry.

"When was it going to involve me? When you decided that it was my turn to die for letting your daddy coerce me into bed? I don't think so."

"Alexa, stop!" Raoul made a move towards me, and I raised a hand in defense. Before I could throw another energy ball, my dark vampire took Raoul down with a foot to the back of the knee.

"Wasn't it you that asked for Alexa's involvement in the first place?" Arys hissed. He twisted the bigger man's arm behind his back with an inhuman strength. "You're at the root of this entire mess, so why don't you keep quiet while the ladies fight it out? You'll get yours."

Raoul grunted in pain. His ebony eyes glared at me as he refused to acknowledge the vampire holding him immobile.

I'd winded Zoey with the psi ball, but she scrambled to her feet. "You don't get to kill him!" She screamed like someone who hadn't known sanity for a very long time. It made me stop to consider my plan of action.

"Who's going to stop me?" I challenged.

Fangs filled my mouth. The sticky blood that adorned her wounds was sweetly human. I ached to taste her human blood, laced with the energy of the wolf. I wanted her to rush me, the final push to finish what Kylarai had begun.

I didn't expect her to break so easily. A torrent of tears streamed down her face, and a sob broke from her. Her misery pained and confused me amidst my need to kill.

"I didn't do all of this just to have you take it from me. Kill me if you must, but I'll be damned before I die without killing him first." The girl's determination was admirable. All she wanted was to make Raoul hurt. I could relate to that.

"Does it really mean so much to you?" I met her gaze evenly with my own wolf eyes. "To kill your own father."

I followed her eyes to where Raoul knelt, straining against Arys's powerful hold.

"Yes," she conceded with her chin held defiantly. "I thought I wanted to bring him down, have him locked away in some wretched facility like he did me. But now, I just want this over."

"Zoey please," Raoul ground out through clenched teeth. "We can talk about this. It doesn't have to be this way."

I couldn't believe he was so convinced they could talk it out and live happily ever after like a sitcom family. His reaction was deeply disturbing on a level that I didn't understand.

"You're fucked, old man." Zoey scowled but didn't attempt to pass me in order to reach him. "You never cared about my well-being before I murdered your bitches. Why would you start now?"

She sounded resigned, as if she'd anticipated this discussion for a long time. I wished I could erase the past week and never let Raoul drag me into this in the first place.

Hunger and instinct gnawed at me, and I fought the urge to shift. My mind was running in the "act now, think later" mode.

"I always cared about you. There has never been a day that passed when I haven't thought about you." Directing his temper at me, Raoul shouted, "For God's sake Alexa, could you call off your vampire?"

"I don't think so." I shook my head and my dyed gold bangs fell in my eyes. "You both need serious help."

The deathly glare that Zoey shot me was worth a thousand nasty words. "What do you know about growing up with a deadbeat father who's responsible for the death of your mother? He left me to suffer, surrounded by people that he knew I could never relate to."

She ran a hand through her stringy locks, and I was reminded of Raoul's penchant to do the same. "Do you have any idea what it's like to live each day trapped in this body while your every instinct cries to get out?"

After a moment of silent contemplation, I shook my head no. I didn't. But, Arys did now, and the sympathy shining in the depths of his stunning eyes was too much for me. If we started to identify with her, her death would be that much harder.

"I can't relate to that." I shifted into a stance that appeared less threatening but didn't release the energy I held ready. "But, I can relate to being scared and inhuman. And being in need of a strong leader but finding none."

"Alexa." Raoul's tone rose in warning at the end of my name. Arys jerked his arm enough to make him gasp.

"Shut up." Zoey and I spoke simultaneously.

"Your father is a self-centered egomaniac, Zoey," I said, finding strength in the incredulous expression splayed upon Raoul's finely sculpted features. "As long as I've known him, he's been selfish, conceited and intent on his own personal interests. You were better off not being here during your youth. I can guarantee you that."

"Thanks a lot, you bitch." The hate in Raoul's deep voice struck me to the core. "After everything I've done for you, after I save you from being raped and used like a piece of meat, this is how you repay me?"

My face flamed with the sudden heat of embarrassment. My wolf wanted to throw off this skin and make the short work of him that he so richly deserved. So, he wanted to air our dirty laundry, did he?

"You saved me Raoul? My ass you did. What kind of knight in shining armor do you mistake yourself for? You turned around and took me to your bed. I was seventeen, damn you. You took my innocence, all I had left!"

Overcome with long repressed emotions, I took a step toward Arys and Raoul. I launched my ready energy so that it blasted a hole the size of my fist in the floor between Raoul's trembling knees.

"And don't you dare start with that shit about how I was willing. I was a new werewolf, and you took advantage of that. You're seventeen years my senior, yet you claim no responsibility."

I stood before him shaking as I stared down into his dark eyes. Aware of my bloody desires, Arys released his hold, but Raoul didn't attempt to get up. The power in my eyes had him wary.

My mind was a mass of confusion as my senses were overwhelmed by the lovely sources of energy to consume. I wanted to taste all three.

"What the hell are you?" Raoul murmured. An entranced expression smoothed his face into a look of wonder.

My eyes focused on the pulse in his throat. It leapt so very fast beneath his skin. I moved to brush his hair away and bent to breathe in his familiar scent, the perfect mix of cologne, man and wolf. Desire reared its head inside me, and I almost gagged on it. The urge to taste his hot blood dripping on my tongue was so powerful, accompanied by the need to have him writhing naked beneath me. My mind was swimming as I fought Arys's hunger.

I sensed a sudden motion behind me; in the same moment, Arys sprang into action. I gave Raoul a shove that sent him reeling. The heavy thud of bodies colliding sent a sick chill through me as I whirled around. Arys pinned Zoey successfully to the floor, but a new rage surged through me when I saw the glint of the silver knife handle lodged in his side.

"Arys?" Adrenaline hit me hard, and I dropped to my knees beside him. "Are you ok?"

Zoey was squirming like a junkie on *Cops*, but he held firm with one forearm tight across her airway. "Yeah, just get it out."

As my fingers touched the handle, the jolt of pain in my side was instant, and I nearly lost my grip. The phantom of his pain felt so very real. With one solid pull, I drew the blade from his body. Bright vampire blood shone wet on the knife. The energy within his blood was as delectable as the scent of fresh roses. A crimson stain grew on Arys's t-shirt.

Across the room, Raoul was on his feet, but stiffness limited his movements. I worried that he would shift in order to compensate.

"Get the fuck off of me." Zoey growled. Four sharp canines distorted her words. Arys gave her a backhand that even made me flinch, yet she didn't cease her struggle.

Before Raoul could even consider intervening, I threw an energy wall between him and us. The clear sheet of immoveable power wouldn't last long if I didn't feed it continuously, but it would keep him occupied for a moment or two.

Voices reached me from beyond the broken front door. "Wait," I heard Jez say in her no nonsense, ringleader tone. "Something's not right."

I'd say. The half-breed wolf from hell was a real pain in the ass. With our backup in place, I took a moment to lift Arys's shirt. The wound was already healing.

"It's cool, Jez," I called. "Come on in."

"What in the fuck?" Raoul slammed his large fists against my barrier, causing a faint ripple. The wall held, though. "What do you think you're doing, Alexa? Damn you. Let me out of this damn thing."

"I'm fine," Arys admonished as I studied the healing stab wound. "Trust me, I've had worse." When I raised an eyebrow in response, he added, "Seeing you with my eyes is absolutely heart stopping."

Crap. That's why Raoul had reacted the way he did to me. I was suddenly very afraid to turn and look at Shaz.

"Alexa? Are you guys ok?" Jez's head poked into the kitchen from the front room. She took in the scene before her with little surprise. "My, isn't this interesting?"

Shaz was barely a step behind her, and he faltered when he saw me on the floor next to Arys with my matching blue eyes. Slowly, I got to my feet, brushing non-existent dust from my knees.

"Kill her," I said to Arys, unable to take my eyes from my white wolf. His presence alone was creating the balance that I didn't know I'd been missing.

"No!" Raoul's voice thundered through the house, and my energy wall dropped.

With no hesitation, the vampire forced Zoey's head to the side and bared her beautiful throat. God help me, but I eagerly anticipated the moment her blood would flow. As Arys sunk fangs into her tender flesh, Raoul growled and leapt.

Both Jez and I reacted, but she was faster. Raoul's weight was at least twice that of hers, and they rolled in a ball of flailing limbs. The angry yowl of a pissed off cat filled the silence as they grappled tooth and nail to gain the advantage.

I hung back and waited for an opening. To use metaphysical power would risk injury to Jez. I feared Raoul would overpower her simply because of his desperation to save his daughter.

Turning to Shaz, I found him hovering between the front room and the spacious kitchen. I saw the conviction in his eyes, and it cut deep.

"Shaz?"

"You have his eyes." The disbelief was strong in his tone. He could barely look me in the face.

"Shaz, I need you. Don't you see that?" I positioned myself so that I could see the entire room.

Jez and Raoul took out two of the four table legs with a crash. A decorative fruit basket hit the floor hard enough to send grapes flying like bouncy balls.

Shaz looked at me with lost puppy eyes, and I grew desperate for him to understand. "I need you to balance out what he does to me." I reached for him. I needed his wolf so badly that I could taste it.

"I can't share you with him." His jade green eyes flicked to the feasting vampire then back to me. "Lex, she's shifting!"

When Zoey's human body had ceased fighting for life, the wolf trapped within her was free to take over. The essence of the wolf flowed over her, and she began to shift beneath Arys. Blood spilled from his lips as he put a safe distance between himself and the writhing creature on the floor.

Raoul had Jez pinned beneath him and growled down into her face. He gripped both of her slender wrists in one hand, while the other stroked a claw along the soft skin under her chin. I didn't waste another second. I kicked him in the temple with as much force as I could muster.

He must have been seeing stars from the way that he slumped over with both hands on his head. Jez got to her feet. I watched as she picked a chunk of long black hair from a perfectly shaped claw. Her previously sleek up do was now a mess of long, tangled curls in disarray about her shoulders.

"This isn't good," she murmured, watching the spectacle in the middle of the floor.

I didn't want to watch, but what choice did I have? I whispered a prayer beneath my breath that Zoey wouldn't get stuck in mid-shift, a horror too cruel for anyone to endure.

"Lex?" Shaz's evident worry mirrored my own.

On the floor, Zoey writhed and flailed as if having a seizure. Her hands reached and flexed over and over as clawed fingers became fully formed paws. I wanted to look away from her face, but I just couldn't. Her face lengthened and narrowed into a muzzle. The worst high-pitched wailing filled the house. Her shift was so slow and agonizing.

It dawned on me that shifting might be a good idea right about now. I slipped out of my top and jeans, thankful for the steady rush of power and adrenaline that prevented me from feeling any embarrassment. Once I was furry, the awkwardness would be left to Shaz and Arys.

"Watch my back."

I directed those famous last words at Jez and my two lovers before I freed the side of me that was scratching to get out. Much like springing the latch on the cage at the zoo, I went down on my hands and knees and was wolf before they touched the floor.

This kitchen wasn't going to be big enough for all of us if everyone decided to sprout fur. This had to end quickly. My one weakness was that in this form I had little to no use of my psychic side.

I'd have to trust Arys with that as I trusted Jez and Shaz to be the fangs and claws at my back should I need them. I had a feeling Raoul may be the unpredictable one here.

'If I didn't know better,' a cool velvet voice echoed in my thoughts. 'I might think the lady wolf has feelings for me after all. I'm honored to have your trust.'

'How is it that you're able to do this when I'm wolf?' I thought back to what he'd said in the coffee shop about seeing me running with Shaz.

I knew I'd sensed his presence then, but I had been distracted by Zoey. Our link seemed to vary quite dramatically based on what form I was in. Strange.

'Be thankful for limitations.'

Raoul leaned heavily on the kitchen counter. Heavy lines in his face betrayed his distress. Four ugly cuts marked his neck as well as his face just below his right eye. I doubted if he could stand much more.

He stared in mixed horror and relief at Zoey. With her slow metamorphosis complete, a small black female wolf stood on shaky legs and fought to get her bearings. She was wearing a wolfish expression of absolute shock. She sniffed the air and eyed each of us in turn. With a gentle swish of her thick tail, she shook off the remnants of her shredded clothing. She pawed lightly at the floor and a confused whine escaped her.

Raoul moved with the instinct of a parent to comfort her, and she turned on him in a blur of black with her hackles raised and her lips peeled back in a snarl. Hands up in defense, he stared down into her dark face with a strange look on his hard features.

I wanted to speak, to warn him not to get so close. I wasn't sure how much of her human mind remained. All of it, I hoped.

I glanced at Arys, as if he should speak for me, but he carefully ignored my eyes.

What the hell was Raoul thinking to walk up to her like that? She could tear his balls off and spit them back in his face before he could react. Ok, maybe not. She didn't know how to use her new body yet, but her instincts drove her actions.

"Might want to back up a little, buddy," Arys decided to give voice to my concern.

He had moved so that he stood a few feet behind me, where he could also see the entire room. His fingertips danced with blue energy outlined in yellow gold.

Raoul didn't look up from Zoey's true wolf eyes. "I'm not your buddy, you useless fucking vampire."

Everyone else immediately looked at Arys. I expected him to launch that power ball at the arrogant werewolf, but Zoey and Raoul had eyes only for each other, though they wore extremely differing expressions.

I felt rather than saw Arys bristle because he never moved a muscle. An absolutely wicked smile tugged at his lips, warming my insides against my will. He gave me a quick wink as he sensed my reaction to him. I wanted to glare, but my furry eyebrows wouldn't form the expression. Cocky vampire.

"Zoey please, you have to listen to me." Raoul begged, his tone both pleading and placating. "I can help you through this. But, you have to trust me."

I scoffed mentally to myself. This was ludicrous. The man had truly lost his mind.

"You can't do a damn thing, and you know it. She's not ever getting back into a human body." Jez feigned casual with her crossed arms and relaxed stance against the fridge. She was in a good position to keep everyone trapped within the kitchen with just one step. The double paned glass sliding doors were an unlikely exit for those of us without fingers.

"Shut up!" Raoul snapped. He glanced at the leopard who clearly wanted another shot at clawing his eyeballs out. "None of you have any right to be here."

"We were invited. And now, we're not leaving until somebody's dead, or Lex decides you're not worth all this trouble." Jez nodded in my direction.

A sliver of guilt nagged me. I shouldn't have dragged my friends into this personal drama.

'You know she didn't mean it that way.' Arys's voice was soothing in my mind. 'We're all going to call in our favors down the line.'

'Stop that.' It felt like a mental fly that I wanted to swat. 'I don't even want to hear your favor.'

Arys chuckled aloud, and everyone but Zoey turned and looked at him. She took advantage of the moment to lunge her newly gained weight into Raoul. The fool never saw it coming. She hit him hard in the chest and took out his legs easily. They slid together in a heap across the tiled floor. With a snarling wolf in his lap, Raoul did the only thing he could with less than a second to react. He threw his arms up to protect his face and throat. All four of Zoey's fangs sank in the tender underside of his forearm. Dissatisfied, she released her hold and struck again.

I winced inwardly at Raoul's blood and crossed the twenty feet separating us in a leap. I threw all of my weight into Zoey, taking her down in a frenzy of snapping jaws. She twisted beneath me in a struggle to get to her feet. When I got a mouthful of thick flesh at the back of her neck, I held tight.

Shaz dragged Raoul to his feet. The bigger man was bleeding from both arms, long red rivulets that fell to stain the white tile.

When I felt Arys's reaction to the fresh blood, I was glad that he'd sated the worst of the bloodlust. I wasn't sure that I could have maintained control otherwise. I resisted the urge to look at Shaz, my stronghold of control.

Powerful jaws closed around my front right leg as Zoey scrambled to get a hold on any part of me. I gave a small yelp of pain, certain this would result in a broken wrist.

A scuffle broke out behind us, and I worried. I could only see the top of Zoey's head from my angle. I let her go so that she would let me go, and we sprang apart. My leg ached. Even the minor bite left my ash colored fur with bloodstains.

I wasn't expecting Shaz and Raoul to be throwing punches like they were in a bar fight. Raoul had a heavier fist, but Shaz had actual brawling experience. I could only assume Shaz had been watching my back while I fought with Zoey.

Raoul let loose with a fist that knocked Shaz back on his heels. Shaz's instant reaction was an elbow to Raoul's jaw, followed by a head butt that sat the large man down on his ass.

Arys stepped between them before I could ask. Jez stood her ground in the doorway, but her watchful gaze never missed a thing.

Despite my attack on her, Zoey really didn't want me. She was all about her father. Seeing him down, she rushed me but veered to the side as I moved to meet her. I fell for her fake out, and she had no problem clearing my reach. With fangs bared, she covered the space between her and Raoul.

Arys released a blast of power straight at Zoey. At point blank range, the shot hit her square in the chest with enough force to move an elephant. I never had time to react before her body struck me and knocked my feet out from under me.

We were airborne, a tangle of fur that snarled and growled. The sound of shattering glass screamed through my sensitive ears. The world rolled before my eyes, and I identified the patio doors as we smashed through them. I did my best to tuck and roll as the shards sliced into me, leaving a hot burning sensation everywhere they touched.

Upon clearing the doors, Zoey and I were thrown apart. Each of us hit the wooden deck hard. I landed in a heap against the massive barbeque, my legs splayed, and my body aching.

Jez called my name as she fumbled to get to me without cutting herself. I lifted my head to indicate that I was ok, but the red blotches staining my fur said otherwise. I caught sight of the particularly large chunk of glass protruding from my side and panic set in.

As I scrambled to my feet, I noticed the growing pool of blood beneath Zoey's still body. I began turning circles in a desperate attempt to dislodge the glass shard from my side.

The entire frame of glass had shattered out of the side that we'd gone through. Shaz and Jez had ducked through but stepped carefully as the broken glass crunched beneath their weight. Shaz peeled off his shirt and began tearing it into strips while Jez approached me with her hands held up in caution.

I whimpered softly to let her know I was alright, not wound up enough to attack. With a gentle hand against the side of my face, she turned my head away from my body so that I couldn't see them picking the glass out of me.

A fresh commotion erupted inside. The unmistakable sound of bodies colliding carried through the broken door.

"I'm going to watch the light fade from your eyes as I drain every last drop from you, wolf." Arys's voice shook with a menace that I'd never heard from him before. "If Alexa's hurt, consider yourself a walking dead man, Raoul." Another series of smacks and bangs were followed by a grunt of pain.

Please God, I thought. Just let this end.

I yelped when Jez withdrew the largest shard from my side. Shaz came to hold my muzzle lightly in his hands. One finger stroked the side of my nose. When she pressed a piece of his torn shirt to my side, I whimpered and tried to pull away.

"It's ok, Lex," he whispered, but his voice betrayed the worry that he tried to hide. The stink of fear on him tantalized my senses as it chilled me to the core. "Just hang in there."

The sound of more glass crunching reached me as Raoul stumbled through the hole where his patio door had been. His eyes went to Zoey, and he fell to his knees beside her, unaware of the glass digging into his legs.

With the faintest twitch of her tail, I knew Zoey wasn't dead. I watched Raoul bend down to bury his face in her silky fur, and I held my breath in anticipation.

Arys appeared in the shattered doorway. His shoulders sagged when he saw me. "My beautiful wolf…"

He never moved closer. He merely stared at me with a sadness that looked so wrong in his blue eyes. With my face in Shaz's hands, I could only look up at my dark vampire as the pain began to set in on a deeper level.

"I think that's all of it," Jez said, tossing a chunk of glass aside. "You have some nasty cuts, Lex. You need stitches."

Hell no, I thought. I don't do needles.

I took a tentative step, and the pain slashed through me. I think I had a broken rib or two. My leg was numb, and fatigue was setting in from the blood loss.

I sensed Zoey's movement before she even twitched a muscle. I made as if to lunge, but I wasn't close enough.

She opened her eyes and leaned into Raoul's exposed throat with fangs bared. My eyes widened in horror and disbelief. Blood, warm and lupine spattered my face as I cleared most of the glass debris in a jump.

I stopped short of an attack when I saw clearly that all four of her fangs were buried to the gum, a gruesome, mortal wound. He'd bleed out in a matter of minutes at best.

Raoul stared at me as the blood gurgled in his windpipe. I recognized the challenge in those coal black eyes even as the light ebbed out of them. He was willing to fight me away from his daughter even as she killed him.

My heart constricted with emotion and blood loss. I took a respectful step back as guilt washed through me. I'd known she wasn't dead.

'No, my love,' Arys's honey sweet voice came from the shadows of my mind. 'He chose this death. He doesn't even struggle.'

Arys was right. Raoul clung to that stupid wolf as if he were a boy and his dog, stroking her black fur, so like his own.

I whimpered and growled, unable to watch this without being able to act. A key player in my life, no matter how positive or negative, was dying before my eyes. I couldn't do this. Zoey had to die.

"Alexa, don't." Shaz's command was softly spoken but a command nonetheless.

Shaz stood behind me as if he'd grab my tail to hold me back. I didn't give that wolf enough credit for how well he knew me. "It's not your fight anymore. It's over now."

How could it be over? The bitch was lying in a pool of blood and still wasn't dead. In seconds, Raoul's body went limp, his hands relaxed in Zoey's fur.

My continuous growl became a snarl when she struggled to her feet, leaving Raoul face down in the broken glass. She stank of blood and death. My every instinct demanded that I finish her off.

"She's not going to make it far," Jez came to stand next to me, and I longed for my human voice. "Let her go."

Were they all completely mad? This was insanity. I looked to Arys for support but he gave no indication as to what he thought was best.

'I can't let her walk off this property alive,' I conveyed.

'That's your decision to make, but she'll be dead before she reaches the edge of town.'

I couldn't stop the snarling and snapping at the air. I was infused with this hate that filled me to capacity. My very nature demanded that I kill her after everything she'd done.

Zoey met my eyes with a look of clear understanding. She was running on borrowed time, and she knew it. Even if she survived the coming day, I would come for her.

Her muzzle was matted with Raoul's blood. One leg dragged awkwardly behind her, and she was a mass of cuts. The few steps down to the grass below the deck proved to be an obstacle, and she stumbled a few times while looking back at us, expecting an attack.

The battle between wolf and human raged inside me as it had so many times before. I wrestled with conflicting urges and emotions. I hated myself when she disappeared from sight.

I padded up beside Raoul, and with my muzzle in his hair, I sniffed for any sign of life. Nothing. I felt physically ill. Something broke inside of me, deep down, in a place that I hadn't acknowledged in so long.

If this all had nothing to do with me, why did I feel like it was my fault? I should have killed her the moment I stcppcd in the house. *I'm sorry, Raoul*, I thought, *Sorry it all had to end this way. If only you'd told me sooner*. If Arys was aware of my thoughts, he gave no indication.

As the adrenaline began to subside, the pain reached intolerable. My side continued to trickle blood, and a wave of dizziness led the blackness to close in on me.

"Shaz," Jez's voice sounded so very far away. "She's blacking out."

I went down on my face in a slick puddle of blood and crushed glass.

Chapter Twenty

In my incoherent dreams, I saw the black wolf, the one that I so admired in my wistful youth. Images sputtered and jumped from one to another. The past flashed by, in all of its horridly disappointing glory.

I'm still not sure if it was my guilty subconscious or really Raoul, but the scent of him was so real. I wanted to reach out and touch him, to sink my fingers into his soft fur. I'd curled up against that fur when the change was still so new and surreal. I couldn't touch it, though; my fingers went right through him when I tried.

The pain of my broken heart far surpassed that of my battered body. In my unconscious state, I mourned the loss of the black wolf as surely as if it were the loss of some great part of me. How would I go on without him?

At some point, I had the vague sensation that I was held tight in loving arms. The scent of my white wolf soothed and lulled me into deeper sleep.

I'd shifted back to my human form. I had a moment of worry as I wondered where my clothing was, but soft material wrapped around me, and the thought vanished. I allowed the scent of Shaz to comfort me as I accepted the returning darkness.

When I finally awoke, with a blinding headache, I was safe in my own bed. Shaz held my arms pinned above my head so that I couldn't lash out at Fox as he went about cleaning and stitching my wounds. Sheets covered my breasts and pelvic region, but the rest of my lacerated body remained exposed.

The faint light of the approaching dawn cast a pretty, pink glow on Kylarai who sat at the foot of my bed. Her encouraging smile was a welcome sight.

I resisted the urge to fight off the two men that insisted on poking and prodding me. Fox was just doing what we paid him well to do, and Shaz was ensuring his safety as he did so. I let out a low moan as pain stabbed through my side. A white bandage was wound tightly around my ribs just below my breasts. I hurt when I breathed.

Ky was injured but clearly ok, which made the agony more bearable.

"You may have a concussion. Take note of any extreme headaches, vomiting or dizziness over the next day or so." Fox's touch was as gentle as his soft, brown eyes. This wasn't the first time he'd tended my wounds.

"Where's Arys?" I coughed as the words stuck in my dry throat.

When Shaz was sure I'd behave, he released my arms and handed me a glass of water from the night table. He frowned in response to my words, but I wanted to know.

"It's sunrise," Kylarai's gentle voice was soothing. "He spent the last few hours cleaning up at Raoul's. He said he'd take care of everything. No worries." Though she directed a smile at me, her grey eyes went to Shaz in apology.

"There we go." Fox gave a tug on the final stitch, and my stomach turned at the sensation. "No shifting for three days. You should be well enough by then."

"Thank you, Fox," I whispered, reaching out to accept the fuzzy blanket that Shaz drew up over me.

Fox rose to leave but paused on the threshold to the hallway. His cheeks flushed, and his eyes were downcast. "I'm sorry about Raoul. This is all very unfortunate. Call me if you need anything else at all." Before we could reply, he ducked out of the room. His feet scuffed down the hall in his hurry to leave.

Ky made as if to follow him, but Shaz motioned for her to stay seated as he followed Fox to the front door.

"How do you feel?" I asked when we were alone. "I was worried."

She laughed softly then winced in pain. "You were worried? This is just a flesh wound. I hear you challenged the patio door."

"It challenged me." I fussed with the pillow at my back, careful not to move too fast. The thought of ripped stitches was creepier than stitches in general.

"Lex," she touched my ankle through the blanket. "What happened with Raoul ... it's not your fault." Was my self-blame so common that it was now expected?

If I closed my eyes, I could see the ebony wolf running to take down my attacker before he could steal my innocence away. I saw him as the hero that he'd been to me as a teenage girl, a blossoming woman.

The truth was, I had indeed given myself to him, my reward to the prince who'd rescued me. It was my own youthful naivete that led to my first heartbreak. I had expected a fairytale romance, and he'd been a werewolf. He acted on instinct and accepted my gift.

I confessed none of this. I accused him of manipulating and taking advantage of me because I'd never been able to deal with being nothing more than a bedmate to him. My childish picket fence dream had gone up in smoke. It wasn't meant to be, or at least, not for me.

But ultimately, that hadn't been Raoul's fault. He was the most selfish man that I knew, but he had died willingly. The paradox made my brain throb.

I accepted the hand that Ky extended to me. "I just wish we'd cleared the air."

She nodded; she understood the absence of closure. "Arys said he'll be by after sunset." She hesitated and looked at the doorway as if expecting Shaz to appear. "They got into it pretty bad. Playing the blame game. You know. Arys wanted to heal you but Shaz wouldn't let anyone but Fox touch you."

I sighed. There was nobody to really blame for the drama and tension between Shaz and Arys but me. How did I get myself into these situations?

"Did Kale take care of you? He better have." I grinned when a full-fledged blush accompanied her reluctant smile.

"He was a perfect gentleman. I didn't once get the impression that he was wondering what I taste like."

"Oh, he was. He's just had a few centuries to practice hiding it."

We laughed lightly together but it was strained. Forced. I could tell that Kylarai had cried upon learning of Raoul's death. Her eyes were bloodshot, and the tangy scent of salt lingered on her skin.

When Shaz returned, she gave my hand a warm pat before excusing herself despite my insistence that she stay. As soon as we were alone and those green eyes met mine, I started to come undone.

On the bed with me, he took my hand so that it lay clasped within his. "Are you ok, Lex?"

"Yeah, I'll live. I promise. Don't blame Arys. It was all circumstance."

"That's not what I mean." He shook his head, causing his platinum hair to fall into his eyes just the way I loved it. "Are you ok? Do you want to talk about what happened with Raoul?"

He gave me a look that said he knew there was so much more than I'd been letting on. Tears flooded my eyes, and I made a pathetic attempt to blink them away.

"I let him die thinking I hated him." My lower lip trembled, and I felt the sob seconds before it broke from me.

I couldn't say anymore, and he didn't push me. As he pulled me carefully into his arms, I sunk against his comforting embrace.

For the first time in a long time, I dropped all my guards and allowed myself to feel raw emotion as I sobbed into the hollow of his neck. So recently, I'd held Raoul in much the same way as his hot tears streaked moist paths along my skin.

I hated that I hadn't realized. I hadn't known it was the last time we would ever have a chance to leave our bitterness aside. Perhaps, that was our closure. If only I'd known.

The entire day passed in bed with my white wolf at my side. When Arys came by that evening, I had just convinced Shaz to go to work. I insisted a day of healing had already done wonders for me. He didn't want to leave me, but after I promised to stay home with Kylarai, he begrudgingly went and swore that he'd be back after last call.

Arys filled me in. He'd arranged Raoul's house to look like a break in. The authorities labeled him a missing person of interest in the murders of his lovers. They could launch a nationwide manhunt, he would never be found.

Arys grasped my chin so that I was forced to meet his eyes. I felt the quiver of power begin deep down inside.

"I know it's my fault that you were hurt so badly. I can't tell you how terrible I feel." The strange silence surrounding us thickened. "Your wolf is right. I don't deserve to have what it is we share."

His admission, though touching, was wrong. "Arys, that's not true. I know you'd never do anything to intentionally endanger me. I trust you."

I realized then that we were all carrying around guilt. And whatever for? It wasn't doing any one of us a damn bit of good.

Arys was careful not to touch me too much. His sly, mischievous tendencies were absent, and without them, his comfort felt shallow. Still, he refused to leave my side until Shaz returned.

Once Shaz's blue Cobalt turned into the driveway, the vampire leaned in so close that I was unable to resist him. He pressed his lips firmly against mine and pushed healing energy into me as he had before.

My pulse quickened and leapt as my blood pressure rose. Our auras blended and a rejuvenating breeze swept throughout my insides. The warm tingle that began in my stomach slowly spread to encompass my entire being, and I gasped when he broke the contact and rose to leave.

"I have to go." He looked like he wanted to stay as badly as I wanted him to. "I have to feed this bloodlust before dawn. I don't want it to rise between you and your wolf when you're in such a weakened state."

"I can't shift for three days. Promise you'll come to me if you can't go that long." I could see that he was itching to go before Shaz made his way inside, but I wanted his word.

He gave a silent nod but didn't touch me, as if he didn't trust himself. I longed for him and the energy humming around us, so I appreciated his restraint.

"Will you come by tomorrow if I'm not up to going out?"

"I promise." He drew an X over his heart, blew me a kiss, and disappeared through the door. His footsteps were silent as he went.

Shaz's frown told me that he'd passed the vampire on his way in, but when I held my arms out to him, the complaint died on his lips. I needed the comfort that only came from him. I never wanted to make the mistake with Shaz that I had with Raoul by hiding my true feelings.

"I need you," I whispered when he closed the bedroom door and turned to me. "Just hold me."

When his warm nakedness curled around me, I snuggled in close and enjoyed the scent of Shaz and his intoxicating wolf. It was a comfort all its own.

"Never leave me." I heard my own sleepy voice murmur the words against his ear with candid and vulnerable but honest emotion.

"Never." His embrace tightened just enough to be possessive, and my wolf relaxed, satisfied.

I was right where I wanted to be. The world could have stopped right then, and I would have died happy.

Chapter Twenty-One

I never did find Zoey's body. Oh, I tried. The trail ended two blocks from Raoul's house, at the creek. Despite a vampire attack and one hell of a beating, she'd survived. I knew it.

Since that night at Raoul's, I've picked up her scent more than once in the forest where we run. It's always days old and never too strong, as if she'd been there only briefly.

Was it a taunt? An open challenge to destroy her? Or was it a desperate plea for help?

I don't care. The need for her death is deep in me. Only the challenge in Raoul's eyes as he lay dying stops me, though I don't know why. I wonder all the time why he chose to give his life to her. The real estate career, fancy house and flocks of women that had ruled his existence had meant nothing in comparison to what Zoey believed.

He'd wanted her to believe in his love, and he felt the only way to show her was to give her vengeance. At the end of the day, my feelings didn't really matter. He simply waited too long to reach out to her. But, I know all too well that the reasoning behind some of our decisions doesn't stand to reason at all.

I was back on my feet within the three days that Fox had estimated. An ugly scar marked where the largest shard had impaled me. That, too, would eventually fade to nothing.

Over a week after Raoul's death, Arys shared with me what he'd found. He had called for me, adamant that I come to see him at his house.

Instinct told me, without a doubt, that it was bad news. He made me promise to run first to "get the wolf out" before arriving at his place after midnight, alone. I was filled with dread, shaking all the way down to my little black sandals when I rang Arys's doorbell.

His solemn expression did nothing to ease my anxiety. He drew me into the well-lit kitchen, took my light jacket, and offered me a hot chocolate. I couldn't stand this beating around the bush.

"Alright, spit it out." I tossed my hair out of my face and took a deep breath. "Whatever it is that you have to say to me, get on with it. The suspense is driving me mad."

He wouldn't meet my eyes, and I followed his gaze to the white envelope lying on the round, wooden kitchen table.

He picked up the envelope and fingered it lightly. "I found this in Raoul's study, taped to the bottom of a desk drawer. I was combing the place for anything unusual that the cops would be better off not finding."

He paused, and I knew that he'd already read it. "It wasn't sealed or addressed to anyone from the outside so I opened it. I have to warn you, Alexa, what you read here will change you forever."

My mouth went dry, and I stared blankly at the stark white envelope in his hand. "Why bring me here? Why not give it to me when you came to see me?"

"I wanted to be sure you were back on your feet. This just seemed safer."

"Why?" My heart was racing, and I was truly afraid.

"Read it. Unless you don't want to."

Of course, I had to. Raoul had left something for me, something, perhaps, that he'd wanted to say to me. I stared at the letter warily but accepted it from Arys's outstretched hand.

My hands shook, and I fumbled to slip the lined paper from the envelope. As I unfolded it, a battle waged between my head and my heart. To open or not to open.

The letter was recent, dated the same day as our last real discussion. As I began to read, everything in me gradually came undone.

Alexa,

A part of me prays that you never learn of this while I live, but I fear my time will be cut short, and I cannot go to my grave with this haunting me.

I have always loved you and regard you with more respect than you will ever believe. I know that you feel little for me, and for that, I am both saddened and relieved.

After Naomi's death, I swore never to love again. Love had become a plague to me, one that withered everything it touched. But then, I met your mother, and I loved her at first sight.

Trapped in an unhappy marriage, she came to me for the comfort and attention your father no longer gave. She grew to love me, too. Upon discovering this, your father became desperate to save their marriage. I did all that I could to hold on to her, but her vows and family came first. She soon told me it was over. I would have done anything for her. She meant so much to me, and I only wish I could have walked away and allowed her to be happy like she so deserved.

Instead, I gave in to my weakness, the possessive nature of the wolf inside. The bitter taste of rejection brought back terrible memories of Naomi, and with it, all of the pain and rage that I'd suppressed for so many years. I flew into a jealous rage and committed the most horrendous act of my existence.

After all this time, I still cannot believe you do not recognize me, the monster behind my eyes. I murdered your family and made you a werewolf. Words won't express my regret. I never imagined that I could take the life of someone I so loved.

You may hate me, but I assure you, I have hated myself more than you can imagine. I will never forgive myself for what I've done.

I need you to know that I would beg your forgiveness, if I thought it would earn me even a little. There is nothing I can do. I know this.

I have altered my will to leave you everything except a small trust fund set aside for Zoey, should she ever accept it. I'm sorry, Alexa, because I know I am your worst nightmare come true.

I never deserved your loyalty.

Love Sincerely,
Raoul

It couldn't be true. It just couldn't be. No, not Raoul. Of all of the werewolves in the world, please God, not him!

When I collapsed against Arys, I was overwhelmed with anger, pain and shock. I sobbed but failed to identify the rage-filled shrieks as mine. My fangs and claws appeared instantly, and I scratched at the floor, pulling uselessly to break free of Arys's strong embrace. Snarls and growls became part of my cries as I screamed in a wordless wail.

I lost all sense of reality as I reacted to everything that I'd just learned. I wanted to kill, but my victim was already dead, which fueled my agony in the worst of ways.

Raoul should have bared his throat for me. I should have torn through his hot, living flesh in search of retribution. I felt hate in a whole new way, and I knew that I'd never truly hated before.

The power between Arys and I rose in a sudden storm, fueled by my rage. He'd wanted me here to keep me from harming myself or someone else. I so badly wanted to. At home, it would have gone very horribly wrong. I wanted to become absolute destruction.

I fought against Arys, but he held tight. I lashed out with a good right hook, and we both stopped grappling and stared at one another. Blood welled up from a cut on his lip, and I felt both shame and excitement.

"Arys, I'm sorry. I don't know how to control this."

My words were inaudible to me, but he nodded in understanding. "Go ahead and let it out. I'm here."

Tears rolled down my cheeks, and I took a long shuddery breath before licking the blood from his lip. The tiny drop shifted my frustration and pain into another outlet.

I tore his t-shirt using clawed fingers. I couldn't stop there once his well muscled chest was bare before me. The urge to hunt, to kill, drove me as I took him down like prey, naked beneath me.

Our lovemaking was anything but loving. It was rough and raw. I released all of the pain that would never truly go away. I couldn't shake the thought of Raoul taking my mother's love and life. I shook with the need to tear him apart myself.

At some point, I sobbed again, and Arys accepted the angry energy admirably. I'd never felt so vulnerable, and yet I knew this was safer, here with my dark vampire. He readily accepted the tornado of my emotions and the physical assault that I launched. Shaz couldn't witness this side of me. The very thought was frightening.

The energy that we created was stronger than before but was also somehow easier to control and direct back to the natural elements. Not a single thing went awry. Talk about progress.

For hours after the sun rose, we lay together in his giant, fluffy bed. The TV on the antique bureau was on low. I stalled, unwilling to go home because that meant showing the letter to Kylarai and making everything real all over again. This was something that I had to share with those close to me. Otherwise, it was going to eat me alive.

When I finally did leave Arys's, I hit the drive-thru for coffee before heading to the little park just off the highway. I loved that park, with its full bridge over the pond and the fountain in the middle.

I walked around the large pond to the bridge. People sat near the playground or went in and out of the tourist office, but the bridge was all mine. I sat down so that my legs hung over the side with my arms crossed against the railing.

I read that damn letter over and over, feeling something different every time. I briefly toyed with the idea of letting it flutter from my hands to the water below.

I cursed aloud, a vent that had nothing to do with vampires or werewolves and everything to do with human nature. I ranted and raved my confusion and dismay to Raoul as if he could hear me because I feared that I'd lose my mind if I didn't let it out.

In my time on the bridge, staring out over the park with my half-consumed coffee, I gave voice to the betrayal and disappointment inside, but no forgiveness. That mercy escaped me. I wept hot, salty tears that carried no trace of blood, just the pure cleansing release of my sorrow. I could not shake the insane anger I felt over the fact that Raoul was dead and, with him, the final confrontation I desired.

The conversation with Kylarai was easier than I'd anticipated. I handed her the letter and watched her grey eyes grow misty. After a long silence, she choked out, "Are you ok?"

I shook my head no, because I wasn't, but forced a bitter smile anyway.

"Oh, honey." Her arms went around me, and I allowed myself to soak up her sisterly affection. I didn't realize how bad I'd been craving the comfort of pack, of family.

Kylarai and Shaz had been my family for several years, but now they felt like so much more. The knowledge of why my mother died did nothing to make me miss her less, though it did bring everything full circle by answering the question that I'd carried for years.

The fact that Veryl knew all of this wasn't lost on me. I debated on whether or not to call him. As soon as the sun fell, I dialed his personal number. With the pain so fresh, I had to call.

"So, he told you." Veryl didn't sound in the least bit surprised. "He had said that he planned to."

I bit my lip so that I wouldn't say anything to him that I'd regret. "Veryl, I need to know more about Raoul. You've known he was the one that attacked me all this time. Why not tell me?"

He took a moment before answering, and I knew he was weighing his answers. "Alexa, there is much that I must keep quiet for a reason. I'm sure you understand. However, in this case, I worried about your well-being."

The wheels turned in my brain as I tried to put it all together. "My well-being? How long have you known about me? I'm guessing it's been much longer than the last five years I've worked for you."

"Of course. Raoul atoned for what he'd done by taking you into his small town pack. He was to keep you safe as you developed into womanhood."

And, as my abilities developed. I could almost hear the unspoken words that he wasn't saying.

"You knew I could work energy."

"Everyone can work with energy if they choose, Alexa. You were born conducting it, natural. That ability in a werewolf is priceless, of course I was interested in you." His firm tone held no placation. He remained the practical businessman.

I felt burned that he had kept me in the dark, ultimately for his own purpose. Though Raoul hadn't been the ideal role model, Veryl had ensured that I'd been safe through my first difficult years as a Were. None of this was really Veryl's fault. It was Raoul's.

"Can I ask you why you didn't just kill him after he murdered my family?" My hands were sweaty as I tightened my grip on the phone.

"Those decisions are never the same for each situation. It was an isolated incident. And like I said, he and I struck a deal."

Business, like everything, my fate was just business with Veryl. Did that vampire ever make decisions based on emotion or instinct? Was he always straight practicality?

"A deal? He killed my family in a fit of rage and almost killed me as well." Bitterness was hard in my voice, but I knew he wouldn't react to it.

"He didn't... and now, he's dead." A short pause as he spoke quickly to someone in the background. "What do you want to hear, Alexa? I am sorry for the loss of your family, but I made the choice that I felt best at the time."

I sighed. There was no point in taking out my undying resentment for Raoul on Veryl. That wouldn't earn me anything. I couldn't blame Veryl for treating it like he would any other situation. He wasn't personally involved.

"Nothing. I'm just having a hard time handling this." There, I was honest. I couldn't see any reason not to be. "I think I need a few days to myself before I'll be any good to you."

"Take as much time as you need. And please, let me help with any expenses involved with this whole situation."

I thanked him for his offer and said that I'd see him next week. After hanging up the phone, I sat on the edge of my bed and hung my head in my hands. I probably would have cried if I'd had the tears left to do so.

As it was, all I wanted to do was spend time alone in my room. I couldn't recall the last time I'd been all alone with nothing but my thoughts and quiet contemplation. Unfortunately, life altering news had brought me to this moment of solitude.

How in the world was I going to come out the other side of this? I felt trapped in the middle of a problem with no solution. My solution had died with Raoul.

Epilogue

Life passed one day at a time. I struggled to accept the truth about my past. It was hard to move on. I'd gone from a delusional teenager with hearts in my eyes to a mid-twenties power hungry wolf with a new appreciation for the dangers of love.

Arys and I continued to discover the delicate balance of our bond. As trying as it may be, it isn't without benefits. After more than three centuries, he sees the sun through my eyes. While we have managed to control our conjoined power, the effort remained a challenge, to say the least.

Compared to Arys and me, Shaz hadn't adjusted any better to the link, but he accepted that it isn't going away. My heart belonged to Shaz like all of me that is wolf, but the root of my own personal power longed for Arys as if we'd always been a part of the same flame. It was complicated. The frequent dreams about Raoul didn't help the confusion.

After postponing our date night for almost two weeks, Shaz and I went out for the classic dinner and a movie. It was amazing how something as mundane as a real date could mean so much to me.

We asked Kylarai to join us for a run, but she just smiled and said that she'd agreed to help Kale nail a target. I'd asked her if "nail a target" was code for anything and received a nice open handed slap on the arm. A blade between the ribs hadn't been so bad for Kylarai.

Outside, in the dark of night, I saw a black wolf framed by trees in the field. A sliver of moonlight cast a soothing glow, and I was sure my keen eyes were not playing tricks on me. When I blinked, the ghostly wolf was gone.

I sensed Shaz's welcome approach and turned to admire his form as he stripped. Upon reading the letter from Raoul, he had responded with a fury to match my own. I felt amused that he, too, wished Raoul was still alive to take the beating that he deserved. Slowly I would learn to live with Raoul's confession. It was a betrayal I never expected to get over.

I gently scraped my fingernails along Shaz's firm shoulders, down his chest to his navel. He shivered in response, and I licked my lips invitingly.

With the most delicate touch, he traced the line of my jaw before nibbling ever so softly on my lower lip. His white blond hair fell across my nose, and I giggled in that girlish way that I so despise. Naked with him felt so right.

"Before or after?" His whisper tickled the inside of my ear so that I had to rub the feeling away.

"After, otherwise you'll say you're too tired to run. Again." I gave him a playful shove and turned away to embrace the change to wolf.

Before I could shift, his arms snaked around my waist. I gave a small squeal and fought back by reaching behind me to the ticklish spot in his side that made him come undone. He released me immediately, and I turned to continue my assault with both hands.

"Alexa!" He tried to sound mad, but it didn't come out that way. "Ok, ok, have it your way." The desperation that comes from being tickled made his voice high on the last two words, and he grimaced.

Unable to resist such a cute expression, I pulled him close for a heart melting lip lock that I knew would get him panting. He tasted of mint and smelled of wolf.

"You little tease," he called as I walked toward the field beyond the back gate. "I can't wait to sink my teeth into you."

I paused long enough to tap my bare bottom in invitation. He answered with a growl that added a spring to my step.

I ran and leaped, arching my body, gracefully becoming wolf in midair. Though it may have had the finesse of Hollywood graphics, it took Shaz and I almost three years to perfect the move. I couldn't count the number of naked spills in the dirt that we'd both taken.

As I'd anticipated, Shaz was only a few seconds behind me. His paws kicked up dirt as he scrambled to catch up, and I poured on the speed as we raced to our tree.

I knew I had to go forward regardless of mistakes and lessons learned the hard way. Though life would be a lot simpler without the drama, power, and bloodshed, I have a sneaking suspicion that's not about to end anytime soon.

Alexa O'Brien Huntress Series Book Two: The Wicked Kiss

Alexa O'Brien is a magnet for trouble. Due to the power she shares with bad ass vampire, Arys Knight, power hungry creatures are eager to get a taste of her. That includes Arys' sadistic sire, a vampire that sees her as a toy, perfect for his personal collection. If he doesn't kill her, she just might wish he had.

Alexa is in danger, something her wolf mate Shaz blames entirely on Arys. The tension runs high when an argument blows up into a full physical confrontation between the two men. Alexa learns there is one way to protect herself from those who see her as a walking, talking power trip. Now she is faced with her biggest decision yet.

But can the two men she loves put aside their differences when it matters most? Because this is one sacrifice that will forever alter her very mortality.

Excerpt at: www.TrinaMLee.com

About the Author

Trina M. Lee has walked in the darkness alongside vampires and werewolves since adolescence. Trina lives in Alberta, Canada with her fiancé and daughter, along with their 3 cats. She loves to hear from readers via email or twitter.

For news and book information please visit:

www.TrinaMLee.com

4793619R00142

Printed in Great Britain
by Amazon.co.uk, Ltd.,
Marston Gate.